"You've Got Your Mother's Courage . . ."

The buggy up ahead had made the turn now into New St. Clair, and as Mary turned too, they heard Alice scream. Both buggies halted.

"What is it, Jim?" Mary shouted.

Jim started to jump out, but Alice jerked him back. "Snake! There's a rattler in the road!" he called back helplessly. "Alice won't let me get out! And there's the baby. . . ."

Before her father could move, Mary was on the ground, the buggy whip in her hand.

"Sister, don't try it!" Jim shouted. "Let's drive on." But the snake could strike at the horses' legs. Then . . .

Mary was out in front of his buggy now, not five feet from the snake coiled in a pile fully a foot high, its flat head moving warily from side to side, tongue flicking. The first whistle of the whip struck it on one side of its heavy body and drew blood, but did not loosen the coil.

"Do it again, Mary—for God's sake!" Jim yelled.

The second crack of the whip shot the snake to its full length—at least six feet of angered reptile as thick as a man's wrist. Before Mary could swing again, the rattler had sensed the movement of her feet and was recoiled to strike. . . .

A Solid Success...

"This book about the return of young Horace Gould to the family plantation . . . his marriage, his family life, his concern with slavery . . . is a solid success. Miss Price . . . knows her period and her people well enough to bring them alive in exciting circumstances."

—*Cleveland Plain Dealer*

"In theme, characterization, vividness of setting, language, and emotional appeal, this work stands apart from some current trends in novels in its adherence to high standards of writing . . . Eugenia Price will please her myriad current admirers and add to that number with *New Moon Rising*."

—*Atlanta Journal-Constitution*

"[In] this warm and sympathetic novel of the old South . . . the author has drawn real people and real ancestors taken out of history."

—*Miami Herald*

A Beautiful Documentary Novel . . .

"This beautiful documentary novel is proof that in the hands of a true artist and a committed Christian, the sordid tragedies of war, the fears and frustrations of blacks and whites, and their complicated family problems there is no need to resort to salacious language, filthy words, or vile and suggestive descriptions in order to create a realistic atmosphere . . . "

—*Augsburg Publishing House*

"Miss Price possesses a unique ability to make the antebellum South come to life in all its color, charm and individuality. And she is particularly effective in portraying the fascination of the Golden Isles in that bygone day."

—Frank G. Slaughter

"In Deborah, especially, Eugenia Price has given her readers much to be thankful for—I'm very glad Deborah once existed. She is certainly one of the most vividly charming and courageous heroines of recent fiction."

—Faith Baldwin

Don't miss these books by EUGENIA PRICE

The St. Simon's Trilogy
   The Beloved Invader
   New Moon Rising
   Lighthouse
Margaret's Story
Maria

And coming soon
Bright Captivity

Available from Bantam Books

NEW MOON RISING

BY EUGENIA PRICE

BANTAM BOOKS
NEW YORK • TORONTO • LONDON • SYDNEY • AUCKLAND

For my valued friend
Commander Horace Bunch Gould II

This edition contains the complete text
of the original hardcover edition.
NOT ONE WORD HAS BEEN OMITTED.

NEW MOON RISING
*A Bantan Book / published by arrangement with
Harper & Row, Publishers Inc.*

PRINTING HISTORY
*Lippincott edition published June 1969
Word Incorporated edition published June 1969
Christian Herald's Family Bookshelf edition published
August 1969
Bantam edition / June 1970*

ISBN 0-553-26848-1

Published simultaneously in the United States and Canada

*Bantam Books are published by Bantam Books, a division of Bantam
Doubleday Dell Publishing Group, Inc. Its trademark, consisting of the
words "Bantam Books" and the portrayal of a rooster, is Registered in U.S.
Patent and Trademark Office and in other countries. Marca Registrada.
Bantam Books, 666 Fifth Avenue, New York, New York 10103.*

PRINTED IN THE UNITED STATES OF AMERICA

RAD   33 32 31 30 29

PART ONE

1

From the sky, there was only a feeling of light. The strength of the clear, magnifying lens of the wheel-house lantern, showing an arc of twenty points through the compass, was barely enough for navigation on such a night. The clouds hung cloaklike, motionless, heavy with unfallen rain. Familiar landmarks along the twisting inland waterway were almost blotted out. The low, bulky steamer moved, but seemingly toward nothing.

Three of the four passengers aboard the *South Carolina* had looked forward to a moonlit trip down the coastal waters of Georgia from Darien to St. Simons Island, and south to St. Mary's at the border of the Florida territory. Cheerfully, almost, the three talkative passengers—two men and a woman—had accepted the more-than-two-hour wait for the tide to free the packet from a sand bar on which she grounded after leaving the dock at Darien. When they had come aboard at 3 P.M., the sun had hung bright and high in a flattened dome of hot, August blue. Everyone knew it would be dark long before they reached St. Simons Island, some twenty water miles away, but in such clear summer weather, the full moon would turn the flat stretches of salt marsh, cut for miles around by serpentine coastal rivers and creeks, into an enchanted landscape.

The fourth passenger seemed to look forward to nothing, and even during the long wait on the sand bar, the others had given up trying to draw the young man into their conversation.

It was after six o'clock when at last the packet was free to move down the short neck of the Darien, through General's Cut into the somewhat wider Butler River. And even with the threat of Georgia's predictable afternoon rain, the three optimistically expected the weather to clear before the moon rose. Instead, the sky had lowered, and by the time the steamer had passed through Wood Cut, to swing into the red water of the South Altamaha, the pilot and his crew and passengers had settled down to make the best of the slow, treacherous trip through the murky, semitropical night around and between the enormous cypress trees which stood in the channel of the South Altamaha like dour statues.

Inside the small passenger cabin, its dark varnished walls shifting in the circles of light from the coal-oil lanterns, young Horace Bunch Gould sat hunched on one of the wooden benches. He would have preferred darkness, not only because he wanted to be left alone, but because he knew the landscape so well that he could have judged by watching it slide by how much longer his reprieve would last. Even from the lighted cabin, he could see an occasional cypress in the river, and he knew they were on the South Altamaha. He would hear the shouts of the crew when they began to sound the depth of the water above the tricky shoals a mile or so from the entrance to Buttermilk Sound. From Buttermilk Sound, they would enter the Frederica River. Then his reprieve would be almost over. He would be home again in less than two hours once they had swung into the Frederica—back on St. Simons Island—forced to tell the whole ugly story to his father. Because he had been what he considered weak enough to come straight home after the trouble, he now had to find a way to justify himself, face to face, to the man he both respected and feared. Feared? The word shocked him. Could he fear the tall, gaunt, sad-eyed man who had always been as kind as he had been firm? Or did he fear that, facing his father, he would for the first time feel guilt over what he had done?

He twisted nervously on the straight bench, turning his back to the others, pretending to peer out the cabin's small, shuttered opening. If there really was a God, he

(4)

thought, who decreed human relationships, He had certainly worked out a strange arrangement with parents and their offspring. When a son got into trouble, it wasn't enough that he carry his own burden; he also had to worry about his father. One problem turned into two if a man had a father who cherished plans for his son's life. Almost ashamed of himself, for the first time since he had been away from home he longed for his mother. His young, lively, pretty British mother. She had gone away to Savannah to get well when he was six and never returned. She had died suddenly the week they expected her home, and because the hurricane season that year was too severe to bring her body back to St. Simons Island, they buried her in the Savannah Cemetery.

He shivered in spite of the damp, clinging heat and reached for his shoulder cape, ashamed that his hands shook, relieved that the other passengers were too absorbed in their own vacuous talk to notice. He was, after all, almost eighteen years old. He had been away at school with men his own age long enough to have learned how to shut out older people. Oh, he was courteous to them, but in his freshman year, during the first student rebellion, he had lost respect for most adults, except for his father and Jeremiah Day, the President of Yale. Even Dr. Day had not understood the students' viewpoint during the last trouble and, in his heart, Horace had marked him off too.

He pulled the cape up around his ears in an attempt to escape the idiotic chatter of the obese, obviously ignorant and obviously wealthy planter from St. Mary's and the other two nondescript passengers. He needed quiet in which to think through what he would tell his father, and the harsh, whiskey rasp in the big man's voice irritated him. Thank God, they were not St. Simons people. He could be as rude as he liked. Not one of them would be curious about why he was coming home from college two years before graduation. The heavy-jowled planter had a right to talk; he had paid his fare, too. But what he said sickened Horace Gould in a new way—though it might not have affected him at all before the years at Yale.

"Yes, sir, an' yes, ma'am," the planter declared. "I picked this boat for its name—*South Carolina*. Now, there's a state! The only state in the consarned Union with guts enough to take a strong stand against the mountin' tyranny of the Fed'rul Gov'mint in this danger-filled year of our Lord eighteen thirty."

The other two passengers, man and wife, Horace assumed, agreed warmly—the woman with quick, self-righteous nods, the man with short little speeches when he could manage to edge one in: "Makes a God-fearin' person pray an' wonder. I say, it makes a person pray an' wonder."

"What makes a decent, God-fearin', freedom-lovin' person pray an' wonder, m'frien'," the planter went on, pulling at one hefty leg to cross it over the other, "is how much longer the Cotton States kin put up with them frazzlin' Fed'rul tariffs! Somepin's got to *give*—an' it ain't gonna be the Fed'rul Gov'mint, 'cause all it knows how to do is *take!*"

The man guffawed at his own joke. Horace cringed. Although there was still a south Georgia flavor to his own speech, the boy had become keenly aware that it set a man apart from Americans who lived in the North. During his two years at boarding school near New Haven, and then at Yale, he had grown aware of much about the South and the North of the country his Massachusetts-bred father had taught him to revere as a Union. With all his heart, Horace had loved New Haven, Connecticut; he quickly felt at home there, even though he had been barely fourteen when he left St. Simons Island. Many of his classmates spoke with his father's crisp New England burr, and Horace felt comfortable with them. Comfortable and at home in a world where he had swiftly become his own man.

All the way south from New Haven, he had struggled with a bewilderment of anger and grief, unable to convince himself that it was all over. Even during the long

(6)

hours of rehashing events with his roommate, Alex Drysdale, who had come with him as far as Savannah, he found it difficult to believe he and Alex would never again settle down for an evening in their familiar dormitory chamber in old North Middle, their feet on the study table, their Latin texts propped on their knees, the wood fire scorching one side of their faces, the old brass lamp smoking, in spite of repeated adjustments, until their eyes stung. He had slept in his beloved, lopsided bed for the last time; through the last spring, he had watched the buds open into leaves on the elms that lined both sides of College Street. There would be no more crunching across campus toward Old Brick Row through the crisp, fallen leaves, the autumn air sharp with the smell of wood smoke—the New England smell of wood smoke was different from any other. During five-o'clock morning chapel just a week ago, he had whiled away the boring hour of Prayers and Scripture by carving on his favorite bench his first two initials, intending to whittle the G the next morning. The blow had fallen that afternoon in Conic Sections class. He never went to chapel again.

"I did get my initials cut into The Fence, Alex, did you?"

"Indeed I did," Alex laughed. "Of course, carving one's initials on the lowly sophomore side is not like carving them on the senior side of the dear old Fence." The bravado went out of his voice. "Oh, well, Horace, if we'd stayed around, we'd have sat on The Fence with a load of guilt because of those nine fellows."

The Fence, a homely wooden structure on whose comfortable round rails Yale students had perched for over fifty years—arguing, swapping jokes—still seemed more real than this cabin bench. He would never sit on The Fence again. . . .

He had been with Alex only yesterday; that was real. That he was alone and almost home had no meaning. He tried concentrating on the good times at Yale, even as a lowly freshman, when the famous Bread and Butter Rebellion had struck him as more exciting than dangerous. At first, his early training had kept him from throwing crockery in protest against the bad food in Commons; but he had finally entered in, relishing the sound of smashing dishes, cheering the student who dared to toss a whole platter of leathery roast beef out the window of the Hall. He remembered the hilarity and the bloody noses and the flying rocks when someone provoked a Town and Gown riot; the fascinating hours spent getting acquainted with sailors from foreign lands and watching the big ships come and go at the docks on Long Island Sound; the long, stimulating debates in Linonia meeting—the only outlet a student had for his own opinions, since no one dared speak up in class. He hummed a few bars of "Here's to Dear Old Yale" under his breath and stopped abruptly. It was all over, for him, and for almost half the Class of 1832. Forty-three young men would never set foot on the Yale College campus again.

He stared into the wet blackness outside, and the one subject he had avoided with Alex during their trip south flashed into his mind: President Jeremiah Day's remarks about Southern students. "It is the history of school rebellions," Dr. Day had declared, "that often the disturbance is led by Southern planters' sons who despise obeying orders, who consider orders fit only for slaves." Bitterly, Horace still resented that. Oh, he admitted there might be some grounds for it, but to generalize was unfair; there had been as many Northern students as Southerners involved in the recent trouble. More, he felt sure, as he recalled the determined faces of some of his Yankee classmates—men from New England, Ohio, Pennsylvania, New York. They were all one—North and South. *Omnes in uno*. True, Grimke and especially Steiner, both Southerners, had spearheaded the protest, but Hoppin, a New Englander, had been a leader too.

Alex Drysdale had been so infuriated by President Day's sweeping criticism that Horace had deliberately not brought it up on their trip home. His roommate was defensive about the Cotton States in a way Horace was not. He sighed. There was so much to think through

(8)

when he could be alone on St. Simons. Arguments about the North and South with Alex or anyone else bothered him. Men argued the subject from emotional allegiance, not from logic. Suddenly he fought back tears. His classmates were the same as dead. Right or wrong, he would never feel as close to any group of people again. Not even his family. He was proud to be a planter's son; he loved the South as any man loves the place where he was born, but part of his heart had stayed in New England. The history of the Northeast excited him as much as the familiar stories of the founding of the Colony of Georgia at Fort Frederica on the Island where he was born—maybe even more. After all, less than a hundred years had passed since General James Oglethorpe had defeated the Spanish just three miles south of his father's plantation, along Bloody Marsh on the Cater land at Kelvin Grove. All his life he had lived with the beginnings of Georgia's history; in a little while this boat would dock at the ruins of old Fort Frederica. General Oglethorpe had seemed almost one of his own ancestors, but now that he had spent school holidays visiting Bunker Hill and Independence Hall, had traveled the same route Paul Revere rode, he was proud that his Grandfather Gould had died in the battle of Saratoga when his own father was six. Colorful as he was, General Oglethorpe had been forced to make room for Grandfather Gould and a whole new set of heroes from the North. Horace's horizons had widened almost frighteningly. He didn't fully understand why the St. Mary's planter angered and frustrated him. There were people on St. Simons Island who talked like this man, whose ideas were as shallow and bigoted. People he hadn't thought of while he had been away. People his father, a Northerner, had accepted with no apparent difficulty as his neighbors and friends. How could James Gould, born in New York and reared in Massachusetts, be neighborly with self-righteous Southerners like this planter whose locked, airless mind reeked even more than his person?

"Wouldn't s'prise me a-tall," the man was saying, "if South Carolina didn't go right through with all the nul-

(9)

lification talk around Charleston these days, if this Fed'rul tyranny keeps up. I just come from up there an' the folks are seein' red. After all, if a state had a right to decide to go into the consarned Union in the first place, don't it have the right to nullify for itself whatever it don't like that Congress does?"

"An' another thing," the planter went on, "all this abolitionist talk makes *me* see red! If a man wants to own slaves, it's a free country, ain't it? Let the Yankees do what they please an' let us do what we please, I say. The Cotton States has got to keep their *rights*. The same rights we had when we went into the consarned Union in the first place."

Like an echo, Horace heard the vigorous, convincing, cultivated voice of one Southern classmate at Yale as he made a fiery speech the night they drew up the petition of protest against the faculty. "We had the right to make our decision to enter Yale, did we not? So don't we still have rights? If too much is being demanded of us in too short a time in our study of conic sections—if the authorities are making impossible, inhuman demands on the sophomore class, don't we have the right to protest? Must we live under the tyranny of the faculty of the school we entered of our own free wills? Isn't this a free country?"

Horace jumped up, hurried across the cabin, shoved open the swollen wooden door and strode out into the rain.

On the starboard side, he could hear the crew using the lead line, which meant they were about to enter Buttermilk Sound. He stared into the darkness, waiting for his eyes to grow accustomed to it, knowing he would recognize a familiar landmark as soon as the packet entered the Frederica River. If the rain kept up, he would be soaked anyway by the time he reached New St. Clair, his father's cotton plantation. Unless he could borrow a horse from Mr. Frewin at Frederica, he would have to walk the two miles. At least there would be no one at the dock to meet him. Even though the faculty had written to his father, the family would have no idea when to expect him.

Staring down at the swirling white foam churned up by the wooden side wheel, he thought of his family, snug in the big tabby house that James Gould had built so proudly for Jane Gould the year before she died. Only one bedroom on the second floor would have a lamp burning at nine o'clock at night. His mother's sister, Aunt Caroline Harris, in her late twenties now, he supposed would be reading alone in her room. Down the wide hall, next to Aunt Caroline, the door to his younger sister's room would be closed, the shutters drawn even in the daytime. Janie was still attending the Moravian Female Seminary in Bethlehem, Pennsylvania. His older sister, Mary, after graduating from the same school, had been home almost five years. This, at least, gave him some hope. Unlike Janie, Mary would not badger him with questions. She might try to decide his future, being Mary, but she would not pry. She might not think he had done the right thing, but she knew how a man thought. To see Mary again became suddenly urgent. Happy-natured, loyal Aunt Caroline saw to the housekeeping while, more and more, Mary ran the plantation. Except for Horace, the most important mission in Mary's life was to watch over their father. She would be sitting across from him tonight, reading, plumping the pillows under his legs propped as usual on a stool in front of his deep, brown leather chair. Mary was beautiful, but so devoted to James Gould that, as far as Horace knew, she had no time for young men. Every night during the years he had been away, Horace could think of his father and Mary and know they were together.

For a moment, he felt drawn toward that love and warmth and security, but he had changed. Horace Gould, as he was now, was not really being drawn to his family, merely back toward his childhood. At least, he thought, his brother Jim would not be there. They may have passed, in boats, going in opposite directions, sometime last week. Jim had agreed to come home to help his father with the plantation, but his wife—a New

Haven girl whom he had married right after his graduation from Yale—hated the South; early every summer Jim had to take Alice back to Connecticut, then go again to bring her south in the fall.

"You'll be shocked when you see Papa, Horace," Mary had written in her last letter. "It's good Jim is settling here for Papa's sake. The old darling is so crippled now, he has great difficulty mounting his horse, and you know what he will be like when he can no longer ride his fields every day. I don't want to alarm you, brother, but he is very, very lame. And he looks old—seventy or more—instead of not quite sixty!"

The *South Carolina* had passed Hampton plantation at Butler's Point on the north end of St. Simons and Pike's Bluff, Dr. Thomas Hazzard's plantation. Horace could see ahead to where the river cut inland to pass close by West Point, the neighboring plantation to the south, owned by Colonel William Wigg Hazzard. The packet would begin to blow her whistle soon and Colonel Hazzard's deerhounds would bay. Horace ducked inside the cabin for his valise and then went back on deck to watch for the first flare of the pine knot fire someone would be trying to light on a pile of wet sand on the Frederica docking platform. The steamer plowed steadily ahead, and he wanted to hold it back. He was afraid, and he was going home, and the two facts did not belong together.

The dread of facing his father deepened as the packet, whistle blowing, rounded the big bend toward Frederica; the pine knot docking flares were blazing higher than he remembered. As though everything was being hurried, the gangplank creaked and jerked over the side of the boat and seemed to fly into place as the steamer bumped the old wooden dock.

Sprinting across the platform to get away from the lighted area, Horace stood for a moment in the darkness looking up at the Fort Frederica landmark—the crumbling ruins of Oglethorpe's ammunition battery rising against the low, wet sky at the edge of the point of high land by the river. He was sure none of the Negro

(12)

stevedores had recognized him. He had grown taller, and the cape thrown over his dark green cutaway made him look heavier than he was. He might be a successful young cotton factor, visiting the Island on business. The waving strands of wet moss beckoned him, but he was a stranger and the whole Island felt unreal. He was in a nightmare, where familiar things and familiar people were set down in foreign places, all lost, all strange.

There were cheering lights in Mr. Frewin's tavern on the other side of the dock. It would be snug and dry in there, and on impulse he turned toward it. He had never taken a drink on St. Simons Island, but he was a man now. Why not?

As he passed the big Frewin house on the way to the tavern a tall man hobbled down the front steps and limped toward him, waving both arms.

It was his father.

2

Back and forth from the easy chair where James Gould sat, to the tall side windows, streaming with rain—Horace paced the familiar, high-ceilinged sitting room. He had forgotten how sticky even upholstered furniture became during an Island August. He ran his forefinger around his green silk cravat, to loosen it. He was home, walking again on the bird-and-rose patterned carpet, aware of the dark wainscot and the blue wood-block wallpaper his mother had selected thirteen years ago, but he was still in his damp traveling clothes, as though to make it clear that he had only come for a short visit.

"Make me feel a lot better," his father said, "if you'd sit down, son. We've got some talking to do."

"Tonight, sir? Do we have to talk tonight?"

James Gould moved stiffly, hunting a comfortable

position for his legs. "No. No, we don't have to talk tonight."

His voice was so kind, Horace sat down abruptly in the wing chair opposite him. "I'm sorry, Papa. If you made the effort to meet me in your condition, the least I can do is talk if you want to."

By the light of the candles in the iron candelabra on the table beside his father's chair, Horace could see the hurt in the older man's eyes. "Am I so crippled-looking when I walk, son?"

Horace forced a smile, tried to think of something light and reassuring. Nothing came.

"Mary wanted to make the trip to Frederica every night to look for you, but I wouldn't let her."

"Every night, Papa? You've been going *every night?*"

"Well, I didn't want you coming home with no one to meet you."

Horace wondered why James Gould had never learned to enjoy talking the way most Southerners do. After all, he had lived in the South since 1796; on St. Simons among the warm, gregarious coastal planters since 1807, the year he won the Government contract to design and build the first lighthouse on the Island. He had loved St. Simons too much to leave, but he had never quite become an Islander.

"I just rode up in the buggy and waited at Frewin's for the boat to come in," James Gould said. "Got home before dark most nights. Tonight was the first time she was so late."

At Yale, one of his professors had a dry, matter-of-fact voice like his father's. He had never felt as though he were getting through to the professor, either, but he liked him.

"I wish you hadn't come! I mean—don't you think I know the way down Frederica Road to our house?"

James Gould had been staring at the carpet. Now he looked at Horace. "I don't think you've changed that much, son."

"Oh, but I have changed, sir. Isn't that why you sent

(14)

me to college? Did you want me to stay a provincial country boy?"

"Why don't you have a glass of this good, cold buttermilk while we talk?"

That was the trouble, Horace thought. He had never really talked with his father, and now that there was so much that was hard to explain, how could he suddenly begin? He took a sip and set the glass down, wishing his sister hadn't left them alone.

"What are the other boys going to do now?" his father asked.

"The other boys, sir?"

"Yes. The forty-two classmates who left Yale when you did. What will they do with their lives?"

"I doubt if most of them know yet. We've pledged to keep in touch with one another." Horace fingered a thick gold ring on his right hand. "We had these rings engraved just before we left New Haven. We vowed to wear them for the rest of our lives."

"May I see the ring?"

Horace held out his hand.

"*Omnes in uno*," the older man read aloud from the inscription on the gold band. "In brotherhood, eh?"

"Yes, sir."

"A few of the others must have some plans," James Gould said.

"Alex Drysdale says he's going to another school. We're good friends, but we don't see eye to eye on a lot of things."

"Which school do you want to enter, Horace?"

The boy set down his half-emptied glass. "None, sir. I'm through with it. If the faculty at Yale is so unfair, what must the others be like?"

For a long time, James Gould was silent, then, "A man makes a mistake to dream for his sons. A father should help his sons, give them an education if he can, encourage their dreams, but he should stop there."

"I'm not sure I know what you mean, Papa."

"I dreamed of both my sons practicing law. Jim got

(15)

married—unwisely, too soon. Don't think he ever had any idea of becoming a lawyer." He took a deep breath. "I haven't written this to you, Horace, but I bought the adjoining land, Black Banks—seven hundred and fifty acres. I'm deeding it to Jim to get him to come here to live. When he and Alice get back this fall, they'll start building their home. But I should never have done it."

"Why not? Jim's lucky."

"No, he isn't. He's trapped—between his wife and his crippled father who needs him to help with the land. Alice hates it here. She's afraid of the Negroes and she hates our moss hanging from the trees." James Gould leaned his head back and said as though to himself, "No, Jim had no notion of studying law. If I hadn't made him an offer he couldn't afford to turn down, he'd have gone into the hotel business with his father-in-law in New Haven."

Horace, his lean, angular face tense, began to pace around the room again, picking up a figurine, opening and closing the cover of the family Bible, flicking imaginary dust off his father's tall planter's desk—suddenly desperate to bring the talk back to his own trouble. Wanting to make his explanations and be done with it. "Don't you want to hear the facts about why I left school, Papa?"

"Mostly, I want to know what you will do now, son."

The boy sat on the arm of a settee across the room, clasping and unclasping his hands. "Oh, I'll be all right. I'll do something. You see, I learned to *think* at Yale."

"Is that right?" Horace had forgotten his father's favorite noncommittal phrase. It had more often than not left him dangling, unaware what was intended by it.

"What I mean to say is that I learned to think for myself. Otherwise, I would never have been a part of the protest. I entered into this thing with my whole heart and mind, Papa. But I thought it through first."

"Is that right." This time it wasn't even a question.

"Aren't you going to ask me what happened, sir? I'm sure you got a letter from the almighty faculty, but don't you want to know the truth of it?"

A mosquito sang past Horace's ear, and he slapped at it too hard.

"The faculty did write to all the parents. I know what happened."

"You know *their* side of it! We knew they'd get their version to you before we had a chance."

"I believe, since I am your father, that the college had an obligation to inform me." He felt in the pocket of his old tweed jacket and handed Horace a folded letter, worn from rereading.

Horace crossed the room, took it, then laid it still folded on the candlestand. "I don't need to read it. I've heard it all a hundred times."

"It seems to me you should read it. If I am to be fair with you, you should know what has been told me."

The boy opened the letter. " 'Thirty-one July!' " He laughed. "They didn't waste time, did they? That was the same day we knew they were forcing us to leave! You must have gotten one of the first copies of this masterpiece."

His father's voice was quiet. "Read it aloud, son."

"Yes, sir. 'A part of the Sophomore class in this college have entered into organized and repeated combinations to resist the laws and regulations of the institution as to the mode of conducting recitations. It became necessary at length to admonish them in a formal manner, in the name of the Faculty, that such proceedings must have an end. I regret to say that they have been again repeated and that your son has been concerned in these measures. In entering the study of Conic Sections, a petition was presented for liberty to depart from the ordinary method of reciting in that study; that instead of demonstrating from the figures and reciting from memory in the usual way, they might simply *read* the demonstrations from the book and explain the steps.' "

Horace threw down the letter. "Papa, that's *their* side of it! And it's only half truth."

"Son, I'll have to ask you to read without comment."

The boy's face flushed and his hand trembled as he began to read again. " 'The apparent reason for this

(17)

requested change was not the length of the lesson, but the *entire uselessness* (as it was claimed) of the ordinary mode of recitation here and elsewhere.' "

Horace hit the page with the back of his hand. "That proves my point! They are telling only half of it. The lessons *were* too long. They had scheduled the whole study of conic sections too late in the term. Later than with any other class in the history of Yale College! Most of us were already half sick from overwork, lack of sleep—five-o'clock compulsory chapel, Papa, every morning all summer—we were stifling in the heat of the dog days and—"

"Finish the letter," his father interrupted.

"All of it, sir? It's three pages of rot!"

"You will stop being disrespectful, Horace. The second page is only a copy of your student petition. At least finish the first page. You need to know how this all appears to me."

He took a deep breath and read rapidly. " 'The Faculty, believing themselves more competent judges of the method of recitation, decided not to depart from the long established principle of the College on this subject. They assured the petitioners, however, that on long and difficult processes, their request would be complied with in accordance with usage; that we had no intentions of making the lessons long or difficult and that if a student should be unable, from any proper cause, to make himself master of the whole lesson, the Faculty would be satisfied with the part which he had actually got.' "

"That seems fair to me, Horace."

"Yes, doesn't it?" he sneered. "But, Papa, they were not to be trusted."

"The faculty of Yale College are all honorable men. All ministers of the Gospel."

"Oh, I don't mean morally, Papa!" He sighed. "Listen to this again—they tip their hands right here: ' . . . if a student should be unable, from any *proper* cause, to make himself master of the whole lesson . . .' Do you see? *They*, the almighty faculty, would be the judges of what the 'proper cause' would be. But, *we*, not

(18)

they, were the ones who saw some of our classmates almost in hysterics at night out of sheer exhaustion and desperation over the impossibility of learning so much material! We, not they, knew the facts. And our over-load this year was not the same as in other years. They had already squeezed in spherical trigonometry and still expected us to memorize conic sections before the term ended."

"Explain that matter of your having called the usual college method of recitation 'useless,' son. Do you think a bunch of boys not yet twenty are apt to know best about that?"

"Papa, will you listen to me one minute? Will you, sir?"

James Gould nodded.

"I know how it appears. They have worded it in a way that puts us entirely in the wrong. We were not in the wrong, and the future will prove that we were not! Time is going to change this senseless recitation method. Why, even the dullest student can memorize, if there is time—as a child commits a Bible verse to memory. That isn't learning; it's repeating. We wanted to *learn* conic sections—not memorize the wording of a textbook. If there had been time before the term ended to do both—to satisfy our own desire to master the meaning behind the demonstrations *and* to satisfy the faculty's old-fashioned zeal for rote memorization—we would have complied. There wasn't time. We were exhausted and so we petitioned for help. They asked an impossible thing of us and then lacked the grace to admit it—to give in. They were like stone walls. That's the way it is, you know, when the weaker young confront the stronger old. We were doomed from the outset, but we loved Yale so much, we couldn't believe its faculty would not give us the help we needed."

"Help, son? Did you boys really want help or were you rebelling against authority?"

"We wanted help, Papa! We were worried half sick at the prospect of failing. We filed a legitimate protest in the proper manner, signed by us all—all of the forty-three who had courage enough to stand up to the injustice of what was being done to us." Horace sighed, sat down, his head in his hands. "But we were all such babes in the woods, we expected understanding, not trickery."

"You feel you were tricked, do you?" his father asked.

Horace jumped up. "Sir, you won't *believe* what they did. The names of nine of the men who had signed our petition were drawn at random from a box containing all forty-three names. This was the usual method for selecting students for recitation, so we still suspected nothing—not knowing, of course, that there were only our forty-three names in that box! Then, those nine chaps —picked by chance, remember—were asked to recite conic sections according to the orders of the faculty—books closed. They were, in other words, asked to turn traitor to the rest of us, to recite as though they had *not* signed the paper. All nine refused, stating that they wholly concurred with our written protest, repeating that they believed the faculty demands to be unfair." Horace sat down again, looking his father in the eye. "Those nine men were expelled on the spot!"

"Expelled?"

"Dishonorably dismissed! It was only by chance that I was not among them. But wait, that isn't all. The rest of us were then told that *if we agreed* to meet faculty demands—if we would back down utterly—knuckle under—we could then go on with our studies at Yale as though nothing had happened!"

"And what about the nine boys whose names had been drawn by chance?"

"I told you, Papa, they were expelled! They were booted out because they had backbone enough to stand with the rest of us. We all kept trying to convince the faculty that we needed help—just help—but always we ran up against those stone walls! Even those nine unfortunate chaps tried to make them understand—right up to the day they had to leave in disgrace. And, sir, the faculty will see to it that those nine men can never enter another college in America."

"Is that right?"

"By any law of fairness, could you have stood by, Papa, and watched the lives of nine friends ruined while you went scot free? Could you hold your head up knowing you had allowed nine classmates, no more guilty than you, to take the entire punishment for you? We even agreed to back down—all of us, right or wrong—if only they would reinstate our classmates. They refused. Even Dr. Day."

James Gould sat shaking his head, struggling, Horace could see, with something. Had he appealed to his father's logic? His sense of fair play, of loyalty to one's friends? "They treated us like small boys in a low-grade boarding school, sir." He smacked a fist against his palm for emphasis. "Not like responsible college men. On the morning we were given another chance, those nine were excluded! Offered no chance to recant. I swear to you we agreed to concede everything, *if* the same chance was given our classmates who had been so unjustly singled out for punishment. We agreed to everything but the dishonorable, unfeeling desertion of our friends. We would not do that and we had to go."

Horace walked back to the window, exhausted, relieved. He had made his case; now let his father decide. His own mind was made up. He would never go back to school.

The rain had almost stopped, and through the spattered window pane he looked for a long time at the swaying outlines of his sister Mary's double row of orange trees boarding the long walk. He raised the window and listened to the almost forgotten Island night sounds—the croak and whistle of the marsh frogs and the lonely call of the chuck-will's-widow.

After a while, he heard the older man groan a little as he pulled himself up out of the chair. Then his father was beside him, one arm thrown around Horace's shoulders.

"Son, you'll make an outstanding lawyer."

Horace stiffened.

"I think I have the picture now," his father went on.

(21)

"It's a tragedy, but in the final analysis you did the honorable thing. Sometimes there is no black or white in a situation. Now and then we have to choose gray. You do have an honorable dismissal, though, and you are free to enter another school this fall and go on to fulfill your dream of becoming a lawyer."

Horace did not take his eyes from the wet, shadowy trees outside. His voice sounded flat, almost hard. "Papa, I meant what I said. I'm through with school. Those nine men are no more guilty than I. They can't go to school. I won't. And at the risk of hurting you still more, it wasn't my dream to become a lawyer anyway. It was yours. I don't know what I want to do."

Slowly, James Gould turned and hobbled back to his chair. He sank into it, his thin, bent shoulders slumped forward, his hands hanging limp between his knees.

From across the room, Horace said, "Don't try to convince me, sir. There's no use."

His father spoke steadily, without emotion. "I knew there wasn't any use before I made the suggestion. I don't rightly think you need another stone wall to bump up against. I forced your brother. I won't force you— even though you're under age."

"And I'm not staying here on St. Simons, Papa."

Horace watched his father's face; there was no change of expression. After a moment, the old man got up, rubbed his knees, stretched, and limped toward the stairway off the front hall. He picked up a chamberstick from the supply on the candlestand at the foot of the stairs, lit it from another burning there, said good night and began the laborious climb. About halfway up, he leaned over the railing to look at Horace. "I doubt if I'll have trouble finding a job for you, son, at the cotton market in Savannah. My factor, Frank Lively is stopping on his way back from St. Mary's tomorrow. I'll speak to him about it."

3

Mary Gould was awake before the plantation bell rang at five the next morning, but she made herself stay in bed. Until the bell rang, there would be no one else stirring in the big house or any of the quarters. She planned what she would wear, which Mary seldom bothered to do. But Horace was home and this day was unlike any other. She would put on her new blue cambric dress, barely to her ankles, as were all her dresses, because Mary hated being hindered; and short sleeves, in spite of the new wrist-length style. And with the blue dress, she would wear her soft, yellow fichu. Pinning it into place was a nuisance, but in every way she could think of, Mary was going to kill her fatted calf in celebration. Even if Horace had come home because of trouble at Yale, she would make him glad to be here.

At the first clang of the bell, she jumped out of the high bed, ignoring the steps, and ran in the dark to throw back the India print curtains at the open windows. There was almost no acrid smell of the rags kept smoldering on the ground to discourage mosquitoes. The rain had put out their fire. Mary breathed deeply and stretched. She could hear drops still falling from the live oaks and cedars at the curve of the lane, but the rain had stopped.

The tall, slender young woman lit a candle, threw aside her nightgown and began to bathe at the washstand with an unfeminine, energetic splashing of water and soapsuds.

Mary, at twenty-one, had for five years assumed most of the heavy responsibility that normally fell to the master of the plantation. Her dead mother's sister Caroline, twenty-nine, ran the house. She was too afraid of snakes and too annoyed by deer flies to spend much time outside, especially in summer. Mary and Caroline liked each other and were satisfied with the division of work that had become their lot because of Jane Gould's death so many years ago and James Gould's crippling rheumatism. As she stood before the looking glass over the lowboy she used as a dressing table, Mary thought of her mother. The thought came often since she herself had turned twenty-one. Her mother had died while still in her twenties, and Mary, in private, found herself wondering how this could have happened. To the mind of a nine-year-old girl, Jane Gould had not seemed old enough to sicken and die. Even later, as she had stood sadly by the cold, frozen, oblong holes they dug to bury her schoolmates at the Moravian Seminary up North— young girls who died five or ten a year from fever or tuberculosis—she was sure it could never happen to her. And now, as she neared her mother's age, death was still inconceivable.

Mary jerked at the yellow fichu. The silver pin her brother Jim and his wife had given her last Christmas was too heavy. It kept pulling the thin material to one side. She sighed, as much about Jim and Alice as about the troublesome fichu. They would be back sometime this fall, and poor nervous Alice would start in all over again complaining about the South and praising the North. Papa kept saying he had made a mistake in buying the adjoining land for Jim, but he had done it, and he showed no signs of changing his mind. She squared her shoulders and approved the fichu at last. Whatever her father did was almost always right, or would turn out to be. Mary lived by that. And whatever he had said last night to her favorite brother had probably been right too. She would see her father at breakfast, but that was no guarantee that she would learn anything at all; nor would she try to. If he sat like a bump on a log while they ate, she would do the same until he was ready to tell her about Horace—or until she found out for herself. Secretly, she wished there could be some way for her younger brother to have the new

(24)

Black Banks land and stay on St. Simons. If only she could talk to him first thing this morning. She brushed her wavy black hair hard and bit her lower lip as she did when an idea struck. She would take breakfast to Horace's room! This would be the perfect way to get the facts straight from him. Certainly he would sleep late after his long trip, and there would be time to eat with Papa and Aunt Caroline, make a count of the hands heading for the fields, check on the milking and pay a quick visit to the quarters to see if any of the children were ill. Then she would ask Maum Larney, who had raised all four of them, to fix a big, beautiful breakfast for Horace and she would carry it up to him herself.

As she hurried down the stairs and back through the wide, center hall toward the kitchen built off to one side of the big house, Mary stopped from habit at the small window in the enclosed pass-through, just to make sure the "people" were up and stirring, having breakfast back in the quarters. Her father was adamant about punctuality. He expected his Negroes to have done four good hours' work by ten. He insisted upon a prompt start for the day, but he also insisted upon rest and refreshment. She must not forget to check the churning of yesterday's sour milk, so that cornbread and buttermilk could be carried to the fields for the hands when they stopped to rest at ten.

She had dressed too hurriedly. Candles were burning in the slave cabins, the people were up, but it would be half an hour before they would parade by on their way to the northwest fields where they were to pick today. Maum Larney was in the kitchen. Mary could hear her rattling around but, dreading the barrage of questions the devoted servant would surely ask about Horace, she stood a long time at the small window in the kitchen pass-through and tried to imagine what had happened that her quiet, sensitive brother should be dismissed from college. An honorable dismissal, her father had said, but a dismissal just the same. Only her bred-in-the-bone respect for other people's privacy had kept her from eavesdropping at the top of the stairs last night. It was Mary's way to have a solution for everything where the family was concerned, but how could she arrive at a solution when she knew so little about what had happened?

She looked at her mother's small gold watch pinned to her waistband. It was a quarter to six. Any minute now, the field hands would be coming by. The time she would have in the kitchen with Maum Larney had been whittled down, but it had to be faced. There was no chance that the woman who still mothered them all had not heard Horace was home. Maum Larney knew everything, even before it happened. Mary walked rapidly toward the kitchen, determined to be casual.

"Good morning, Maum Larney," she called, breezing into the spacious room, its high windows open to the moist, scattering darkness outside. The night silence was disappearing too. The gulls and terns cried, hunting their breakfast, roosters crowed, a hound dog barked, a wren shouted "sweetie, sweetie, sweetie," and a single marsh hen chattered somewhere down along the Black Banks river.

"Mornin', Miss Mary," Maum Larney mumbled over her wide shoulder, without looking around, without missing a beat on the batch of dough she was kneading. "It stop rainin'."

Mary could feel the burden hanging over the kitchen. She had expected questions, not this glum comment on the weather. Whatever Maum Larney had troubling her own heart, she never shared with her white folks until they asked. "Maum Larney, what's wrong with you?"

Mary watched her turn around slowly, her broad, strong features drawn and heavy, as though she hadn't slept all night.

"What wrong wif mah boy?"

"Oh. I was sure you knew." Mary tried a light touch. "My goodness, Maum Larney, it was almost eleven o'clock when Horace and Papa drove in last night. How *did* you know?"

"Ah caught m'se'f listenin' on de grapevine."

(26)

Mary deserved that answer. There had never been any point in trying to fool Maum Larney; no one had ever managed to put her off with a joke or a pat on the head. Most of the other Negroes went along with that sort of thing, but not Maum Larney.

"What wrong wif mah boy? Why Mausa Horace come home? He ain' sick, is he?"

More to avoid looking at Larney than to check on the workers, Mary's eyes were on the sandy, wet road that ran toward the fieldhand quarters. "No, of course Horace isn't sick. He's fine. You should see how handsome he looks in his Northern clothes. And he's so tall! His shoulders have filled out, his voice is deeper, and—" Mary tried a laugh. "He's got whiskers. Oh, not a beard, but when I kissed him last night he scratched! Can you imagine?"

Without a hint of a smile, Larney walked heavily across the kitchen to the open window where Mary stood. "Ah knows deys somepin' bad wrong wif 'im, Miss Mary. Ain' no use tryin' to fool Larney. Twelve day ago somepin' bad happen to Mausa Horace. Twelve night ago, when ah was walkin' to mah cabin down dat road you watchin' now, a night bird—a chuck-will's-widow—flew acrost mah path. Quick as a wink, Mausa Horace come up befo' me. Ah hurried aroun' in de dark till ah foun' me a brittle stick. Ah broke it in two pieces an' laid one on top de other to make a cross right dere in de road where dat bird crossed mah path. The nex' day when ah look fo' mah sticks, dey was gone!"

Mary knew better than to laugh. She didn't want to anyway. This woman was their rock. She had belonged to her father since his arrival in Spanish East Florida before the turn of the century to begin his first big surveying job. Larney was the only slave James Gould owned until he married Jane Harris in Charleston and brought her back to East Florida, where he designed and built the first house for her. Maum Larney had become the matriarch of all the slaves he bought in Florida, and after they moved to St. Simons Island, the years had only strengthened her lofty position in the

Gould household. As James Gould's wealth grew, Maum Larney increased in pride and dignity and importance. Her husband, Papa John, the father of her two children, Ca and July, was the plantation's head driver.

Mary accepted Larney's superstitions as gospel truth—for Larney. She didn't have to believe them in order to believe what came to Maum Larney from all her signs and haunts and evil omens.

"You say the night bird flew across your path twelve nights ago?" Mary asked.

"Dat when de trouble hit him fo' sho'."

"I'll admit that's about when the trouble started at school in New Haven."

"Dat boy didn't do *nuffin'* wrong! Larney kin tell you right now, Mausa Horace didn't do nuffin' wrong."

The straggly line of field hands was in sight and, automatically, Mary began her head count. They would all be coming, thirty of them. There wasn't a no-good worker on the place this year, but her father would ask and she could say she had seen them all heading for the northwest field before six o'clock. Mary counted the men and women and older children, the tow-bag ropes around their necks, the empty bags hanging behind them, slapping against the backs of their legs as they trudged along, almost in silence. Their silence didn't register on Mary at first, but suddenly it did. "Maum Larney, is something wrong down at the quarters?"

Larney had no intention of allowing Mary to change the subject. "Ain't nuffin' wrong a-tall. Larney done pass de word to dem fiel' niggahs to keep dey moufs shut dis mornin' when dey pass de house. Mah boy need his sleep! Miss Mary, what happen to 'im?"

Mary turned from the window. "Maum Larney, there's no use trying to find out from me. All I know is that there was some kind of trouble, and Horace and about forty other students had to leave school."

Larney went back to her dough board and began venting her feelings on the dough. "You ain' talkin' 'bout dat boy when you talks 'bout trouble," she muttered. "Dat a good boy. He didn't cause no trouble—*no* trouble.

Lawd, I knowed mah boy, July, shudda gone wif Mausa Horace to school to look arter 'im. July be a smart black boy, Miss Mary. He might cudda he'p some." She pummeled the dough with her fists. "How'd it look anyway, fo' Mausa's younges' son t' be goin' off jis' fo'teen year ol' by hisse'f wifout no servan'?"

"Larney, I've told you a dozen times that Northerners don't have body servants. Papa didn't want Horace laughed at. Jim wasn't allowed to take a servant, so why should July have gone with Horace?"

Larney gave her dough another thump, slapped it in a big brown crock to rise, stood to her full height of almost six feet, and declared: "Dey mus' be white trash up Norf. But you ain' white trash, an' ah's axin' you to answer mah queshun lak a lady. Mausa Horace is mah boy jis' the same as black July, an' ah got a right to know."

Mary touched Larney's arm. "Of course you have a right to know, and I swear to you I'm not hiding anything from you. Look, Maum Larney, you and Horace have always been so close, you know good and well he'll be right down here in your kitchen to talk to you as soon as he gets up."

Larney looked toward the ceiling in the direction of Horace's room. "He gonna' hab dat talk wif me fus' thing, all right. Miss Mary, *ah's* de one carr'in' his breakfas' up to his room!"

Mary's surprise and resistance kept her silent for a moment, and in that moment, she knew she had lost. "You're right, Maum Larney. You should be the first one to see him today. I imagine he needs you more than he would admit to anyone in all the world—but you."

At nine o'clock, Larney was climbing the stairs carrying a large tole waiter in both hands. On it she had placed a thick slice of country ham with red-eye gravy, hot biscuits, a whole, hot sweet potato, split and floated with butter, a bowl of grits with more butter, a pot of steaming coffee and a compote of her own pear preserves. Outside his door, she set the tray on the hall chest for the moment it took to smooth her long, full gingham skirts and her starched apron. She even gave her bright blue head scarf a quick adjustment, took a deep breath, knocked on the door, then stood back smiling, holding the tray out, ready to surprise him.

There was no sound from inside the room. She knocked again, balancing the heavy waiter on one arm.

"Who is it?" The voice behind the closed door was sharp. "Who is it, please?"

"It be Maum Larney, Mausa Horace! Maum Larney! Open de do', chile, an' see what ah's carr'in' to ya'."

After what seemed a very long time to Larney, the door was opened a few inches, and the tall, thin young man, wrapping the sash of his silk dressing gown around him, barely peeped out.

"Mausa Horace!" The woman poured her heart into his name. "Open de do' wide, honey. Maum Larney got yo' fav'rite breakfas'!"

He admitted her, then, but stayed four or five feet away, and Larney felt the strength drain from her arms so that the loaded tray shook.

"Hello, Maum Larney," he said politely.

She could see he had been up a while. The shutters were open to the bright morning outside. He had bathed, his brown hair was neatly combed—different from the way he used to comb it; he had the wave in front slicked straight back. She stared at him a long time. "Be dat all you gon' say t' me, chile?"

"Uh, no, of course not. Here, let me take that tray. It must be heavy as lead."

"Take yo' han's off! Larney carry dis food up here to ya an' she inten' to serve ya, jis' lak she allus do."

"Oh, no, that won't be necessary. Thank you very much. I can handle it myself."

Stunned, Larney let him take the tray. Her head began to swim. She stared, unbelieving, as he set the loaded waiter down on the table by his bed, easily, as though he had always taken care of himself.

"I'm glad to see you again, Maum Larney. It's been a long time. And this is very thoughtful of you."

She took a step toward him. "Why wudd'n' ah' carry yo' breakfas' to you, Mausa Horace? Larney ain't change none." She was studying his eyes, for the moment unmindful of his discomfort. They were the same pale blue eyes, but their expression was strange to her.

"Well, I guess I'd better eat while it's hot," Horace said stiffly.

Larney stepped back, her head high, her voice little more than a whisper. "Be you dismissin' me lak dat, chile? *Maum Larney?*"

"Well, yes, I suppose so. You must have work to do. But this is good of you, and—thank you very much. I'm sure I don't need anything else."

Larney began to back slowly toward the door, still looking at him, her heart pounding, making her voice tremble. "Yes, sir." She straightened her shoulders. "Yes, sir. If—if dat's *all* you needs, Mausa Horace, ah'll be gittin' on back to mah kitchen." She stopped her slow progress toward the door and tried once more, pointing to the tray, smiling almost shyly. "Ah made riz biscuit, an' dey's a dish of mah own p'sarves."

He glanced toward it. "Thank you, Maum Larney. Thank you very much. I won't need another thing."

His words were like a thick door closing on all the years they had been through together. Years in which they had been close as only a motherless white boy could be close to the Negro woman whose heart had been big enough to include him through every minute of every day, as though he had been her own flesh and blood.

Larney had reached the door of his room, and there was nothing to do but go through it, pull it shut and begin the long walk back to her kitchen.

She went down the stairs one heavy step at a time, looking straight ahead, her eyes so full of tears that she had only a glimpse of Mary darting into the parlor out of sight. Aloud to herself, halfway down, Larney said, "Miss Mary know how he was wif me. Thank You, Jesus, she know. An' thank You she know enough to stay outa mah way till ah git past dis."

At the last step, the woman's hand slipped from the railing as she crumpled up, sobbing, and rocked herself as she would have rocked a weeping child.

4

Looking slimmer than ever in a loose-fitting gray cotton shirt and tight buff nankeen trousers with matching gaiters, Horace slipped downstairs, across the front veranda and hurried around the clump of century plants at the north corner of the house. He passed Mary's garden fence, heavy with pink multiflora roses, and headed toward the stables behind the screen of mulberry trees. At ten in the morning, July would be grooming the horses. Maybe if he were lucky, he'd have to see no one but July, at least until the family dinner hour. One thing had obsessed him since he had roused from only two hours' sleep when the plantation bell rang at five—he must get away by himself. Avoiding a family as gregarious and warm-hearted as the Goulds would not be easy. He had waited until he was fairly sure Mary was busy with the accounts, his father riding his fields, and Aunt Caroline supervising the day's cooking in the kitchen with Maum Larney. These would be the only persons likely to stop him.

He had grown up with July, Larney's stocky son, almost exactly his own age; had played with him every day until they were twelve. Then July became his body servant. When he had left for boarding school at fourteen, saying good-bye to July had been almost the hardest of all the farewells except to Maum Larney. He frowned a little, walking swiftly down the damp sandy road, hidden from the house, he was sure, by the high border of white oleanders in full bloom. It had been awkward having Maum Larney bring his breakfast. People down here don't change, he thought. And they make no allowances whatever for the fact that those who go away do change. There should be a new way to come home. A way that doesn't require the one returning to make all the adjustment. A bridge should be built from both sides. Last night, his father's kindness and lack of irritation had made him feel uncomfortable and young again, indecisive. The calm offer to find a job for him made him feel pushed. Time alone this morning to think, to get things back in focus, would help, he told himself, as he turned in at the stable road. July would be the same too, he supposed, but he liked the way his old friend was with him. He had always been comfortable with July. The watermelon-pink crepe myrtles that lined Mary's carefully laid out back-garden walk caught his eye as a breeze moved through them. Home. For a moment, he felt caught, his whole being choked by love for this place. But was it love? Wasn't it merely dormant childhood memories stirred by the sudden sight of those crepe myrtles rocking against the blue Southern sky? Fiercely, he wished again, as he had when they were twelve and could no longer play together, that July's rich brown muscular body had been white like his own.

He was in sight of the stables, and they were as beautiful as ever. Even there, his father had insisted upon beauty for his young wife. "I was much older than she was," Horace remembered his saying. "The least I could do was surround her with beauty." The tabby walls of the well-proportioned big stable had cracked a little, and the thick, tiny-leafed fig vines which Horace himself had planted covered the entire side away from the sun. The hand-hewn cedar-shingled roof, sloping steeply into its protective overhang, had turned a lighter silver gray with the years. Its curling shingles sheltered moss now, and clumps of resurrection fern, revived after the rain last night. He listened. July was inside, singing as he worked, the soft, velvet voice as confident and musical as ever. Horace walked through the high open double doors.

Standing in the shadows of the large feed room, he

looked for July and saw him in the familiar back stall, grooming Dolly. The mare saw Horace first and began to stamp, so that July looked up, surprised.

"Good morning, July," Horace managed to say, sounding like someone else.

July sprang toward him, his square, strong-boned face lit with the old smile. "Mausa Horace! Ah sho' be glad t' see you, sir!"

They shook hands long and vigorously.

"Ah been dressin' up Dolly for ya', Mausa Horace. How you think de ol' girl look?"

July had made the bridge. Horace went to the restless coal black mare and threw his arms around her strong, arched neck, patting and laughing and hugging, being glad as he hadn't been able to be once since he got home. "Oh, July, she's still the most beautiful animal on earth! And you've taken perfect care of her."

"S'cuse me, Mausa Horace, but wif Dolly to take care of, it was lak habin'somepin' ob you here, sir."

Horace was still rubbing Dolly's long, aristocratic head. "It's good with horses, isn't it, July?"

"Yes, sir. It sho' is."

It was going to be the way it should be with July.

"Oh, July, she looks fine. Is she ready to ride?"

"Yes, sir! Ah been workin' on her all mornin'. Ah guessed you'd be wantin' to go soon."

Horace led the mare out of her stall and, from habit, started to the yard to saddle her himself. He stopped, quieted Dolly, and whispered, "Uh, July, I was so happy to see her, I almost forgot. I'm sneaking away from the family. I want to ride alone."

"Yes, sir. Ah'll saddle 'er."

"Good. And bring her around back. I'll slip out the feed door."

Horace saw the frown that crossed his old playmate's face. July had come as far as he could. If they were really going to talk, he would have to go the rest of the way. "July," he began, and stopped.

"Yes, sir?" July's face had the look of a hopeful child. "Kin ah he'p some way, Mausa Horace? Jis' *any* way?"

"No. No, thanks. I'll be fine. All I need is a good hard ride on Dolly."

July did not hide his disappointment. "Yes, sir."

"Where are the people picking today?"

"De norfwes' field, Mausa Horace. You bes' ride souf."

James Gould, tracking sand on his heavy boots across the downstairs hall, looked old and discouraged but intent on his mission. "Mary!" he called. "Caroline! Where is everybody?"

"I'm in the dining room, James," his sister-in-law answered. "Oh, look what you're doing to our nice clean floors, James! Couldn't you take off those muddy boots at the back door?"

"Where's Horace? I haven't seen that boy all morning, Caroline. Thought he and Mary would ride out to find me. Has he had his breakfast?"

"You know Maum Larney saw to that. Why, she even took it up to him in his room."

"He couldn't still be in his room at this hour."

"No."

"Then where is he?"

"Mary and I saw him ride off alone on Dolly about half an hour ago."

"By himself? What way is that to treat him on his first day back home?"

"He slipped away. But I doubt that he's alone now. Mary dropped everything and galloped after him."

"Which way did they ride?"

"I'm not saying. The boy evidently wanted to be alone or he wouldn't have sneaked off. I tried to tell Mary, but she's as stubborn as you."

James Gould turned and hobbled back toward the hall.

"James!" Caroline called sharply. "You're not going after them, do you hear me?"

He stopped, but the helpless look that almost always melted Caroline's heart did not melt it this time.

"My dear James, I know how you feel. You're doing all you can do for Horace by trying to get a job for him.

(35)

Don't you think we owe it to the boy to leave him alone for a while? After what happened, coming home isn't easy."

He smiled weakly, looked down at the trail of wet sand and brown leaves he had tracked across the polished floors. "I did make a mess, didn't I, Caroline? Mr. Lively will stay for dinner, of course."

Mary rode after her brother toward the blackberry-covered earth embankment that formed the boundary line between New St. Clair and the Black Banks land. July had been close-mouthed, as she knew he would be. But she had seen Horace galloping Dolly down the shell road south, and with the woods standing with rain water, she was sure he would not leave the road. She kept to it herself, urging her colt, Peter, to a full gallop. Muddy splotches spread across the hemline of her new blue dress; she hadn't bothered with a riding overskirt. Only one thing mattered—to catch up with Horace. He had frozen poor Maum Larney, but he would not freeze her. Mary had decided her brother needed her; whether he knew it or not was beside the point.

The winding Black Banks river was in sight now, curving in to drift close to the spot Jim and Alice had selected for their house. Why couldn't Horace build his house there instead of Jim? She was fond of Jim, but always somehow on guard with him. Horace, even as a small boy, had understood things that mattered, like new red at the tops of the camphor trees in spring, the marsh turning green suddenly at the end of May; he knew the way she loved roses, the scrappy bright-colored little nonpareils standing up to jays and red-wings at the big tray of crumbs and nut meats and cracked grain kept near the dining-room window. Her father had told her not one word about his talk with Horace last night, except that he was going to talk to Mr. Lively about a job in the cotton brokerage in Savannah. Mary meant to find out if Horace wanted a job in Savannah or anywhere else. That would be a far cry from becoming a lawyer. She had no choice, as she saw it, but to charge after him and find out the true state of things; not if she were going to protect both Horace and her father from themselves.

All she could tell about Horace when she had seen him for those few minutes last night was that he seemed tired and wet and somewhat affected in his speech. Today she would get at the heart of the trouble. Any minute now, she would find him, and they would talk as only the two of them had ever been able to talk.

Nearing Jim's house site on the river, she reined Peter to a trot. Horace had dismounted and was standing right on the spot where the new Black Banks house would be built. He couldn't have known that, Mary decided. The spot drew him. No one had planted the Black Banks land in years and the woods had taken over. It was friendlier, more sequestered than her father's plantation, which stretched for nearly a thousand acres between the Black Banks river and Frederica Road—planted almost solidly with Sea Island long-staple cotton. "Whoa, boy," Mary said softly to Peter. She found it hard to believe her brother hadn't heard her ride up, but he still stood, his back to her, his hands in his pockets, watching the river.

She dismounted and walked swiftly through a little grove of scrub oaks, tangled all the way to their tops with wild grape vines, their small, heart-shaped leaves showing only a touch of the pure gold they would be weaving through most of the Island trees a few weeks from now. There was no one to *look* at autumn on St. Simons when Horace was gone. Well, there was one she felt would see autumn as she saw it, but she was not sure of him or herself, for that matter. The others took it for granted, agreed pleasantly when she pointed out a flaming black gum against a yellow hickory. Horace saw it with her.

The fallen pine cones and heavy, rough palmetto roots along the woods floor hurt her feet, but she was glad she hadn't stopped to put on her outdoor shoes. The Chinese cotton house slippers she wore would make less noise. It was suddenly important to come upon Horace quietly, gently. Not so much to surprise him as not to intrude. If I can only just be with him, as his sister, she thought, not as an outsider.

"Hello, brother," she called softly. "Isn't this a perfect spot?"

Horace turned around.

"Will I be in the way?" Mary asked.

"Yes."

She stopped abruptly and her hands flew to her hips. "Well! I must say that's an impertinent way to greet your older sister whom you have scarcely seen for four years." She could have bitten off her tongue.

Horace turned back to the river. "I'm sorry, Mary. I heard you ride up. I'd just hoped to be alone a while."

And here I barged in, she scolded herself, feeling suddenly nervous with this unpredictable young man, so sleek in his city clothes, so intent upon remaining a visitor. "Look here, Horace, honey—this is *Mary*. What's happened to you? Oh, I'm not prying about the trouble at Yale. What's happened to *you*, my favorite brother? Where are you? It isn't like you to ride off alone like this without telling anyone." She had begun softly, but now her voice was rising and she couldn't stop it. "We all want to help you, but all you do is shut us out. Even Maum Larney. You hurt her this morning and you don't have a right to hurt her. You're a Gould, you know. You're one of us and there isn't any point in trying to act as though you're not." Mary caught her breath. "Horace, honey, can't you come home—even halfway?"

He whirled to face her. "What in the name of heaven do you *want* me to do, Mary? Act like someone I'm not?" He tried to laugh. "On second thought, that should be easy—I don't know who I am any more."

She stared at him, more stunned than hurt.

"What *do* you want me to do?" he repeated. "If a man can't ride alone on his own horse without being accused of being strange and cruel—without being accused of hurting the good ol' homefolks—" His voice broke. "Why is it all up to me? Why is everyone treating me like a—a mental invalid who has to be handled with kid gloves? I

(38)

want to come home, sister. I want to—but how do I do it overnight?"

A nonpareil, his feathers colored scarlet and royal blue and golden green, swung from a joe-pye stalk, straining toward its seed. Mary pointed to the tiny bird. "Look, there's our favorite little bird, brother. Remember how the nonpareils scrap in the spring and early summer? Look at the poor fellow now. He's molting—see? Half his green shawl is gone. His whole personality is changed— no fight left in him at all."

Horace sighed. "I'm not a six-year-old any more, Mary. I'm not even fourteen and leaving for boarding school. I'll be eighteen next week, and none of this talk works. You didn't change when you went North to school be- cause you knew you were coming back here to stay. This place has always been yours. You've refused every offer of marriage, every teaching position—everything, just because you want to stay with father and run his planta- tion."

"What's so wrong about that?" she flared and thought, you don't know everything about me, baby brother.

"Nothing. That's what I'm trying to tell you. You know who you are and what you want to do. I don't care what anyone does so long as he knows that's what he wants to do."

"You knew once. You've always wanted to be a law- yer."

"*Papa* wanted me to be a lawyer. I hadn't begun to think for myself, but he had it all decided. Oh, being a lawyer would be as good as anything else. I could grad- uate from another school and go on and be the best all-fired lawyer in the country!"

"You'd better watch your language in front of Papa."

"Don't worry, I will."

Mary studied his thin, sensitive face, the dark circles under his deep-set eyes, the new thrust to his jaw; but mostly she was arriving at what she felt to be the solution. "Horace, I'm convinced that you should do just that. Graduate from another school and show those peo- ple at Yale! I don't really know what happened, but I'm convinced that's exactly what you should do. Then you could come back and open your office near home—maybe Brunswick will be large enough by then if Papa and Mr. King and Colonel duBignon get their canal started."

He whirled and ran toward the river. Mary caught up with him, grabbed his shoulders and tried with all her might to shake him. He didn't budge. He was a man now, no longer her baby brother. Tears, as strange to Mary as Horace's behavior, stung her eyes. And then his arm was around her shoulder and they were both crying, clinging to each other until the strangeness and the tears were over.

"I'm sorry, Mary," he said finally, blowing his nose, his eyes almost smiling for the first time. "But if I had to act like a baby, I guess it's better with you than anyone else."

"That's a silly thing to be—sorry. I think I'd have exploded if you'd kept on acting so peculiar with me. Do you want to tell me what happened at school? If you don't, it's all right."

He looked at her a moment, and then said, "Yes, I'd like for you to know, but then that ends it."

They sat together on the scaly trunk of a big fallen pine, back from the river, where they would be out of sight. He told her the whole story and seemed relieved, quiet, Mary thought, when he finished.

"Well, sister, what do you think?" he asked at last.

"I think the faculty was unfair, that's what I think!"

"I don't mean that," he said. "Do you really feel *I* could have done anything other than what I did?"

"No, I do not. And if you're carrying a lot of guilt, Horace Gould, drop it right now!"

He laughed, picked up a pine cone and tossed it at a squirrel. "I guess I'm not as grown-up as I thought I was."

"What kind of talk is that?"

"Just your saying I'm not to feel guilty makes it a lot easier not to. I should have been able to reach that on my own. I thought I had. Then I got mixed up again here at home."

"Fiddle-faddle. Now, let's talk about how long you might be able to stay and about which school you'll—"

"No, Mary! I'm through with school, and even you can't change that. Get it clear once and for all and don't bring it up—not ever again."

She stood up. "But, Horace, if you don't go back to school, Papa's going to get you a job—just an ordinary job on Factor's Walk in Savannah. Old bald-headed Mr. Lively is probably at the dock at Frederica now. Papa says he's going to talk to him today about a job for you in that dumb cotton market!" She tried to make him look at her, but he was hard and strange again. "Do you want a job in Savannah, Horace? Is that what you told Papa you wanted to do?"

"I didn't tell Papa anything except that I was through with higher education. He decided about the job on his own—the way you're deciding I don't want it." He grabbed at a piece of Johnson grass and jerked, but it wouldn't break off. "Don't I matter? Doesn't it matter what I think? Maybe I want to do something entirely different from what either one of you wants me to do! Did you or Papa ever stop to think that maybe I might want to find out about myself—for myself?"

"Horace, honey, I only want to know what you want so I can take your side."

His shoulders sagged. "You know good and well, sister, that if Papa gets a job for me in Savannah, you'll decide it's the thing for me to do."

"I will not!"

"You will, too. You wouldn't cross Papa because you couldn't. There isn't anything in you that would go against whatever he wants—for me or for anybody else. You wouldn't be here if that weren't true."

"Oh, yes, I would be!" she snapped. "This is the one place on earth I want to be, Horace Bunch Gould, and don't you ever doubt it. I'm here taking care of Papa and New St. Clair because I want to be."

He laughed. "Then you're lucky. At least you know."

"But you must know what you want, too. That's all I'm asking. I can try to influence Papa, if you'll tell me what it is you want. Maybe if you stayed here with us a while, you'd find out whatever it is you need to find out about yourself. Just tell me what it is you want to do right now."

He jumped to his feet. "I don't *know* what I want!" he shouted. "Can't you get that through your head, sister?"

She didn't go after him this time as he ran out of the woods toward the river and back up the slight rise to the spot where the Black Banks house would stand. He paused there a moment, then raced toward Dolly, swung into the saddle and rode back toward his father's house.

Talking to herself, Mary walked slowly to her horse. "I wonder if what he really wants is to stay here?" She mounted Peter easily from a fallen tree and sat looking out over the marshes and the Black Banks river, toward the sea. "No point in dreaming." She shrugged. "Papa would only say Horace is too young to own land. What poor Papa doesn't realize is that Horace is different— different from Jim, different from Janie, different from me. And maybe," she said, as she started Peter trotting toward home, "he's better than all of us put together."

5

It was four o'clock, dinnertime, and Larney, in a fresh apron and head scarf, moved around the big mahogany table, holding the company dishes filled with steaming food, while each one helped himself. She did it all slowly, more carefully than usual, giving herself plenty of time to observe and listen. What if mah boy don' want no job in S'vannah? she thought. Ever since they had sat down, her master at the head of the table, that dried up Mr. Lively to his right and Horace to his left, her boy hadn't said a word. He had politely seated first his aunt, then his sister, but he didn't have anything at all to say. Larney was glad Miss Caroline had a mind to keep jumping up and running to the kitchen for things they needed. She was a cricket, anyway, and had a hard time staying still. But best of all, it meant Larney didn't have to go. She could stay where she wanted to be, in the same room with Horace, praying under her breath, watching his every change of expression.

"Well, so you have a mind to go into the cotton business, son!" Bespectacled, bald Mr. Lively made his statement as if butter wouldn't melt in his mouth.

To Larney, it was as though he had it all decided ahead of time from high up on his perch. She stopped in her tracks as Horace looked up surprised, quizzical, but he didn't have a word to say.

"My son needs a job," James Gould filled the silence. "Savannah isn't too far away and I think he'd enjoy the work."

Larney clamped her mouth shut. What was the matter with Mausa Gould? she thought, looking from her master to Horace. They didn't so much as exchange glances. She looked then at Mary and saw that she was watching her brother as closely as Larney watched him.

"Well, as I was telling your father out at the gin a while ago, it so happens we do need a new man—and right away. An enterprising young man of sterling character." Lively's steel rimmed spectacles slipped down on his long, pocked nose, and he readjusted them with a flourish. "I'm delighted to tell you, son, the job's yours if you want it."

What right did that man have to call her boy "son"? Larney frowned and went on serving the rice.

"Could you tell us what the job entails?" James Gould was asking. "And would he have time to come home now and then?"

"Of course he could come home," Mr. Lively clucked. "It would be better in every way, son, than being way up there at the North among strangers. You'll be close

(43)

home, mixing with your own kind—cultivated coastal Georgians. You won't find better people anywhere than our Savannah people." He poked at his spectacles again. "Now, there will be some traveling involved. You'll like that, I'm sure. Mainly it's a clerk's position with a private desk—a golden opportunity, I'd say, for a boy as young as you are."

Larney saw Horace look helplessly, first at his father, then at his sister. Miss Mary seemed about to bust to say something, but wonder of wonders, she kept still. Maybe because Mr. Lively kept on talking.

"I'll tell you what it amounts to, Gould—keeping track of cotton shipments, and when one gets lost, as one will now and then, even with a fine firm like Lively and Buffton, it would be your job to track it down. Now, doesn't that appeal to you?"

Larney stood behind Horace, a little to one side, waiting. He looked down at his plate, and mussed the rice around with his fork.

"How about it, Horace?" his father asked.

"Well, I—I suppose it's all right, sir."

Larney had never seen him look so alone, so in need of comfort.

Frank Lively cleared his throat several times. "Well, now, I can assure you, Mr. Gould, senior, that as a rule a firm such as ours does not offer a responsible position like this to a mere boy—an inexperienced one at that." He cleared his throat again. "In all due respect, I am surprised to say the very least at this—uh—lack of enthusiasm."

When Horace suddenly pushed back his chair, Larney spilled water on the carpet trying to fill a goblet without looking at it. Halfway to his feet, the boy seemed to fold up, like a hurt bird, slipped back into the chair slowly, replaced his napkin on his lap, and said, "All right, sir. I'll take the job."

Lively peered over the rims of his glasses, touched his bony fingers together at their tips and smiled benignly. "Good! You won't be sorry a day, son. Not a single day.

Now then—can you be there to start in bright and early Monday morning?"

"Monday!" Mary gasped. "That's day after tomorrow—before your birthday!"

"Yes, sir," Horace said flatly. "I have only a valise with me. I left my trunk in New Haven until I knew where I'd—be. I'll take the boat up Sunday afternoon."

"Good!" Mr. Lively said again, more emphatically. "Now then, we've plenty of splendid boardinghouses in Savannah. You'll have no problem at all. In fact, I'll gladly meet your boat, young man, and escort you personally to what I consider the best place for you to board." He slapped the table. "Well, then, it's all settled, and I prophesy you're going to like our big city. Thriving businesses, many cultural advantages—splendid theater, opera, concerts. Steeped in history. Our six lovely squares, right in the heart of the city, you know, were laid out by the great General Oglethorpe himself. Oh, my, yes, we are prospering in Savannah—well over eight thousand people according to our eighteen-thirty census!"

"Is that right," James Gould said.

Larney watched Horace start to get up from the table again, his face so set and determined, her heart ached more than ever.

"I'm grateful for the chance you've given me, sir." He stood up. "May I be excused now, Papa?"

"Why, I—suppose so, son. And I'm relieved you decided to take the job."

"It's easy to decide, sir, when you don't really have a choice."

As Horace strode rapidly out of the dining room and up the front hall, Maum Larney stooped over to wipe up the water she had spilled. There was nothing for her to do but the hardest thing on earth—let him go again.

6

On Sunday morning, dressed for church, Mary and Caroline drove up Frederica Road in the new green phaeton, ahead of Horace and his father in the old buggy, toward the Island's only church. It was already hot, with not enough breeze to stir the hanging moss, and the deer flies were so thick that two Negro boys rode importantly—one on the back of each vehicle—swinging long, leafy branches over the heads of their passengers.

"Can't you go any faster, Mary?" Caroline kept her palm-leaf fan going against the flies, too. "I'm being eaten up!"

Mary, who hated wearing hats, was more beautiful than ever, her aunt thought, with a lovely piece of black lace draped over her dark hair. But, oh, she looks so grim today, poor child.

"I'll go faster if you've got it all figured out what we're going to say to people at church this morning when they begin asking questions about why Horace will go to work in Savannah suddenly, instead of finishing school. Papa and Horace aren't in a hurry behind us, and I don't relish the idea of having to talk to anyone without Papa beside me. This is all his idea."

"Oh, Mary, honest to goodness! Do you really think they're going to be nosy about it?"

"It wouldn't be natural if they didn't ask questions."

"Well, I hadn't given that a thought."

"I think of everything," Mary snorted, "but a lot of good it does."

"Now, what do you mean by that?" Caroline slapped at a deer fly on her white lace mitt and made a stain.

(46)

"Aunt Caroline, I know good and well Horace does not want to leave the Island now."

"How do you know, Mary?" she asked, rubbing the spot on her mitt. "How can you possibly know he wants to stay? He hasn't said a dozen words since he arrived."

"Because I know my brother. He shouldn't be forced to leave when he really doesn't know yet what he wants to do. Especially not to be sent to Savannah to work for old Baldy."

"Hush," Caroline whispered, glancing back toward skinny little Adam, a field hand's son who, by his tenth birthday, had won the coveted spot as July's helper. Adam was waving his branch over their heads and listening intently. "Maum Larney picked Adam to ride with us and Joe to ride with Horace and Papa for a reason—you know they're both all ears!"

"What do I care what Maum Larney finds out? Her heart's as heavy as mine is."

Caroline turned in the buggy seat for a better look at her niece from under her own straw scoop bonnet. "Do you mean to sit there and tell me that you actually disagree with your father about something, Mary Gould?"

"I certainly do," Mary said. "And I'd give anything I own to know what those two are talking about in the buggy behind us."

"Dey ain't talkin', Miss Mary," Adam called. "Dey's jis' settin' up lookin' straight ahead. Joe ain' goin' hab nuffin' to tell Maum Larney when we gits back."

"Since you know so much, Adam, did you see Master Horace say good-by to Maum Larney?" Mary asked over her shoulder.

"No, ma'am. She was waitin' fo' him too, at de kitchen do', but he don' come."

"Now, why in the world does Horace want to hurt poor Maum Larney?" Caroline wondered.

"He doesn't want to hurt anyone, Aunt Caroline!" Mary snapped the reins in exasperation, then remembered and slowed the horse again. "He's so mixed up,

(47)

he's just doing as little of anything as possible. Everything's happened too fast for him. He needed a long time at home to think things through. Papa may be sorry to the last day he lives."

"Well, I never thought I'd live to see the day when you would disagree with your father. But I'm sure James thinks he's doing the kind thing for Horace. The boy refuses to go to another school and he needs to be busy. The last thing he needs, in my opinion, is to sit around and mope about what happened. If you ask me, Mary, I think your father's being considerate and understanding—and wise."

Horace stared into the quiet woods as his father drove the old buggy along the narrow, winding shell road. He felt numb, almost relieved that a decision had been made, right or wrong; dreading the good-by and the two hours he would have to kill before his boat was due; feeling the pressure of so much left unsaid between him and his father; puzzled by how this man sitting beside him could love him so much and understand him so little. He would work at the new job. He would not hurt his father any more than he had already hurt him, but every minute he would be on the lookout. Savannah was the largest city in Georgia. Hundreds of people came and went daily. There would be chances for new job openings. A bedraggled cardinal with only one tail feather left popped onto the budding bloom of a devil's-walking-stick by the roadside. Horace half smiled at the molting bird. All the joy of living is over for you too, isn't it, redbird? You just fly about hunting what you need in order to exist—losing your feathers, no more song. The big difference is that you're free—you can come and go as you please, as your instinct prompts. I'm caught. I can't bear the thought of staying and I don't want to go where I'm going.

The bell at Christ Church Frederica began to ring.

"Be good to sit beside you in our own pew again, son."

Horace felt his throat tighten. *Did his father think he was going to church?* He had assumed they would all say good-by in front of the church, permitting him the dignity of going on to the dock alone. His father couldn't be forcing him to make polite, neighborly conversation with their Island friends!

"We refinished the sanctuary floors last month," his father was saying. "Put a new coat of white paint on the outside. She's a beautiful sight now, back under all those big old oaks."

In less than a minute, they would be across the wooden bridge over the savannah at the curve in Frederica Road, in sight of the little white church built when Horace was eight. Mr. Bartow, the rector, would be standing out front in his vestments, greeting the eight or nine planters' families driving up in their Sunday best, their buggies and carriages clean and polished, their children scrubbed and excited, since this was almost the only time they got dressed up to go any place. His father had not given a thought to the humiliation it would cause him if he had to talk to any of those people who had known him all his life.

They could see the tiny white building now, set far back from the road, dwarfed by the tall oaks. Horace would have to think of something fast. He saw that Mary and Aunt Caroline had stopped the new phaeton across the road and were still sitting in it.

"Let's ride over there by Mary, Papa," he said nervously.

Aunt Caroline waved to them, but Mary sat stiff and motionless. The people and Mr. Bartow had already seen them and were drifting in their direction down the long path from the church.

James Gould drove the buggy to the opposite side of the road and drew up beside the phaeton. Horace jumped to the ground, helped his father down, shook his hand—hugged him briefly, raised one hand in an awkward farewell to his sister and aunt, leaped into the driver's seat of the old buggy, and with Joe still hanging

(49)

on the back, drove as fast as he could make the surprised horse travel, up Frederica Road, past the churchyard, and out of sight.

If Mary or his father followed him, he could do nothing about that, but he could get away from the familiar faces of the parishioners, and soon, in less than two hours now, he could get on that boat and go away.

Seated on a wooden bench, the only passenger in the cabin of the *Magnolia*, Horace kept his back to the window. The steamer, loaded with bags of raw cotton, packed to rock hardness by bare black feet on plantations from St. Mary's to St. Simons, was entering Buttermilk Sound, north of the Island. He had sent Joe back with the buggy, and no one had followed him. He felt weak with relief, but he dared not watch the Island slip by as he moved away. The family would be almost home from church now, he supposed, and tried not to think of his father driving back down the road alone in the buggy.

At last he looked out the window. The Island was gone; only water and marshland stretched ahead and behind as the *Magnolia* crossed the Sound. In spite of himself, he had cried alone in the woods at Frederica. His eyes still smarted. Tears had come with an unexpected, irrelevant thought of the beautiful tract of land called Black Banks. Why should thinking of his brother's land make him sad?

Stretching out his long legs in an ungentlemanly fashion, he looked around the cabin. It was much the same as the *South Carolina's*—more peaceful, because the St. Mary's planter, who had talked all the way from Darien to the Island, was not there. "We're probably carrying a few hundred pounds of his cotton to market, though," he mused aloud, enjoying the freedom of being alone. He had meant to discuss politics with his father; to find out how his father felt, what he said when one of his St. Simons neighbors ridiculed the Union. He smiled a little. "Papa probably stays true to his nature, and says nothing." Today, in the quiet, empty, sunlit cabin, he was ashamed that the ignorant planter had somehow reminded him of his Southern classmate who had led their rebellion. "That's nonsense. No grounds for comparison." It was impossible that an uneducated, loud-mouthed bigot could in any way think like his brilliant friend at Yale. Unless, of course, education doesn't go as deeply into a man as it is claimed to. Maybe it just shines up a man's exterior. He rather liked that idea; it justified his determination never to enter another school. Still, he had agreed with his crusading classmate, had taken the same stand against the tyranny of the Faculty. He sighed. He would think that through another time. Now he was still too tired. Too tired and too anxious about what lay ahead in Savannah. Perhaps he would invite Alex Drysdale to his boarding house some night and discuss the real effects of education on a man. He and Alex looked at almost everything from opposite points of view, but it would be good to see old Alex again. It had only been four days since they parted in Savannah. It seemed at least a year.

He studied his short black boots, the trouser straps beneath them pulling the legs of his dark gray trousers taut. Maum Larney had sponged and pressed his clothes. They were his favorites—a pearl-gray, short waistcoat, cut straight across the front, a dark green cutaway with fashionable, extra wide lapels, and a white shirt with a crisply plated frill; his cravat was pearl gray too, and fastened with a silver stud. He would have to be careful of his limited wardrobe until his trunk could reach Savannah, but once it did, he guessed he would look as well as or perhaps better than most. He took a deep breath. Maybe Savannah wouldn't be so bad after all.

7

The service and the food were excellent at Miss Susan Platt's boardinghouse on the corner of Bull and Congress. Horace liked his attic room with two dormer windows, and Miss Platt was kind and attentive. He would have to say that Mr. Lively had done well for him. His employer's intentions appeared to be genuinely solicitous. So solicitous that much of his free time was spent in dodging invitations to join the "lively Lively family" for an evening at the theater, a dinner at their home, a picnic on the Strand. He had found no way to escape attending Christ Church with them on Sunday mornings. It was obvious that Mr. Lively had his eye on Horace as a prospective son-in-law. To Horace, Tessie Lively was a cow, even duller than her father and as homely as her ten-year-old brother, Bubba.

The job would not have been unpleasant if Horace had been born with a bent toward detail and routine. He had mastered the work swiftly, and the first week, when cotton shipments were heavier than usual, he had rather enjoyed the excitement of the huge schooners and brigs coming and going on the Savannah River below Commerce Row, where the Lively and Buffton Cotton Brokerage was located. Part of his job was to scan the distant stretches of the river with powerful glasses for the arrival of the ships whose cargoes he was to check off. He watched from one of the ornate wrought-iron balconies that hung above the dockside of Commerce Row, and this part of his work he liked. The majesty of a four-masted sailing vessel rounding the big bend in the river never failed to excite him. He loved boarding one of them when she docked beside the wharf at the foot of the steep, sandy bluff that formed Savannah's Strand between Bay Street and the water. Checking off a cotton shipment, tow bag by tow bag, bale by bale, grew monotonous, but there was the satisfaction of seeing his careful list tally with the list at Commons. And there were always the idle times of waiting for the city-owned black stevedores to swing up more cargo, when he could hang over the railing of the big ship pretending he would be sailing away on her. Daily, Mr. Lively assured him that travel might begin for him at any time. "We've been fortunate so far, Gould, but one never knows about these things. A shipment could be lost tomorrow."

On Thursday of his second week in Savannah, Horace went to the Drysdale home on State Street. The two classmates greeted each other with bear hugs and slaps on the back. "Why in the world did you wait so long to look me up?" Alex complained. "I've been so lonely to see a familiar face from old New Haven. If I'd known you were nearby, we'd have been in one of our famous arguments long ago. I find the social life of Savannah pretty dull, Horace, do you? Or haven't they captured you yet?" Alex stood back, inspecting him. "A fine gentlemanly specimen like you—why, the young ladies of Savannah will spin with joy when they discover you! Stay for dinner, and let's live life together again for a few days. I'm leaving in three weeks for school at the North."

This had begun a changed life for Horace and some relief from the Livelys. Alex might have been bored with Savannah society, but he was in the midst of it, and in no time so was Horace. He particularly relished being safely in the company of Alex and his friends when, at intermission time at the theater, he would see Mr. and Mrs. Lively, young Bubba, and thick-waisted Tessie. For diplomacy's sake, he continued to attend church with them, but except for that, Alex had saved him. Every night they were in the company of attractive girls at parties or concerts or alone together arguing hotly.

Early on the last evening before Alex was to leave for school, the two made certain they would have some time alone. As soon as Horace finished work at six o'clock, they walked to the livery stable, rented mounts and rode down East Broad to Liberty and across the commons toward the thick pine forest at the edge of town. When they reached the wide, steep-banked ditch that drained the city's streets, Alex slowed his horse. Clopping over the wooden bridge spanning the ditch, they entered the virgin forest in silence except for the soft thud of their horses' hooves on the carpet of pine straw.

"I used to play here when I was a boy," Alex reminisced, as they dismounted and stood looking up at the long-needled pines. "It was a great place to play. I still miss these tall pines at the North. Pines are different up there. You know you're going to be sorry, Horace, that you aren't going back to school with me—even though the other colleges are putting us ex-Yale rebels on probation for the first six months."

Horace frowned. "Alex, this is our last evening together for a long time."

"All right. I won't mention it again. It's just that I have pride in you, my friend. You stood firm at Yale. You showed what you're made of. You've a fine mind. The South needs your kind of man. I hate to see you going to waste following the Lively family fortunes."

"Don't worry about that," Horace snapped. "This is only a stop-gap job with Lively."

"But what else can you do? You're only partially educated. You're not equipped to do anything of importance—your splendid mind and loyalties notwithstanding. Some of those fellows didn't amount to much, but you matter."

"Thanks," Horace said, grinning. "Say, Alex, I've been meaning to ask your opinion on something. Did you consider Steiner a troublemaker?"

Alex looked puzzled. "You mean because he was the orginator, more or less, of our so-called rebellion? No, I did not. Why?"

Horace dreaded a real argument on their last meeting, but he had to tell Alex about his reaction when the St.

Mary's planter on the *South Carolina* had spoken critically of the Federal Government. Of how he had suddenly heard overtones of their friend, John Steiner. "How could that man have reminded me of Steiner? Do you think it could have been something of the same spirit motivating both men?"

"Both men were kicking against the goads of tyranny," Alex said quickly. "Any honorable, free man will do that!"

"I agree. But it bothered me. This planter *was* the kind who would make trouble when resorting to reason might avoid it. It made me face something in myself I didn't like. I was dismissed from Yale for the same reason Steiner was."

"Look here, Horace, you're a planter's son. It should be easy for you to see that planter's point of view. His lack of education has no bearing at all. You can't be willing to acquiesce in the way the North is attempting to take over control of the Federal Government by starving us out down here! I admit we're still fairly strong economically, but if these impossible tariffs continue to be heaped onto the load the South is already carrying, our whole Cotton States economy will collapse. You agree, don't you?"

"Yes, I suppose I do, but—"

"But what? The Northern theory of government by majority rule is coarse, materialistic—wrong. Only the well-born have real political power down here. We in the Cotton States venerate the Union for its sublime moral principle—States' rights! The North worships the Union in a crass spirit of commercial idolatry. You're not using your head."

"On the contrary, I think I'm just beginning to use it," Horace said. He could see Alex was going to argue, not from logic, but from his own emotional viewpoint. "Maybe we'd better just forget the whole thing."

"Not on your life. I don't intend to stand by and hear you disagree with me on the all-important subject of States' rights!"

"Did I say I disagreed?"

"*Do* you believe in the high and sacred principle of States' rights, Horace?"

"Yes, of course I do. It's constitutional. But I also believe in the *Union* of all the states. And anyway, I wasn't trying to start a political discussion."

"Your question led right into one! Tyranny is tyranny, isn't it? Whether it's found in the Federal Government or on the faculty at dear old Yale."

Horace felt uncomfortable. He said nothing.

"And before you deliberately change the subject, Horace, I need to be sure that you are not taken in by any of the abolitionist talk from the hypocritical North. In spite of your intelligence, you're something of a romanticist. I think it's highly possible you could be taken in by what they're saying. It all *seems* humane. They shout and circulate pamphlets on how inhuman it is for us to own slaves. You can bet your shirt they would own them too, if the weather up there weren't too inclement for agrarian life! Don't forget the slave trade is carried on—and for big profit—by Yankee ships."

"That's a superficial observation," Horace said. "All Northerners do not own slave ships and all Northerners are not abolitionists."

Alex sighed. "I just want you to keep your perspective clear where the Cotton States are concerned. You're much too sentimental at times. It can throw your mind out of focus. Where would your father be without his slaves? For that matter, where would they be without him?"

Horace wished Alex hadn't brought up the subject of slavery. The people at New St. Clair seemed so content, such a part of life there, he could neither imagine New St. Clair without its people, nor the people without New St. Clair. They were one. Still, at Yale during arguments for and against slavery, he had been the only Southerner to keep silent. I'm gone from the Island now, anyway, he thought. I'll never be a planter. None of it is my concern.

"You didn't answer my question, Horace," Alex broke

into his revery. "Where would your father be without his slaves?"

"I don't have an answer yet. I haven't thought it through. I don't think I'm on either side of the slavery question."

"That's impossible! You have to be on one side or the other of a question as vital as the right to own any kind of property."

Horace was not going to be trapped. "I could jump into an emotional argument *or* agreement with you right now, but it would be only that—emotional. Respect my right to think a while, old boy." He grinned at his friend.

"Of course," Alex snorted, "although I don't want to. We're Southerners, Horace. We may have Northern educations, but we're Southerners, and proud of it, aren't we?"

"Yes, sir," Horace agreed warmly. "The way I feel these days, I might end up living anywhere on the face of the earth. But I guess part of me would always be hanging around under the moss, smelling the jessamine in the spring."

"The man's a poet, as well as a foolish, cautious idealist," Alex laughed. "Say, do you think we'd better ride back? It's getting dark. Wanta' race?"

"You bet!"

They galloped like Indians, shouting at each other, dodging cows and push carts in the streets and laughing all the way back to the livery stable.

"That's a bad neighborhood on East Broad around the stable," Alex said as they turned onto President and began walking toward the Drysdale house. "Wherever seamen congregate, they attract a rough element. I don't like being over there at night."

"I do," Horace said. "I go often. I like seamen."

"Better watch your pocketbook. Say, Horace, you will visit my mother often when I'm gone, won't you?"

"Well, yes, Alex, if you want me to. Of course, I could be leaving any day."

"No lost shipments yet, eh?"

"Not yet. But I may not wait for one, if I can find a

place I want to go and something I want to do after I get there. And don't start lecturing me on the values of higher education."

"I won't. I've finished that lecture. I can see you're not going to settle down anywhere for a while. I don't understand what's troubling you, but I accept it."

They were at the corner of President and Bull, in the circle of light from the whale-oil lantern which had just been lit beside the water pump. Alex stopped short and put his hands on Horace's shoulders. "Look, friend, we stay in touch once in a while, eh? *Omnes in uno.*"

"*Omnes in uno,*" Horace said, and they walked on. At the front steps of the Drysdale house, they shook hands, but neither young man said anything more until they were inside. Horace meant only to pay his respects to Alex's parents and go back to his boardinghouse. With warm, hospitable people such as the Drysdales, this was impossible. He was swept into the parlor full of guests, where a beautiful woman in a soft blue gown was singing.

Before her song ended, Horace was in love.

8

Horace kept his promise to visit Alex's mother. It was impossible not to. If he went often enough, he was sure one day—one shining day—that *she* would be a guest there again and he would see her, maybe even have a brief conversation with her. He had been presented to her in the crowd that night; he knew her name and it was magic: Linda Thatcher. The Widow Thatcher, Mrs. Drysdale called her, and he had resented it. Widows were not necessarily old, he knew, but the word sounded old, and Linda Thatcher was ageless. Older than he by a few years, perhaps, but what did years matter when a man's heart was suddenly alive with love?

After Alex had been gone a week, he called again at the Drysdale house.

"How nice you've come by tonight, Mr. Gould," Mrs. Drysdale greeted him. "We're having another musical evening. You may not remember her—I know how boys are—but the Widow Thatcher is singing for us again tonight."

For Horace, the high-ceilinged, dark-paneled entrance hall began to slide to one side; he felt his face burn. Mrs. Drysdale seemed not to notice, because she went right on trying to refresh his memory. "It was the night before Alexander left for school. You'd been riding. You popped in right in the middle of an aria. Oh, my dear boy, we are so blessed in Savannah! This talented lady is planning to make it her home."

Horace was suddenly, unreasonably panic-stricken. Linda Thatcher hadn't arrived yet, and somehow he must find an excuse to leave before she got there.

"Come right on in, Mr. Gould," his hostess was saying. "There's a nip in the air this evening, and perhaps you'd like a cup of hot tea or mulled wine."

"Oh, no, thanks. I can't stay, ma'am. Much as I'd love to hear her sing again. I—uh—have other plans for the evening."

She smiled knowingly. "Someone lovely and suitable, I hope?"

There was no one on earth lovely and suitable except Linda Thatcher, but he let it stand. "Thank you for being so gracious, Mrs. Drysdale. I wouldn't have come if I'd known you were entertaining. I'll stop another time, if I may. It—it's marvelous that Mrs. Thatcher is going to live in Savannah."

"Isn't it, though? A lovely person, from a fine Northern family. Massachusetts. Has the most adorable little girl, Harriett. Frail and pretty. A head full of golden curls. To see the child enter a room with her raven-haired mother is a picture! Well, now, I must run back to my guests. But do come again, Mr. Gould."

(59)

He stood under the shadows of a big cedar across the street from the Drysdale house until her carriage arrived. And for a fleeting moment, he saw her again. She laughed as she gave instructions to her driver, and her laugh was as musical as her singing. And wonder of wonders, she was alone. Rarely did a lady go anywhere at night alone, but she was unlike anyone else, and his heart took wings at the thought that there might be room in her life for him.

Even Mr. Lively received a warm greeting the next morning when Horace met him in front of the coffeehouse.

"You seem in fine fettle, young man," his employer said.

"Oh, I am, sir. It's a beautiful day, isn't it?"

"Indeed yes, and it bids fair to be another on the Sabbath tomorrow. Will we see you at our house for the usual stroll to church, Gould? My dear family has come to expect you."

"Yes, sir. I'll be there."

"We have a splendid treat in store at the service tomorrow, have you heard?"

"No, sir, I haven't."

"The Widow Thatcher is going to sing! Surely you know this magnificent artist is in Savannah to stay."

"Yes—yes, sir, I've heard that."

"Well, she's an Episcopalian too, fortunately for us at Christ Church, and from now on she'll be blessing us with her divine voice each and every Sunday morning!"

They had crossed Bay Street and were turning in at the wooden walkway that led from the Strand to the Lively and Buffton entrance, and Horace saw a way to escape. "If you'll excuse me, Mr. Lively, I have to go below to check on something first thing. I'll be back at my desk right away."

He ran down the wooden stair to Factor's Walk, the canyonlike passageway that connected the warehouses along Commerce Row. There was nothing to check except his pounding heart. He leaned against the steep, sandy bluff and tried to imagine why he should be so fortunate. When everything had seemed wrong, in a moment's time life had become not only right, but full of promise, high expectation, joy. If he could get his mind on prayer at church tomorrow, he would pray—oh, how he would pray—that there would be no lost shipments. He could not leave Savannah now that she was here to stay.

Horace straightened his desk early that evening, eager to leave promptly at six. This Saturday night he would not wander around the city, hunting for interesting sights. He would bathe, wash his hair, lay out his best clothes and polish his new black dress boots. All the way home he planned what he would wear to church. Of course, he would choose his dark gray cutaway and the new gray striped trousers he had bought the week before with his first month's salary. Should he be conservative? Would a waistcoat of the same color make him look more mature? Or should he wear one of a contrasting color? His white silk cravat would be perfect, either way.

At Johnson Square, the line of people at the water pump reminded him that he might need more water that evening than the maid normally left in his room. And then he heard a shrill voice calling his name. It was Tessie Lively, waving frantically.

"Oh, Mr. Gould! I just knew if I kept coming to this old pump, I'd meet you some day."

"Good evening, Miss Lively." He bowed.

"Aw, come now, don't you think you know me well enough to call me Miss Tessie?" Her cheeks puffed into a coy smile.

"Well, I suppose so. Nice evening, isn't it?" As a gentleman, he would have to offer to wait with her and carry her firkin of water home. "May I help you, Miss Tessie?"

She shivered with delight. "Oh, that's asking an awful lot, isn't it?"

"Not at all," Horace lied. "Here, give me the firkin. You're next."

He took the wooden bucket, pumped furiously, filling it as fast as he could, and started toward her house on St. Julian.

"My goodness gracious, you walk rapidly, Mr. Gould," Tessie said.

"I'm in something of a hurry. If you'll excuse me, I have to move right along."

"Oh, in that case, I'm more honored than ever that you offered to help me, sir."

No matter what he said, he knew she would twist it to mean what he didn't mean, but he made small talk as best he could. "How does it happen you have to come for water, Miss Tessie? Can't one of the servants bring it?"

"Of course! One of our nigras usually keeps the water supply up. But I told you, Mr. Gould, I knew if I kept coming to that old pump, some day you'd come by on your way home."

"Well, here we are, Miss Tessie. I'll see you in church tomorrow morning."

"You're coming here so we can all walk over together, the way we always do, aren't you?" She was being coy again, her big head tilted to one side.

"Yes, indeed. I'll be here right on time." He said goodnight, accepted her thanks and ran all the way to his boardinghouse to clean up for dinner.

When he came downstairs a few minutes later, Miss Susan Platt met him at the entrance to the dining room, her kind face crinkly with excitement. "Oh, there you are, Mr. Gould. I've been watching for you. I want to ask a favor."

He liked Miss Platt. "Certainly, ma'am."

"We have a new guest in our house, Mr. Gould, and since the others are more or less set in their table arrangements, I wondered if you'd mind taking your meals with our new guest and her little girl. That's she in there at the corner table by the window. It's the Widow Thatcher. We're ever so honored that she's chosen our establishment to be her new home."

Unable to answer, Horace stared into the dining room.

Linda Thatcher was already seated, her dark head bent as she spoke with her child.

"Mr. Gould?" Miss Platt prodded gently.

"Oh, yes, ma'am. I'll—be happy to sit at her table. You—honor me." Susan Platt didn't seem to notice that he labored over each word. She was already sailing across the room toward Linda Thatcher, and Horace was somehow following behind her.

Formal introductions were made and acknowledged, and before he was ready, there he was—where he had dreamed of being—seated at a table with the woman he loved.

"This is kind of you to keep us company at our first dinner here, Mr. Gould." She looked straight into his eyes, smiling.

She was so warm, so natural, so at ease, he found himself surprisingly at ease too, his panic almost gone. He could talk to her. What was more, he wanted to. It's as though we've lost enough time away from each other, he thought, but he said, "This is my pleasure, Mrs. Thatcher. It isn't often a gentleman has the honor of dining with two such beautiful ladies." He bowed toward them both and little Harriett smiled and then made an ugly face at him.

"That means she likes you already," her mother laughed. "And so do I."

This would have been a forward thing for a lady to say, had the lady been anyone but Linda Thatcher.

"Miss Platt tells us you've just moved to Savannah, too. Do you like it here, Mr. Gould?"

"I'm growing to like it, ma'am. Oh, I like the city very much. What I mean is, I'm learning to like being here more and more."

"There isn't any snow here!" Harriett piped.

Horace laughed and Mrs. Thatcher explained that Massachusetts winters had been bad for Harriett's health. "Since my husband's death, Harriett and I have just been wandering around—wherever I happen to be singing—looking for a healthful place to light. I think we've found it. We feel right at home already."

(63)

The impish child did look frail. Horace supposed she was perhaps five, though tiny for her age; her big, dark eyes were too shadowy for one so young. He didn't exactly like her, but he could learn. "I do hope you grow strong and well down here, Miss Harriett," he said. "I pray you grow big roses in your cheeks."

"You mean that, don't you?" Linda Thatcher's directness had caught him off guard again.

"Yes, I mean it," he answered simply.

"Thank you."

He felt that with those two words she had handed him the gift of her confidence. She helped her daughter cut her meat in silence for a moment, then turned her attention back to Horace. He was leaning toward her, his own food untouched. "I've heard you sing," he said.

"You have? That surprises me. Where?"

"At the Drysdale home not long ago. We met, but very briefly and there were other people around."

"Do forgive me." She was so honest, so without artifice, he knew he could never doubt her. "I'd be untruthful if I said I remembered," she went on. "I don't. But I'm awfully glad I know you now, Mr. Gould."

"It's a dream come true for me, Mrs. Thatcher."

"Is it really?" She laughed. "Well, even if you're just being the gallant Southern gentleman, I'm pleased. I'm not a Southerner, you know."

"Yes, I do know. My father is from Massachusetts, too."

"How interesting. You were born in Georgia, though, weren't you?"

He grinned. "My speech?"

"Yes, but I find it charming. I do like Southerners."

"My cheeks would be a dumb place to grow roses," Harriett shouted.

They all laughed, and then the child stuck out her tongue at him. Horace went resolutely on. "My mother, who died when I was about Harriett's age, was a British subject. Born in London, grew up in Nassau, New Providence—" The child's tongue was out again and she was pulling the corners of her eyes down grotesquely. "Uh—

(64)

my mother grew up in Nassau, met my father in Charleston," he struggled on, "and they eventually settled on St. Simons Island, Georgia."

"Harriett, you'll spoil your face," Linda Thatcher said lightly, then turned back to Horace. "An island! Tell me, is it a beautiful island?"

"St. Simons? Oh, yes, ma'am. The most beautiful spot I've ever seen." He grinned again. "Of course, I haven't been everywhere yet, but I do hope to travel—or, at least, that's what I've had in mind up to now."

"Oh, you don't like your work on Commerce Row?"

He shrugged. "It's a job. But how did you know I worked on Commerce Row, Mrs. Thatcher?"

"My dear young man," she laughed, "Miss Susan Platt gave me all your credentials before she asked to seat you at our table. I know you're a clerk in the firm of Lively and Buffton, that you're somewhere near twenty, that your father is a successful cotton planter, that you know the Drysdales and that you've gone two years to Yale."

He was so comfortable with her he began to feel hungry and tackled the roast beef on his plate.

"I should stop chattering and let you eat your dinner, but will you be returning to school?" She laughed at herself. "Just answer me between bites."

"No, ma'am. I won't be going back to school."

"Mama, I'm finished," the child broke in, and this time Horace was relieved. It wasn't good form to talk too much about oneself at a first meeting.

"You must say 'excuse me' when you interrupt a conversation, Harriett. But all right. I know you'll be sleepy soon."

Horace jumped up to pull back Linda Thatcher's chair. She wiped the child's mouth, smoothed her curls and lifted her down.

"If we're dining together, I'll have to learn how to help little girls, won't I? I haven't been around children much," he said apologetically.

Harriett hit him on the hand. "I like to eat with you, man!"

(65)

"Harriett, I'm ashamed of you. That's no way to show Mr. Gould you're fond of him. I've spoiled her, I'm afraid," she said to Horace. "She's been ill so often. But since she likes you that much, let's go on having dinner together—except, of course, when we each have other engagements." She held out her hand. Horace took it, bowed over it, dropped it reluctantly, and said he would be delighted with the arrangement.

"I'll be waiting eagerly to hear you sing tomorrow, Mrs. Thatcher. I attend Christ Church, too." Perhaps this would detain her a golden minute longer.

"Then why don't we walk to the church together? I leave Harriett with her nurse. She fidgets during a long service. Of course, the church is only across the street, but it's awkward—a lady going alone."

He thought of the Livelys and dismissed them at once. "If I could go with you, I'd—well, what I mean to say is—I am more than honored."

"Good. Shall we meet on the front porch say, at ten-thirty? I won't be at breakfast. I never eat before I sing. Good night, Mr. Gould. I'll see you in the morning."

After watching her leave the dining room, Horace sat down and tried to finish his meal. Even the blackberry cobbler, which he loved, was difficult to swallow. The Livelys! He would have to walk to their house tonight to tell them he would not be meeting them for church tomorrow morning. Halfway down the front steps he thought of the extra water he would need, ran back inside, down the rear hall, grabbed up a firkin and hurried to St. Julian Street to get the Livelys settled first.

At their front door, he felt foolish holding the empty bucket, but luck was with him. He gave his message to their butler, raced back to Johnson Square, filled the firkin at the pump, sloshing water in a trail behind him as he took the front steps of Miss Platt's boardinghouse two at a time. He did slow down in the entrance hall out of respect for the carpet, but as fast as he could manage, he mounted the three flights to his attic room and began to prepare for tomorrow.

The trouble at Yale seemed a part of another life. He was ready for the future. A man could meet any challenge with a wife like Linda, and she had asked him to escort her to church.

9

On that first hallowed Sunday she had sung "O Thou That Tellest Good Tidings," and her presence and her rich contralto voice had filled the old red brick church with beauty as the late September sun filled it with light. They had walked together back to their boarding-house and he felt she was pleased that he knew her aria was from Handel's *Messiah*.

To please Linda Thatcher had become the one aim of his life. She had not only set him free of having to attend church with the Livelys; he was certain that escorting so respected a newcomer to Savannah had freed him from mediocrity, too. Until Linda came, he had been just another young clerk on Factor's Walk.

He and the Thatchers ate their meals together. When the child was with her nurse, Linda walked with him occasionally through the falling leaves up and down Savannah's tree-lined streets; one Sunday afternoon they drove for two hours in a rented carriage—and they talked. Hour after hour, mostly about him. He had almost stopped trying not to confide in her. She made confidences too easy. Telling about the trouble at Yale had been as natural as breathing, and Horace was convinced beyond any doubt that she had willingly become a permanent part of his life when she asked to go with him to visit his mother's grave in the Savannah Cemetery.

"Being with you is like lighting a bright lantern, Miss

Linda," he said one evening in early November as they drank their after-dinner coffee in Miss Platt's dining room; the nurse had fetched Harriett to get her ready for bed.

"That's a lovely thing to hear, Mr. Gould, but it makes absolutely no sense to me."

"I mean it," he insisted. "You have a way of making me see myself as I've never done before."

"Is that good?" She was smiling.

"Yes, of course it is. Oh, I don't mean that I like everything I see, but somehow since I told you about the trouble at college, it's lost its sting. I can believe now there are better things ahead for me." He smiled too. "I tend to take myself too seriously, don't I?"

Linda tilted her head and studied him closely. "Yes, you are a serious young man. But that isn't bad—if we don't take the wrong things too seriously, we get by."

He leaned toward her. "Miss Linda, do you think I should go back to college?"

"Oh, heaven forbid that I should meddle that much in anyone's life!"

I've gone too far, he thought, and said less seriously, "Well, I just wanted you to know you're making me think. I was all awash when we met."

"Nothing has real meaning until we begin to think for ourselves. We own what we learn then. You've a good mind. Whatever you do, don't waste it. But, you know, I have a theory that a man—or a woman, for that matter—does not need to go in for great public achievement in order to use a good mind. Good minds are needed everywhere, in all circumstances of life. In big circles, but also in very small ones."

He could feel the blood rush to his face. "You mean even wharf clerks are to use their minds."

She looked at him with what appeared to be genuine affection. "My dear friend, I meant no such thing. I forget how young you are. It's natural for the very young to be sensitive. Forgive me for forgetting."

Horace knew he was acting insufferably young. Desperate to find a way back to their old closeness, he blurted, "I'll be nineteen my next birthday! I don't call that young, do you?"

Linda was smiling again. "Yes," she said in a low voice, "I'm afraid I do. You see, I've had my thirty-fifth birthday. I'd lost three children before Harriett came."

He had supposed she might be twenty-five. To have her suddenly middle-aged stunned and fascinated him. He wouldn't have expected it, but the very fact that she was sixteen years older than he bound him to her even more strongly.

"I've shocked you, haven't I?" she asked. "You thought me younger, and I suppose I should be flattered. I think I am."

For once he wasn't listening to what she said because all he could think of was how much he wanted to take her in his arms. More than ever, he wanted her now.

"Age has come to be rather irrelevant to me," she was saying. "It's what's inside a person that matters, and you're fine, Mr. Gould." She sighed. "I've tried to be. My daughter has given me something to live for."

Most of the time Horace had forgotten her widowhood, in spite of having spent so much time with her child. To think of Linda belonging to another man frightened and confused him, and he had rejected it. But she had helped him begin to understand himself— shouldn't he try to help her, too? Perhaps this courageous, lone woman needed to talk to him. "Miss Linda, you're just the right age! And, can you forgive me for being so absorbed in myself all this time? I'm—I'm your friend. I'd be honored if you cared to confide in me sometime."

Her smile was warm. "Thank you. I've almost forgotten what that's like. I just go about singing my heartaches. That way all people have to do is compliment my voice."

"I remember the first song I heard you sing," Horace said eagerly. "It was 'What Is Life?' "

"Was it really! That's a favorite of mine, and I've been criticized for singing it. A widow who is so brazen as to flaunt her grief in public, or words to that effect."

"That's cruel!"

"Of course. But life is cruel—often." She smiled a little. "So, you heard me sing Gluck's *Orpheo* aria."

"I'll never forget it. I remember the myth Orpheus and Eurydice from when I studied Virgil and Ovid."

"How good that you do." Her eyes were soft, tender. "That really pleases me. .... And now I must go and tell Harriett her bedtime story."

He had found her again where she would always be found, on a higher plane than other women. His heart leaped. He had pleased her. Another bond had been formed between them. It was better, far better to talk about her and not himself. She needed him. Perhaps the next time they could be alone together without the child, she would tell him more. If he lived a thousand years, he would never have enought time to discover all he longed to know about Linda.

To Horace, as he walked to work, the cloudy December morning might have been May and sunny. He was so happy he wondered at the people who passed him on Bull Street with only a curt nod or a complaint about the weather. Tonight he and Linda would be alone at dinner; at long last, Harriett was to spend the night at the home of a friend. There would be no bedtime story and Linda could stay in the parlor late. He had thought almost constantly about how he could draw her out, induce her to confide in him about her life before they met. To know more about her had become an obsession. No matter how she hurt him in the telling, it would only increase his caring, his conviction that she needed him.

Striding across the Strand toward Commerce Row, he welcomed maturity. Years don't matter, she had said. He would be mature enough for her. He would find a way to be the kind of strong man Linda needed to fill her life.

In his corner cubicle at Lively and Buffton, he riffled through the notices of the day's incoming shipments. Then, whistling, hung up his overcoat and changed into the heavy mackinaw he wore to board the ships.

He stood for a moment on the deck of the new fast schooner *Mary*, looking her over, admiring her fine, sleek lines. She had come from New Orleans, picking up additional cargo at Darien. In her hold would be cotton and rice from St. Mary's, Jekyll Island and St. Simons—transferred, he knew, at Darien from the *Magnolia* or the *South Carolina*. His trips on both boats, his anger and heartbreak, his blank and empty future—all lay behind him because the future seemed so safe now. Perhaps, he thought, I can work my way up right here in Lively and Buffton. Better still, I might find a connection with another firm on Commerce Row. I can be happy in any kind of work as long as there is Linda.

A stiff wind snapped the *Mary's* flags and vibrated the ropes that held the hoisting derrick, the iron gaffs, the heavy boom, so that the ship groaned and creaked. The salty chill off the water stung his face. It was invigorating. He enjoyed a day like this on the big ships, even at anchor.

In a few minutes, the stevedores had heaved a pile of cotton bales out of the hold. He began checking, moving quickly, laughing and joking more than usual with the heavy-shouldered dock slaves, who called him Mausa Clair, because he had shown them bales and tow bags marked New St. Clair, and had told them his father had grown the cotton. Checking had become automatic for him and he allowed himself to think about home. He felt guilty for having written only two letters. A letter from Mary yesterday was full of their anticipation of his Christmas visit. Savannah was so close, if he had time off, he would have to go, though all he wanted was to spend Christmas with Linda. She would need him at Christmas, the loneliest time of the year for someone with no real home. He shivered, more against the turmoil of his thoughts than against the cold.

The last two hundred and thirty-five bales to come up out of the hold were marked: Gould, New St. Clair. His father was progressing. He no longer shipped partly in the old tow bags. These were all bales, ginned in the

Gould gin behind the stables. Grade A, long-staple, Sea Island cotton. His father's land produced the best.

A big stevedore named Enoch scrambled out of the hold, his tattered linsey-woolsey shirt soaked with sweat.

"What are you doing up on deck, Enoch?" Horace shouted over the dock hubbub and the wind. "Where's the Mississippi shipment? I'm almost finished with the St. Simons load."

"Dey ain' no Miss'ippi load, Mausa Clair. What you sees right dere be all."

"There has to be more, Enoch! We had three due in today."

"It ain' dere, sir." The big man grinned. "You done got yo'se'f what you been wantin'. You got yo' fus' los' shipmun', Mausa Clair!"

Horace pushed past him and down the rope ladder into the musty hold of the ship. The Mississippi cotton had to be there! The checkers at Darien were always careful. He raced from one shadowy bin to another, paying no attention to the other stevedores still in the hold, waiting for orders from him. The shipment would be on the starboard side. There was nothing there.

He climbed back on deck, where Enoch stood frowning and scratching his head. "You got yo' fus' chance to trabel—all de way to Noo Orleens, Mausa Clair, an' you don' seem one bit happy."

Without a word, Horace streaked by him across the wide, crowded wharf, taking short cuts over bales of cotton and bags of rice, ducking between towering piles of meat barrels to the wooden stairs that led up to Factor's Walk. He ran, slipping on the smooth cobblestones, to the back entrance of Lively and Buffton. There had to be a mistake! Maybe he had picked up a shipping invoice with the wrong date. Upstairs at his desk, he shuffled papers right and left, hunting another invoice, refusing to believe the shipment was lost.

"Something wrong, Gould?" It was Lively, peering through his spectacles over the low partition which separated his big square office from the clerk's room.

Horace took a deep breath before he turned around, then exhaled helplessly. "Yes, sir. As wrong as it can be. We've lost the Mississippi shipment. Must not have left New Orleans."

Lively made the short trip around the partition to where Horace stood. "Now, see here, Gould, it isn't your fault. We do appreciate your concern for the funds of the company. A trip to New Orleans is no small matter, but that's why we hired you. We'll pay all your expenses from the moment you set foot on your ship until you're back with us again."

"But, sir, I—"

"Now, now, now, not another word! This kind of thing happens. We expect it. You're not to feel bad. Just square your shoulders, pack your things and be on your way. The *Talma*, under Captain Charles Pool, sails early tomorrow. Excellent accommodations." He snapped his fingers. "I do believe there's a boat sailing this evening, if you can make it."

"No," Horace said quickly. "I couldn't possibly make it tonight."

"Well, then, I'll be at your boardinghouse bright and early tomorrow morning with the carriage. I tell you what I think I'll do. I just think I'll bring Tessie and Bubba along to give you a proper send-off. They'll cheer you up. And they'll both be tickled pink at the idea!"

10

As he waited for Linda at their corner table, Horace tried to decide how to tell her he was leaving. The thought of not seeing her for three or four weeks depressed him so he would surely show it. Being Linda, she would sense that something terrible had happened.

He took out his watch; she was late. Unusual for her. He walked to the wide front window and looked out into the dark street. Perhaps she had gone shopping down on Bay. The two best emporiums were just across the street from Commerce Row. If only she had told him, he could have escorted her home, could have carried her packages for her. He returned to their table, afraid she might come in at any moment and he would miss a glimpse of her.

"Good evening, Mr. Gould," Miss Susan Platt trilled.

He stood up.

"We've delicious fried chicken tonight *and* your favorite—blackberry cobbler. May we serve you now?"

"No, not yet, thank you. I'll wait for Mrs. Thatcher. She should be downstairs any minute."

"Oh, I'm afraid she won't be, Mr. Gould. Mrs. Thatcher went with her adorable child to visit friends across town. The little girl isn't staying the night as planned. They'll be in late this evening. About nine, I believe she said."

Horace stared at her.

"Too bad you have to eat alone, but since Mrs. Thatcher won't be here, may we serve you now?"

"Yes, I suppose so. Thank you."

At the front window again, while he waited for his food, he fought for control of himself. True, he had been at work when she decided to go with Harriett, but the least she could have done was leave word for him. She hadn't even asked Miss Platt to tell him. Nine o'clock. It was barely seven now. Two precious hours lost from their last night. Well, she would see him when she came in because he intended to wait in front of the house—he would be there when her carriage drove up. Back at his table, he reminded himself that it wasn't as though he had to leave without seeing her. He would have to wait while she took the troublesome child upstairs to her nurse, but he would see her. One hour of the two could be passed, he supposed, in the dining room. He could walk the second hour away, up and down Bull Street, keeping the entrance of the boardinghouse in sight. He took a sip of water, drummed on the tablecloth. Of course, he could pack while he waited, but if he did that, he might miss her, and once she reached her room, he couldn't get in touch with her without causing talk.

He ate as slowly as he could. The chicken first, then the rice, then the English peas and turnip greens—one after the other, to make the meal last as long as possible. He swallowed the last tender bit of cobbler and looked at his watch. Only half an hour had gone by! If he smoked cigars, he could loiter another half hour, but he didn't smoke. A second cup of coffee should last at least ten minutes.

Then he remembered a letter from Mary in his pocket, still unopened. He looked at it for a long time without breaking the dark green blob of sealing wax stamped with the monogram MG. Dear, loyal Mary, who kept writing no matter how negligent he was. I should write to them before I go, he thought, knowing he wouldn't. Writing a letter home in his present mood was the last thing he would be likely to do. After all, it was a hurried trip. No time for letters. He broke the seal: "Dear Horace, We know we'll be hearing from you soon and we can almost not wait. Everyone wants so much to know how things are with you. Especially Maum Larney and Papa. It seems you were with us just long enough for us to begin to love you more than ever." He scanned the rest of page 1 and looked at the end to be sure nothing bad had happened, then went back to reading slowly and carefully. Good old Mary. She was even helping him pass this endless hour. "Papa is as well as he ever is, but a little irritable now and then from the pain in his legs and from not hearing from you. I'm not fussing, honey, just reminding you to write to him when you can. He doesn't say anything about it, but I can almost read his thoughts by now. Sometimes I think it's a good thing I can, since he seems to talk less as the years go by. Well, at last Jim has got Alice to agree to come back to St. Simons. They were to come in September, then October, then November, but now, Jim writes that they will arrive in December for certain. I dread it in a way, knowing how unhappy Alice is down here, but the Black Banks property is in Jim's name and the house laid out according to specifications they sent us. Wish us well. Our sister, Janie, writes that she is fine and excited about spending the holidays at a classmate's home in Baltimore. We are still fervently hoping you will be here for Christmas." Horace stopped reading. Christmas! If he had any trouble finding the lost shipment, he wouldn't be back for Christmas at all. He grabbed at one small ray of hope: he could, with any luck, time his return so he would make it back only as far as Savannah by December 24 or 25, which would give him a legitimate excuse to stay with Linda. ... He went back to Mary's letter. "It's time to cut out fourteen dresses for the children down at the quarters, so I must close. We all send you our love, and our prayers and our best wishes are with you every day. Your affectionate sister, Mary Gould."

Horace left the dining room, picked up his overcoat from the hall tree and went outside. A cold wind was rising. He would stay clear of Johnson Square and the pool of light around the pump lantern. No point risking a meeting with Tessie Lively. He could walk south on Bull, keeping within hearing distance of an arriving carriage. Walk south, then back to Miss Platt's, then south again and back.

He walked one long hour away and his mind was made up. He knew what he must do. She was already fifteen minutes late, but the cold night air cleared his thoughts and, having decided, his patience returned. He knew exactly what he would say. Somehow he would keep his courage high until she had taken the child upstairs and had come down to be with him. They would have less than an hour together, but he was going to make it count.

A carriage rattled toward him along the rutted, muddy street. He was waiting in front of the boardinghouse when it stopped.

"I know something's wrong," Linda said, seating herself on the edge of the love seat in the guest parlor. "You might just as well stop walking up and down and tell me, Mr. Gould. I must get back upstairs soon."

Horace's courage was still high, but the words were lost. He tossed a small pine log on the smoldering fire.

"You wouldn't have waited in this chilly night air just to be polite, would you? You've scarcely spoken since I came in. Can't you tell me what's happened—what's bothering you?"

"Miss Linda," he began, his voice thin and squeaky. "I intended this evening to be so different from the way it turned out. I had hoped we'd have dinner together alone and the rest of the evening to talk. I—I wanted you to talk to me. I've been so selfish always talking about myself." He sat down on the arm of the chair nearest her, his hands clenched together. "I wanted you to feel free to tell me anything that might be important to you."

She smiled. "How very nice and thoughtful of you. I am grateful."

He jumped up. "It *isn't* 'nice and thoughtful'—it's more than that, Miss Linda. I know there isn't time now. Everything's turned out all wrong, but—" Her frown frightened him. "You see, I'd planned a beautiful evening—just the two of us. And then—" He broke off, sat down limply. "I thought you might have left a message for me." He could hear the petulance in his voice. Had he turned from a man with his mind made up, into a complaining child?

Linda leaned toward him. "I want to be very certain that I understand, Mr. Gould. You feel I should have left a message that I wouldn't be dining with you tonight? Did we have plans beyond the usual boarding-house dinner—pleasant as they have been?"

"Well, I—I just took for granted we'd, that is, since you said your child would be away, I—" He cleared his throat.

Linda's laugh was the one usually reserved for little Harriett. "Oh, I see. Your feelings are hurt. I'm sorry. I apologize, but that's about all one can do, isn't it? At least when I've hurt you without knowing it."

Without knowing it. She had to have known! It could not have mattered so much to him and never have crossed her mind.

"Miss Linda—Linda—I'm being sent to New Orleans tomorrow morning, early. This is good-by for us. Maybe for a *month.*"

She sounded relieved. "Oh, well, now, that's really good news, isn't it? A long time ago you told me you were looking forward to traveling, when and if it ever happened. And now, here it is!"

He could have dealt more easily with a slap in the face.

"You'll adore New Orleans," she went on. "Full of history and beautiful girls and lovely houses." She lifted his chin with her forefinger. "I'm glad for you."

Horace grabbed her hand, moving quickly to sit beside her on the love seat. "Miss Linda, before I go, tell me you'll be waiting for me."

She moved away a little, but he clung to her hand.

"Why, I expect to be here when you return, Mr. Gould. I have no plans to leave Savannah."

"Miss Linda," he blurted. "Did you love your—husband very much?"

She withdrew her hand and Horace thought she looked faint. In a moment, she recovered her poise. "My dear young man, listen to me. I owe you much more than an apology. Unless I'm very mistaken, I owe you much, much more."

"Love never owes anything, Linda. I love you. With all my heart, I love you!"

Linda Thatcher sat erect for what seemed an eternity, and when at last she stood up, he stood beside her. "It's late," she said, her voice firm, almost disciplinary. "But somehow I must make you understand that you've taken me completely by surprise. Our friendship, while it has been most enjoyable and stimulating, has been just that. Nothing more. Why, you're the age of my baby brother, and I think of you that way. I'm sure this will seem utterly cruel to you, but better to know it now and know it well. I do apologize for not having realized—but you're just a pleasant young man to me. There will be the right young lady for you when the time comes. Now, have a successful journey. And don't hate me. It won't help at all."

He backed away slowly, staring at her, reaching behind him for the knob of the door he had carefully closed when they came in.

"Can you forgive me? I've been the selfish one." She held out her hand.

Horace found the door, jerked it open—looked at her one last time and ran up the three flights of stairs to his room.

11

At six-thirty the next morning, his trunk stood locked and ready, his box of favorite books beside it. He had packed everything, because he was never coming back. With him he would carry only his valise. No one, least of all Mr. Lively, must know of his intentions until after he was safely in New Orleans. When he had found a place to live, Miss Platt could send his trunk and books. He would tell her a white lie on his way out—that he had packed things away so his room might be more easily cleaned in his absence. He would pay a month's rent in advance. Coolly, carefully, he laid his plans.

When he had finished dressing, he studied his face in the mirror and was shocked to see how old he looked. He blew out the candles on the dresser for the last time, picked up his valise and walked numbly down the stairs, not even slowing as he passed her closed door. To have managed this strengthened him.

Outside, the Livelys would be waiting in their fashionable carriage to take him to the boat. He smiled cynically. Maybe I'll give Tessie a thrill this morning, since I'm leaving. She deserves to be hurt as much as I deserved it. The idea gave him a kind of energy. He paid his rent, said goodbye to Miss Platt and went, almost enthusiastically to meet the Livelys.

Passengers were boarding the *Talma* when they reached the waterfront. The last of her cargo, Horace knew, had been put aboard late yesterday. Yesterday. How many years had gone by since he had discovered the lost shipment?

"Need to drop by your desk for anything before you go, son?" Mr. Lively asked cheerfully. Horace had not only caused Tessie to squirm with delight by seating himself beside her in the carriage, he had delighted his employer, too.

"No, sir," Horace answered, smiling at Tessie. "I have everything I need."

Tessie giggled, and Mr. Lively made a speech about how they would all be following him with their prayers and how he knew the trip would be a rousing success.

At the dock, after he had shaken hands with Lively and Bubba, he took Tessie's thick hand in his, bent over it, kissed it longer than was customary and disappeared inside the big schooner without looking back. "Better to learn it young, Miss Tessie, than to go on making the same stupid mistake," he said aloud in his cabin as the *Talma* moved away.

And then he threw himself on his bunk and sobbed.

Amiable John Couper, the Scotsman who owned Cannon's Point plantation at the northeast end of St. Simons Island, was the postmaster at Frederica. Since everyone likely to receive mail attended Christ Church, it was Mr. Couper's custom to ride to the Frederica dock early on Sunday morning to pick up the week's post. He would then establish himself with his letters and papers in the churchyard under a big oak, and greet his neighbors as they made a beeline for him on their way to the service.

"Best way I know to get people to church on time," he

laughed, as his old friend, James Gould, limped toward his tree on the second Sunday in December. The men shook hands and John Couper's handsome, laugh-lined face grew grave. "There's nothing for you, neighbor. Nothing you're looking for, that is," he said in his warm, Scottish brogue. "I've never longed so to hand a man a letter, but I've looked through the lot. Nothing here but the newspapers and an invoice on the last provision shipment from your factor in Savannah."

James Gould took his mail, scuffed at a mole cricket with the toe of his boot. "Well, the boy's busy, no doubt. Of course, I've had two letters since he left, you know."

"Indeed I do know. Not long after he got there."

"The last time Frank Lively was here in October, he said Horace was doing fine. Weather kept Lively away in November. Won't be by now till January. To tell the truth, I half expect Horace to come home for Christmas."

"Now, you may be right, James! The lad may be planning to surprise you."

"I hope so. My youngest, Janie, won't make it, but Jim and his wife will be back soon. Be good to have the boy with us, too."

"Good morning, Mr. Gould—Mr. Couper. I'm sure you both know my sister-in-law, Mrs. Richard Abbott—and this is her little daughter, Deborah."

The men bowed and greeted Mrs. George Abbott, the widow of their old friend whose plantation at Orange Grove had steadily deteriorated in the five years since his death. In answer to an urgent plea for help from Mary Abbott, George Abbott's younger brother, Richard, and his wife, Agnes, had come from Ireland to live on St. Simons.

"How happy you must be to have them here with you, Mrs. Abbott," John Couper said, kneeling down to talk to the child. "How old are you, Miss Deborah?"

"She'll be two on New Year's Eve," her mother said.

Deborah twisted shyly on one foot and hung her head, although John Couper's big friendly face so near hers made her smile.

"Take your finger out of your mouth, Deborah," Agnes

Abbott scolded. "That's no way to greet a nice gentleman like Mr. Couper."

He stood up, patted the child on her brown curls, then grabbed dramatically at his heart. "Of a truth, she is going to be a charmer, Mrs. Abbott! A veritable charmer!"

"Don't spoil her, Mr. Couper," Mary Abbott laughed and then grew solemn. "But isn't she pretty? God sent her, I say. It's not only a blessed thing to have her parents here; it's like a gift out of heaven to have another little Deborah in my house. She's almost the age of my Deborah I lost, you know."

The child was looking up at James Gould now, who smiled down at her. "Come here!" she piped.

He flushed and explained that his knees hurt and he couldn't stoop down. "I can't get to where you are," he chuckled, picking her up, "but you can come up to where I am."

"Do you see what I mean?" John Couper laughed. "The bairn's a charmer!"

"Indeed she is, but we must be moving toward the church," Mary Abbott said, holding out her arms for Deborah. "I want to say a word to poor Mrs. Wylly. I understand she's having some trouble with Dr. Hazzard over their joint property line, and Captain Wylly isn't well enough to be of any help. It's made her terribly nervous."

"You should see that child more often, James Gould," Mr. Couper said after the women left. "She made you laugh!"

James smiled sadly. "I *am* turning into an old goat."

"A gross exaggeration, friend. You're a reserved man by nature, and you've a lot to weigh you down. But isn't that little Irish miss a delight? What's so special about her? Is it her eyes? Her smile? I wonder which of these briggledy Island boys will grow up to win her!" John Couper laid his hand on his friend's shoulder. "Cheer up, James. Your boy's all right. I'm sure he is."

"I trust Horace," James Gould said simply.

"Well, good morning, gentlemen!" The Widow Shedd

swept up, her wrinkles well-powdered, her plumed bonnet and silk dress the same bright green as her slippers. "Lots of interesting mail for me, Mr. Couper? I'm such a poor correspondent, I declare it's a miracle when I get one single letter!"

The men exchanged glances as they bowed, both aware that she spent her days writing letters. John Couper counted out seven.

"Oh, how nice! Hm-m. Four from Savannah, Mr. Gould. I wouldn't be at all surprised to find some news of your son in one of them." She pressed his arm. "I know you don't hear from Horace often, poor man, so I try to help when I can. Loads of friends in Savannah from the days before my dear late husband and I came to St. Simons, you know. Miss Susan Platt, who runs the boardinghouse where he stays, is a long-time friend. Knew her and all the Olmsteads so well. Marvelous family. Of course, Susan Platt will not stoop to gossip about anyone in her lovely establishment. I like that. I do despise a gossip. But I have other friends there, and—oh, yes. Here's a letter from one of them. Would you be interested in a bit of second-hand news about your son, Mr. Gould?"

"No, thank you, Mrs. Shedd," James Gould bowed to her and hobbled away.

"Oh, I shouldn't have offered, poor man. His heart is heavy," she muttered to herself, then turned to Mr. Couper. "Something very strange about that boy just dropping out of Yale. If you ask me, he's broken his father's heart. And they say his oldest son, Jim, has finally persuaded his Northern wife to come back to the Island. I'm so afraid it won't work. She hates it here. Poor Mr. Gould. Did you ever see a man age so?"

"Oh, I don't know," John Couper said mischievously. "I think he's doing well for one who's so crippled. You should have heard him sing a solo at our St. Clair Club meeting a few weeks ago."

Mrs. Shedd's eyebrows flew up. "James Gould sing a solo? He's such a quiet, retiring man!"

"Not at our meetings at St. Clair, my dear lady. Performing at the gathering, when it's a member's turn to be the host and provide the food and libation, is one of our rules. He sings or recites or dances a jig or he's out of fellowship. The Gould servants brought a magnificent dinner—and, you may take my word or not, but James Gould sang a good portion of Robert Burns's 'Jolly Beggars'! Not gloriously, but he sang it. The man's got courage." He threw back his gray head, laughing. "Believe me, it takes courage to sing for our membership!"

"Is that so?" He had lost her attention. "Excuse me, Mr. Couper. There's his daughter, Mary. I think I'll go visit with her. Such a responsible, lovely girl. Mary Gould! Mary Gould!"

"Bless her old heart, I saw her coming, waving a sheaf of letters," Mary told her aunt a few minutes later. "If Papa didn't want any secondhand news, I did. And guess what? Horace has gone to New Orleans!"

"Whatever for?"

"He's tracing a lost shipment. It's a part of his job. Won't Papa be glad to know that's why we haven't heard? But, Aunt Caroline, that isn't all." Mary held her aunt a moment outside the church door and whispered. "The Widow Shedd read in another one of her Savannah letters that the Lively girl is telling all over town that Horace is in love with her! Isn't that dreadful?"

"Dreadful, Mary? Why, I don't know whether it is or not."

"Well, I do! Unless old Lively's wife is a goddess—which I doubt—their daughter has to be obnoxious. Horace *couldn't* fall in love with her."

"Sh! Lower your voice, Mary. It's time for the service."

The tiny congregation had grown silent in the sanctuary of the church and the quiet spread across the churchyard. The rector intoned: "The Lord is in his holy temple; let all the earth keep silence before him."

"We must go in, Mary!"

"I know it. But let's pray Horace comes home for

Christmas. I'm not really worried about the Lively girl—but for some reason I'm suddenly worried about Horace. Let's pray hard. I'm getting one of my feelings."

12

Horace pinned his cravat in place, combed his hair for the third time, slipped into his cutaway and surveyed himself in the looking glass of his room on Chartres Street in New Orleans. He would be making his first appearance at the Théâtre d'Orléans and it was important to look his best. His new friend and employer, the theater impresario, Mr. John "Toto" Davis—French, he vowed, in spite of his name—would approve the way he looked.

"Nothing gaudy, *mon ami*," Davis had said on their last night at dinner on the *Talma* before she docked in New Orleans. "You will be living in what the frontier evangelists call 'the City of Sin,' but New Orleans is a lovely, gracious, subtle sinner. Even her professional gamblers are never flamboyant as on the river boats." John Davis had leaned back in his chair, savoring his own description of the Creole City. "New Orleans is a queen and her taste is superb—as I believe yours to be. You and New Orleans will fall in love, *mon ami*. Real men, *gentlemen* with poetic souls and a lust for living, never fail to fall in love with the Queen." Speaking in the confidential tone which inevitably had the effect of making Horace feel older, he had added, "Track down your silly cotton shipment, write your letter of resignation to your firm in Savannah, and meet me in my office at the Théâtre d'Orléans at seven sharp one week from tonight. I'll put you to work as my head usher, responsible for seating the wealthiest and most socially

(85)

prominent people in all New Orleans! After a week or two of that, if you please me, there will be something far more fascinating, far more lucrative. Now, you *must* have a brandy with me and a toast."

Horace had met John Davis at the Captain's table during the voyage to Louisiana. On a stroll around the deck their second night out, in the glow of his first after-dinner brandy, he had even told John Davis about Linda Thatcher. "Not your type, my good fellow. Her age should have made no difference. But—" Davis shrugged, "she's the sort of person who would pall on a man like you in no time. Thank your lucky stars and forget her." He would never forget Linda, but this confident, stimulating man had given him his first impetus to live again, and Horace was in awe of him. Nothing, he had discovered, stiffened his spine more than to be thought mature. In less than a week in New Orleans, the lost shipment had been found and was on its way, his letter of resignation was in his pocket, and tonight he was meeting Mr. Davis at the theater to begin his new job.

Still observing himself in the glass to be sure he did it all correctly, he picked up his overcoat and hat, drew on his gloves, took them off, in order to put them on again downstairs in a more casual manner. Then he settled his tall beaver hat on his head and walked briskly toward a new life in the bustling, beautiful, bawdy city he had already come to love. On his way to the Théâtre d'Orléans, he would post his letter of resignation to Lively. Tomorrow, perhaps, or the day after, he would think of what to write to his father.

December fourteenth was so cold Mary convinced her father that she should meet Jim and Alice at the Frederica dock. With Adam beside her on the high seat of the wagon, she drove the team at a rattling clip up the shell road as the big, flame-colored winter sun was sliding behind the trees toward the flat marshland to the west. No one but Maum Larney seemed as worried as she was about Horace, and once more she tried to convince herself that he would find the lost shipment and be home in time for Christmas. She had grown irritable and jumpy, and having Alice and Jim back wouldn't help matters. Poor Alice. So beautiful, so genteel, so helpless and ill-equipped to cope with life. Especially life on a plantation, where a woman needed courage and fortitude and, above all, a sense of humor. Alice was not only afraid of the snakes, the jumping spiders, the lizards, she was downright terrified of the Negroes. Even the occasional bird that flew by mistake through an open window put her in a panic. Mary wondered how Jim had finally persuaded her to come back. I guess the time just ran out. She sighed. It's run out for us, too. They're almost here. I wonder if I feel sorry for the family or for Jim and Alice. For everyone, I suppose. She sighed again, loud enough for Adam to hear.

"You feel bad too, Miss Mary?"

She glanced at the boy, who was staring straight ahead, his peaked face glum. "Now, why do you ask a thing like that, Adam? Do you feel bad about something?"

"Yes, 'um. Ah sho' do feel bad when she come back."

"Mr. Jim's wife? Shame on you for saying a thing like that!"

"But ah been so happy wif' dem gone."

Mary realized she had never thought one way or the other about Adam's happiness. About his welfare, yes, but not his happiness. He was a good boy. He worked well for his age; would certainly grow up to be valuable to them, but it had never occurred to her to think that Alice could be a source of unhappiness for the Negroes, too. Oh, she knew how earnestly Maum Larney had tried to win Alice over, but the others had merely tried to stay clear. Even the house servants would slink away when she entered a room. Still, I hadn't thought about her return making them unhappy, Mary mused. Well, they're not going to go around as if Alice is poison this time. I won't have it. She's Jim's wife, and we all have to make the best of the fact that she's going to be a part of our lives from now on.

"What Mausa Jim's wife askeered ob, Miss Mary?"

"Oh, just about everything, Adam. But you must always do everything she asks you to do."

"She don' ax' nobody to do nuffin'. Effen she would ax' me to do somepin', ah sho' would do it, but she don' do nuffin' but open her eyes wide an' look at me when ah's anywhere 'roun. Miss Mary, July say she skeered ob colored. Be she skeered ob me, too?"

"Adam, wouldn't you like to drive the team the rest of the way?"

The boy was so delighted that he said no more about Alice, and they rode up to the dock at Frederica in a merry mood, chattering about how well Adam drove and laughing as though they were meeting someone they'd both be happy to see.

Mary hopped down from the wagon when Adam pulled up at the dock. "I'll wait for the boat at the Frewins', Adam. You mind the team."

As Mary started to walk away, he called, "Miss Mary, be she gonna' stay fo' Chris'mas wif' us?"

"Why, of course."

"Well, does we 'Chris'mas gif' her like we does ever'-body else?"

Mary went back to the wagon. "Adam, I want you to stop worrying. You leave all that to Maum Larney and me. We'll tell you how everything is going to be in plenty of time."

Climbing the steps to the Frewin house, she wished she knew how everything was going to be.

A week passed and Mary took heart. Alice Gould seemed to be making an effort toward adjusting. True, she stayed in her room most of the morning, and Jim, not one of the house servants, took her breakfast upstairs every day, but plans for the new house at Black Banks interested her.

"It's going to be tabby all over," she explained to Mary as they spread the plans on the dining-room table. "I want as little wood as possible. The whole idea of fire down here in this wilderness terrifies me."

(88)

"Tabby takes a lot longer to build," Mary said. "You know, the shell and sand and lime have to be mixed and poured a section at a time. The first section has to dry before they can even set the form for the next one."

"I know how eager you are to have us out of here, Mary, but the Black Banks house is going to be *tabby*—upstairs and down." She pointed to the plans again, and Mary said nothing as Alice traced the architect's sketch of the wide piazza to run all the way around the house at the first-floor level. "Jim and I will have our bedroom on this floor, and of course the parlor and sitting room and a sewing room. And, here, on the ground floor, will be the kitchen, dairy, storeroom, dining room and wine cellar. Then, in the second story, two bedrooms for the children. Here's the entrance—wide, generous steps from the ground to the first-floor level. All across the front, thick tabby posts. Do you like it, Mary?"

"Of course, I like it! And in that gorgeous setting under the oaks by the river—oh, Alice, I hope you'll be happy."

The two women looked at each other. "Happy? I have grave doubts, but I am going to try."

"Well, it's Saturday," Mary said cheerfully. "My day to give out the supplies for the week to our people. They bring their baskets and firkins and crocus sacks and we have a good time while I'm 'dolin','' as they call it. Want to come out to the back porch with me and help?"

Alice tensed. "No, thank you, Mary. Your father has promised to drive me to the house site this morning."

Every trip to the house meant that Mary or Jim or their father must drive Alice. It would have paralyzed her with fear to ride through the woods in a buggy with July. Gentle July. I'll never understand it, Mary thought, as she hurried to the back porch to meet the people, who were already gathering noisily for their week's provisions. She would have to stop trying to figure out how a woman could run a plantation house without contact with the Negroes. That would be Alice's problem, not hers.

13

"Sit down, sit down, my dear Gould, and stop prattling like a schoolboy," John Davis said, leaning back in the big leather chair behind his office desk at the Théâtre d'Orléans. "*Everyone* carries firearms in New Orleans! Don't you?"

"No, sir, I do not and I'm not going to sit down and I'm not talking about carrying firearms for protection. I'm talking about murder—cold-blooded murder!" Horace rapped his knuckles on the desk. "I saw a young man murdered this afternoon. It was a friend of yours—don't you care? Don't you care that he didn't even have a chance to draw?"

"Toto" Davis began to laugh uproariously, all trace of the suave impresario gone. Horace thought he would never stop and felt his own skin prickle with revulsion.

The whooping laughter ended abruptly, and Davis leaned toward him, his eyes hard. "Listen, Gould, what are you? Are you a man or a boy? It wouldn't be New Orleans without a few duels a day. This sudden change in you is sickening. Why, I've been a principal in seven duels myself. Your time will come *if* you're a gentleman with any honor and any guts!"

Horace pressed both clenched fists against the top of Davis's desk. This man was his security. He had to control himself. "Did you—kill anyone, Mr. Davis?"

"Dead as mackerels. All seven, of course," John Davis said, bored. "Look here, Gould, you can go far with me, but you've got to grow up. Gain a little gentlemanly finesse about the so-called sordid side of life. It's a dogfight—not a taffy pull. What kind of men do you have on that little wilderness Island where you were born? Are they lily-livers or are they men?"

"They're men!"

"You will continue to address me as 'sir,' Gould."

"They're men, *sir*. But they're gentlemen. We'd kill for a just cause, but there isn't a white man on St. Simons who would be brute enough to kill another man in cold blood. I grew up where men are really honorable."

"Then why don't you go back to that insulated little province? You're not indispensable to me, you know."

Davis's voice was calm again, but his eyes narrowed to slits and Horace felt panic, as though he were being suffocated: a nightmare suffocation, slow, gentle, steady, all evil, from which there was no escape. He bit his lips in silence.

"Well, Gould? Do you want to go home to Papa and his soft-bellied neighbors or do you want to talk about the new position I'm offering you? At least, I think I'm still offering it."

He could not go back to St. Simons. The reasons wouldn't come singly during this nightmare interview, but they were there, in a thick bundle. He had to stay in New Orleans. The reasons for that were not clear either, but he had to stay. Its fascination seemed stronger than ever. He was obligated, somehow, to learn to live with the brilliant, wicked rhythm of this turbulent city and its river. It was too late for him to leave.

"Interested?" Davis prodded, smiling.

Horace's clenched fists opened. "Yes, sir. I'm interested. I'd like to make more money."

"I thought so. Sit down."

Horace sat in a straight chair near the big desk and waited. Davis was in no hurry. He opened a lower desk drawer, took out an ebony box, unlatched its brass catch. Slowly, methodically, he selected a long, slender cigar, sniffed it, smiled to himself, clipped the ends, and lighted it—inhaling and exhaling with pleasure, as though he were alone in the office.

I'll listen, Horace thought grimly, but he has no hold on me. It's only New Orleans and the river I care about. "Toto" Davis is just one small part of New Orleans.

As he waited for Davis to speak, he thought of the

long walks he had taken up one narrow street and down another, admiring the singular architecture of its galleried houses bedecked with lacelike iron traceries of leaves and flowers and vines. The Mississippi waterfront had drawn him daily—the vast stretches of crowded docks, the people who poured on and off the snow-white pleasure palaces, coming and going from Ohio, Kentucky, Missouri, Tennessee, Alabama, Mississippi. Someday he wanted enough money to take a trip on one of those luxurious river boats. More than anything else, he wanted to do that. He would hear Davis out.

"Well, now," Davis said at last, "if you have no further objection to offer, I will tell you what I have in mind. As you know, I also own the Salle d'Orléans next door."

"Yes, sir. Gambling below, ballroom above."

"Correct. Very profitable to me, very enjoyable for the public. Have you been there?"

"No, sir. I've never had money enough."

John Davis laughed. "Then I'll fix that. I intend to put you to work in the most important position presently open, Gould. That is, if you're convinced you want to learn to live and work in New Orleans. I wouldn't want you fainting at the first shot that might be fired by one of my more impetuous clients." He leaned toward Horace, all business. "Remember, I'm not trying to coerce you. I'm merely offering. You're free to tuck your tail and run home at any time—*before* you begin this new position. You are not free to resign afterward! And I trust it is abundantly clear to you what I am saying. You are *not* free to leave once you have begun." Davis was watching him intently. "I see that has shocked you. Well, it needn't. If a man likes his work, why not stay on?" He flicked a long ash from his cigar. "I need a polished, handsome, genteel-appearing broker for my Salle d'Orléans' quadroon balls."

Horace frowned. "A *broker*?"

"A broker. These scheming black mothers who bring their not-so-black beauties to be uh—chosen by my gentleman clientele are smart as the whips that fall across the backs of their less fortunate sisters, say at the hands of kind gentlemen planters like your father."

Horace jumped up, his eyes blazing. "My father has never laid a hand on any Negro who has ever worked for him!"

"Oh, naturally not. That's the well-known story all over the gallant South." His voice rasped. "We are not discussing the virtues of slave owners, my impetuous, very young man. Sit down and let me talk!"

Horace sat down again on the edge of the chair.

"As I was saying, these black mothers are shrewd. They drive a hard bargain. A young gentleman who looks as you look can serve me well. Can gain and hold the confidence of both the black daughter-sellers and the white mistress-buyers. Do I make myself clear? Oh, it's all very refined, Gould. The entire atmosphere of the Salle d'Orléans is one of elegance. The best French champagne, superb brandy and absinthe, the most excellent cuisine in town. Our orchestra is as good, perhaps better, than any playing for the whites."

Horace was staring at the cockaded head of a bird in the Persian carpet, as he struggled against the nausea sweeping over him like a wide green wave.

"I will pay you seven times your present salary," John Davis was saying. "You would be able to buy yourself a slave and an entire new wardrobe. I've noticed your weakness for personal finery. The Salle d'Orléans closes during the slow months and you would be free to travel if you like. On second thought, I'll make it ten times your present salary."

Horace could feel the blood pounding in his head. It was as though "Toto" Davis leveled a gun at him. "Do you mean *I* would actually *sell* these young women?" he asked hoarsely.

"I thought it would interest you." Davis looked triumphant. "They're really lovely creatures. Many of them come handsomely gowned in authentic Parisian fashions."

Horace got to his feet slowly, cleared his throat,

(93)

reached deliberately for his hat and overcoat and gloves.

"I can certainly understand if you want to think it over, Gould." Davis's voice came as if from a great distance. "You are still free to go back to your Papa, you know—*as of this moment*. So far, I have told you nothing most of New Orleans doesn't already know. But if you're accepting this promotion, you are to make your decision *now*."

"I've made my decision, sir."

"Good. Then sit down."

"I'm not taking it. And I resign from my job at the theater after tonight's performance. I know you don't have time to find a replacement."

"Toto" Davis ground out his cigar with such fury in his eyes that Horace edged toward the door, afraid to turn his back. "Get out, Gould!" He struck the desk with his open hand. "Get out now! To hell with tonight's performance." His voice rose to a shriek. "Get out and never let me lay eyes on you again. I need a *man* to work for me—not a pink-mouthed baby! Don't just stand there staring—get out!"

Davis was still screaming curses after him as Horace ran down the flight of wide stairs.

It was only a little after six o'clock, but the sky was blue-black glass, glittering with big and little stars, and the thin sickle moon made Horace think, as it always had when he was away from home, of July. They had sat one night, when they were still young enough to be playmates, on the bottom step of Maum Larney's cabin looking at the sky; wondering about what made the stars shine, what kept them hanging up there. Wondering why sometimes the round old moon melted into a new moon, sharp pointed and platinum white, barely a sliver of moon. Neither boy had spoken for a long time; lost in the marvel of black sky and brilliant, silent lights. Then July had whispered, "God bless the new moon!"

The oil lamps of the city were burning up and down the narrow, crowded streets, but they flickered dim yellow, artificial, when one looked at the sky. The sickle moon over New Orleans was as white and bright as the enormous, gleaming star that hung near its lower point. July would be in his own cabin now, his evening meal over, his day's work done, carving delicate wooden horses out of soft whittling wood. July is at home, safe, Horace thought. July is a slave without a last name. I, Horace Bunch Gould, am free. He laughed and walked rapidly down Orleans Street through the throngs of people out for their night's business. At Chartres, he slowed his stride. There was no hurry.

He cut through the narrow alley alongside the Cathedral, out into the openness of the Place d'Armes and stood wondering where to go. The wind was too cold for loitering, and he desperately felt the need of a destination. There would be a way to handle what had happened, but first, he needed a place to go—not a building, not a house with an address, but a place, any place, so long as it was *his* choice.

Striding across the Place d'Armes, he headed for the now-familiar waterfront. The four miles of lighted levee bustled even at night with ships and men and goods, all on the move in or out of the port of New Orleans. Some of the sickening horror he had experienced with "Toto" Davis faded, as he hurried between towering stacks of cotton bales and meat barrels, his eyes fixed on the curving line of ships and boats which lay two or three deep along the levee. As far as he could see, vessels were jammed together, hull to hull, from ports all over the world. Vessels of all sizes, all colors, all shapes. The gray sails of ocean-going ships were furled, their flags cracking in the wind, and he wished he could talk to each foreign sailor who ran down the gangplanks, to find out in the space of a few minutes what it was like in the land each one called home. He too was alone in an almost strange city, needing to find a place where he could feel at home.

Farther up the levee, toward the American part of town, the flatboats and keelboats and smaller, bulky river craft rode the dark waters of the Mississippi, their decks swarming with coarsely dressed, uncouth Westerners as ready for a quick fight as for a quick sale. He walked around and between the stacks of tobacco, hemp, kegs of pork and pickles, rum, tar and coffee. The unmistakable aroma of coffee made him homesick, but not for his father's house, for his own place—the place he hadn't found. With the far end of the levee in sight, he turned and retraced his steps, two miles or more, back past the French Market toward Canal.

The wind had changed and the flares and lanterns and lamps along the waterfront seemed suddenly focused on the white line of steam packets, haughty and palatial at their own landing at the foot of Canal Street. Horace stared as though he were seeing them for the first time. The quieter, more sedate river-palace landing was familiar. He had dreamed there of walking aboard for a long, leisurely trip on any of a half dozen dreamlike river queens. Now, the boats were no longer dreamlike and he was moving toward them with one thought in his mind. He shoved his way through gangs of sailors and sightseers, past Spaniards hawking flowers and black stevedores scurrying from one landing to another, seeing none of them, his eyes riveted on one proud, brightly lighted pleasure palace called the *Princess*.

Knowing full well he could be stopped for trespassing, he hurried down the wooden steps to the dock, up the wide gangplank and onto the deck. He would act the innocent if anyone caught him, would explain that he was fresh from Georgia and didn't know he wasn't welcome to look at the magnificent boat. Up and down the wide, varnished lower deck he strolled, gawking at the fancy turned-wood scrolls; peering into the brightly lighted ballrooms, their crystal chandeliers spreading shadow patterns across the ornate dark-paneled ceilings. Many passengers were already aboard, most of them expensively dressed, laughing and talking with the excitement that precedes a long pleasure trip. Affluent men lined the bars, their polished boots on the polished brass rails; their ladies strolled the decks, or sat in the comfortable lounges, chatting together. Through one wide window, he could see the ever-present, professional river-boat gambler, already at work at a gaming table in the corner of the largest saloon.

At the railing of the quieter upper deck, Horace looked toward the big curve in the Mississippi, around which the *Princess* would move tomorrow morning. His heart raced, and even in the chill night air little beads of sweat stood on his forehead. He was alone. There would never be another woman for him, but there was a new urgency pushing him from within, very like falling in love. He laid his hand on the *Princess*'s polished railing, caressing it, then he strode quickly across her noble deck and mounted the narrow wooden stair to the Captain's quarters.

He knew the captain of a Mississippi River boat was a king, untouchable by common man, never to be disturbed, but he had no power to stop himself. The heavy mahogany door bearing the gold letters CAPTAIN'S QUARTERS loomed in front of him, and he knocked—more briskly than he meant to—and without waiting for an answer, opened the door and stepped inside.

The Captain, a tall, red-bearded man with a haughty face, jumped to his feet, his hand on his pistol. "Who gave you permission to enter my quarters?"

"I'm terribly sorry, sir," Horace said, "but I have fallen in love with your boat and I want to work for you."

The ship's master sank slowly into his chair, his heavy, pinkish brows pulled together. "Who told you I need a purser?"

"No one, sir. Do you?"

"What's your name? Where you from? And how do I know you're not a scoundrel?"

"My name is Horace Gould. My father is James Gould of New St. Clair plantation on St. Simons Island, Georgia. I've been at Yale two years and I'm not a scoundrel. I just want a job on the *Princess*."

The Captain grunted.

"I need it and I'm sure I'd make a good purser."

"But how the devil did you know I needed one?"

"I didn't, sir."

"Well, I do." The Captain pushed his heavily braided

cap back on his head. "This is my big Christmas cruise, and since I have to leave port in the morning, and my new man hasn't shown up, I have no choice but to hire you. My old purser was shot on board the *Princess* last week. You will take his place."

14

Before she left for church, Mary went to the kitchen to give Maum Larney some last-minute instructions. The Thomas Butler Kings were taking dinner with them, and since Mrs. King set such a splendid table, everything at New St. Clair that day must be right.

Larney looked Mary over from the new black morocco ankle boots to the green velvet bonnet to match her new velvet dress with leg-o'-mutton sleeves. "Miss Mary, you looks as purty as yo' mama, Angel Miss, ever look!"

"Well, thank you, but you should approve. You helped me make my new outfit. What about the pies Ca baked? Did they turn out all right?"

"We ain' servin' no pie today! Larney cudda tol' ya' dat mah girl Ca don' know how to make piecrus' yet. Today we gon' serve Larney's apple cake." She dried her hands on her apron and walked toward Mary. "Miss Mary, don' make me wait till after dinner to tell me effen dey's a letter from mah boy."

"Maum Larney, you know I'll tell you the minute we get home."

Larney turned away. "Mausa James done give up on hearin'."

"You mean because Papa's stopped riding to Frederica every day? He just hasn't felt like it. I'm sure we'll have a letter today. Since he didn't come home for Christmas, I'm sure we'll get a letter."

"Lessen he's sick or dead. . . ."

"Maum Larney!"

"Yes-um."

Suddenly there was a clatter of carriage wheels on the road at the back of the house and Adam shouting: "Miss Mary! Miss Mary, come see de new carriage—got it all hitched up fo' church. Two story high—bottom fo' de white folks, top fo' de niggers—all gilsey gold!"

Mary ran to the door, and there stood her father's fine new carriage, with July on the high driver's seat, Adam beside him, their faces shining.

"Oh, July, Adam—it's magnificent! But we can't go to church in the carriage. You'll have to hitch the horses to two buggies instead." It was an uncomfortable moment. "I know how disappointed you both are, but will you do as I say?"

"Yes, ma'am," July said. "Two buggies."

"And hurry. We should be starting right now."

She watched them drive back toward the stable and then turned to Larney. "July knows about Miss Alice! Why did he do that? Why did he put me in the position of having to—spoil their pleasure? I can't help it that she won't ride with—"

"Wif niggahs?" Larney said gently. "No, Miss Mary, you sho' can't he'p it, chile."

"But why did July do that? He's no dumb darky, Maum Larney. He's your son. And he knows!"

"He know all right. But since Mausa James buy de new carriage wif room fo' Mausa Jim an' Miss Alice too, I reckon July was jis' hopin'. He gon' hear from me after you done gone to church. He gon' hear plenty from his mama!"

"Promise you won't say a word to him. I shouldn't have said anything to you." Mary made herself smile. "Let's forget it. Oh, Maum Larney, I'm trying so hard to believe we're going to hear from Horace!"

Mary tethered the horse at the hitching rail across the road from Christ Church and sat a moment before jumping down to help her father. They had ridden in silence most of the way, Caroline sitting quietly between them. Finally Mary asked, "Papa, would you like for me to run over to Mr. Couper's tree and find out this time?"

She looked at her father's drawn face. "Yes," he said wearily. "Yes, daughter, if you please."

John Couper was holding out a letter, smiling.

"Good morning, Mr. Couper—is it from Horace?"

"That it is, Miss Mary, I'm happy to say. From New Orleans."

She took it, curtsied to Mr. Couper, and ran back to the buggy.

Her father did not reach for the letter. "He wrote to us at last, didn't he?"

"Yes, Papa. Do you want me to read it aloud?"

"If you please."

"Oh, Mary, do hurry," Caroline said. "I suppose you need to catch your breath, but—careful, dear, don't tear it breaking the seal!"

Mary unfolded the single page and began to read: " 'Dear Papa and Family, I know I should have written before I left Savannah, but I'm sure Mr. Lively has told you the details of my hurried departure. I was sent to find a lost cotton shipment. I found it rather easily and I want you to know I made sure that I fully dispatched my obligation to Mr. Lively before I tendered my-letter-of-resignation.' " Mary's voice faltered.

"Resignation!" Caroline gasped.

"Go on, Mary," her father said.

" 'You see,' " she read, " 'on the schooner coming across from Savannah to New Orleans, I met a gentleman by the name of John Davis, who is the impresario (quite famous and well-connected) of the popular Théâtre d'Orléans. He offered me a job as head usher in his theater and I took it. I have a nice room in a nearby boardinghouse and I am enjoying the city and the fine performances at the theater. They are of a much higher caliber than Savannah. I hope you had a good Christmas. Affectionately, Horace Gould.' "

Mary turned the letter over, unable to believe that was all. She looked first at Caroline, who was on the verge of tears, then at her father. He said, "Help me down, daughter. I need to go into the church."

Jim and Alice drew up beside them, but Mary and her father walked on across the road and up the narrow path to the church door.

"What's wrong with those two?" Jim asked. "For that matter, what's ailing you, Aunt Caroline?"

"We've heard from your brother at last, Jim."

"Good! But why is everyone so funereal? How is the little rebel? What's he up to?"

"That's just it, Jim. He's taken a job as head usher in a theater in New Orleans, and that's all we know."

"Horace a head usher?" Alice laughed.

"Yale would be proud of him for that noble accomplishment." Jim was laughing too, as he helped Alice from the buggy.

"Both of you stop making fun this minute," Caroline scolded.

Jim swung his aunt ceremoniously to the ground, and when she had regained her dignity, she commanded, "Not one word of ridicule of your brother to either Mary or your father, do you hear? Their hearts are heavy enough. And who knows? The Théâtre d'Orléans is probably quite an elegant establishment."

"Oh, it is, dear Aunt Caroline." Jim chuckled. "And run by one of the most famous impresario-gamblers on the frontier. Did I say 'famous'? I meant to say 'infamous.'"

"Gambler, Jim? Did you say 'gambler'?" Caroline whispered.

"My dear Aunt Caroline, everyone gambles in New Orleans—everyone. The rascal may come home a rich man yet." He offered an arm to each. "To the church, ladies. If my baby brother is settling in New Orleans, we really have something to pray about."

PART TWO

15

Except for the steady rattle of rain on the tin roof above the bay in the dining room where Mary sat over breakfast coffee with her father, the house was quiet. They had just exchanged sections of the Savannah newspaper of September 3, 1831, and neither had spoken for a long time. More and more often, they sat together without talking, except about casual things—the probability that Thomas Butler King would represent Glynn County in the legislature next year, the price of calico and linsey-woolsey, the new ruts in Frederica Road after the last hard rain, the need for more oyster shells on their own lane, a new rose blooming, the Wylly-Hazzard boundary dispute. Horace had been gone from Savannah for almost ten months, and in that time, he had written to them twice. It was September, and the last note, like the one before—saying almost nothing—had been dated May 21. Over and over Mary had asked, "Papa, do you suppose he's still at that theater in New Orleans?" Horace had given them merely a New Orleans post-office address and had said he liked his work. He had not written even once for money, was apparently in good health. Beyond that, they knew nothing.

James Gould stirred his coffee, sipped it and went back to reading, slapping the folded sheet into the shape he wanted. "Well, it looks as though the cotton market is holding steady at Liverpool," he mumbled, without looking up. "Our long-staple is still at fifteen."

"Papa!" Mary's cup crashed against the edge of her saucer and her hand shook replacing it.

"What is it, daughter?"

Her eyes were wide with shock, the color gone from

her face. "Didn't you read it? You've seen this part of the paper—didn't you read it, Papa?"

James Gould sighed heavily. "Yes, Mary. I did."

"Then how can you just talk about the cotton market?"

"Guess I didn't know what to say, honey."

She stared at him, her dark eyes demanding some explanation.

"What is there to say, daughter? Except that it's a fearful thing. Fearful for the whites and fearful for the blacks who took no part in it." He sighed again. "Fearful for the ones who did."

Mary let the paper slide to the floor and sank back in her chair. "Fifty-five white persons—*massacred*. Some of them in their beds!" A new fear, totally strange, had begun its slow crawl over her. "The Negro who led the uprising was always considered a good slave." She spoke almost to herself. "One family he belonged to named Turner had even taught him to read."

"It wasn't the family he turned against, but we can't know the whole story from the newspaper, Mary. Only the bare facts. Not the heat on both sides, nor the possible cruelty—there's no way for us to know the real conditions up there in Virginia."

"But, Papa, what could white people do to make their darkies plan a thing like that? Are they so cruel on the mainland? Or is that just Northern talk?"

James Gould turned his half-empty cup round and round in its saucer and did not answer.

"Papa, I asked you a question! Do you think there are white folk who mistreat their people so that an intelligent slave like this Nat Turner would be driven to murder? And not just one man—these Negros didn't just shoot one white man in a fit of anger—they hacked off people's heads! They murdered women and old men and little children! Papa, answer me!"

"Well, there's Northern talk and there's cruelty, too."

"Like whippings?"

"Like whippings—and worse."

"But don't they know how valuable slaves are? I

(106)

mean, even if they don't care about them as human beings, don't they care about breaking their spirit so they won't work?"

"Daughter, I only know some of our plantations here in coastal Georgia. I can't rightly answer your question about other slave owners anywhere else."

Mary knew he had said all he meant to say, but she couldn't let go. "Can you imagine July doing something like that to us? Can you? By the widest stretch of your imagination, can you believe our July would—murder you? Or me? Or Jim? Or Aunt Caroline?"

"No, I can't believe that, daughter."

Mary stood up and began collecting the breakfast china. Suddenly she set the stack down and clutched the tall chair back with both hands to steady herself. "Papa, there are almost two thousand darkies on this isolated Island and only a hundred whites!"

"That's right."

"Does it make you afraid?"

"No. Not after I sell Burt, it won't."

Burt! The surly, flat black face criss-crossed with crooked scars like white silk cords. ... Never July, but she could see Burt standing over her bed, a broadax upraised.

"I got Burt right after Horace left Savannah, when I went up early this year to question Lively about what happened," her father was saying. "Eight or nine months is long enough for a darky to get used to a new place. Burt's a bad one. Larney's John is at his wit's end with him. He's an evil influence on the other people. I won't permit a whipping—wouldn't change Burt anyway. So he goes back to the market the first time a trader comes by."

Mary felt faint. Only heaven knew when a trader would stop at St. Simons. Island planters almost never sold their people. She had never known a Negro family to be broken up by a sale. She had never heard of a whipping on the Island. Maybe there had been some, but she had never heard of any. Just last week, good-natured Tab and mild, shy Jasper had fallen under

Burt's goading. Both young men had, for the first time, refused to finish their day's task, had forced her father to resort to the most extreme punishment he would allow at New St. Clair. "Give them all three a rest," he had told his driver, John. And Tab and Jasper and Burt had been locked up in separate quarters, with plenty to eat, but separately housed, so they could not talk to each other. Unable to bear the solitude, in less than two days, Tab and Jasper had given the signal to John that they were ready for their hoes again. But not Burt.

"Burt's still locked up," her father said.

"Don't let him out!"

"I don't intend to, even though we need him the worst way right now to finish picking the south field."

"*Don't let him out*, Papa, and help me keep Alice from learning about any of this, do you hear?"

"I pray she won't find out, daughter, about Burt or about what happened up in Virginia."

Mary began stacking the china again, noisily, to bolster her courage. "One more big scare, after that mockingbird in her room last week, and Jim's baby could be marked. It's just two months away."

Her father pulled himself slowly to his feet. "You've done mighty well with Alice, Mary. Their house will be ready in January. That might help some."

"It'll help us here, but it can't help Alice. She's going to have darkies over at Black Banks too."

"Tell Maum Larney that was a good breakfast. And don't be afraid. I'll send for a trader right away."

"I am afraid," Mary whispered when he had left the room. "*I am afraid*."

Alone in the kitchen, still holding the stack of dishes, Mary leaned heavily against the wooden safe, her heart pounding. In a moment, Larney appeared, tall and dark, framed in the porch doorway. The black woman walked slowly toward her and it was all Mary could do not to back away.

"You dun hear somepin' bad 'bout mah boy!"

"No, no—it's not about Horace."

"Den, what's wrong wif you, chile? You look lak a haint chase you thru de house!"

Mary set the dishes down and threw herself weeping into the arms of the woman who had fed her and Horace and Janie from her own breasts. The long, brown arms were around her, one broad hand soothing the middle of her back with firm, circular strokes as Larney had done through every childhood crisis.

"It got t' be somepin' bad to make Miss Mary cry," she said tenderly. "But jis' go on, go on. Not long nuff t' make yo' eyes red, but long nuff."

Mary wondered how an article in a newspaper about something that happened hundreds of miles away in Virginia could cause her to feel strange with Maum Larney. To feel suddenly despised because her own skin was white. To *feel* white and different with the most familiar person in her whole world. There couldn't be any secret, dark bitterness in Maum Larney! She was one of them—proud to be a Gould.

"A band of Negroes in Virginia turned on their white folks, Maum Larney, and murdered them in cold blood. Some of them at night in their beds. With swords and broadaxes. They hacked up women and children and old people!" Her voice rose. "In one house after another, they murdered every white person in sight. Why? *Why did they do it?*"

Larney stepped back two or three steps. She picked up a cloth and gave an already clean table a hard swipe. Then she looked straight at Mary. "Does ah seem stubborn an' brassy standin' here lookin' right in yo' eyes whilst ah talks to you, Miss Mary? Answer me, chile. Darkies ain' s'pose to do dat. A good darky neber look a white pusson in de face when he talk."

Mary frowned. "I didn't know it was any sort of rule."

"Well, it be a rule, all right. An' a good 'un, too. All mah chillurn been taught neber to break dat rule. Dey be plenty ob white folks git mad effen a niggah don' look at de groun' or de ceilin' or de flo' when dey talks. *Nice* white folks, too. Larney's lookin' right at yo' eyeballs. Is ah bein' a no-good, brassy darky?"

"Maum Larney, no! Everything's different with you."

The deep-set brown eyes held Mary's for a moment, then Larney went on. "*Right dere*, you done give yo'se'f de answer to yo' own queshun, honey. Diffurn is diffurn. Don' you fo'git it. What happen up dere in V'ginny don' happen here on S'n Simons. We's all diffurn down here on dis Islan'—black *an'* white."

Mary sat down on Larney's caned chair. "You knew about what happened up in Virginia before I told you, didn't you?"

"Ah caught m'se'f listenin' on de grapevine."

"But how *could* you have known it?"

"Ah don' mean no disrespeck, but dey's things white folks don' know nuffin' 'bout, Miss Mary."

Mary felt suddenly afraid again. "Maum Larney, do you ever think about being a—slave?"

"Wha's de good?"

"I need you to tell me the truth! Does it ever make you—hate us because, in a way, Papa owns you?"

Larney wiped the clean table a second time, then laid down her cloth. "Be yo' Papa de one dat pilot de fus' slave ship, chile? Be he de one dat buy de fus' scared niggah an' set him down in a strange lan' where he don' know one word dat's bein' hollered at 'im? Be Mausa Goul' de fus' one dat put a hoe in a black man's han' an' say 'go chop mah fiel'? Be yo' Angel Miss mama de fus' white lady to put a dishrag in a black woman's han' an' say 'scrub mah dirty dishes'? Oh, chile, chile, res' yo'se'f. We'se all right on dis Islan'."

Mary thought a minute. "You mean—since there *is* slavery, the St. Simons people are as content as possible. Is that it?"

"Far as ah knows, dey ain' but one niggah here dat don' know he's well off."

"Burt."

"Mah John done beg Mausa James to sell 'im. He come from up V'ginny, close to where de trouble happen. De lan's done run out up dere. All de white mausas is mad at de worl'. Burt's striped-up black back is how mad dey is. He been *made* a mean niggah. Maybe he was bo'n a mean niggah, but dey be a han'—maybe a black driver's han'—wif a whip in it to he'p his meanness grow lak a wil' cucumber vine." Larney was wiping her clean table again. "We bes' git rid ob him right quick. Burt be a black debil."

Mary looked out the kitchen window. The rain had stopped and the trees tossed their shadows again across the green grass—black trunk and branch patterns forming and reforming in the suddenly bright, windy day.

"Maum Larney, is it really so bad other places? Were any of your people—before you came to Papa or any time—ever treated cruelly by a white owner? I mean—a whipping or worse? You were already a young woman when Papa bought you. Had anything horrible ever happened to *you*?"

Larney squared her wide shoulders. "Miss Mary, effen dey's somepin' dat needs t' be talked 'bout, Larney's here. Not unless. Go on, chile. Ah got mah work t'do. So hab you."

16

"Oh, Jim, I told you to bring me a lot of butter! I'm *so hungry* for butter!"

"Alice, there must be a quarter of a pound of butter on that plate."

"You don't know what I'm talking about. I know I shouldn't expect a stupid man to understand when a woman craves a certain kind of food, but—" Her voice rose sharply. "Isn't it enough that I have to live in this Godforsaken place, surrounded by peering black faces and snakes and bugs and lizards—with that horrible, howling wind that hasn't let up for three whole days? Am I expected to starve too?" She threw her napkin into Jim's face. "I'm having a baby! I'm scared to death every minute of the day, and I'm starving, Jim. I'm starving for butter!"

When she began to sob, Jim tossed the napkin back at her. "Here, dry your eyes and eat your breakfast. You're not the first woman who ever had a baby, but I'll bet you're the first woman whose husband leaves his work in the middle of the morning to carry her food up to her with a houseful of servants who could do it just as well." He sat down abruptly on the bed and smoothed her hair. "Alice, I'm sorry, but my nerves are frazzled too."

"Go on back to your precious work!" she snapped. "I won't eat a bite of food until you get out of this room."

"That's fine with me." He started for the door.

"Jim, wait—where are you working today?"

"Papa and a trader from Savannah are waiting for me downstairs. We're selling a man. Why?"

"Nothing. I just wanted to know where you'd be."

He came back to the bed. "Does it make that much difference to you, poor Alice?"

"No, it doesn't! And there's nothing poor about me, except—"

"Yes, I know," Jim said, striding toward the door again. "There's nothing poor about you except the snakes and the wind and the darkies and the moss and the lizards and the bugs! Eat your breakfast. And get dressed and come downstairs in time for dinner, do you hear?"

He slammed the door, and Alice forgot him as she crammed the entire lump of fresh, sweet butter into her mouth, and leaned back on her stack of pillows, her wild craving momentarily eased. The strong northeast wind banged her wooden shutters with unbroken monotony. She shivered, picked at a pancake. Without butter, it was tasteless, and moving the almost untouched tray to her bedside table, she jumped up, struggled into only two petticoats and a loose cotton dress that would no longer fasten around her distended waist, threw a cloak over her shoulders, slipped downstairs and out the front door then ran, bent against the wind, toward the spring-house. "I'll get my own butter," she said half aloud. "If

(112)

they won't give it to me, I'll steal some and hide it in my room."

She took the path that led to the servants' quarters, chancing the ordeal of meeting a black alone in the woods, then cut through a grove of scrub oaks and cassina and headed for the spring, at an angle where she was hidden, she hoped, from the big house. The rough, woolly moss whipping from the sapling trees brushed the back of her neck, and her flesh crawled, but her craving drove her. Out of the tangled grove at last, she hurried along the path under a water oak that stood between a small, thick-walled tabby hut and the spring. She had never even wondered what was kept in that stolid tabby hut with its one high window. Now, about to pass it, she was struck with terror when, over the wind, she heard a rapping and a coarse, husky laugh. Frozen, she stood staring into the flat, scarred black face peering at her through the high window.

"Wha's yo' hurry, white wench?" Burt called, then laughed again.

The last sound she remembered was her own scream, until Jim's voice broke into her consciousness. Her husband was bending over her where she lay on the ground beside the tabby hut, his voice rough, angry, demanding to know if she meant to kill his baby.

"Son, the darky's been sold—he's gone," James Gould tried to reason with Jim. "It was a bad experience for Alice, but you saw the trader take him away. There'll be no more trouble."

Jim paced the sitting room from the front windows to his father's easy chair. "If you didn't stand to lose six or seven hundred dollars, I'd have shot the black pig through his ugly head!"

"And that would have been murder. Son, listen to me. Alice seems fine. She had a bad scare, but she seems fine except for—"

Jim whirled from the window. "Except for her usual complaining. Go on, say it, Papa. I don't even try to defend her any more."

"I've noticed that and I'm ashamed of you."

"Ha!"

"Did I say something funny?" The older man studied his son's face—the jaw set, eyes like flint, every muscle in the tall, lithe body tensed—always ready to jump, he thought. But where? "Did I say something funny, Jim?" he repeated.

"No, it just struck me that way."

"What's really troubling you, more than usual?"

"What is required, Papa, to please people? If I please you, I displease my wife. If I please my wife by taking her back North to have the child, I displease you. I'm going to ask you something just once. If you refuse, I promise I'll never ask again."

"What is it?"

"Get Horace to come back here to help you. He's nineteen—and, lucky man, he's foot-loose and fancy-free—at least so far as we know. How about it? Will you let Alice and me go back to Connecticut and bring my brother home to take my place?"

As always, when his trouble ran deep, James Gould fell silent. After a long moment, he asked, "What about your new house at Black Banks?"

"Let baby brother have it. You can give him the land. I'll sell him the house—cheap."

James covered his face with both hands. "I suppose we could locate Horace. But I forced you. I won't force him. You knew, before you asked, I couldn't grant your request, didn't you, son?"

"Yes, I knew. Maybe that's why I asked. It cleared my conscience. You see, Papa, even with all the hell she causes me here, I want to stay. I don't want to go back to Connecticut. St. Simons is my home. Until she spoils it utterly for me, it will be. This way I can blame you. I can tell her I tried."

James Gould looked at his elder son. Jim had always been headstrong, but he had never known him to be cruel. Worse than cruel, what Jim had just tried was weak. "Well, it's all right to blame it on me, if you think that's the only way. It is my fault you're here, and I'd do anything within my power to set you free. Anything but force Horace."

"Papa, do you want me to write to him?"

"What for?"

"To give him a piece of my mind for not keeping in touch with you."

James took a deep breath. "No, I don't think it would help. Mary writes him a good letter every week. He doesn't answer, but she keeps on writing. He knows we want him home with us. I guess the boy isn't ready to settle down."

"But this isn't like Horace."

"His heart is broken over what happened at Yale."

"After all this time? That makes no sense whatever."

The older man tried to pull himself to his feet and fell back in his chair. "Give me a hand, Jim?"

"Of course, Papa."

He leaned on his strong son to steady himself.

"Jim?"

"Sir?"

"Try to stay with us if you can. You're all I've got."

"My sister Mary wouldn't care for that remark." Jim grinned.

"Mary is part of _me._ I never think of losing Mary." Tears sprang to his eyes. "Janie's going to teach in Baltimore—I think about losing you at times and I've lost Horace. But Mary will stay."

17

October 20 was an almost perfect day, mild, still. The deer flies were gone. The sunlight had become the warm, burnished gold Mary waited for at the end of each hot summer. She stood in the yard at the north corner of the rose-laden picket fence that closed the

(115)

Gould house into its orderly garden. On a slight knoll, separated from the palmetto thickets and stands of tall trees and cotton fields, the house stood an unpretentious, sturdy symbol of her father's Yankee industry and pride of dwelling. It was a symbol of Mary, too. She was its mistress, and because of the beauty of her rose gardens, the people who came from all over Glynn County to get slips from her specimen plants had begun to call her house Rosemount. Mary liked that and felt quickly at home with the name. It was a tribute to long hours of hard work under the hot sun battling sand gnats and deer flies and red bugs and yellow jackets. Her garden had become the creative center of her life. "Rosemount," she said softly to herself as she set the big basket filled with pine straw mulch on the ground beside the first thick-caned multiflora rose at the fence corner. She stood a moment, loving Rosemount, pushing aside the thought of the turmoil it housed this day—the day Alice's baby was due. Turmoil that would end soon, she reminded herself. In two months, Alice and Jim would be gone to live in their own home. Rosemount would remain and she would remain its mistress for as long as she lived. And that would be enough. She would see to it that Rosemount would be enough.

From far down in the south field, she could hear bursts of high-pitched Negro laugher and frequent puffs of work songs as the changing sea breeze nudged the familiar sounds toward her and then away. It was midmorning, and automatically she looked down the lane that led from the back porch to the south field. The straggly little procession was underway: eleven-year-old Adam, lugging a big brown jug of buttermilk, trudged ahead of three more children in their shapeless everyday garments, toting baskets of cornbread—kicking pine cones as they hopped and jounced along, giggling, screaming with delight or yelling in exaggerated pain when their bare feet struck an oyster shell on edge in the road. Rosemount's day was in progress. She liked the feeling. "Well, this is not getting my roses mulched," she scolded herself, propped the basket of pine straw on her hip and squeezed in between the bushes to do the hard part by the fence first.

She had piled the fragrant, long needles around the canes of two bushes when a scream shattered the quiet morning. Mary jumped to her feet. Alice! She had been a little girl, not quite seven, when her baby sister, Janie, was born in this same house, when Rosemount was brand new. Through every minute of that long-ago, strange day, she had waited for something dreadful to happen. Rhina, the leathery, coffee-brown midwife from Mr. Couper's plantation at Cannon's Point, had ruled the household with a deft, bony hand: moving silently upstairs and down, her head tied up tightly in her "birthin' band"—a piece of white cloth folded smoothly above her forehead and knotted behind with the ends hanging over the back of her neck. Their new baby was born and nothing dreadful happened. Her mother did not scream once, and by evening there was laughter and excitement and noise in the house.

Alice screamed again—sharper than before—and Mary's whole body prickled with anxiety and dread. With Alice, something unpleasant was bound to happen. She stooped down to her roses once more and piled big handfuls of straw furiously around their roots and up their green canes, as the screams grew louder.

"Mary! Sister! Where are you?" Jim was running across the yard, his eyes wild, his usually clean-shaven face bristly with black stubble.

"Here, Jim—behind the roses," she called.

"What an idiotic time to mulch roses, Mary! Don't you hear her?"

"Of course, I hear her. Maum Rhina will be here soon. July went for her early this morning."

Jim clutched his head. "I should have gone along to keep that nigger driving. Mary—what if Rhina is sick or tending someone else? What if she isn't coming?"

"She'll be here any minute. And that wasn't a nice thing to say about July. You'd better not let Papa hear you call him a 'nigger,' and you know he's hurrying as fast as he can. Maum Rhina's hard to get started."

"Don't lecture me, and come out from behind that infernal rose bush! How can you be so callous as to mulch roses when Alice may be dying?"

"She's not dying and I'm not callous. I'm nervous. What else is there for me to do? It isn't time—Aunt Caroline's with her. Larney would be too, if she'd let a darky in her room." Mary pushed her way around the big bush. "Jim, Rhina's black, too."

"My Lord, sister, don't you think I know that?"

"Does she know the doctor can't come? Will she let her in to help?"

Jim grabbed her arm. "That's your job. You're the only one who can convince her that Rhina means the difference between life and death—for her and the baby. You're going to handle her, aren't you, Mary?" His fingers dug into her arm. "You're going to do it for me, aren't you?"

"I'll try. That's all I can promise. I'll try."

The buggy rattling up the long lane sent them both running. Mary reached it only one step behind her brother, helped Rhina down, then pushed and pulled her toward the house and up the stairs to Alice's room.

Inside the yellow, sunlit bedroom, Alice's screams were almost unbearable. Her eyes were squeezed shut and she clawed at the bedclothes like an animal hunting for a place to hide. Rhina seemed not to notice. Taking her time, in full charge and on long familiar ground, the black woman checked Caroline's preparations: "Clean clofs, warm blankits, bilin' water." She enumerated each item, sniffing the blankets and cloths for cleanliness— poking her gnarled finger into the water to test it. Mary began to wonder if Rhina would ever do something definite. "Tuhn yo' backs," the granny woman ordered. Caroline had warned Mary about this. Rhina's rituals had to be kept, and so they turned their backs, pretending they didn't know she was removing her "birthin' beads" and a sharp knife from her apron pocket. The "birthin' beads" she placed inside her own white cotton blouse. Then she got down on her knees and tossed the knife well back under the bed to cut down the pain. As the black woman raised up, Alice opened her eyes and shrieked, "Get out of here!"

Mary watched Rhina hoist herself up, peer calmly with her slanting, squinted eyes at her patient, then hobble to the nearest chair to sit down and wait.

"Mary Gould, get her out of here! I'll die if she touches me!"

The screaming began again; more hysteria now than pain. Mary looked helplessly at Rhina and her aunt, then made up her mind. Just short of a slap, she clamped her hand over Alice's mouth, silencing her. "You'll die if she doesn't help you! You'll die and your child will die. There is no one to help you but Maum Rhina and she is *going* to help."

Alice's eyes were so wild and full of fear that Mary almost relaxed her grip, but she held firm. If she could keep her sister-in-law under her control for a few more minutes, maybe the poor woman could begin to control herself. "Alice Gould," Mary repeated with all the authority she could muster, "Jim can't get the doctor. If Maum Rhina does not help you, both you and the baby can die. I won't permit you to do this to my brother!"

Mary watched as Alice's terrified eyes circled the room, stopping for a long moment on Rhina, rocking quietly in her chair by the mantel. Rhina met Alice's look head on, nodded her head briefly, raised one big-knuckled hand as though in greeting and smiled politely. Mary felt her sister-in-law relax. When at last she took her hand away, Alice closed her eyes and big tears of submission slipped down her cheeks.

"Not for Jim," she whispered, so that only Mary heard. "Not for Jim. For the baby."

Mary straightened up. "She'll let you help her now, Maum Rhina," she said.

Rhina nodded. "Ah heerd she don' lak niggahs."

"Well," Mary stammered, "she—you see, this is her first baby, and—she's afraid."

(119)

Rhina worked her loose, toothless mouth as though she had a bite to chew and swallow before commenting again. "Ah neber los' no babies yit."

"Not one?" Caroline asked in amazement.

"Not ary one," Rhina replied. "Some ob 'em dies, but 'tain' mah faul'."

Mary caught Caroline's faint smile, felt her aunt and Rhina could handle matters, and with her heart stretching toward Jim, she left the room. No one must ever know what Alice had said, but Mary would never forget it.

She found her brother in the front yard, mulching her roses. "Alice is going to let Maum Rhina help her, Jim."

He sighed and for the first time since he was a small boy, Mary saw tears in his dark eyes. "What in the world did you say to her, sister?"

"I held her mouth shut long enough for her to get hold of herself, that's all."

"That's *all*! That's a miracle. Is the baby—?"

"No, it isn't coming yet. Maum Rhina was calmly waiting in the rocker when I left. Aunt Caroline is there. Alice is quiet. I saw no reason to stay. I think you need me more than Alice does."

Jim grinned halfheartedly. "I guess you're right. I do."

Mary squeezed back behind the rose bushes with him and they went on mulching together. "I think everything is going to be fine, Jim. Maybe letting Maum Rhina see her through this will help Alice—in other ways, too."

He passed a handful of pine straw to Mary. "I suppose it could help." He sat back on his heels. "How does she look, Mary? Do you think she's—going to make it?"

"How much do you love her, Jim?"

"How much? Enough so that if I lost her, I would lose every reason I have for waking up in the morning."

"That much? Does she know it?"

The muscles in Jim's face tightened. "Yes, she knows it. And she knows our being here has nothing whatever to do with the way I love her. We've been married three years, and I still get excited when she walks into a room. If Alice dies, I'll quit."

"What about the baby?"

"You heard what I said. If Alice dies, I'll quit." He stood up, suddenly anxious. "Why did you ask, Mary? Do you think—?"

"No, Jim! Nothing like that. It was just that somehow—today—it's very important to me to know how much you love her. That's all. I swear, that's all."

They both turned to watch a horse and rider gallop up the driveway toward them. "It's a darky," Mary said. "Must be carrying a message from some of the neighbors."

They went to the gate in the picket fence. The merry wave of the young Negro's hand told them nothing bad had happened.

"It's the Kings' man, Robert," Jim said.

"Mornin' Miss Mary—Mausa Jim," Robert called, reining his frisky mare.

"Good morning, Robert. You look happy today," Mary greeted him.

"Yes, ma'am. Yes, ma'am. An' ain' it a purty day? All bright an' reddy-gold.' Robert dismounted, doffed his straw hat, and stood looking around at the scarlet and yellow sweet-gum trees, tossing their colors in the rising breeze from the ocean.

"We know you've come on some important mission," Mary smiled. "The Kings never send anyone but you when it's important. Aren't you going to tell us?"

"Yes, ma'am, it sho' be one beautifulest day." He was in no hurry, and although it was too warm for a jacket, he was wearing one, buttoned all the way. Now, he unbuttoned it slowly, deliberately. "Yes, ma'am, an' yes, sir, ah be carr'in' a mos' valuesome message from Mausa an' Madam King," he proclaimed, ceremoniously drawing a note from his jacket.

Jim began to scan it silently.

"I think Robert wants to hear you read it aloud, brother, I know I do."

(121)

The King servant stood beaming as Jim read: " 'To my friends and good neighbors of St. Simons Island. Twentieth October, eighteen thirty-one. It is my pleasure to invite you to honor us with your presence at King's Retreat on Thursday, seventeenth November, at a barbeque to be prepared for the purpose of presenting to you, our friends, our new son, Lord Page King, born twenty-fifth April. It has been God's good pleasure to strengthen the child so that he is now healthy and along with his parents, eager to see all of you. The gentlemen will, at the same happy occasion, be able to discuss some issues of political importance. Mrs. King and I will look forward to welcoming you once more to our home. Please find it your pleasure to accept. Signed, Thomas Butler King, Esquire.' "

"Well, now," Mary smiled, "that is good news. You may tell the Kings we'll make every effort to be there. A party at Retreat is always something to look forward to."

"Yes, ma'am! Dat's de truf. Dat's what eberbody say."

"If my wife's all right, we'll be there, too, Robert," Jim said.

"Yes, sir, Mausa Jim."

Alice screamed, and Jim whirled and ran to the house.

"We're having a baby, too, Robert." Mary dismissed him by the tone of her voice.

Back on his horse, Robert sat holding his straw hat, staring at the window where the screaming grew louder. "Dat mus' be a *curse*' woman to holler lak dat. She sho' mus' be. Po' Mausa Jim. You better hurry, Miss Mary."

As Mary went toward the house, the screams ended as though they had been cut by a knife. She stopped to listen, and in a moment, the heavy silence was punctured by a first, lusty cry. Mary waved to Robert. "Tell the Kings we have a new baby too!"

18

"And my dear Caroline, listen to this account of Nat Turner's capture!" The Widow Shedd sat on the edge of her chair in the Rosemount sitting room, holding a sheaf of newspaper clippings. "Now, let me see—this one is from *The Norfolk Herald* of November second: 'On Thursday last, Nat was startled out of a fodder stack by a Mr. Francis, who fired at him with a pistol, but missed and he escaped. This circumstance being made known in the neighborhood, a number of persons collected together and went in pursuit of him. On Sunday last, one of the party, a Mr. Phipps, came upon him in a coverture of brushwood, so suddenly that he had not time to escape, but at the risk of being shot down, he surrendered without resistance, and was conducted to Jerusalem, where he was committed to the county jail.' Oh, my dear," Mrs. Shedd fanned herself with her clippings. "Did you ever hear of anything so ghastly? Shall I read more?"

"No, thank you," Caroline said. "It's too horrible. But I'm sure the countryside around Southampton is relieved they've caught the poor man."

"Poor man, indeed! He's a cold-blooded murderer, Caroline."

"I know he is, but he's human, too."

"Human? Yes, I suppose so. Frightened within an inch of his wretched life, I imagine. You're very Christian to think that way, my dear. I'm ashamed to say I hadn't considered the nigra's feelings at all. But what kind of man is he? White or black, how could a human being made in God's image slaughter so many innocent people? Might I have another cup of tea? This is all so unnerving."

Caroline poured tea for her guest. "It is unnerving, and I think we should change the subject. My niece may be bringing our new baby downstairs to show you, Mrs. Shedd, and we don't talk about the slave rebellion before her. Will you remember not to mention it at all?"

"Of course, my dear. How thoughtful of you. I promise not to say a word. I do despise blabbermouths. How is dear Miss Alice? Is she gaining in strength since the little fellow arrived?"

"Yes," Caroline said, passing her the cream. "She's made remarkable progress, thank you."

"Such an ordeal, childbirth. How it marks a woman. Believe me, *I* certainly have never fully recovered."

Caroline looked up, startled. The Widow Shedd couldn't be a day under seventy-five. "I don't believe I knew you had children, Mrs. Shedd."

"Oh, my dear girl, yes." She sighed. "I'm the mother of a manchild, but without any of the joys—just all the heartaches." She sipped her tea. "I do hope that wonderful Mary comes in from the fields before I have to leave. She's like a rock, isn't she?"

"Indeed we could never manage without her. Mr. Gould's rheumatism is worse and Mary rides out every day now. Has for many months."

"That poor man, with two plantations and only one son here to help him. Oh, that reminds me. I had so much other news to share, I forgot the most important item. I've had a lovely long letter from my dear Creole friend, Mme. Beauvoir, in New Orleans—with first-hand news of Horace!"

"Well, good afternoon, ladies," James Gould stood in the doorway with the baby in his arms. "Miss Alice is resting, so my grandson, Jamie, and I thought we'd join you."

"Good afternoon, Mr. Gould"—she struggled up—"Oh, my, let me have that precious little bundle right here in my arms this instant!"

James looked helplessly at Caroline, knowing Alice would object, but the Widow Shedd was already cradling Jamie in her arms. Then she held the child's face against hers and fell silent for so long, neither Caroline nor James knew what to say. They watched her begin to pace slowly back and forth across the big room, as though part of a strange unseen procession, her steps measured, her nearsighted eyes filling with tears that spilled down her cheeks.

Suddenly she said, "Take him, Mr. Gould." She handed over the infant. "Take back your grandchild and be glad you have lived to hold him in your own arms."

"May I pour tea for you, James?" Caroline asked.

"No, thank you, Caroline," he said, still standing.

"I'll have another cup, my dear." The Widow Shedd sat down again, the baby apparently forgotten. "I have most important news for you and I do need a bracer."

It was going to be news of Horace, and Caroline would have done anything to stop it.

"I was just telling your lovely sister-in-law that I've had a most interesting letter from my beloved friend, Mme. Beauvoir, who has just returned from one of those leisurely, luxurious cruises on the Mississippi. And, my dear Mr. Gould, she saw and spoke with your son, Horace!"

James looked at the Widow Shedd, his face expressionless.

"Mme. Beauvoir and friends departed New Orleans on the elegant river palace the *Princess* not long ago, and on the very first night out, she discovered the handsome young purser's name—Horace Gould. Your son, Horace, is the purser on the Mississippi River boat, the *Princess*!"

Caroline caught her breath, kept her eyes on James.

"Mr. Gould, I said—"

"I heard what you said, Mrs. Shedd, and it's a lie."

"James!" Caroline whispered.

"Forgive me if I speak brusquely to a guest, but I know my son, Horace. I also know something of the nature of the work of a purser on a river boat. It's a lie. Your friend is in error. My daughter, Mary, and Miss Caroline both choose to think that you mean well, Mrs. Shedd. I will keep my thoughts to myself, except to say once more that what you have just reported is a lie, and from now on, I would deem it a favor if you keep your gossip to yourself."

Caroline got up. "James, please control your temper!"

"My temper is controlled. I'll take Jamie back to his mother. And I'll take this last minute to suggest to you, my good woman, that you tell no one else this miserable piece of false gossip. Good day."

When he had gone, Caroline turned anxiously to the Widow Shedd, who was slumped in her chair, her soft, sagging face suddenly full of grief and sorrow.

"Don't be upset, Caroline, my dear." The old voice had lost its dramatic vigor. "I wouldn't want you to be upset at all by any of this. What I told Mr. Gould is true. Mme. Beauvoir did talk with Horace." She smiled wanly. "You see, I had written her to keep her ear to the ground for news of the boy. I know I seem like an old busybody. I'm not entirely. My son went away too, when he was seventeen, and I've never seen or heard from him since. He's fifty now, if he's alive. I've had people looking for him all these years. It's a habit with me to keep people looking for lost young men."

Caroline sat down limply. Her guest had changed before her eyes from a rather lovable, but often annoying, Island gossip into a sorrowing woman whom she pitied and wanted to comfort.

"I know I brought shocking news. I thought, I suppose, that his father would be glad for some word of the boy. Didn't stop to realize that his pride would be hurt. You see, when the years pile up and there has been no word, it would be wonderful just to hear he is alive somewhere—doing anything. Just alive. Horace hasn't been gone quite a year. It's too soon. Too soon."

"Oh, Mrs. Shedd, I'm so sorry."

"I'm sure you are, my dear. You're very kind and I must be going." She got wearily to her feet, and held out her hand. "The news I brought is true, no matter how it hurts. . . ."

"I believe you."

"Thank you."

"James will too, once he talks with Mr. James Hamilton Couper. He's on a trip now to Natchez and Mobile to look over some property there and has promised to locate Horace, if possible."

"Good. Just so the boy is rescued in time. The purser, you know, is the young man who sees to the wants and wishes of the passengers, and their wants and wishes are not always of the highest moral nature. I'm glad he'll hear it from Mr. Couper. He'll believe a man. Well, hand me my cloak, my dear, and give my best to dear Mary."

Caroline draped the long blue silk cloak over her guest's shoulders, hugging her as she did so. "Will we see you at the Kings' barbecue next Thursday, Mrs. Shedd?"

"Indeed you will. Be a fool to miss a party at the Kings'! And, uh—before I go, just in case Mr. Couper hasn't made contact with young Horace, Mme. Beauvoir wrote that this young purser told her he was from St. Simons Island—that his father owned a plantation called New St. Clair."

19

When the Goulds arrived at the Retreat barbecue on November 17, Mary, as usual, first made sure her family was comfortable. She settled Alice, who still refused to leave the baby in Maum Larney's care, in a rocker under an ancient cedar tree on the lawn, Jamie in one of the Kings' cradles beside her. Mary knew the neighbors would be coming by to see the new infant—Alice would not lack company—and after steering the Ben Caters in her direction, she hurried to her father, who stood alone, looking, she knew, for James Hamilton Couper.

"Papa, there's no use fidgeting. Mr. James Hamilton Couper is here. I asked Mrs. King first thing."

"Well, where is he?"

"With Mr. King down at the landing. The Wyllys are arriving by boat. Jim and Mr. Couper went along to meet them. Now, there's a nice, high-backed chair over there under that oak—come on, you need to rest."

"I don't want to rest. I've got to find out if young Couper saw your brother."

"Papa, listen to me. I don't want to be watching you like a mother hen all day. I intend to have a good time. Are you going to be sensible and take that chair?"

He was peering toward the King veranda, shading his eyes with his hand. "I see his father in there. You go on and enjoy yourself. I'll talk to John Couper."

Mary watched him limp away. Why did he have to hear from a Couper what he had already heard from Mrs. Shedd? She bit her lip. Her father was going to be troublesome today. Today of all days. She had so looked forward to the party, it was difficult not to be annoyed with him. Mary stood on tiptoe for a better view of the little knot of people approaching slowly across the wide beach. She could see the Wylly sisters, she recognized Jim and her host and Mr. Couper—and, as she had hoped, oh, how she had hoped—there was John Wylly, helping his mother through the soft sand. She would see him, talk with him. Perhaps, if his mother felt well, they might be alone a few minutes. Might even take a walk together. Well! She couldn't just stand there watching John Wylly come toward her up the beach. She would have to pretend interest in someone else. The Frewins and their pretty niece, Sara Dorothy Hay, were nearby. They would do—until the Wylly party arrived.

Seated in a veranda rocker, James Gould went right to the point. "Did your son see my boy, Jock?"

"Aye, he saw him, James Gould, but I wish you'd wait to let my son tell you of their talk."

"Was Horace all right? He was well, wasn't he?"

"Oh, aye. Very well, it seems. Looked grown-up, older, more the man than my son remembered him."

"Where was he?"

"On the boat from Natchez to Mobile."

(128)

James Gould stiffened. "On a boat, you say?"

"Aye. The *Princess*."

"Was he taking a trip?"

"Well, in a way. He was taking a trip, but he was also working."

"Don't try to spare me, John Couper."

"My son will be back any minute. Wouldn't it be wise to get the story firsthand?"

"I said—don't spare me!"

"Aye, I heard what you said." John Couper took a deep breath. "Horace was the purser on the boat, James."

It was a lie. James Hamilton could not have seen Horace as the purser on any Mississippi River boat. He jerked himself out of the chair, and as fast as he could manage, limped down the steps, across the lawn and the garden and headed for the beach. He would prove it was a terrible mistake—*or a lie*.

Sweat poured down his face from the effort and the wind off the ocean smarted his eyes, already wet with tears of fury and anxiety. "Not Horace. Jim, maybe, but never Horace!" The people coming toward him were laughing. Well, they could stop laughing, he thought, long enough to prove him right. Long enough for young Couper to set the record straight. His head swam; he lurched, stumbled, then felt the sand rough against his face as he pitched forward—and, after one excruciating twist of his left leg, nothing.

Mary sat beside the bed where they had laid her father in the big downstairs bedroom. She was frightened. He looked very old, his proud Gould nose more prominent than ever, embarrassed by what he had done, swiping with the back of his hand at the tears that kept rolling down his cheeks.

"What a thing for me to do, daughter—and away from home. I've spoiled the day for you."

"You've done no such thing! And you're going to be fine. Dr. Hazzard says you just fainted from the exertion of trying to run like a deer through that loose sand. Your leg isn't broken. All you need is rest, and we've got the whole day for that."

"Where's James Hamilton Couper, Mary?"

"Can't you rest first? We already know about Horace's job, Papa. I talked to darling old Mr. Couper while the doctor examined you. He's heartsick. He even blames himself for your fall." She took his hand. "What if Horace is a purser on a river boat? He's alive, isn't he? And he's well."

"I'd almost rather have him dead."

"Papa!"

"Those men—who—cater to the needs of river boat passengers—cannot keep their self-respect."

"But Horace is different!"

"Send James Hamilton here."

She got up. "All right. I'll see if I can find him."

"Don't stop to talk to anyone—hunt till you find him. I want to know what my son had to say for himself."

Mary managed to reach young Couper just as Thomas Butler King was clapping his hands for quiet.

"Can you go to my father, Mr. Couper?" she whispered. "He's not going to rest until he talks to you."

"Of course, Miss Mary. You stay here for the presentation. I'll slip away now before it begins."

She thanked him and joined the crowd around the long wooden tables set up a few yards from the fragrant barbecue pit. Mr. King clapped his hands again and the people grew quiet. Mary looked for the Wyllys as their host began his speech: "We are all deeply sorry that our good neighbor, Mr. James Gould, met with an accident, but we are grateful to Almighty God that he was not seriously injured. We plan, of course, if he is well enough, to make our presentations to him in his room, just as soon as we make them here to you."

Mary saw John Wylly leaning against a tree, two tables away. He smiled at her.

Mr. King motioned to his wife, who stood nearby holding the new baby. "First, to you, our beloved neighbors and friends, I am proud and happy to present our youngest son, born the twenty-fifth of April this year, Lord Page King!"

Up and down the lines of smiling well-wishers, the Kings walked, Anna Matilda showing the baby to each guest, receiving their congratulations and compliments. After the child had been presented to Mary, she began trying to move unobtrusively through the crowd in the direction of the Wyllys. She was stopped, when their host once more clapped his hands for attention.

"Now, it is my pleasure to present to you another new infant, who, because of the nearness of their ages, and the faithfulness of its mother, will be reared as a foster brother to our own son, Lord Page. Hetta? Will you come here with your child?"

From the edge of the crowd walked black Hetta, her plump face beaming, her head as high as any queen, carrying her new son, Neptune, in her arms. She too, circulated among the people, nodding, saying, "Ah thanks you, ma'am," and "Ah thanks you, sir," as each guest admired the perfect little dark face beneath its still soft thatch of hair.

As the guests began to line up at the long tables, Mary pushed on toward the Wyllys. She would take a plate to her father later. Food would be the last thing on his mind now, anyway. Mr. Bartow began to ask God's blessing on the food, and when at last he said "Amen," Mary opened her eyes to see John Wylly elbowing his way toward her.

"Miss Mary," he called. "I'm so sorry about your father."

She curtsied, he kissed her hand, and for a moment, their eyes met. "Thank you, Mr. Wylly," she managed at last. "I was—on my way—to greet your mother. Is she feeling better?"

"So-so. In a stew constantly over our property line, but—" he laughed. "As long as I give her plenty of attention, she does well. How is your father, Mary?"

She tried to remember if he had ever called her

(131)

anything but 'Miss' Mary before. "He's going to be all right, thank you." Then she laughed too. "You and I have a time, don't we—playing nurse?"

He grew serious. "Yes. Yes, we do."

Did she only imagine that John Wylly seemed to be studying her face?

"How about joining us?" he asked. "Mother agreed right away when I suggested inviting you."

"Why, thank you, sir. I'd love to."

John offered his arm and as they started toward the table, Robert, the Kings' man, rushed up to tell Mary that Mr. Couper thought she should go to her father at once.

She looked at John, took a deep breath—held out her hand.

"I'm disappointed," he said, quietly.

All afternoon Mary sat by her father in the darkened room. Two plates were sent in—piled with chunks of juicy pork, red beans, rice, Brunswick stew—but neither of them ate.

He had not sent for her, but his silent agony was soon palpable in the room, she understood why Mr. Couper had thought she should be there. Now and then, she had pulled the curtains aside to look out at the festivities. Once she saw John strolling alone along the cedar plaisance. An hour or so later, she watched the Wyllys start for the landing where their oarsmen waited. Others were leaving too, and the Kings stood at the carriage entrance, saying good-by, as one group after another drove away. Her father felt better. They could go too, now, and she went to find Jim to help her get him into the buggy.

Mary drove as steadily as possible on the long bumpy trip home. Caroline had offered to hold the baby and ride with Jim and Alice in the buggy ahead to give James Gould more room. Anna Matilda King had brought pillows and a blanket and had tucked him in herself. He was preoccupied, saying only what he had to say to anyone. They had ridden the length of the Kings' avenue of oaks and were passing the Demere place at Mulberry Grove, when Mary could bear his silence no longer.

"It's been a long day for you, Papa," she said.

He didn't answer until they turned on to Frederica Road.

"The longest I've ever spent, I think, except the day I learned your mother had died."

He was not going to talk about Horace. Mary vowed not to force him.

"I keep wondering, daughter—for some reason, especially this afternoon—if she hadn't given birth to Janie, would your mother still be with us? After all this time, I wonder about it."

"Mama died of pneumonia! Janie's birth had nothing to do with it."

"I know, but having the child must have weakened her. I wonder too, if our Janie is all right up there in Baltimore. She seems so young to be away."

"Of course, she's all right! And a most successful teacher. We should just be happy she's doing the kind of work she likes."

He sighed. "I suppose so. At least, we know where she's living—the kind of people she sees. Her work—is honorable."

Mary waited for him to say more. He didn't.

"Do you want to tell me what James Hamilton had to say about Horace?"

"Not now, daughter."

The sun was setting behind them and as they passed Kelvin Grove, the trees and the Caters' cotton fields glowed rose and red-gold.

"Are you comfortable, Papa?"

"I'm doing all right. But I'm not being fair with you. I know how anxious you are to know about your brother."

Mary said nothing.

"I owe Mrs. Shedd an apology. He's a purser on a river boat, all right."

"I know that, but what did Mr. Couper say about

(133)

Horace? How did he act? I mean—what did Horace say about having such a peculiar job?"

Her father waited so long to answer, Mary leaned toward him to be sure he was not ill.

"I'm coming to it. It's hard for me to tell you." After another silence, he said, "Horace told him he was doing what he wanted to be doing—right now."

For a while there was only the rattle of the buggy and old Tom's steady clop, clop. Finally, Mary spoke. "It makes *me* hopeful if Horace said 'right now.' Do you suppose that could mean he's just—well, sort of experimenting with life? Maybe just—temporarily?"

"I don't know. I don't know."

"Did he send a message to us?"

"Sent his love, I believe Couper said. That he'd write."

"Well, I think *that's* hopeful, don't you?" She sat up straight. "Even if you don't think it's hopeful, I do. And I'm just going to go on writing to him—telling him all about us here, keeping him in touch—and maybe one day he'll have enough of it—whatever it is he's trying."

"You've got your mother's courage, Mary. That's like something she'd say."

"Oh, I'm lucky. I've got your courage, too."

They had passed Black Banks and the sun was gone, the shell roadbed darkening, its two tracks harder to see.

"The days are certainly getting shorter," Mary said, urging Tom a little, since Jim had done the same in the buggy ahead.

"What did you think of Alice today, daughter? Did she seem to enjoy herself at all?"

"I thought she did very well for Alice. She and Jim ate with the Frewins and Mrs. Shedd. Alice talked quite a bit. I even saw her laughing once with the Frewins' niece. You should see Jim's face when Alice laughs. It makes him so happy he looks foolish."

The buggy up ahead had made the turn now into New St. Clair, and as Mary turned too, they heard Alice scream. Both buggies halted.

"What is it, Jim?" Mary shouted.

Jim started to jump out, but Alice jerked him back. "Snake! There's a rattler in the road!" he called back helplessly. "Alice won't let me get out! And there's the baby. ..."

Before her father could move, Mary was on the ground, the buggy whip in her hand.

"Sister, don't try it!" Jim shouted. "Let's drive on."

But she was out in front of his buggy now, not five feet from the snake coiled in a pile fully a foot high, its flat head moving warily from side to side, tongue flicking. The first whistle of the whip struck it on one side of its heavy body and drew blood, but did not loosen the coil.

"Do it again, Mary—for God's sake!" Jim yelled.

The second crack of the whip shot the snake to its full length—at least six feet of angered reptile as thick as a man's wrist. Before Mary could swing again, the rattler had sensed the movement of her feet and was recoiled to strike. Once more she swung the whip and once more the snake uncoiled, its body cut deeply now, the white flesh gaping. Mary's arm ached, but the whip slashed the fourth time, then again and again. The snake lay writhing in the road, scattering shells and sand. With all her strength, Mary struck again, this time exactly where she wanted to strike—behind the head. The body still twisted into quick spasms of loose coils, but she knew it was dead.

"Hit him again, sister!" Jim shouted, and it infuriated Mary so, she grabbed the snake by its tail and slung it out of sight into the woods. She could hear the baby screaming.

"I wanted to shoot it," Jim said lamely. "Then I remembered how frightened she is of guns."

"That's right," Alice cried. "Blame me—go on, blame me!"

"Better let me carry the pistol next time," Mary said. "Shooting would be a lot less work."

Back in the buggy beside her father, she wanted to cry from exhaustion, but he looked so stricken that she laughed instead. "Well, Mr. Gould, how did your pupil conduct herself on that one?"

"Jim must feel like two cents."

"He does, and I don't blame him. Poor Alice. Poor Jim."

"Poor all of us," her father mumbled.

"Not at all! I can't seem to do anything to help Alice and Jim, so when they move in January, I'm just going to wish them well and welcome being alone again with you and Aunt Caroline. There's nothing 'poor' about the three of us. Not a thing."

They rode up the lane in silence. When they were in sight of Rosemount, her father said, "I think I'll go to New Orleans and take a trip on that boat."

Mary turned in the seat to look straight at him. "You'll do no such thing! We're just going to wait. We're not going to do anything we might regret later. When Horace comes home, we want him to *want* to come back, don't we?"

He gave in. "Yes. Yes, I guess so."

"We're going to wait for as long as we have to wait and I'll go on writing letters."

"You do have your mother's courage."

"—and yours," Mary said again, as she reined Tom in beside the gate.

20

18 January 1832

Dear Horace Bunch,

Do you remember we used to call you that when you were a little boy? I hope you haven't worried about us, since I'm a few days late writing to you, but last week was the big exodus. At last, poor Jim and Alice have moved into their new house at Black

Banks. Rosemount seems empty, but I confess blessedly so. Papa gave them a present of ten Negroes, Adam and Ca among them, I'm sorry to say. Sorry for us, that is. Ca is learning to be a wonderful cook and life won't be half as interesting without Adam, who is twelve now and smarter every day. We can only pray that the ten who went will learn how to get along with Alice. She will never understand Negroes. She wants them to do their work in total secrecy, never showing her their puzzled black faces. Jim left in fair spirits, but fearful of the future. My head wants to say it is their problem, not mine. My heart is not so detached.

We miss you, brother, and hope you are well and enjoying your work, whatever it is.

Your affectionate sister,
Mary Gould.

Horace folded the letter, then unfolded it, angry with Mary for trying to remind him of when he was a "little boy"; angry with himself that he had not been able to tell them he had been working on a river boat for almost a year. They knew it anyway by now, from James Hamilton Couper. Why did Mary pretend they didn't know? Folding the pages once more, he raised the lid of his trunk and tossed the letter in the top tray with the rest.

He looked around his cabin on the *Princess*. It was crowded, but private. His salary was three times what old Lively had paid on Commerce Row—almost twice what "Toto" Davis had paid at the theater. He was supplied with tailored uniforms and braided caps which became him well. The work was not hard. He was meeting all sorts of people, gaining experience he could not get anywhere else, learning about life. He combed his hair, set his cap in place, and looked at himself in the glass for a moment. His face was a bit angular, perhaps too thin, but he rather liked what he saw and walked briskly out on deck to the Captain's quarters. This job was certain for as long as he wanted it. The Captain approved of him, of the way he handled himself with silly, giggling old maids; with planters off on a lark without their wives; with bawdy, coarse Westerners, eager to throw their money away for cheap liquor with expensive labels, for pretty girls, for introductions to the plantation aristocracy aboard. He despised the river boat gamblers who used the *Princess* as their place of business, but he got along with them, learned to speak their language, and kept his opinions to himself. When an elderly man committed suicide on the *Princess's* polished upper deck because he had gambled away the money he was taking to his dead daughter's children, it had made Horace ill, but the next time a man was shot, he had not been ill. He was doing all right. None of it was touching him. He remained himself, and it angered him that he had not found the courage to write home about the nature of his job. Climbing the stair to the Captain's quarters, he put it out of his mind, knocked on the Captain's door, ready for another raucous, busy night aboard the *Princess*.

23 May, 1832

Dear Horace,

Papa appears to be somewhat less nervous now that we have been alone at Rosemount for three months. Good news! He has agreed to become a charter member of the new Agricultural and Sporting Club just organized. Since you left, he has almost stopped attending meetings of the *bon vivant* St. Clair Club. I understand why. Their meetings are so hilarious, a man in constant pain, as he is, can tire of it. Papa never was a reveler at heart, anyway. The new club will meet at the old St. Clair house, as the social club does, but the "agricultural" angle appeals to Papa. The men will write and read papers on various aspects of cotton growing, and the old darling will do well with his papers. He seems to grow wiser about long-staple Sea Island cotton every day. So, be happy with me

(138)

that he has not only joined, but is their first Secretary, a tedious job he will adore.

We pray you are happy and prospering and thinking of us all back here now and then.

Your affectionate sister,
Mary Gould.

12 August 1832

Happy Birthday, beloved Horace Bunch!

I can almost not believe my baby brother is twenty! If you were here, we'd give the biggest party in the history of St. Simons. Papa hasn't mentioned you today and probably won't, but Aunt Caroline and Maum Larney and July and I have all wished you a Happy Birthday and Papa too, in his heart, I'm sure.

I had better write of a less important event now, or I might get too sentimental for you. Latest marital news: Colonel William Wigg Hazzard has, at long last, taken himself a wife! Maum Larney learned of it first by "listenin' on de grapevine." No amorous signs yet from Dr. Tom. The whole Island might sink into the sea should Cupid ever smite him! The Hazzards are such cultivated men, but Dr. Tom is still quarreling with the Wyllys over a few feet of land. You know how headstrong he is. I spoke for a minute at church with John Wylly. Captain Alexander Wylly is ailing again, and John fears for his mother's health if the trouble goes on.

Being August, it is hot, hot, hot, but my oleanders are high clouds of pink and white and so are the crepe myrtles. July had a summer cold, but he is better now. Our sister Janie writes fairly often. She is successful in her work, and especially in her Baltimore social life. Every Sunday Papa hurries to Mr. Couper's tree, hoping for a letter from you, but I am not scolding. We know there is a reason why you do not write. We hear rumors, of course, but we wait to hear from you direct. And always, we wait with love.

Your affectionate sister,
Mary Gould.

Horace read this letter while standing on a street corner in New Orleans. The *Princess* was in dock for a new coat of paint and for three days he had nothing but time on his hands. He could not put off writing any longer. There was no excuse with which he could live. A box of writing paper under his arm, he walked slowly to the Place d'Armes, found a bench under an oak tree and sat down to try to decide what to say. He was glad his father had joined the new club. He could say that and be honest. It seemed funny to him too, as to Mary, that one of the bachelor Hazzards had married. He could say he was glad Jim and Alice were living in their own house and that he hoped they would appreciate the beauty of Black Banks. He could send love to Janie in Baltimore.

He could also admit at last that he was a purser on a Mississippi river boat.

A mockingbird experimented up and down the scale, and his heart tightened. Mockers would always mean St. Simons Island to him. Hoping to forestall another wave of homesickness, he lighted a cigar. As long as he remained tied to his past by maudlin sentiment, a man would never find himself. A pretty quadroon smiled at him as she undulated past. He winked at her, the homesickness disappeared, and he hurried to his cabin on the *Princess* to write the letter and get it behind him.

21

12 July, 1883

Dear Horace,

You won't believe this, but Papa made me read your letter to him again at breakfast this morning—almost a year after we received it. It is just about worn to shreds. I lost count of how many times I had to read it to Maum Larney, and Aunt Caroline kept it for weeks in her room. Aren't we funny? I try not to burden you with my letters, but when you write to us again sometime, please tell us that at least it relieved you somewhat to know that we already knew you worked on a river boat and that our love did not change or even shift. I feel you *were* relieved, but it would help Papa if you told us. A year is so long for him to wait for word of you.

Death has visited our Island twice lately. Captain Alexander Wylly and the Kings' handsome first-born child, William. Captain Wylly was old and ill, but Mrs. Wylly is bereft, and we all fear Dr. Hazzard will make still more trouble now. She is thankful, as she should be, that John is still unmarried and at home, so her land will keep producing. His sisters are still unmarried and at home, too—but John will be her real comfort. He is a good and remarkable man. Of course, the death of such a small boy as William King is heartbreaking. Mrs. King was so courageous at the churchyard when they buried her child. Thank heaven, her husband was at home from the legislature in Milledgeville when it happened. He is almost always away these days. You know, I don't cry easily, but I cried at the boy's funeral. Why is it hard to bury the very young? Is it because we feel they are cheated to have missed life? I wonder. Life looked all clear and conquerable to me such a short time ago. It seems harder now and sometimes puzzling. Do you realize I am twenty-four? Time to ride out to the fields. As usual, I will write again next week.

> Your affectionate sister,
> Mary Gould.

24 November, 1833

Dear Horace,

I'm sure I've written about the nice Irish couple—the late Mr. George Abbott's younger brother and his wife—who answered the Widow Abbott's plea to come here from Ireland to help her. Energetic Mr. Richard Abbott and his pretty wife, Agnes, an adorable child named Deborah, and a fine Irish nurse. Things looked so much better for dear Mrs. Mary Abbott, but the poor woman seems jinxed! A month ago, Agnes Abbott died giving birth to baby Annie, and yesterday the Irish nurse died, leaving Mary Abbott with two extra children to care for. She is all alone again, since the grief-stricken young father went to Darien to work. Mary Abbott is a courageous woman, though, and seems to love both the Irish children as much as her own two girls. Deborah, the older little girl, is particularly fetching. I find myself riding over to Orange Grove as often as possible, just to chat with this winsome child. She's four now, but as smart and grown up as six.

Our little sister, Jane, seems permanently settled in Baltimore. She is thriving. Jamie, our splendid nephew, has learned how to declare that he is two years old and does it vociferously and often. I don't write much about Jim and Alice. What is there to say? It is all only endurance for her. Even when I carry her roses from my garden, right while she is smelling their fragrance, a spider is sure to crawl out on her arm or her neck and on come the hysterics. How I wish, oh, how I wish Jim could take her home to

New Haven. Only God knows how Papa and Aunt Caroline and I would miss the child, but Jim is aging so—his hair is graying over his temples—and what was once real love for Alice has turned into something I wouldn't know how to describe. Still, the Black Banks land produces well, and financially, we are all fine. I must close, brother, before I write something I am determined not to write.

Your affectionate sister,
Mary Gould.

Mary had accused him more definitely than if she had spelled out the whole thing. Horace crumpled the letter and threw it into a corner of his cabin, irritable with her and with himself for what he now saw for exactly what it was—his own selfishness. He had been calling it by another name, but he *was* selfish. A man who passes the years of his life deluded by his own motives could never hope to find peace. Peace. He laughed dryly. Peace had never interested him before. He had demanded life—all of it, *his* life, with his imprint on it. He still believed that he could never find this at home on St. Simons. He would be smothered with kindness and love and family and provincialism and security. No chance at all there for a man to gamble on his own ability, to find his special place. At home, he would simply become another cotton farmer—without his own land. Of course, his father needed him. The thought of Mary forced to do a man's work—*his* work, brought on such a spasm of self-hatred, he kicked his desk chair across the tiny cabin, ran down to the *Princess*'s lower deck, sprinted across the gangplank and headed for the nearest tavern on the New Orleans waterfront.

24 February, 1835

Dear Horace,
Guess what? Janie is home for a visit! She loves her teaching in Baltimore as much as she likes the social life—but the big news is that she is *in love*. A

(143)

Mr. Orville Richardson, who she claims is the world's most marvelous man. Papa is so glad to have her with us that he is almost pathetically attempting to pull his funny little pranks the way he once did. Now that I have told you the happy news about Janie (who says she will write to you, but don't sit up waiting!), I must tell you the bad news. A week ago we had one night of unprecedented cold—8 degrees! Poor Mr. John Couper lost his olive trees, and of course, I just sat and watched my beloved orange trees freeze and wilt down. They are all lost. Janie's visit is a gift from heaven because seeing my orange trees die was almost like a death in the family. I was practically inconsolable. As I am at times when I'm alone, and thinking of how much I long to see you, to know about you. It has been six months since your last letter, which said so little. Do I sound cross? Janie just brought tea to me and sends you love.

Your affectionate sister,
Mary Gould.

Janie. Horace smiled a little, remembering his pretty younger sister. Janie would mean to write to him, but would never manage to do it. He had not seen Mary in five years and yet she wrote as though he were still a part of life on St. Simons. Janie would never do that. She respected another person's freedom because she had always taken her own. And yet, Janie was merely his happy-go-lucky little sister. Mary was his friend, and he found himself wishing for the first time that he could be a friend to someone. To whom? To Mary? To his father? He leaned back in his chair and looked out the tiny window at the big curve in the Mississippi around which the *Princess* would move in a few hours. Same old scenery again, same old waterfront along the same old river. Romantic to his passengers, routine to him. He had some money saved. He could move on to something else. He crossed the cabin to stand by the window. New

Orleans too was old to him. The Queen had lost her charm. Feeling lonely for the first time in months, he tried to remember Linda Thatcher's face. He could almost remember it, but not quite. She was to him now what she had really been then—an older woman, who meant to be kind to a foolish boy. Perhaps Linda had been his friend, after all. The word had infuriated him then, but Mary's last letter forced him to admit that he would like to be a friend to someone. Even alone in his cabin, he was embarrassed to remember how he had longed to comfort Linda, to take care of her. But wasn't that just to make *him* feel important? Did his desire to look after Linda spring from love for her or for himself?

After a long time, he stretched out on his bunk. "I have—never—been a—real friend—to anyone." He spoke aloud, his voice sounding squeaky as it used to sound when he struggled to say something important to Linda. He cleared his throat. "I admit it. *I have never been a friend to anyone.*"

22 June, 1835

Dear Horace Bunch,

Your old friend, Hugh Fraser Grant, was married and has now taken over Dr. Grant's Elizafield plantation on the mainland. Dr. and Mrs. Grant have moved to Oatlands, their St. Simons summer home, to live the year 'round. Hugh told me at the wedding that he had so wanted you as his best man, but had no hope that you would come. Janie is still with us, but seems fidgety to get back north to her Mr. Richardson. We are sure she will marry him before the year ends. I wish I knew you at least had someone to love you where you are. You never mention your friends. I am tired tonight. Forgive me if this is short and somewhat downcast. I feel downcast. You may never be planning to come home to us again, but I do not give up hoping.

Your affectionate sister,
Mary Gould.

Horace read this a few minutes after the *Princess* had tied up again at the levee in New Orleans. He had begun to look forward to her letters and, for some reason, he had feared there would be none this time. It would have served him right after all the years he'd dreaded finding them. The fact that he had never been a friend to anyone in his family did not change any of them at all. His family went right on loving him as he was—went right on hoping he'd come back. Slowly, he folded the single sheet and slipped it in his waistcoat pocket. He could not tell Mary about his friends, because he had no real friends. No one to love. No one to love him. The laughter and confusion and shouts on the New Orleans levee shut him away with himself until he felt that if he could not escape, he would suffocate. He walked rapidly away from the Canal Street dock, across the Place d'Armes and straight into the Cathedral. It had been four years at least since he had been inside a church. He knelt, in the silence, feeling conspicuous and awkward, glad for the high backed pews and the shadows.

He may have stayed there five minutes, half an hour, an hour. He did not try to pray, and only one thing came clear. He was just as shut away with himself in the silence as he had been in the hubbub of the levee.

22

Mary laid her quill down on the table in the big bay of the dining room where she had been writing to Horace and stared for a long time out into the pale pink light of the coming day before she reread what she had written. During the first two or three years, she had dashed off whatever came to mind, never rereading. She had not seen her brother for six years, and writing to him was growing increasingly difficult. At least Horace had written five or six times this year instead of once or twice. She was determined to believe that was a good sign, even though his letters told little of his work and no hint of the kind of person he had become. She sighed. Maybe he has grown so far away from us, he writes only from duty—saying all there is to say. She found page 1 of her letter and began to reread her swift, angular script:

21 October, 1836

Dear Horace,

I am up before dawn to write to you. Yesterday was a happy day for us all—even Alice, I think. It was little Jamie's fourth birthday. Ever since he has been old enough to understand, I have kept him aware of his Uncle Horace Bunch, have shown him your picture every time he comes to Rosemount, and yesterday, in the midst of his party, he began to cry because you didn't come! We invited all the Island children anywhere near his age—the young Coupers, Demeres, Kings—and of course, the Abbott girl, Deborah, who is seven now and more winsome than ever, with large, black-fringed eyes of the softest, gentlest gray (never without a twinkle!). If I had ever borne a child, I should have hoped she would be like Deborah. Maum Larney baked her famous yellow birthday cake and the party was a success, although I can't recover from the fact that little Jamie missed you, whom he has never seen and may never see.

Janie has been Mrs. Orville Richardson for five months, and seems happier every day. We wish she could live nearby, but to know she is content makes us happy too.

Brunswick is booming still. Papa and the other charter members of the canal project—Thomas Butler King, Col. duBignon and Dr. Hazzard—seem really hopeful. Once the canal is finished, Brunswick—funny little lean-to Brunswick—will, they believe, become a thriving metropolis. Mr. King's beloved railroad is in progress too, although they seem to have endless trouble with the state-owned slaves running away. We have an Aquatic Club now, and plans are already under way for our locally owned boats to challenge boats from as far away as New York. Those Northerners are sure to lose their Sunday shirts betting against our plantation oarsmen, though. Mr. James Hamilton Couper is in the midst of it, hiding his disappointment at having to close down his cotton-seed-oil mills in Natchez and Mobile. Selfishly, I'm sorry he had to, because he did see you once in a while and always rode to Rosemount to tell us how you were looking. Oh, Horace, Horace. And there I stop. Except to say that Alice is talking of going to New Haven for an extended visit. I wonder if that's all it is.

> Your affectionate sister,
> Mary Gould.

She was not happy with her letter, but there was no time today to write another. What difference did it make anyway?

8 May, 1837

Dear Horace,

Big local news and sad Gould news. Brunswick, Georgia, now has its own newspaper, *The Brunswick Advocate*. Papa says he is subscribing for you and maybe it's a good thing, since my letters seem to be petering out in spirit. The sad Gould news is that Alice took Jamie and went back to New Haven last week. Jim tries to convince himself and us that it is only a visit. That she will be back. We all know she won't. Jim should face the truth, but he can't. My grief for their hopeless marriage is great, but not so great, I confess, as my grief over you. Now, I've said it after all these years. My self-control failed me. I do die a little inside, though, when I think of poor Jim alone in that empty house at Black Banks.

Your affectionate sister,
Mary Gould.

10 August, 1837

Dear Horace,

Day after tomorrow, you will be twenty-five. I am too weary to write congratulations, etc. A fearful hurricane struck the Island about ten in the morning on 6 August, and battered us all that day and night and into the next. Both Black Banks and Rosemount were damaged—we are not sure how much. I do know the beautiful shingle roof on the stable was mostly blown off. July, at the risk of his own life, saved Dolly. All crops are flattened— cotton, corn, peas, potatoes, beans—a total loss. The *Brunswick Advocate* prophesies financial disaster for us this year. We are too stunned to believe it yet, but at least no one was killed. Maum Larney barely escaped with her life, though, trying to help July save Dolly. Part of the stable roof struck Maum Larney and knocked her down. We lost seventeen cows, nine sheep and countless chickens, guineas, turkeys, and our beautiful peacock. I still find his broken feathers around. But again, no one was killed. At least we have heard of no deaths among blacks or whites. Now there is much work to be done.

Your affectionate sister,
Mary Gould.

With July in the high front seat, driving the team, Mary rode in the carriage with her brother, Jim, her father and aunt to church on the second Sunday after the hurricane. Alice and little Jamie had not returned, and there was no more need to harness two buggies.

(149)

The sure-footed horses picked their way around fallen tree limbs on Frederica Road, their hooves trailing great clumps of broken branches and moss. The Goulds rode in silence, looking at the destruction around them as they passed their own fields and those of their neighbors to the north.

"Well, we can be thankful no one was killed," James Gould said for the tenth or twentieth time since it happened.

"I'm going to try to be thankful today, James," Caroline promised. "I'm going to *try*."

"I don't feel enough of anything yet to be grateful," Mary sighed.

Jim said nothing.

James Gould took a deep, heavy breath. "We're all ruined so far as I can tell. Look at the Wyllys' west field."

No one said anything more until they reached the church. "Want me to see if there was any mail for Mr. Couper to pick up this week, Papa?" Mary asked.

"If you please, daughter. But I doubt any got through."

Expecting nothing, Mary walked slowly across the wide churchyard, her head down except to say good morning to the few parishioners who had found the courage to come out.

"I see you made it to worship this morning, Miss Mary." John Couper's smile weathered everything. "And 'tis good you did, since I'm too old to ride all the way to Rosemount to deliver this important letter in person!"

Mary stared at him. "Is it—from Horace?"

"Aye, that it is, bonnie Mary Gould."

Holding the letter, blinking back tears, she stood for a moment, then hugged Mr. Couper, turned and ran back to the Gould carriage.

"Well, Mrs. Shedd, are you ready to go inside the church?" Mary Abbott asked. "Mrs. Shedd, I said, are you—"

"Sh! I heard you, Mrs. Abbott. Of course, I'm not

ready. Don't you see what's happening in the Gould carriage? They've gotten a letter from their wandering son, Horace, and the way they're behaving in the face of what's struck us all on this Island, it can only mean one thing—the boy's coming home!"

"What? I hope so, but you can't possibly know that."

"James Gould was wiped out by the storm. That man would not be looking so pleased right now if Horace had not had a change of heart. The Goulds were ruined by the hurricane."

"Well, who wasn't?" Mary Abbott demanded. "We all were, but long faces won't help."

"Don't you see, my dear friend, they are *happy* about the letter they're reading. And when old James Gould can smile, it's got to be news of his prodigal. Of course, I'd be glad for the Goulds too, but it could be very awkward having that boy back here on St. Simons after the kind of life he's been living! Don't you agree?"

"We have absolutely no reason to think anything one way or another about Horace Bunch, Mrs. Shedd, and I don't intend to form any snap judgments. I'm just glad for whatever's happened to make the Goulds smile, bless them. The good Lord knows we all need something to smile about."

"Mary, it's a very unusual letter. Can you read it once more quickly before we have to go into the service?" her father asked.

"You'd better hurry, sister," Jim whispered. "The Widow Shedd is bearing down on us."

Mary's hands shook as she read again in a loud whisper. "Twentieth August, eighteen thirty-seven. Dear Family, I am not going to try to write a lot of nonsense that has no meaning this time. I am in good health and have saved some money and am still doing well in my work, but I am not happy. Even before your letter telling about the hurricane damage, Mary, I had faced the humiliating truth that I have been fooling myself all these years. I guess the real purpose of this letter is to ask you to forgive me—all of you—for my selfishness. That seems to be all I can say right now and remain honest. Please keep writing to me and thank July and Maum Larney for saving Dolly. I hope Maum Larney is all right now. Affectionately, Horace Bunch."

"He even signed it Horace Bunch!" Caroline exclaimed.

"This letter is about *Horace*—every line," Mary was almost shouting. "He isn't writing a lot of nonsense this time. He's sharing himself with us. What did I tell you, Papa? He's getting homesick!" She twirled around for joy. "Horace is getting homesick!"

"Sh! Here she is," Jim warned, as the Widow Shedd came toward them, smiling.

"I just know by your happy faces that you've had news from that handsome son of yours, Mr. Gould, and I'm also sure that the dear boy is coming home! I'm so glad for you, I could cry."

Everyone waited for James to answer her. He scrambled down from the carriage without assistance for the first time in months, straightened his thin shoulders and looked her in the eye. "No, Mrs. Shedd, he didn't say one word about coming home. Sorry to spoil your prophecy, but it's fake—as usual. Come along, children, Caroline—time for church."

23

Standing alone on the starboard side of the Savannah-bound schooner, away from the crowds saying their good-bys, Horace reached in his pocket for Mary's last letter. He unfolded it carefully in the brisk October wind, his hands trembling. He was apprehensive, but he was alive again. Until he had received this letter—limp now, and wearing at its creases—he had almost stopped reacting to anything. For a few days after he had written asking their forgiveness, he had experienced sharp, nearly painful relief. Then, in its place, like a sickness, the apathy had crept in, the dullness, the not caring. The days moved by, impersonal as the river, four ... six ... nine ... twelve ... twenty. And at every port he wished he had given Mary other addresses along the *Princess*'s run.

When at last they had docked again in New Orleans, the letter he had counted on was there—the one he held now. He knew each line.

You have filled our hearts with more joy than you can imagine, beloved Horace Bunch. Of course, we forgive you, but mostly we thank you for giving us yourself again. I have decided not to write a long letter this time—just this much: I'm the happiest person alive because I know you're homesick! For the very first time in seven years, I'm sure you miss us—miss riding Dolly, miss fishing with July. When you mention July and Maum Larney, it sounds like you. Find yourself soon, my beloved brother. The real you is so worth knowing and respecting. When you do find yourself as you really are, you're going to like you just fine. The way I like you.

Mary's letter had freed him to try, at least, to find his way back to what he meant to be so long ago—his own man, but a man he himself could respect. He was going home to start over. No matter how it all turned out, for the first time since Yale, he felt he was doing a right thing, taking a right step.

He crumpled the letter into a tight ball and tossed it into the darkening water. Watching the tiny wad of paper bob in the muddy river until it was out of sight, he took a deep breath of clean, moist air and chuckled to himself because the first boat on which he had been able to book passage to Georgia was the schooner *Mary*.

24

The *Sarah* was a new boat on the familiar run from Darien to St. Simons Island. New to Horace, at least—a trim, squat, all-white steam packet—better cared for than either the *South Carolina* or the *Magnolia*. All through the sunset, he had stood on the small passenger deck, watching the big red ball dim from brilliant gold to orange to rose, as it plummeted toward the marshes, streaking a sky full of thin, strip clouds with pink, edging them with pale green light. The air was brown-gold, warm, soft, welcoming. Home.

He was nervous. To deny it would be dishonest, and he was determined to stay honest with himself; as honest as possible with everyone else. In less than an hour, in weather like this, Captain Stevens would move his proud little packet into the dock at Frederica. As they entered the Altamaha, he remembered all the tall cypress ghosts looming in the darkness of that rainy, rebellious night years ago. He should be more ashamed to go home this trip, but he wasn't. For the first time in his adult life, he was convinced he had chosen to do a right thing. Whatever lay ahead, he would keep remembering that.

Horace was Captain Charles Stevens's only passenger, and it seemed a good idea to climb up to the pilothouse to get acquainted with this hearty-voiced, ruddy Dane who had come to live on St. Simons during his absence. A new friend could be helpful, surrounded as he would be by so many old friends who no longer knew him at all.

At the top of the ladder that led to the pilothouse, he stopped a moment to size up the Captain, who sat singing to himself, his heavy, wide shoulders hunched comfortably over the wooden wheel under full control of his muscular hands. He must be my age, Horace thought, and smiled at the difference in their looks. Captain Stevens was a giant of a man, thick of body and limb. Horace had liked him from their first meeting at the dock in Darien. One would always know where one stood with Captain Stevens.

"She's a tight little craft, Captain," he called over the huffing engine.

The big man turned, smiling broadly. "Come up and take her wheel, Gould. Do not settle for her beauty." He spoke with a thick Danish accent, his laughter always ready to surface.

Horace took the smooth, varnished wheel and settled into the Captain's seat. "You'll have to guide me, Captain. I'm used to the river, but I'm certainly no pilot."

Stooped under the low ceiling, Charles Stevens stood behind him and, for a mile or so, gave Horace expert directions. He knew the waters around St. Simons as though he had grown up there instead of in faraway Denmark. Horace wondered, as he turned the *Sarah's* wheel at Charles Stevens' bidding, if this confident man had ever needed reassurance about anything. Had he ever been afraid of anything or anyone?

They were entering Buttermilk Sound, and Captain Charles took back the wheel. "Better let me have her now, Gould. You enjoy the scenery. You will be home again at last in no time."

Horace frowned. "How did you know I was going home?"

"Do you forget I live on your Island over a year? That is long enough to know all about you, my friend. Everybody on St. Simons knows about you."

A knot tightened in Horace's stomach. "I hope they'll give me a chance to start over."

Captain Stevens maneuvered his packet into the Sound and leaned back in his chair to look at Horace. "To begin again is never easy, Gould. Do not expect it to be. St. Simons is a very little world."

"How do you make out, Captain, with all that plain talk of yours among the sweet-talking Southerners?"

Charles grinned. "I wonder when I first came here—do they mean all those beautiful words? Do they just say words to make music? Ha. Do I insult you, Gould?"

"Not me," Horace laughed. "I've been exposed to Northerners, Southerners, Westerners, Creoles, Europeans, city slickers, country bumpkins—I may have to learn to understand my own family all over again. Coastal Georgians have a language all their own."

"You speak like St. Simons people, but without the—how do I say it? Molasses?"

"Thanks. That still pleases me a little, I guess. Isn't it a wonderful part of the world, Stevens?"

"You like it best?"

"Best of any place I've seen."

"You're happy to be home, Gould?"

Horace hesitated. "I wish I didn't have to see anyone else but my family for a few weeks. But, yes. I'm happy to be almost there."

"I'm happy to be almost there, too. I am in love!"

"Well, congratulations! Who's the young lady?"

"Miss Sarah Dorothy Hay. See?" He pointed a thick finger at the name *Sarah* lettered across the inside as well as the outside of his pilot house. "I name my first self-owned boat for her. Ah-h, she is the belle of the Island. She is the most beautiful woman God ever created."

"Sarah Dorothy Hay? I remember her when she first came here from England as a little girl with her aunt and uncle—the Frewins."

"Well, she is no little girl any longer, believe what I say. She is nineteen and all lovely woman. So, keep a distance, Gould!" He flexed his thick biceps. "I warn you. Keep a distance."

Horace laughed. "On my word of honor. Marriage is the last thing on my mind."

"It was the last thing on my mind too, but Sarah Dorothy Hay turned me around."

They were in sight of St. Simons now, and Horace

(156)

said. "I suppose the good ladies of the Island gossip about the prodigal Gould boy who left his father's house for the wicked life on the river."

"What do you think they do?"

"Gossip."

"They are living ladies. Can they help it?"

"No."

"Be your own man, Gould, and let them talk. They will forget in time once you are back. They will forget for talking about someone new." He chuckled. "Me maybe."

"Have you been made welcome, Captain Stevens?"

"Oh, yes and oh, no. All at once. But I am my own man and I will one day have the most successful shipping business from Charleston to the Florida Territory. When I get my fine schooner, the *Splendid*, they will begin to say 'Ah, this Captain Charles Stevens is a big man!' "

"Got your eye on a new boat?"

"Two hundred dollars paid on her. In four years or less, she will be mine. She will be mine and so will Miss Sarah Dorothy Hay."

"I envy you."

"Why? You can do it too!"

"Do what?"

"Be a big man. Have what you want—what will make you your own man."

"I wonder. But I'm dead sure I'm going to try."

Charles Stevens held out his hand, smiling broadly. "We will be our own men together, Gould."

Horace shook the big, rough hand. "Right. I'm twenty-five. How old are you, Captain?"

"Twenty-six. One year ahead, but one only."

"You're more than one year ahead. But I'll catch up. I don't know how, but I will."

The sky had darkened. The pine-knot flares were being lighted on the Frederica dock, and suddenly, Horace felt he couldn't wait.

PART THREE

25

"Son, you've been back with us ten days. Ten happy days for me. I wonder if we've let you know how glad we are."

Horace looked across the dinner table and tried to smile at his father. Tears came instead. The old man's joy was more difficult to handle than the sight of his constant pain.

"I feel right at home, Papa," he said hoarsely. "You've all been just fine about it. I'm the one who should be wondering."

"Nonsense," Mary said. "No one needs to wonder about anything. I'm too happy even to worry about the money crisis." She patted her brother's hand. "You're home—and if you came back, so will prosperity! Want some more of Maum Larney's huckleberry jam?"

"Are there any more hot biscuits?"

"Yes, sir, Mausa Horace—jis' one minute!"

Horace and Mary laughed.

"She's eavesdropping at the dining-room door again," James complained. "She should stop that."

"Maum Larney only does it for love's sake, Papa," Mary scolded. "That dear woman is so happy Horace's home, she can't bear to miss a single word he says."

Larney hurried back into the room and straight to Horace, lifting the napkin from a plate piled high with steaming biscuits.

"Larney's boy wants more biscuits, an' dey ain' nobody gon' stop 'im—an' ah's got another pan ready to put on de fire."

Horace took two, dug his knife into the butter Larney held for him, and grinned up at her, but could think of nothing to say. Tears stung his eyes again and Larney rescued him. "Ah declare, Mausa Horace, you done got thin enough to see thru t' de other side. Here, lemme spoon out some more hucklesberry jam."

"Hey, Maum Larney, hold up!" he laughed. "I'm just right. If I keep on eating your cooking, I'll have to buy new clothes. Can't do that—we're all poverty-stricken, haven't you heard?"

He watched the old familiar gesture of courage—Larney rising solemnly to her full height. "Larney's heerd, all right, Mausa Horace. But we has riz up befo'!"

Horace stopped smiling. "Of course, Maum Larney. We will again."

"It won't be that easy, son," his father said. "And I think it's time you got the full picture. I want you to drive me to the Kings' tomorrow for a meeting of all the Island planters with Mr. King before he leaves for Augusta."

"What's happening in Augusta, Papa?" Mary asked.

"A commercial convention of planters from all over our state to try to come to some solution before it's too late. I'm glad we have King to speak for us here. These are serious times. I'm sorry you've come home to things the way they are, Horace, but that doesn't alter the facts. Will you go with me, son?"

Horace knew Larney was watching him. He looked at Mary for a clue to what his answer should be. She was watching him too, with much the same expression. Both women seemed to be expecting something of him, but what? Oh, he knew about the high tariffs, the squeeze of the industrial revolution on the Cotton States, but he wasn't ready yet to become involved. As he looked at his father, he felt his first real resistance since his return home. Thomas Butler King was a strong States' rights man. And States' rights to a Southerner meant only Cotton States' rights. Horace had ridden over all the fields at New St. Clair and Black Banks, had seen the flattened crops. He knew specie payment had been stopped and that cotton prices were skidding downward every day. These were facts of which he was totally aware, but it was too soon to expect him to become involved in a meeting of the type he knew would take place at King's Retreat tomorrow. He had been away too long. He needed to get the feel of being home first. He had not even ventured to church on the one Sunday he had been back. If he went to the meeting, he would be seeing Senator King and the Demere and Hazzard men and Ben Cater and John Wylly and John Couper for the first time since he left for boarding school at fourteen.

"I thought it would be neighborly if we took old John Couper in the buggy with us," his father was saying. "He's been a real friend."

Horace knew that every minute he remained silent made any answer more difficult—except a simple yes or no.

"You really mean to stay and help us, don't you, Horace?" his father pressed him.

He didn't look at Larney, but he was sure she was clasping and unclasping her hands, waiting, as was Mary.

"Son?"

"Yes, sir. I mean to stay."

"Then you'll take me tomorrow?"

Even at the risk of hurting his father, he was going to be honest. "May I ask a question, sir?"

"Go right ahead."

"Do I have to take part in this meeting?"

He saw his father's frown. "That's up to you."

"Then I'll go with you to the Kings'."

He heard, rather than saw Larney clap her hands twice softly, in relief. "Here, Mausa Horace, lemme butter another biscuit fo' you."

"No, thanks, Maum Larney." He stood up. "I'm not hungry any more. May I be excused, Papa?"

"Certainly, son," his father said, turning to watch him stride out of the dining room.

Suddenly, he had to know what they would say about him once he had left the room. He stopped on the stairs out of their sight to listen.

(163)

"Papa! Did you have to pin him down like that?" Mary demanded.

"Yes, daughter, I did. Jim's going back North and Horace is all I have now."

"Jim's going back North?"

"Yes. He's taking a boat to Savannah tomorrow morning. Jamie's birthday's coming up in two weeks and Jim says even Alice can't keep him away from his son on his birthday."

"Oh, Papa, no! We need Jim now."

James Gould sighed. "Well, Horace is here, and I believe the boy will come through this time, Mary. He has to. He's all we've got to count on."

26

Horace looked around the large, comfortable living room of the King's eighteenth-century English cottage, which still served as the main house at Retreat. He remembered they had planned for years to build a larger house, but he doubted that the new home would ever materialize. Even without the money problems, Mr. King was so deeply embroiled in politics and away so much of the time, it was certainly all Anna Matilda King could do to run a large plantation alone. He rather hoped the Kings would always live in the hand-hewn, sprawling cottage. For as long as he could remember, parties at Retreat had been happy events, and the look of the gabled roof and shuttered veranda had been part of his childhood memories.

Seated around the room were nine plantation owners besides King—he remembered them all. The brilliant, rather eccentric Hazzard brothers; handsome, congenial young John Wylly of The Village; Joseph Demere of

Harrington Hall; soft-spoken Ben Cater of Kelvin Grove, dependable Dr. Grant from Oatlands; his father's dear friend John Couper from Cannon's Point, and British Captain John Fraser from Hamilton—all familiar faces, growing older now—and all seeming, at least, to accept him as one of them; forcing him by their very acceptance into a sense of strangeness. After all, they had been living on St. Simons all the years he had been away. Their interests, while cultivated and varied for so provincial a life, had remained centered on the land they loved and depended on for their positions and sustenance. He knew that somehow he would have to come back to where they were. He was coming back as fast as he could, but he was not going to pretend an involvement he did not yet feel. He was never going to become circumspect and preoccupied with only the problems of the Cotton States. He was going to remain an American who loved and believed in the Union of all the states, North and South.

Thomas Butler King, in his late thirties, Horace supposed, unremarkable in size, but dynamic, arresting, was standing to one side of the open fire demonstrating his oratorical genius. Point by point, he reiterated to the men, who already knew it well, the sad plight of the South in its battle with the Federal Government in Washington. For the Cotton States' despised dependence upon the North, he blamed the protectionist tariff, the discriminatory financial policy of Washington, and—most of all—the lack of enterprise among Southern planters and merchants. This, it seemed, was the purpose of the Augusta commercial convention where King would represent them, serving on the resolutions committee, entering into debates, and working on pamphlets to make known the new movement that was to free the South from its domination by the North.

"This all sounds fine," James Gould said during a short lull, "but what *specifically* will the resolutions committee propose to do?"

"Yes." John Wylly looked relieved that Mr. Gould had

spoken out. "Words are cheap. We Southerners are known for our garrulity, King, but exactly what are we going to *do*?"

There was a low murmur of agreement. Only the Hazzards sat expressionless, their long legs crossed exactly alike.

"I'll tell you one thing we must do," Thomas Butler King declared. "We must, in order to avoid total dependence upon the North, establish direct trade with Europe!"

Another murmur rose, this time of surprise.

"Direct trade between the South and Europe?" Joseph Demere asked.

"Yes, Demere," King said. "In that way, profits from Southern staples would no longer flow out of our beloved area—they would flow in; and credit and imported goods would be available through our local commercial organizations."

"It seems to me that would take a long time to accomplish." James Gould spoke quietly. Horace was proud of his father's directness, his grasp of reality. There *was* no time for long, wordy negotiations.

"It will take time, Mr. Gould, but this is why we must make our purposes known, must stir up the very blood in the veins and arteries of our fellow planters and merchants—must stir them up to see that we have to *act* to protect ourselves from oblivion at the hands of the Federal tyrants in Washington!"

"It seems to me, Congressman, you're campaigning pretty hard to get elected to work in a city you hate so much," Ben Cater said, grinning.

"I don't hate the seat of our Federal Government, Ben. I was born in the North, don't forget, but I have grown weary of its domination. I am a Southerner by adoption and choice, and I cannot represent my Cotton States constituency in the Congress of the United States, if I am elected, by going along passively with their demise. What I have been trying to say to you gentlemen is not against the Federal Government, it is in *behalf* of our beloved Southland!"

Horace had not been concentrating on every word; there had been too many of them, but he heard that, and with all his heart he hoped it was true.

"If we can accomplish direct trade with Europe," King declared, "we can at least break away economically from the North."

The phrase "break away" brought Horace's attention to full focus.

"We must become economically independent of those people up there. Only *we* know how to handle our own affairs. The industrial revolution in the North presents totally different problems from our agrarian way of life down here. We are a large country—so large that we no longer resemble each other, North and South, in any way but our loyalty to a united form of people's government."

"Excuse me once more, Mr. King," John Wylly interrupted, "but this sounds to me as though you're recommending a kind of Southern nationalism."

Dr. Thomas Hazzard jumped to his feet, glowering at Wylly. "I consider that remark out of order and disloyal!"

"Disloyal to what?" John demanded.

"To our host, first, since the proposal is his—and to the South! Our situation in the Cotton States is unsupportable. It cannot go on—and I for one do not intend to sit by and listen to the young and fiery among us as they deprecate all we hold dear."

John Wylly laughed. Horace wanted to, but kept his face straight. The men were all talking among themselves now, so that he could catch only occasional phrases: "Wylly didn't say that much!" "We need to have open discussion." "A man's entitled to say what he thinks, including you, Doc Hazzard."

King clapped his hands for order. "We are all free to speak our minds peaceably, I would hope. This is a free country and our Constitution guarantees freedom of speech—but it also guarantees the rights of individual states! It is not against our national government that we must declare ourselves—it is for the rights of the Cotton

(167)

States, guaranteed by the Constitution. We oppose only the *tyranny* of our present Federal administration, plainly in cahoots with the industrial North against us."

Driving home that afternoon with his father and John Couper, Horace waited for what he knew his father would say.

"Well, son, you kept pretty quiet through the whole thing."

"Yes, sir."

"So did I, James," John Couper said. "But I'd like to know how we looked to you, Horace, after all those years away."

"Yes," his father agreed, "what did you make of us?"

Horace grinned, wondering how to answer. "You seemed like Southerners with your dander up—in varying degrees."

John Couper chuckled. "I thought young Wylly and Doc Hazzard might take a poke at each other there once, didn't you?"

James sighed. "It's their properly-line trouble that caused Hazzard to spout off like that. John Wylly couldn't open his mouth without saying the wrong thing as far as both Hazzards are concerned. I sometimes think they hate the boy."

"Aye, and John Wylly bursts into flame pretty fast around them too," John Couper said.

"I thought they'd have that all settled by now," Horace remarked.

"Nope, still at it." His father shook his head. "Harder than ever, if anything. I'm afraid it's a personal hatred between the two families now."

"Aye, it is, James, and I don't like it. I don't like it at all. Hatred like that, festering for years among neighbors, can poison the lot of us."

"What did you think of King's idea to establish trade directly with Europe, Jock?"

Mr. Couper took a deep breath and exhaled slowly before he answered. "I'm not sure. On the surface it sounds as though it might accomplish what King claims.

He's a brilliant man. But I also saw young Wylly's point. It did sound a bit like nationalism—Southern nationalism. I'm against that."

"So am I," James Gould said warmly.

Horace was relieved. The whole concept of this independent action by the South disturbed him, although economically, it sounded good—for the South.

"Well," James Gould philosophized, "they talk a lot, Southerners."

"Aye, James, that they do. I wonder if they'll ever act. I suppose I should correct myself and say, 'I wonder if *we'll* ever act.' "

"Did you come away with a half-finished feeling, Jock?"

"Aye, James, I came away with a half-finished feeling."

So did Horace. But, against his will, he had become involved. At least enough to hope for a better way to handle the problem.

27

On New Year's Day, 1838, Rosemount saw a steady stream of visitors, calling to wish the Goulds a Happy New Year—and to have a look at Horace at home in his father's house again.

"Don't mind them, brother," Mary kept saying between visitors. "They'll be accustomed to you again soon and you'll be just a part of the landscape like the rest of us."

Horace smiled and tried, for Mary's sake, to be indifferent. "It's all right. Let them peer and let them see I still have two legs, two arms, two ears, two blue eyes and one proud Gould nose."

They laughed and touched the tips of their noses with

their forefingers in the old childhood gesture of defiance when anything Gould had been threatened. But Horace did mind. The careful sidewise glances of the young ladies, the not-so-guarded scrutiny of their mothers and grandmothers and aunts, made him wonder what they might be expecting him to do. "I'm sure I disappoint them. They all appear more interested in me when they arrive than when they leave."

"I try to know how you must feel," Mary said when they had seen the Demeres and the Grants to their carriages. "But don't let it change the way you are toward them. Please try to see their point of view, too."

Mary's dark eyes pleaded with him and he realized he was at least beginning to understand her predicament as his sister—utterly loyal, uncomfortable for him and for their neighbors.

"Mrs. Abbott didn't even come, did she?" he asked dryly.

"Oh, but not for any reason that has anything to do with you, Horace. If there was one woman on this Island who remained loyal and fair to you through all those years, it was Mary Abbott. Don't let me hear one peep out of you about her."

He laughed. "All right, ma'am. She's just the only one who hasn't shown up yet today and I was merely remarking."

"You'd better be 'just remarking' because she's been wonderful about you. Never critical, never trying to make us believe a lot of sentimental talk about your coming home any day—just right. She's one of the few people I know who can see things as they are, with no twists, no wild imaginings—never, never condemning."

"You make her sound like a plaster saint."

"Well, she isn't. You just wait till you get to know her again."

"I'll do that," he grinned. "How about a gallop through the woods?"

At the stable, while July saddled Mary's horse, she stood watching Horace saddle Dolly, her eyes drinking in the sight of her brother stroking and patting his beloved mare again.

"Oh, Horace, will I ever get used to it?"

"To my awkwardness with Doll's saddle? I'll get the hang again. She doesn't seem to mind."

"No, silly. Not Dolly's saddle—you." She hugged his shoulders impulsively as he bent over to test the girth straps. "Horace, Horace, you're home to stay!"

He stood up. "Yes, sister, for better or worse. I'm home."

"Here we is, Miss Mary," July said cheerily, leading Peter from the stable, his chestnut coat gleaming. "It sho' be good t' see you two saddlin' up agin t' ride out together."

"Oh, July, isn't it good? Isn't it just the best thing there is?" Mary stretched her arms over her head and pirouetted so fast her riding skirt swirled about her in wide loops.

"You two make me feel like a returning hero instead of a prodigal, and I think it's time you stopped. I might get so relaxed I'll turn into what they're all hoping for."

Mary stamped her foot. "Horace Bunch Gould, that is the last time you are to make such a remark, do you hear?"

"Yes, ma'am," he laughed, "I hear. How did you stand her all this time without me, July?"

"She be right, Mausa Horace," July answered solemnly. "Miss Mary right. You pay 'tention only to us's. Me an' her knows what's right 'bout you."

"There," Mary gloated. "Does that settle it?"

A short, startled shriek from the direction of Frederica Road stabbed the quiet of the drowsy afternoon. The three stared at one another, too stunned to speak. Another shriek, louder, full of animal fear—a second, a third—staccato, primitive—and then a sustained descending wail, submissive, almost relieved, faded at last into silence.

"What was it?" Mary cried.

Without a word, Horace swung up on his horse and galloped toward the road. Quickly, July cupped his hands for Mary to mount, and she rode after her brother down the Rosemount lane and out into Frederica Road, where Horace had reined in Dolly to get his sense of direction.

"Down that way," Mary called. "I know it came from down by the spring!"

"Go back to the house, sister!"

"No!"

Peter lunged off at a gallop, with Dolly right behind, their hooves scattering shells and raising clouds of dust for the few hundred yards to the drinking-water spring, and neither horse had to be stopped. Both reared on their hind legs, whinnying and balking at the sight and scent of the mangled little black body, sprawled like a rag doll, face down in the road, its arms twisted under out of sight, one thin leg bent back, and blood flowing like syrup from five knife gashes that exposed muscle and white backbone.

"Dear God, it's little Tuesday! Horace, she's been murdered!"

He stared at the broken form, wondering irrelevantly at the volume of those screams from so small a girl. "Who did it, Mary? Who would do a thing like this?" Horace ran to the edge of the thick woods. A clump of brown sedge and a few seedling gums had been freshly broken. "Whoever did it must have run into the woods toward Abbotts'," he breathed, suddenly unwilling to speak aloud.

Someone called Mary's name and they turned to see Mrs. Abbott and little Deborah half running up the road toward them. They hurried to their neighbors and Horace steadied the older woman, who seemed about to faint. Mary put both arms around Deborah and turned her away from the bloody scene behind them.

"He's—he's in our woods!" Mary Abbott whispered. "We heard the—screams—and we—saw the—nigra—run off into—our woods!"

"Put the child on Dolly with you, brother," Mary said, "and take her to our house. I'll bring Mrs. Abbott with me. You'll have to get a gun and some of the men to go with you."

Horace helped Mrs. Abbott up onto the horse with Mary, lifted the frightened child onto Dolly, leaped on himself, and with one arm securely around Deborah, rode back to the stable as fast as he safely could.

In less than an hour, Horace and July and his father, Larney's John, had fanned out along the edge of Dunbar Creek on the Abbott land. Each man was armed— Horace with James Gould's pistol, July and John with flintlocks. It was against Georgia law for a Negro to carry firearms, but July and John were trustworthy, and he needed their knowledge of the woods and marsh. It was no time to argue a law.

They had decided to begin their search in the tall rushes along the salt creek and in the dry marsh itself— a man could hide there, lying flat on his stomach. For the first few minutes after they separated, Horace could hear July's footsteps crackling in the dry brush to the south and John's to the north. Then they were too far away, and the realization that he could meet the murderer alone hit him like a blow. His heart pounded as he reached the north bank of Dunbar Creek and crouched down in the high grass to listen. He had never noticed how many sudden noises there were in the marsh. Each kind of grass rustled or rattled a different way, as the wind rising from the tide change swept here and poked there through the dry, stiff stalks. The sudden cackle of a marsh hen caused his whole body to tingle. A flock of redwings rose from somewhere in the marsh not a hundred feet from him and began to jingle and whistle in flight like a hundred broken bells and pipes. They flew south and settled in the marsh again, and he was relieved. One could hear nothing over the racket that blackbirds made. Fiddler crabs scuttered around his boots as he plodded along the water's edge, keeping his eyes trained on the tall grass on the other bank of the narrow creek. The man might creep up behind him in the dry marsh, but he could watch in only one direction at a time. He was glad the tide was rising. If the Negro was hiding somewhere in or near the wet marsh, the tide would flush him out. Horace waited, his pistol cocked, feeling the thud of his own pulse in his throat. He saw nothing and decided to creep steadily, slowly down the creek bank until he was satisfied the killer was not hiding in the grass on the opposite side. He could retrace his steps later and search the marsh behind him. The thought that the man might at that very minute be watching him from the rear chilled his blood. But he made himself go on.

He had seen men die in duels and by their own hand in New Orleans, but this was different. This had to be a madman. That he had committed his atrocity on St. Simons somehow added to Horace's fear. It was horrible to be so full of fear—at home, on the Island, where everyone felt safe.

In the tall grass to his right, his eye caught motion; then he heard the rushes rattle. He began breathing through his mouth in order to take in more oxygen. Slowly, the marsh grass was pressed first to one side and then the other. Not large enough for a man, he told himself, but he dared not fire. It moved too slowly, too steadily for a wild boar; it was too big for a coon or a possum. It has to be a big snake, he decided, and stepped back cautiously until he was sure. It was a snake, an eight-foot water moccasin crawling slowly toward a sunny spot in the mud. Horace could do nothing but silently circle the moccasin and hope it would be content to sun itself a while in the fading afternoon light. He returned to the creek bank fifty feet or so farther on, just in time to see another, bulkier form shoving through the tall grass toward him. Not away from him—toward him. He knew an alligator would not move that clumsily. And then he saw the black, woolly head, the ragged shirt, the lean brown arms. It was the Negro, pushing his way along on his stomach. Horace's hand shook as he aimed the heavy pistol and waited, taking the chance that the man was armed with only his knife. Cold streams of sweat trickled down Horace's face. There had been no sound from the shapeless form wriggling toward him through the dense grass. Horace moved a step or two nearer and a whimpering, gurgling noise came from the man's throat as he raised his head so that Horace could see his contorted face. He was crying.

"I see you," Horace called. "Get up on your feet!"

"Mausa!" the man sobbed. "Don' kill me, Mausa!"

When Horace said nothing, the creature rolled over on his back, clawing at the sky with his mud-caked hands, crying out in a thick Geechee dialect most of which Horace could not understand.

"I'm not going to shoot you if you'll stand up and talk to me like a man," Horace shouted. "Do you live on St. Simons? Who owns you?"

Almost feebly, the black man rolled over and struggled to his feet. He looked past middle age, although one could never tell with a Negro—slight of build, exhausted, perhaps ill, his thick, purple lips sagging with fear.

"Where do you live?" Horace demanded.

The voice was little more than a wheeze: "Ah lib—Butler. Ah be Butler man."

"When did you run away?"

"Fibe day 'go. Be you sh-shoot—me, Mausa?"

"I told you I wouldn't, if you'd talk. We know you killed one of our girls. Why did you do it?" Horace tried to fight down a surge of pity. "Why did you kill her?" he shouted.

The murderer fell to his knees and held out his clasped black hands toward Horace. "Debil git me, Mausa. Big green debil git me. Mercy, Mausa! Mercy! Hab mercy!"

"Stand up," Horace commanded, unable to bear the sight of another human being on his knees begging him for mercy.

"John, July!" He shouted as loud as he could. "John! July!"

They were black too. They could tell him what to do.

28

Waiting impatiently for Mary in the sitting room, Horace tossed a small, twisted oak branch on the fire, then another, for something to do. The house was closed against the chill, damp night, but he could hear the mournful voices singing down at the quarters. He envied them. Negroes knew how to vent their grief. Their rhythm was full of sorrow, but they sang loudly, easing the pain in their hearts. He stood at the window for a long time, then slumped in his father's leather chair and tried not to think until his sister got back from the quarters. This strange New Year's Day had stirred old conflicts, and new ones were beginning to form—too soon. All of it too soon. What the runaway from Hampton plantation at Butler's Point had done was enough to turn a man inside out, but the wretch's own condition sickened Horace as much as his deed.

He walked to the front door to look for Mary and saw her lantern bobbing up the tabby walk between her new orange trees.

"Is Papa in bed?" she asked, blowing out the light, stamping sand from her shoes on the veranda.

"Yes, about an hour ago. Did you have to pull all the children's teeth that need pulling tonight? I thought you'd never get back." He closed the door and hung her cloak on the hall tree.

Mary shivered. "It's chilly outside."

"I've got a good fire. Come on in and sit with me. I don't want to ride to Black Banks yet. I want to talk."

"I only pulled four loose teeth," Mary said, sinking thankfully into her chair. "Did Papa seem all right?"

"Calmer than I am," Horace sat on the edge of his father's chair. "How's Tuesday's mother taking it?"

"Just the way you know Matty would. Like a stoic. That's why I was gone so long. Maum Larney and I were trying to make it easy for her to cry. Matty's like me—tears don't come easily. She just sat there in her cabin, staring at the fire. I could almost see sobs welling up inside her. Then she would hold her breath, gasp and choke, as though she were drowning in tears. But she couldn't cry. Most darkies cry freely."

"Maybe Matty can't believe it happened."

Mary kicked off her slippers. "She believes it, all right. They accept death as part of life. They're better about it than we are. Horace, he might have killed you too."

"Not in the shape the poor fellow was in by the time I found him." He rubbed both eyes. "I'll never forget the look of Tuesday's little bleeding back—but neither will I forget the look on his face when he came crawling like an animal toward me." He jumped up. "Oh, Mary, what a system!"

"System?"

"Slavery! I hate it!" He walked to the window and stood looking out, his back to her.

"Horace?"

"Hm?"

"You read about the Nat Turner massacre in Virginia, I suppose—back in eighteen thirty-one." Her voice was tentative, unlike Mary.

Returning to the fire, he slumped in the chair. "Yes, of course I did. It worried me half sick for weeks thinking of you all here on this isolated Island—a hundred or so whites and two thousand blacks. Then I convinced myself that St. Simons planters are too good to their people for something like that to happen here."

"Do you really believe it couldn't happen to us?"

"No. It could happen anywhere. Our Negroes are docile, obedient—especially the ones born into slavery—never knowing any other life. Oh, some of them lie by the yard, steal—but so do children. That's what most

(177)

black people are, you know—children. We've kept them that way. It's wrong."

"But, Horace, even Maum Larney would be lost without us! She bosses us now, but if Maum Larney suddenly had to go away and live without us, she'd be as lost as a little puppy dog."

"That's just what I mean, Mary. We've kept them so dependent, who knows what they're really like inside? How do you know what Maum Larney actually thinks of you? Of Papa? Of me?"

"Horace Bunch Gould, you need to have your mouth washed out with lye soap for saying a thing like that! Maum Larney loves us."

"Of course, she loves us. I'm not doubting that. But what does she *think* of us inside that wise old head of hers? Aside from the fact that we own her body, what grounds do we have to expect perpetual submission and loyalty from her? From any of our people? That poor black, demented devil is probably lying on the bare ground in the prison hut at Hampton right now with his back cut to ribbons by Mr. Butler's new overseer. The man committed a murder; he should be tried and convicted by a judge and jury—as I would be if I had murdered someone. Who is that overseer to judge him and mete out his punishment?"

"Horace, do you think because Pierce Butler is an absentee owner, the Butler people are—*whipped*?"

"I don't know, Mary. I've been gone eleven years except for those few days after Yale—how would I know what goes on here? Don't you know?"

"Papa says no one mistreats his people on St. Simons. Hardly anyone ever sells a slave, except from one of our own plantations to another. I think our people are all— well, contented. Maum Larney thinks so, too. She told me."

"I wonder." He sighed and stretched his legs toward the fire.

"What do you mean, you wonder?"

"Nothing. When are they going to bury Tuesday?"

"Next Tuesday."

"But that's a week away!"

"The child was born on Tuesday and Matty wants to bury her on Tuesday. What can we do?"

"Nothing, of course. I suppose Maum Larney cleaned her up and laid her out."

"Yes. I helped. She looks real pretty."

"Her troubles are over."

"Horace, have you changed?" Mary asked anxiously.

"I don't know. Yes, I do. I haven't changed. I'm just finding out bit by bit what's been inside me all along, I think."

"Are you worried about the money crisis we're supposed to be in?"

"We're in it, sister, make no mistake about that. And I'm more worried than I meant to be. Six months from now Thomas Butler King and the others are holding another commercial conclave, and no more will come from that than came from the first. Something has to be done. Cotton planters are at the mercy of New York shipping merchants far more than they're at the mercy of the Federal Government. But most of these planters, sincere as they are, more knowledgeable by far than I'll ever be, can't seem to keep the real issues out of the political arena. Result? Just more talk and increased bitterness. Well, I can't help—I'm not a planter. I'm just a substitute for Jim until he gets back. After that?" He stood up. "Who knows what I'll be doing?"

"You're not going to leave again, are you?"

"No. I'm here to stay. And if I'm born to be merely a helper, maybe I can learn to be a good one." He kissed her forehead. "Do you know it's nine o'clock? I've got to ride to Black Banks."

"Do you hate living there alone?"

"Hate it? I'd hate to tell you how much I'm coming to like it. I'm rascal enough to hope brother stays at the North a long, long time. While the cat's away, this little mouse is playing in that wonderful house, and he couldn't be happier." He sobered abruptly. "Hadn't you guessed how much I love it down there, honest? Hadn't you?"

"Of course I'd guessed! Oh, Horace, it's always been all wrong for Jim and Alice to own Black Banks."

"Good night, sister. For 'tomorrow and tomorrow and tomorrow,' at least—it's mine."

Horace had lived in the Black Banks house four months when his first visitors came to call. He had been in the fields all day on horseback and had just cleaned up for an early dinner when a buggy clattered up to the front entrance. His heart sank when he saw two women and a child being helped ceremoniously to the ground by Adam, seventeen now, and calling himself proudly the "Black Banks butler." There had been no need to assign special duties to Adam. The boy seemed so glad to have Horace living there, he had taken over the polishing of the Black Banks silver and mirrors, the grooming of the horses and the leaf raking; he served Horace's meals, and now, in his new white jacket, he was receiving guests. Adam seems pleased they've come, even if I'm not, Horace thought, as he grabbed his own coat and hurried through the parlor.

The Widow Shedd and Mrs. Abbott and little Deborah were climbing the wide front steps when he greeted them—courteously, he hoped.

"Good afternoon, Mr. Gould," they chorused, and Adam, standing behind the callers, saluted Horace proudly, as though he had arranged the whole thing.

"We trust we're not intruding," the Widow Shedd caroled. "We just thought it was high time your neighbors paid you a friendly visit."

"That's very kind of you."

"It seemed a good hour to call," Mary Abbott said, smiling so warmly that some of Horace's irritation melted. "We hoped you'd be in from the fields and not too busy for three neighbors to visit with you a little while. Say good afternoon to Mr. Gould, Deborah, dear."

The child curtsied and Horace bowed. "You do me a great honor, Miss Deborah. Will you come inside, ladies, or does this March afternoon sunshine tempt you? We can sit right here on the piazza if you like."

Adam was still loitering around the front steps, jiggling first on one foot and then the other. "S'cuse me, Mausa Horace, but does you want me to serve dinner on de piazza?"

"Dinner! Oh, my, no," Mary Abbott exclaimed. "We didn't come for dinner. Just a friendly visit—and a brief one at that. The piazza will be fine."

Adam looked crestfallen when Horace dismissed him and muttered in a voice easily overheard that he would try to keep dinner hot. Horace vowed to give Adam some training that very evening, as he held chairs for the ladies and Deborah, who smiled her thanks with the softest, most alert gray eyes he had ever seen.

"May I have tea brought out?" Horace asked.

"No, thanks, Mr. Gould," Mary Abbott laughed. "We're really not staying that long, and we don't want your dinner to get cold."

Mrs. Shedd had been unusually silent simply because she was busy looking—scrutinizing the chair cushions, covertly swiping a finger over the wooden arms for dust, peering over her shoulder to catch a glimpse of the interior of the house.

"Is this your first visit to Black Banks, Mrs. Shedd?" Horace asked pointedly.

"What? Oh, no, no. I called on your sister-in-law as often as I possibly could. She seemed to need friends, poor dear. Do you know her lovely pale hands used to tremble so that I was sure she would drop the hot pot when she poured tea—simply because a darky brought it in?"

"I know," Horace said.

"Was she afraid of black people?" Deborah asked.

Horace smiled. "Yes, she was. Isn't that a strange thing to be, Miss Deborah?"

"It certainly is. I'm not afraid of them. I like them."

"So do I." He was still smiling at her. "You've grown, I swear, young lady, since you and I had that wild ride together a little over two months ago."

"Oh, we'll never get over that dreadful murder, Mr. Gould," the Widow Shedd declared, pressing her temples at the memory. "I hope the Butler's overseer got rid of him—one way or another."

"He got rid of himself shortly after that, ma'am."

"*What?*"

"Yes, the poor fellow slashed his own throat and bled to death."

"You never hear of a nigra killing himself. He must have been feeble-minded," Mary Abbott said pityingly.

"He was, I'm sure." Horace turned to Deborah. "How old are you now, Miss Deborah? Or is that a rude question for a gentleman to ask?"

"I'm glad to tell you, Mr. Gould. I'll be nine years old next New Year's Eve." She sat very straight, her hands folded in her lap.

"Why, I would have guessed you were at least twelve! You're certainly grown up for nine."

She smiled. "Do you really live here in this big house all by yourself? Without any wife or any children or anything."

"Without any wife or any children or anything," Horace laughed. "But you know, I rather like it. Oh, I'm lonely sometimes, but this is a friendly house. As friendly as an old house, even though it's only been here a few years."

"Will you live here by yourself always?" the child asked.

"Deborah! That's enough, dear." Her aunt was firm, but pleasant.

"I enjoy her questions. They're good ones. Right to the point. No, I won't be able to do that, Miss Deborah. You see, Black Banks belongs to my brother and his family. They'll be back from the North one of these days and my happy times will come to an end."

Deborah's dark, bird-wing eyebrows pulled together in a sympathetic frown. "Oh, I'm so sorry."

"Thank you," Horace said.

"Upon my honor, I believe you really do like living here alone, Mr. Gould!" Mrs. Shedd exclaimed. "How strange for a young man. Don't you find it impossible to keep the house properly in order without a white woman to make the nigras work?"

"No trouble at all, ma'am. And I like a house well-kept, too. Ca, the daughter of my father's Maum Larney, is turning into a replica of her mother. She's wonderful. I'm spoiled, in fact. Aren't we having a beautiful spring?"

"Spring? Oh, yes, so far, so far. Uh, Mr. Gould?"

"Yes, Mrs. Shedd?"

"Are the men folk on the Island taking care of you? I mean, have they invited you to join their clubs yet?"

"No, ma'am."

"Oh! Isn't that too bad."

"I don't think so. There's plenty of time. I'm enjoying my solitude. Do you ride yet, Miss Deborah?"

"Oh, yes, sir. I'm quite good at it, too, I believe."

"Then we must ride together sometime. That is, if your Aunt Mary will let you."

"I don't call her Aunt Mary. I call her Aunt Abbott. May I go, Aunt Abbott?"

"I don't see why not, Deborah, but I've never known you to talk so much before, my dear."

Mrs. Shedd fidgeted and tried again. "Please feel free to smoke before us, Mr. Gould, if you care to."

"Thank you, Mrs. Shedd. I don't smoke any more."

"Oh, I see." She cleared her throat. "We must seem terribly quiet and provincial to you after your years of—of—"

"Of high living?" Horace chuckled. "Not at all. I told you the truth when I said I'm very happy right here at Black Banks for this interim until my brother comes back. Are you sure I can't order tea for you, ladies?"

"We are sure, Mr. Gould," Mary Abbott said, collecting her mitts and purse. "And it's past time we rode home, too. Come, Deborah, dear—on your feet. We'll see Mr. Gould again soon."

He said good-by to them and walked slowly up the front steps, his hands deep in his pockets. This, he was certain, was the first of what would be a long line of visitors. Now that the Widow Shedd had come, others would be stimulated to examine him in person away from his family.

At the top of the steps, he watched until the buggy was out of sight. He didn't resent being examined for marks of the world as much as he resented having his solitary life at Black Banks disturbed. It would be pleasant, though, to take the Abbott child riding sometime, he decided, and he did like Mary Abbott. His sister was right, as usual.

29

John Wylly's lead oarsman broke his arm, and James Gould offered to take John to Brunswick in the New St. Clair boat when he and Horace made the trip on December 3. All through the autumn months, work on the Altamaha-Brunswick Canal had been going badly. The state-owned slaves stayed in continuous rebellion against Davis, the superintendent. Money was scarce; Thomas Butler King had gone to Boston to try to arrange new financing. The charter members had not met together since last spring, and painful as it was for James Gould to sit cramped up in the long, narrow plantation boat, he felt, with King gone, he should attend the December meeting with duBignon, Dr. Hazzard and the others at the Oglethorpe House, the new hotel in Brunswick.

"I'm certainly glad you're here to go with me, son," he said to Horace, as their oarsmen maneuvered the twenty-foot boat—hand-hewn from a single, giant cypress—toward the landing at The Village, where John Wylly was waiting with his mother.

"I always loved the trip across to Brunswick," Horace said. "Anyway, Mary gave me a long list of Christmas things she needs from Harrington's store. Be interesting to see the old town, too. When I left, it was just a mud puddle and a handful of houses."

"I guess young Wylly's going over to see his attorney," the older man said sadly. "John's changed so in the last year."

"Because of the trouble with Hazzard, I suppose."

"Yes. And the Wyllys do own the land, Horace. Everybody knows they do. Too bad. John Wylly used to be a gentle, carefree sort of fellow. He's bitter now. Not like himself at all. Still, I don't know how I'd be if someone tried to claim a mile long half-acre strip of my land."

The boat was nearing the Wylly landing. They saw Mrs. Wylly hug her tall, dark-haired son, anxiously holding him a moment longer than usual, and as he ran to the edge of the dock to jump into their boat, she waved and blew a kiss to him.

> Row, row, row, Larney—bake de bread!
> Row, row, row, Larney—bake de bread!
> Row, row, row, Larney—bake de bread!
> We'se rowin' home hun-gary as buh-zards!

Skimming over the brilliant blue water of the tidal rivers that separated St. Simons Island from Brunswick, the Gould oarsmen sang their primitive work songs—this one inspired by Larney, the most respected woman in the New St. Clair Negro community. Horace and James applauded each time the men finished another chorus, but John Wylly sat staring ahead of him, smiling absently now and then for courtesy's sake. Between songs, he lashed out about the insulting letter Dr. Thomas Hazzard had written to his mother. "A man can sit still only so long when his own mother is being harassed," he shouted, banging the wooden seat of the plantation skiff. "If the courts can't settle this, so help me, God, I'm going to settle it myself!"

"Try to keep your temper, John," James counseled.

"Flying off the handle won't help with a man like Hazzard. He'll be at the Oglethorpe House for the canal meeting today, and I advise you to keep out of his way. Conduct yourself like the gentleman you are."

Horace said little all the way across, but his heart ached for John Wylly, embittered, harassed, apparently so helpless.

While his father attended the meeting, Horace walked around Brunswick, observing the changes in the tiny city. At Harrington's store, he not only found the thread, bindings, sheeting and bleached shirting Mary wanted, he bought eight loaves of sugar—five for Rosemount and three for Black Banks—three new ax handles and half a dozen corn brooms. For the traditional "Christmas gif' " celebration with the people on Christmas morning, he laid in a supply of the things they would love: large boxes of raisins, half loaves of brown sugar, store-bought wooden pails, a new iron spider for Larney, ribbons and lengths of bright calico, ginger, boxes of sweet cloves, fifty pounds of hard candy and flannels of all colors so that Mary and his aunt could make clothes for the new babies born this fall at the quarters. He hired a wagon to cart his purchases to the dock, strolled back to the Oglethorpe House to wait on the veranda in the warm December sun for his father. Sitting in a white wicker armchair, he admired the large, sturdily built brick hotel, finding it hard to believe a building like this could be situated in Brunswick, Georgia. He watched the people coming and going from the hotel; the once sleepy little town did seem to be rousing. Suddenly he sat up. Two men were shouting at each other on the far side of the piazza. John Wylly and Dr. Hazzard! At the moment he recognized them, he saw his father and Colonel Henry duBignon appear from inside the hotel and hurry toward the angry men. Horace reached them just as John Wylly struck Dr. Hazzard across the face and shoulder with his cane. He helped Colonel duBignon separate the men, led John away and pushed him into a chair. "Man, you can cause real trouble doing a thing like that!

Panting for breath, more from anger than from exertion, John sat, his fists clenched, the veins standing out on his high forehead. "You'd better begin to use some self-control, friend," Horace went on, trying to break through John's fury. "Look, we're all with you. I don't know anyone on the Island who believes Hazzard owns that strip of land. There are people living there whose families have owned property on St. Simons long before the Hazzards came—back to Oglethorpe. There has to be a reasonable way out of this. We'll all help any way we can, but don't, I beg you, *don't* do anything else as crazy as what you just did!"

John slumped in the chair. "All right, Horace. I know, I know. But that man turns something loose in me! I don't even know myself these days. Do you know what a thing like this can do to an otherwise normal man? He's going to kill my poor mother with worry!"

Horace was helping his father down the front steps of the Oglethorpe House half an hour later when they heard the shot. They turned just in time to see John Wylly reel, strike out at his assailant with his cane, and fall. The smoking pistol was still in Dr. Hazzard's hand as he stared down at the motionless body of young John Wylly, who was dead before Horace could reach him.

Mary sat straight in her tapestry chair staring at the fire Horace had built in the Rosemount living room. The whole area was in shock. Every home up and down St. Simons Island was heavy with the same sorrow—disbelief, horror, grief. Everywhere except in the two shadowy Hazzard houses at Pike's Bluff and West Point, the people spoke in stunned whispers. And yet, Horace felt something different at Rosemount this night—an added heaviness he couldn't explain even to himself.

"You and Papa brought him back in the boat?" Mary asked woodenly.

"Yes, and took him home."

"What else will happen?" Mary seemed too quiet, too remote.

"I don't know, sister. I don't know."

"Peaceful, happy little St. Simons has had two murders and you've only been home a little over a year." Her voice was a hopeless, weary monotone—not Mary's voice. "Poor Mrs. Wylly. Christmas is coming. Poor Mrs. Wylly."

"I can't imagine who will plant for her now that John is gone," Horace said.

After a long silence, Mary whispered hoarsely, "I—don't want—him—gone."

Horace stared at her.

"I—don't—*want*—John—up there—in—the churchyard."

"Mary!"

She was looking directly at him, tears spilling down her cheeks—looking and looking as though she waited for him to do something to help.

"Sister! Oh, sister—did you—did *you*. . . ?"

Still sitting up straight, Mary closed her eyes. "I—hoped, Horace. We—John and I—have been so busy—with our families. I doubt that—he even—knew." Her eyes were open now and she was looking at him again. "I hoped. I *hoped*."

30

Driving up Frederica Road under a thick February sky as gray as smoke, Horace tried not to think of what might have been for Mary if he had come home sooner. Would it have freed her from her responsibilities so that she might have married John Wylly? True, he might not have been able to prevent John's death, but suppose she now had a child or two for her comfort?

He was meeting Frank Lively on the morning boat in an hour. He had not been alone with his old employer since his return, and some of the guilt he had believed gone hung over him again as the heavy sky hung over the gaunt, bare sweet gums and maples—mingled branch over branch with the dark pines and live oaks along the road. He leaned his head back and looked all the way to their tops as the buggy rattled and squeaked past. Far out on the tip of each bare sweet-gum branch he could see buds swelling. In a month, they would be green again. The maples were already crimson, their tight, paper-thin leaves uncurling. At the savannah below Christ Church on the western boundary of the Wylly land, he turned to admire the deep pink camellias almost smothering Mrs. Wylly's roadside bushes. There was never a season on St. Simons Island when nothing grew, nothing budded, nothing bloomed. Death came often to its people, but never to the land.

His sister had spent more time alone these past two months. "No one will ever know but you," she had told him after John's funeral was over, and that was the last mention of her shattered hopes. There was time to spare before Lively's boat docked, and when he reached the churchyard, he reined the horse, jumped down from the buggy to the cemetery. He was surprised to see John Wylly's tombstone already in place; a broken column set on a square base of pinkish marble. His cap in his hand, he stood looking, still finding it hard to believe that his friend lay beneath the stone, dead. He read the inscription:

Sacred
to the memory of
John Armstrong Wylly
who fell a victim
to his
generous courage
on the 3rd of December, 1838
Age 32 years and 1 month

To John's grieving mother, he *was* "a victim of his own generous courage." But Horace learned that John had spat on Dr. Hazzard, unable to meet him a second time that fateful day without another show of anger. People stopping to look at the strange broken column in years to come would wonder about that "generous courage" that cost John Wylly his life. Horace had another name for it, but he joined every other family on the Island in sympathy for the Wyllys. *How long had Mary hoped?* Had John hoped too? Courageous, unselfish Mary. Not at dinner today with Lively, when they would discuss the Wylly-Hazzard trouble, nor at any other time would there even be a visible sign of her sorrow. He did not deserve to be her brother, he reminded himself, but alone in the silent churchyard, he wished he knew how to thank God that he was. God. He turned to look at the tiny white church, the only tie he had ever had with whatever lies beyond physical death—his only tie with faith for this life.

The church was locked and empty.

31

Lively had advanced them money against this year's crops, and by early March, the people were preparing to sow the fields of both plantations. It had been a hard day, riding from one field to another, but Horace thought Mary was more like herself than she had been since John Wylly's death. She had raced him through the woods to the New St. Clair road and won. She looked almost happy. No man ever loved planting cotton more than Mary does, he thought, as he trotted Dolly up beside her.

"Dolly's getting old," she teased, brushing her wind-blown dark hair back from her forehead.

"She is not! Dolly's immortal. I'm the one getting old," Horace laughed.

"You're handsome, brother," she said simply. "It seems right for Janie to be married, but what will I do when some lucky young lady steals you away from me?"

"That's impossible."

Her shoulders sagged. "No, it isn't. Nothing's impossible."

"Oh, I may get married some day, but how could that change us? Don't forget, sister, I'm not leaving the Island ever again."

She smiled. "You are growing handsomer every day, and your shoulders are so heavy and broad, you need new clothes. Your coats are too tight!"

"It's Ca's cooking. I'm getting fat."

"That's muscle from plain old hard work. Have I told you how proud I am of the job you've done at Black Banks? You're a born planter. A better one than poor Jim will ever be."

"I wish his life would straighten out so we could stop saying 'poor Jim.'"

Mary sighed. "It won't. You mark my word, Alice won't be back with him this summer, and he'll disintegrate without the child."

By July of next year the price of cotton had dropped on the British market from half a guinea to less than a shilling a pound, and Jim, looking older, had returned alone to conditions far worse than anyone could remember. Money was so scarce, even the determined Thomas Butler King had abandoned work on the canal that was to make Brunswick a thriving port city. James Gould sat in his chair for hours at a time, staring at nothing, talking less and less, even to Mary.

A mistrial had been declared, and Dr. Hazzard had gone scot free, causing still deeper resentment on the Island among the Wylly sympathizers. Brazenly, it seemed to everyone, Dr. Hazzard had married almost at once, and continued to attend Christ Church and to bring his Negroes every Sunday afternoon to the colored meeting. At the morning service, the Hazzard men and their wives entered the little white building in silence, sat alone, and left alone—speaking to no one, no one speaking to them. Out of a sense of decency, Horace tried one Sunday to greet them and was rebuffed. He didn't try again. To him the whole aftermath of John Wylly's death was tragic. The other planters needed the Hazzard brothers' educated minds, needed their ideas; needed their support and cooperation as the financial squeeze grew tighter. It hurt Horace to see his otherwise warm, friendly neighbors turn hard and unyielding. He was disturbed at the treatment of the Hazzard slaves by the other Island Negroes, who now boasted that they were all "Wylly people." When he took the Gould Negroes to church, he watched them straggle into the meeting on Sunday afternoons like haughty children, the women literally pulling their long skirts aside to avoid touching the clothing of a Hazzard Negro. Church was an ingrained habit for all Islanders, but Horace began to dread it. Why did the Hazzards still come? What good did it do for people to read prayers together when they refused to speak to each other?

The months dragged by, with Jim turning more and more of the Black Banks' responsibility over to Horace. In his own heart, a resentment took root against his brother. Why should he, Horace, be saddled with the work while Jim held the planter's privileges in the community? Only Jim was invited to attend the meetings at King's Retreat preceding each commercial conference which Thomas Butler King continued to dominate. Horace could have gone, but the invitations were extended only to planters. He was merely a planter's helper, and feeling out of things, he withdrew from Jim. And from his father.

He had been home almost three years, yet the only white person with whom he felt comfortable, aside from Mary, was Captain Charles Stevens. Eighteen forty-one was a big year for the Captain. His shipping business had grown enough, even in the face of the financial crisis, so that at last, on November 30, he purchased his dream sloop *Splendid* in Savannah, and by special invitation from the new owner, Horace was on hand to sail her home to Frederica. She was 48 feet long, 16½ feet wide and carried 50 tons.

"It's that magnificent tonnage that counts, Gould," Captain Charles declared as they slipped through the twisting coastal rivers on the first of December. "That tonnage is what I will gain on. A trip is a trip, mate, but when a man can carry a big cargo, his bounty increases. Right?"

"Right," Horace agreed warmly. At least he could enjoy his friend's success, could live vicariously in Captain Charles's boundless energy and ambition and happiness.

"You wait, Gould," Charles said, navigating the *Splendid* around and between the cypress standing in the red waters of the Altamaha river. "You wait, mate, until you own your own plantation on St. Simons Island, and then you'll know what happens in a man's heart when he *feels* like a master. Master of a ship—master of a plantation." He pounded his big chest. "All the same inside, where a man's heart beats."

"I wish I could believe that day would ever come," Horace said.

"Ah, but you have to believe it! A man *needs* to own for himself. And to believe comes first. First, you dream and then you work like the devil to make that dream come true."

"I wish I could dream."

"Wish hard enough and you have a dream on your hands."

Had he been wasting his energies resenting his brother when he could have been daring to dream for his own future? He didn't envy Jim. No one could envy a man as unhappy as his brother, but he did resent him—resented his being there, gaunt and older and in the way of his own dream.

"But what makes a dream come and stay," Captain Charles was saying, "is a beautiful woman to love! Now, that's what you must get busy on first, Gould. How about falling in love?"

Horace grinned. "With whom? There's only one single woman on St. Simons a man would want to marry—that is, if he's in his right mind—and that's my sister."

(193)

"But the young ones will grow up! Look around you, man. Use your eyes. Remember what I say to you—a man needs a woman, a place of his own—and a dream."

32

Horace had actually come to look forward to Lively's visits to the Islands. He had even been glad to see Tessie and her children, when they came along at Thanksgiving in 1839. The Goulds and half the other families on St. Simons would have gone under during the panic years of the thirties if Lively hadn't come to their rescue. There had been no relief from the exorbitant tariffs, from the pressures of the New York shipping firms. The members of the now-abandoned commercial conventions had indulged in oratory and lofty phrases, but did not act.

In April, 1842, all over the South, planters—thanks to loans from their factors—were once more sewing seed, believing that because of the never-say-die spirit of the Cotton States, there would be a miracle crop and their troubles would be over. Life would somehow be good again. Horace looked for no miracle. He simply had a tentative plan for himself. He would need Lively's advice, perhaps his direct help. At the Frederica dock, he paced back and forth, eager for what he once had dreaded —a meeting with Frank Lively.

When he stepped off the boat, his old employer was in fine spirits, and Horace meant to keep him that way. He would allow plenty of time for Lively to eulogize the beauties of St. Simons, which he did boringly but with relish.

"Ah, what is more exhilarating than a day in April,

when the verdure returns? Makes a man's heart beat like a return to youth, eh, Gould? Of course, you are still a young man. How old are you, by the way?"

"I'll be thirty in August, sir. And I'd like to talk to you about something, if I may."

"About being thirty?" Lively snickered. "Do you think I don't remember? Well, I do!"

"Oh, I'm sure you do, Mr. Lively. After all, it hasn't been that long ago."

"On a day like this, not long at all. What is it you want to talk about, my boy?"

"Myself, sir. I can't go on being my brother's helper forever."

"Hm. You know, Gould, I've thought about that."

"You have? Well, I've found out at last what I really want to do with my life. I want to own my own place and plant cotton."

"Now, that does *not* surprise me. You're a much better planter right now than your brother. His heart isn't in it."

"You may be right."

"Why don't you buy Black Banks from him?"

Horace turned, surprised. "Me buy Black Banks?"

"Why not? It's valuable land. You'd do a lot more with it. I know what you've done to improve both New St. Clair and Black Banks. Your father has told me, and I've marketed the cotton you've produced. Your first smart move was to insist that the old man begin to advertise his eighteen-thirty-six seed in *The Brunswick Advocate*. That enabled him to float still another loan with me. I know about your experiments in fertilizing with marsh mud, with oyster shells—and I know the yields have increased."

Horace hadn't experienced genuine pride in anything since he left Yale, and it felt good. "What I have in mind, sir, is to find a profitsharing job managing a place for a few years until I can save enough to buy my own."

"Entirely within the realm of the possible, Gould. I commend you for a splendid show of courage. Many young men would expect their fathers to buy land for them. Shouldn't be hard to find an opening at all. People are dying, others getting scared of the hard times—where do you want to locate?"

"That's the problem, I suppose, sir. I don't want to leave Glynn County."

"What about Mrs. Abbott at Orange Grove?"

"Oh, I've been helping her for over two years. But not for money. I just like her."

"There, you see? You have courage, but you're not a good business man. You could work full time for Mrs. Abbott for a share of the profits and be of even more help than you can be now by giving her only what time you can spare."

"Perhaps. But I had something a little bigger in mind, sir, with a bigger margin of profit—an operation at least the size of Black Banks."

"Well, I know of one fair-sized, but very run-down place on Blythe Island. Owned by an old lady seemingly ready to die any day. Her only son in New York will have to retain someone to run it. Of course, the old woman could hang on a while. She's the stubborn type."

"I mean to stay through this year with Jim, anyway," Horace said. "This is just a dream for the future. Will you keep me in mind, sir?"

"Indeed I will, and I'll stake you to what you need when the time comes, Gould. How's that?"

They shook hands. "It's a deal, Mr. Lively, and I can't tell you how grateful I am. You're a good friend."

"In spite of a little touch of trouble once long ago, eh?"

"Yes, sir. In spite of that. But—will you mind not mentioning this to my family? It could be two years before I'm ready. Papa and Mary still need me, too."

"I see the picture, my boy. I admire your loyalty to them. The whole matter will stay between us."

Horace worked harder than ever through 1842 and 1843, riding often to King's Retreat and Cannon's Point to confer with Anna Matilda King and old John Couper, the two most successful owners in residence on the Island.

"Have you ever thought of rotating your crops, Mrs. King?" Horace asked Anna Matilda, as they rode together across the east field of Retreat plantation late in October of 1843.

"You've been talking to that dear old fox, Mr. John Couper, haven't you, Mr. Gould?"

"Yes ma'am." He grinned. "And you have tried it. I can tell."

"Tried it two years ago and it works!" She laughed. "For once, I was relieved my dear husband was away in Government. I doubt he would have agreed to try what he might have called 'Mr. Couper's wild scheme.' But I tried it on my own and Mr. King is the proudest man in the South over the yield we got from just this east field alone. I simply alternated with beans and corn and sweet potatoes. Now, you see the cotton this year."

"It's the finest."

"I intend to keep right on rotating. It looks as though I'll go on being the 'planter.' " She smiled. "My husband is hopeful that when Mr. Clay is elected President next year, he'll offer him a cabinet post."

"That should make you very proud."

She sighed. "It should, I suppose. In a way, I will be proud—if it happens. But oh, Mr. Gould, I wish my husband would come home and learn to content himself with being a good planter. Conditions are worsening for us so steadily in the South, it comes to me daily that perhaps all we can really do is stay down here to ourselves and try to bring about harvests so large they will somehow offset the inequities from the North."

As he rode toward New St. Clair to help Mary with the accounts, Horace decided to try crop rotation in at least one field of his father's land. He might even persuade Mrs. Abbott to let him experiment on a few acres of Orange Grove, so much of which lay fallow, going back to woods. He was sure Mary would agree, and their father was too lame now to ride his fields. Time enough to tell him later.

He rode slowly. The gums and hickories and bullis grapevines on each side of Frederica Road were in color, a subtle beauty softened by the gray moss, and his mind went to New England's unsubtle riotous hillsides, beginning now, he knew, to turn crimson and copper and gold. He would like to visit at the North again some day. He would always love New England, would always feel a part of it, as he was a part of America. More and more his neighbors seemed to relish feeling separate. Even Anna Matilda King had grown weary, longed for her husband to give up and come home. Trouble drove people to stay to themselves. Horace wanted to be a good planter, but one of the reasons, he realized now, was to prove that it was somehow possible to be a successful cotton grower without struggling against the rest of the country. There had to be a way and if only for one man, himself, he meant to find it. Not by running off to the frontier; by staying where his roots were already down. He would have liked a talk with Captain Stevens today, but his friend was piloting the *Splendid*, somewhere between St. Simons and Charleston, on the last voyage before his wedding in November. Horace smiled. Lucky people, Captain Charles and his lady.

Out of the corner of his eye, as he trotted past the Abbott home, he saw thirteen-year-old Deborah in a light blue dress, peeping at him through an opening in the high hedge where the plantation fields ended. He turned Dolly quickly and rode back.

"Miss Deborah?" There was no answer. "Miss Deborah! are you hiding from me?"

Still no sound except a wren shouting and one of Mrs. Abbott's roosters crowing. He walked Dolly to the hedge, and although the blue dress was plainly visible as Deborah sat scrunched up in the pine-straw mulch, he decided not to embarrass her and rode on, smiling to himself. She's a beautiful little Irish leprechaun, he thought, and urged old Dolly to a gallop, not to keep Mary waiting any longer.

The next morning, on his way again to Rosemount, he spotted pink behind the big hedge, but he did not stop.

For the rest of the week, the spot of color changed from pink to blue, then white, then yellow, and on Saturday morning, as Horace rode very slowly past the Abbott place, he saw two spots of color, one red and one green. Deborah's little sister, Annie, called "Hello" from the hedge, and the cat was out of the bag. Annie ran to meet him, and there was nothing for Deborah to do but stand up, her gray eyes wide, her pretty face almost as red as the dress she had thought she was hiding behind the hedge.

Horace smiled at her. "Well, good morning, Miss Deborah! I haven't seen you for a long time."

"Haven't you?" she asked hopefully.

"What are you doing out here behind that hedge? Did you lose something?"

"Oh, no, Mr. Gould, she didn't lose anything," Annie volunteered. "We're *supposed* to be taking a walk before our tutor comes."

"I see. Then you both study all morning, is that it?"

"Yes, sir," Deborah answered.

She was so delicately beautiful in the yellow sunshine, he could have looked at her forever. She held herself so straight—and though she was still blushing—with a quiet composure rare in so young a girl. He frowned. "Miss Deborah, you're growing up."

"I am?"

"I swear, I hadn't realized until right now—you're almost a young lady."

"Is something wrong with that, Mr. Gould?"

"Not at all. Why?"

"You're frowning something awful."

He laughed, annoyed with himself for feeling embarrassed before a mere child. "Well, it's rude of me to frown. You're very pretty, you know, and—you do know, don't you, Miss Deborah?"

"I wasn't sure," she said shyly. "I hoped I was pretty."

He laughed again. "Well, you can stop hoping. You are. But those lessons are more important. Study hard, both of you. My regards to Aunt Abbott."

33

Early in March of 1844, James Gould informed Larney's John that they were taking a trip north together. "You and Horace are needed here, daughter," he said to Mary as he packed the papers he would need in his brass-bound portable carriage desk and deposited some gold in its secret drawer. "John's the one I want to go with me. It's not a pleasure trip. I'm going to get well enough so I can ride my own fields again. I've read they're giving a new kind of massage at the baths in Saratoga. I plan to have John learn how to do it so he can take care of me when we get home. I don't intend to give in to this rheumatism any longer."

When his carriage had rolled out of sight, and all the people from both plantations who had come to say good-by had returned to their work, Horace and Mary walked slowly back to the Rosemount front steps and sat down.

"I hope it helps him," Horace said.

"Oh, so do I. The old darling's had enough pain—too much." She leaned her head against the stair post. "I miss him already."

"Of course you do. We don't need to worry about him, though—not with Larney's John along. Which reminds me: with Papa John gone, I'd better get out to the fields."

"Don't go yet. Everyone's working. I want to know something, Horace." She was looking at him intently.

"Well, what?"

"You're different. Are you up to anything you haven't told me?"

"Not a thing."

"You never could lie, Horace. You don't have any idea of leaving us, do you?"

"Not—well, not any time soon."

"I knew it! Where? Where are you going?"

"I don't know. And I'm not lying. It shouldn't surprise you that I want a place of my own sometime. Living at Black Banks with Jim—as sorry as I am for him, and as much as I've come to love the house—is like living a nightmare. Besides, I don't belong there."

"Yes, you do—hard as you've worked on that land!"

"My work hasn't a thing to do with who owns the land. It's Jim's and it will never be mine, and I'd think you'd want to see me get away before I get any more attached to it."

"Do you—love Black Banks that much?"

"Yes. But what difference does it make?"

"Horace, do you ever think about getting married?"

"Who would marry a man with no land?"

"That isn't what I asked."

"All right—of course, I think about it!"

"It's none of my business, is it?"

Horace slipped his arm around her. "Papa may end up with a bachelor son to match his old-maid daughter. You've spoiled me."

Mary stood up, her brown eyes so solemn, he stopped smiling.

"I know someone who would be perfect for you," she said.

"Don't make jokes."

"I'm not making a joke."

He got up too. "I don't think I want you to tell me. What good will it do? I have nothing to offer a wife."

"I intend to tell you anyway—little Deborah Abbott."

Horace stared at her, opened his mouth to protest, but no words came.

"You can wait for her, Horace. You can wait."

Halfway to the New St. Clair south field, where he had planned to supervise the planting for the day, Horace changed his mind and rode toward the Black Banks house. Jim was in the fields, Ca was making soap in the back yard, Adam was raking leaves; he could be alone in the house. He felt almost foolish, not at all certain of his motives in wanting to return to the family rooms where he had been so happy. Not at all sure of what he would do once he was there. He hitched Dolly at the front steps, mounted them slowly, crossed the wide piazza and turned the knob on the front door.

The quiet, spacious sitting room welcomed him—welcomed *him*. It was his house again, the one place where he had ever felt he belonged. He was thirty-two and late with everything. Captain Charles Stevens owned his own home and two boats and was saving for another. He was married and the father of his first child.

Horace let himself out the French doors that led from the sitting room to the piazza. Clear, radiant spring sunlight caught the new green on the sea myrtles that stood along the marsh margin, picked out the tiny cassina leaves, silvering them; transformed the stiff brown bull grass and plumy sedge into glass patterns—glistening arcs—intricate fairy pencilings of splintered light. Ca sang out back as she stirred the soap with a wooden paddle; Adam's rake scritch-scratched somewhere in the side yard; the guineas down at the quarters complained; mockers and cardinals streaked from tree to tree, staking out their breeding territories, announcing their claims. Spring was the time to stake one's claim, to begin to build a dream. After spring it grew late. How had Mary known what he had not dared admit to himself. Could he wait for this disturbing child? He was late. Could he? Was little Deborah Abbott what he lacked?

He leaned against the piazza railing, his back to the sharp beauty of the spring marsh. Suddenly he touched the rough, shell-spattered tabby wall of the house, laid both hands against it. "Dear Black Banks house," he whispered. "*If only I owned you*. If only I owned you, everything else might fall in place."

All his life he had talked of finding himself. Did a man ever find himself by waiting for life to take hold of him? Didn't a man worth his own salt take hold of life?

Thirty-two years of coasting, of convincing himself that for him there was a special place up ahead; a special thing to do—but always up ahead, never at hand. What had made him think there would be anything special for him? Didn't a man shape the pattern of his own days? How had he been content to work so hard for Jim? To settle for a spare room in another man's house? To wait and wait and wait for the dream to come to him? He turned back to look out over the wide stretch of marsh, down the Black Banks river, toward the sea. Captain Charles was right: "First you dream, then you work like the devil to make that dream come true." Life *should* be stingy with floaters, with those who merely wait for a right time and a right place and a right person.

This time, he didn't settle for a resolve made only within himself. He acted.

Sitting across from Mary Abbott on her vine-shaded front porch, Horace had to restrain himself while she chatted amiably from one subject to another. The futility of his waiting had become so real, so painful, he wanted to blurt out to this comfortable, merry-faced lady everything he had begun to dream. She was mending a rip in a soft, blue cotton dress with a white ruffle—a dress he had seen Deborah wear—not requiring him to comment, enjoying their visit.

"Yes, my husband's family, the Abbotts, came from a long line of distinguished ancestors," she was saying. "One became the Archbishop of Canterbury—his name was George, like my dear husband. Another, Robert—same name as Deborah's late father—was Bishop of Salisbury. And, Horace, one of the things I like most is that this gentleman who became Archbishop of Canterbury was one of the eight divines who translated our Bible under orders of James the Primate."

"Is that right," he said, sounding like his father.

"Maybe I like that so much because the two books he translated are my favorites—the Acts of the Apostles and the Gospel of Saint Luke."

Horace had begun to listen now. These were Deborah's people—long, long ago, but her people just the same.

Mary Abbott finished the mending, broke off her thread, smoothed the stitches over her knee, and laid the blue dress aside. "I wonder where those children are! It isn't like Deborah to be gone so long. Especially when she must have heard you ride up."

He leaned toward her. "Mrs. Abbott?"

"Yes, Horace?"

"You—you're Deborah's legal guardian, aren't you?"

"Indeed I am, and I declare, I love that child as though she were my own. Isn't she getting as pretty as a picture?"

"Prettier than a picture," he murmured, fishing for an opening.

"You should have seen her mother, Horace. Not as lively and spunky as Deborah, but a true beauty. Losing her killed Deborah's father, I believe. At any rate, he died in six months. Tell me, Horace, how's your father making out at the North? Have you heard lately?"

He had lost his chance. "He writes once a week, and seems to feel the baths and massage are helping his legs, thank you." Mary would be waiting; he had to go. "I've stayed too long. I hope you'll give my best to Miss Deborah—and little Miss Annie."

He went every day for two weeks, and only once was Deborah anywhere in sight. One afternoon she raced in to show her aunt a baby rabbit she had found, saw Horace, blushed furiously, tucked the rabbit in her apron pocket and ran away.

"She's acting very strangely these days, that child. I just don't understand her all the time. One has to be patient, though, when young girls begin to pull toward womanhood." Mary Abbott laughed. "The difficulty is that one never knows exactly when or whether they're pulling toward womanhood or back toward childhood—they're so contradictory."

"Mrs. Abbott?"

"Yes, Horace?"

"Mrs. Abbott, I want to marry Deborah."

She let her sewing fall to her lap and stared at him. Then a small frown wrinkled her forehead. "You—you want to *marry* Deborah?"

"Yes. I do."

"But Horace—she's only a child."

"I can wait for her."

Mary Abbott took a deep breath, then let it go into laughter.

"I'm serious. I don't have a home to offer her yet, but I will someday. And until I do, Deborah and I can live with my brother at Black Banks. There's plenty of room. It's a wonderful house."

She stopped laughing, but her smile lingered. "I know it's a wonderful house, and you're a fine man."

"I will be a fine man, if I—if you—" He looked at her helplessly.

"Of course. Every man needs a woman beside him, but she's a child—barely fifteen. Why, she can't really cook or sew—she knows nothing about handling servants or seeing to a thorough housecleaning—she can't nurse your colored sick or—Horace, she has to learn *how* to be a wife to you—or anyone else!"

"Can't you teach her? I mean—can't you maybe just do nothing else for a few months but teach her? I'll help with your other work at Orange Grove."

"I suppose I could. I should be able to after all this time, but Horace—you're in such a hurry so suddenly. How does a man know he loves a woman before she's a woman?"

He swallowed hard. "I don't know how to answer that. I—I love her because she's beautiful, but, of course, I know that isn't enough. I—like the Irish in her, the spunk, as you say. Mostly—I feel close to her. And if I feel this way now when she's so young, wouldn't our closeness grow with the years into something really strong?"

"My dear boy, I don't know. How could anyone possibly know?"

"I need someone to take care of."

"You are pretty much a lone wolf—even with your family, aren't you?"

He let that drop. "I want you to know I'm aware of what people will say."

"About my permitting a young girl to marry a man in his thirties?"

"About the years I was away. I lost all those years, ma'am. But their traces are gone too. I swear there are no scars."

"Would I have even discussed this with you if I didn't believe in you, Horace Bunch Gould?"

"Thank you."

"I didn't say as Deborah's husband—I just mean I believe in *you*. And before I can promise any kind of concentrated wife-training, you must promise me one thing."

"Anything you say, Mrs. Abbott."

"You and I must somehow be convinced that this child wants to marry you." She leaned back in her rocker. "Whew! Now that I've had a few minutes to recover from my shock, I must admit I've seen signs I didn't recognize."

"You have? Honestly? What?"

"She hides every time you come."

"Is that a good sign? I was beginning to worry."

"You're a good planter, Horace—you've helped save both the Gould plantations, and goodness knows you've helped me—but you've as much to learn about women as Deborah has about keeping house."

"May I go find her now?"

They both turned to listen in the direction of the thick oleander clump at the north end of Mary Abbott's porch.

"I thought I heard something there in the bushes, Horace, did you?"

"A coon, maybe. I'll look."

He slipped quietly down the front steps and around to the end of the porch. Deborah was sitting under the oleanders—her knees tucked up to her chin, the mended

(206)

blue dress with the white ruffle spread around her—
smiling up at him as though to smile at him was the
most natural thing in the world for her to do.

"Hello," he said, as calmly as he could. "Don't you
want to join the party?"

He reached toward her, pushing the oleander trunks
aside with one foot. "Want me to pull you out of there,
Miss Deborah?"

Her eyebrows knit into the smallest frown; then the
smile came back as she reached eagerly for both his
hands.

34

Jesus die a happy die
He die fuh sin but not His own

Gimme Him gimme Him until I die.
Gimme Him gimme Him until I die.

Larney's joyful voice carried from the kitchen to the
front door where Mary was hanging up her cloak on the
hall tree. Maum Larney's heart was as light as hers. She
hurried to the kitchen and joined in the last "Gimme
Him gimme Him until I die."

Without a word, Larney, smiling, turned from her
cook pot and began to clap her hands and tap her heels
in the rhythm more familiar to Mary than the hymns at
church. "Is you ready, is you ready, Miss Ma-ry?" Clap-
clap. "I am ready, I am ready, Maum Lar-ney!" Clap-
clap:

Brother Froggy went to town—un hunh, un hunh!
To buy his wife a weddin' gown—un hunh, un hunh!
What you gon' t' hab de weddin' feas'? un hunh, un
hunh!

Two big bread n' not a bit ob grease—un hunh, un
hunh!
Firs' come aroun' wuz Mr. Bug
He fell in de lemonade tub
Nex' come in wuz Mr. Snake
Pattin' all 'roun' dat weddin' cake
Nex' come in wuz Mr. Tick
He eat so much 'til it make 'im sick—un hunh, un hunh!

Mary danced around the kitchen as they sang, slapping with her open hands in time to Larney's beat—first
on the table, then the safe, then the big dough board—
and ended by applauding them both as she had done all
through her childhood when she and Horace and Jim
and Janie had managed to learn one of Maum Larney's
intricate, primitive Sea Island play songs.

"Ah tellin' de truf, we has got us one happified house,
Miss Mary! An' it was pas' time too. We ain' had no play
singin' fo' too long. Mah boy done make us as happy as
he make us sad, ain't he?"

"Oh, I'm so happy I could shout!" Mary laughed.
"Remember how we used to annoy poor Miss Alice
when we sang that song? Just because it had bugs and
snakes and ticks in it?"

Larney stirred the contents of her big iron kettle
hanging over the open fire. "We's celebratin' today fo'
Mausa James too. His fav'rite—mullet stew! Dat good
man kin walk agin' wifout so much hurtin'. Un hunh!
Ain' dat de han' ob de Lord, chile, dat de long ol' trip
he'p yo' papa?"

"Oh, it's the most wonderful thing that ever happened—and wasn't it dear of Papa to borrow a horse
from Mr. Frewin and come *riding* home from Frederica?
To show us he could?"

"Bes' thing to Larney is dat mah John done learn dat
fancy rubbin' at de Norf. Dey bof' claims effen John
rub 'im eber day, dem ol' legs won't go stiff no mo'. Does
you reckon dey's right, honey?" Her eyes were full of
tears. "Does you s'pose mah John gon' be able to he'p
de Mausa sho' nuff?"

"Why, yes! John's strong and smart, and I know he learned well from the masseur at the springs. Papa's overjoyed about Horace getting married, too—and you know being happy again is going to help him most of all."

Larney's eyes twinkled through her tears, as she began to shuffle and bounce lightly, slowly across the kitchen. " 'To buy his wife a weddin' gown—un hunh! un hunh'!"

"Can you believe it, Maum Larney? Can you believe Horace is really going to marry that dear little Deborah Abbott?"

"Tain' but one thing hurt mah heart," Larney said softly. "An' dat ain' nuffin' but Larney worryin' 'bout Larney. He gon' lib at Black Bank' wif mah Ca an' not here wif Larney. Ca gonna' be de one t'nus' Mausa Horace's chillurns."

Mary patted her shoulder. "But we'll all be together. Horace won't be leaving us again—ever."

"Does you think Mausa Jim gon' stay?"

"I suppose so. Where would he go? He has no home but Black Banks." She sighed. "I know what you're thinking. But maybe Horace and Deborah will be so happy it will help Jim."

Larney shook her head. "It don' work dat way, honey. Don' eber work dat way a-tall."

"I won't permit you to borrow trouble, Maum Larney, do you hear?"

"Ah hears, but mah heart don't heed."

"Well, let it! I wonder how Deborah and Mrs. Abbott are doing with their housekeeping lessons? Poor child, her aunt is so determined to make a good wife of her in six months, she must be champing at the bit. Horace says he almost never sees her these days, and when he does take her for a walk or a ride, the little thing is so tired, they can't go as far as they did when she was ten years old. She went sound asleep on his shoulder sitting on a log the other day down by the river."

"But Aunt Abbott, Mr. Gould's sister, Mary, and his aunt have been making all the colored children's dresses and trousers. Can't I let them teach me how to cut out later on—after I'm married to Mr. Gould?" Her voice trailed off dreamily, and she dropped the scissors and stared out the window into the gathering storm clouds rolling across the summer sky. "Anyway, Mr. Gould will be here soon. We're going for a walk."

"Deborah Abbott, what do you see out that window? You're looking right at the sky! Can't you see those thunderheads piling up? It's going to pour. Mr. Gould probably won't come today, and even if he does, you are not going for a walk until you've shown me you can cut out a front panel to match a back. Now, cut."

"Mr. Gould says he likes to eat just anything, Aunt Abbott! I won't have to learn how to bake Brown Betty for maybe years and years! Their cook, Ca, is as good, Mr. Gould says, as Maum Larney any day."

"The way to a man's heart is through his stomach. You're going to learn how to make Brown Betty and a one-two-three cake *and* a Lady Baltimore before this week is over. They're on my list, so you might just as well work on creaming that sugar and butter. Here's the spoon."

"But I've already found Mr. Gould's heart!"

"Then we'll modify the saying: The way to *keep* a man's heart is to keep his stomach happy. Start creaming, Deborah."

"But isn't it the man's place to handle the colored people, Aunt Abbott? I know you have to, but you don't have a man around your house. I'll just be myself with them and they'll like me fine. I already like them. There won't be a smidgen of trouble ever at *our* house."

"Deborah, you must always be kind to the people, that's true. You're kind by nature, but you can't just 'be yourself' with them. It doesn't work."

"Why?"

"Because the colored know us better than we know ourselves. They can size us up far quicker than we can size them up, and if they find out you're tenderhearted and easygoing all the time, they'll run all over you."

"I don't believe it. Excuse me, Aunt Abbott, but I just have to be myself."

"It's very young and inexperienced of you to say a thing like that. Very young. When you're the mistress of your own plantation, some day, you must be wise—not foolish and young."

"Do you think Mr. Gould and I will have our own plantation someday, Aunt Abbott? Do you really? Without that other Mr. Gould, his brother?"

"I hope so, dear. With all my heart, I hope so. But you're not going to change the subject that easily. We're talking today about how to handle servants and that means today is the day for you to learn the fundamentals of how to conduct yourself with them. Darkies are not all alike, as some people try to say. They're smart and intelligent and honest and deceitful and good and evil—just like white people. They respond to kindness, but some of them take advantage of it—like some white people. They're totally dependent upon their owners for everything—their food, houses, clothing, medicines. But these things are due them, and so they don't need to say 'thank you' when you dole out to them of a Saturday. They usually do, but they have it all coming to them. They've earned their rice and meal and sugar and side meat and bolts of cloth. It's a business exchange. But because they are dependent upon you—because you do own them—they respond to genuine authority. They respect strength in you. Here, in a way, I suppose, they're like children. They need to be able to look up to their white folks, to admire them. The darky's world is the world of his white people. If you and Mr. Gould prosper, their world expands too. They have dignity, and it must be encouraged, but they must never be flattered—they know it everytime. And if they fall silent when you're explaining something they've done wrong or left someting undone, don't fall into their trap."

"Trap?"

"A darky's silence is almost always a trap. It doesn't seem to embarrass them as it embarrasses us just to stand and say nothing. We white people can't bear silence, and so, if we're not careful, they trap us into filling the silence—and too often, we fill it with just what they were hoping for."

"I'll try to remember, Aunt Abbott, but it sounds like hard work. Just loving seems so much easier to me."

"Now, Deborah, today we're going to talk about how to be with husbands."

"But, Aunt Abbott, I must know that already or Mr. Gould wouldn't want to spend the rest of his life with me, would he?"

"You know how to look pretty for him and make him happy now, Deborah, but I'm talking about later, when things are not so rosy, when death comes or sickness or failure or disappointment. Those are the difficult times to know how to be with a man. When you see he's made a mistake, in the name of heaven, Deborah, never tell him right out. A wife's place is to be submissive, and this is not going to be easy for you all the time."

"Why not? Whatever Mr. Gould wants is what I want!"

"*Now* it is. But there will be times when Horace Bunch Gould is going to be wrong, is going to make mistakes, is going to be weak, or headstrong, or cross with you."

"Mr. *Gould*?"

"Mr. Horace Bunch Gould. The man you're going to marry the fifth of November. Whenever he does anything that displeases or angers or hurts you—just wait."

"Wait?"

"For him to get over it or come to his senses—but while you wait, love him just the same."

"Oh, that won't be hard. It's never hard to do what I can't help doing, Aunt Abbott. And I can't help loving Mr. Gould."

"Do you know what loving someone means, child? It means you will always care more about how *you* are making *him* feel than about how *he* is making *you* feel. That's love."

"I love him that way, Aunt Abbott. I do, I do."

Mary Abbott smiled at her. "I believe that. Young as you are, I do believe you love the man. You wouldn't have gone through my stiff paces all these months if you didn't want to be with him more than anything else on earth. I'm proud of you, and I expect to stay that way."

Horace heard the floor squeak as Ca tiptoed into the sitting room at Black Banks. He sat still in the platform rocker, his back to her, staring into the small pine-branch fire he had built. Ca was more like Maum Larney every day. He knew she had a problem and that she was standing there figuring out the best way to approach him with it. Almost a minute ticked away on the mantel clock. Ca was silent as an Indian. With any of the Negroes, he would have waited a little longer, then shouted, "Boo!" No one teased Ca that way. As with her mother, her dignity stopped one short of teasing.

"You comfortable standing there, Ca?" he asked quietly.

"Lord have mercy, Mausa Horace! You got ears lak' a rabbit."

"Come on in and tell me what's wrong."

"It's Mausa Jim," she said, coming to stand in front of him, tall, like Larney, her handsome head down, her eyes on the carpet.

"It's usually my brother, isn't it, Ca? Look at me so I can tell how bad it is this time."

"Mausa Jim won' come to dinner, sir. I done call 'im an' he won' come."

"But there's nothing new about that. Is he in his room?"

"Yes, sir. Wif' de do' lock."

Horace got up, stretched, told Ca he'd be back down in a few minutes, and climbed the stairs to Jim's room. He had made the same effort night after night for the past three years. Sometimes Jim would come down, sometimes not. Still, Ca was not an alarmist, and he felt suddenly uneasy as he knocked on Jim's door.

"It's Horace, Jim," he called, as casually as possible.

There was no answer, but in a moment, the bolt slid back and Jim opened the door. He was in his old red dressing gown, his hair disheveled, the circles under his dark eyes deeper than ever. Horace looked around the room. His brother was fully packed. "Going away?"

"Looks like it."

"Before the wedding, Jim? You're my best man."

Jim whirled on him, struggling to keep his voice steady. "I meant to be your best man. I really did. But—now that the time is so short, the wedding so near—I can't go through with it. Can't you put yourself in my place?"

Horace stepped toward him. "I try, brother."

"Well, you don't succeed! If you did, you'd never ask me to do a thing like that." He laughed bitterly. "I do fine with funerals, but—" Jim strode to the window, his back to Horace.

In a moment, Horace said, "Don't feel bad. I—I was thoughtless to ask you. But you are my only brother."

Jim turned around, slumping against the window sill. "I'm going back to New Haven to—try—once more. But I want Adam to drive me to the boat. Just Adam."

Something like pity choked off the things Horace wanted to say to this man who had stood for so many years an indifferent ghost between him and Black Banks. Nothing came but a hoarse: "Good luck, Jim."

Jim held out his hand. "Happy days to you."

"Thanks. I'll try to hold the fort till you come back."

Jim laughed. "Yes, I suppose I'll just—come back again. Like the other time—alone." He cocked his head to one side, a shadowy reminder of the old Jim. "Meanwhile, you and Miss Deborah are de Mausa an' de Missus ob' de ol' plantation."

Early the next morning, Horace was relieved when he found Deborah alone on the front porch at Orange Grove. He had never known her to look so appealing—in the old blue cotton again, the soft white ruffle framing her tender, young throat—standing erect as always, her hands out to welcome him.

"Will you always do that, Miss Deborah?" he asked softly, taking her hands.

She lifted her face, smiling, her sweet mouth inviting his. "How could I ever *not* welcome you, Mr. Gould, dear?"

He kissed her forehead, then held her head against his shoulder. "I have some bad news."

He felt her slender body grow rigid, but she did not pull away. "We will be married, won't we?" she whispered.

"Yes, my beloved. Of course we'll be married—day after tomorrow, but our wedding trip to Savannah has to be postponed—maybe canceled."

"Oh, I thought it was something bad. Don't you have any money?"

He smiled a little. "I'd saved for our trip. It isn't money this time. My brother went North today. I can't leave Mary and Papa with two plantations to look after."

"But I thought Mr. Jim was going to be your best man!"

"He couldn't go through with it. His own marriage is so unhappy, he—"

Deborah put two fingers over his lips. "You don't need to tell me. Our happiness right under his nose would be too hard for him. I know how that is. I used to want to run away because I didn't have a papa, when other children walked along at church holding their father's hands."

How could one so young know so much? And how was it that this beautiful, tender, gray-eyed child wanted to marry him? He would never know.

"We'll just take a long ride in the woods the day we become man and wife." She snuggled against him again. "And that *is* day after tomorrow and when we come back from *that* ride, I won't have to let you go away from me. I can go home with you, Mr. Gould, dear. To stay forever."

Mary Abbott put the finishing touches on Deborah's short-waisted white silk wedding dress the night before the ceremony took place in the parlor of the Orange Grove house, on November 5, 1845, and stayed up late, helping her own Bessie and Larney and Mary and Ca decorate the white-walled room. All of her maidenhair ferns were brought in from the front porch, and where Horace and Deborah would stand to repeat their vows were banks of pear branches, their heart-shaped leaves turned coral, pale green, yellow, black-brown—gleaming like polished leather in their silver and crockery urns—spiked here and there with butter-yellow hickory and trailing crimson creeper.

So many people came the next day, there was no room for dancing, although old John Couper brought his fine fiddling man, Johnny, who played his "violane" after the ceremony, while the guests milled about kissing the bride, congratulating the groom, helping themselves from Mary Abbott's laden tables. The Gould and Abbott Negroes outside pressed close to the open windows, four and five deep, enjoying the merriment, and the punch bowl had to be filled four times because Deborah and Horace insisted upon their sharing it too.

For once, Horace did not mind the occasional sidewise glances from the older ladies, still watching for some sign of his "wicked past." Let them watch. They enjoyed it and he could agree to anything that added to the gladness of this day. Mary was glowing and only he could have guessed what her thoughts might have been when, across the room, he saw her kiss John Wylly's mother. The third time his smiling father got in line to shake his hand, Horace gave him a big bear hug. The old man's heart was broken for Jim, but this time Horace could be sure he had given his father nothing but joy. Becoming one with Deborah had made him one with his family and with the Island. He belonged to them all and they all belonged to him, at last.

He could only manage to grin and nod when his best man, Captain Charles Stevens, said, "Congratulations, Gould! You have made the first dream come true. You will be a hard man to stop now—you watch."

PART FOUR

35

Taking the narrow plantation lane as far as the quarters, Deborah rode hard, then cut into the spring-green woods through a shadowy fern-covered clearing. Aunt Abbott had just said what Deborah had hoped she would say, and the girl sat lightly on Major's broad back, wishing she could fly over his head, above the treetops and into her husband's arms. She rode out of the woods into the newly burned off field by the pond, and there he was on his knees, sifting some soil through his fine, capable hands. One day, she was sure, he would be the outstanding planter in all the Sea Islands. Horace ran toward her, his expressive face anxious.

"Don't worry, don't worry!" she called, and when he had lifted her down and stood holding her in his arms, unmindful of the field hands' smiles and snickers, she put both hands over his mouth to stop his questions. "I'm going to do all the talking, so s-sh!"

He pried her hands loose. "But what's happened to bring you riding like a Creek Indian to find me in the middle of the morning?"

"I said 'Sh'!" She cocked her head to one side, inspecting him. "Are you shushed, sir? Yes, I guess you are." Suddenly both hands flew to her own mouth and her gray eyes filled with tears. "I'm too excited to tell you—help me, Mr. Gould, dear!"

"Help me" meant he would press her head gently against his shoulder and smooth the back of her hair until she quieted down. He did, and in a moment, she said in a loud whisper, "Sometime about the first of September, Mr. Gould, dear, we're going to have our first child." She clung to him, frightened by his silence. "Don't I—don't I make you happy?"

"Oh, yes, little Deborah—but you're still only a child yourself! Are you sure? Are you quite sure?"

"Aunt Abbott made me wait to tell you until I was. Are you angry with me?"

"My darling, beautiful wife, I'm scared! For you. What would I do if something happened to you?"

She laughed and pulled away. "If that's all you can say, I'm going to ride right back to the house."

He grabbed her arm. "You shouldn't even be riding a horse!"

"And do you want me to walk all that way, sir?"

"Don't tease, Deborah. You can't understand things like this. You're too young to grasp what this means!"

She lifted her head. "Mr. Gould, dear, when the time comes, just watch me grasp all it means."

Before he could think of anything to say, she led Major to a burned-off stump, hopped lightly to his back, and waving triumphantly, rode off.

Every hour of every day and night throughout the spring and summer of 1846, Horace worked, ate, slept, breathed for the glorious, frightening day in September when Deborah would give him his first child. He consulted with Maum Larney, with Aunt Abbott, with Mary, with Ca. He rode to Cannon's Point to consult with the Granny woman, Rhina. All spring and summer, Deborah laughed at him, refusing to be pampered. But he would settle for no Island midwife. His baby would be brought by Dr. Troup from Darien, and from late August, he kept the Black Banks oarsmen working in the field near the landing, their new cypress canoe in readiness.

"How can we be that definite, Horace?" Mary asked. "What if you go for the doctor and then we have to wait? He can't just stay here on St. Simons doing nothing."

"He'll stay if I have to tie him up," he declared, and made the rounds again, consulting Rhina, Maum Larney and Aunt Abbott.

Somehow the days passed, and on September 7, at

dawn, he jumped from the landing into the canoe for the long trip up the Black Banks and Hampton rivers, across Buttermilk Sound to Darien.

That evening as the sun was touching the marsh grass along the river, silvering the black sandy banks, Mary met Horace and the doctor at the landing.

"It's here, Horace! Your baby is already here—a beautiful little girl with coal-black hair like Deborah's. You'll have to stay overnight, Dr. Troup, but we don't need you now." She hugged her brother. "Horace, Deborah isn't a child any more. She's a strong, magnificent woman!"

After Larney's John massaged his rheumatic legs, James Gould rode every day to Black Banks and waited on the piazza or in the sitting room for Deborah to bring his new grandchild to him. Then he would sit for an hour or more, the baby cradled in his arms. Sometimes Deborah sat on a low stool at his feet; most days he just visited with his granddaughter.

"This is your birthday, Miss Jane," he said on the seventh of December. "My beautiful little Jennie is three months old today. Then she will be five and seven and nine months old, and before we all know it—one whole year of her life will be lived." He studied her drowsy eyes. "Blue, like your father's, Jennie. Light, light blue. Blue, too, like your grandmother's eyes, and you have her name, Jane. She would be so proud to have a granddaughter like you." The baby scratched her tiny straight nose. "Heh! Looks very much like you're going to have a Gould nose. That makes me happy. Your papa declares he hopes not, but he doesn't mean that. One thing I know about you, young lady, you've got a fine father. It took him a while to settle down, but now that he has you and your sweet mama to love, I'll never have to worry about him again."

James Gould looked toward the river, sparkling under the late morning sun. "When a man loves a place the way your papa has come to love Black Banks, it ought to belong to him. I made a bad mistake giving it to your uncle." He sighed. "Uncle Jim will be drifting home one of these days. I dread to see him come back."

With no warning, Jim did return early the next January, explaining that he had stayed in New Haven to be near his son until Jamie had entered boarding school on his fifteenth birthday. For two months, Jim had traveled aimlessly. Now, he slept in the big room he had shared with Alice, rode to the fields every other day or so, attended church with the family and usually stayed for Sunday dinner at Rosemount. But he was a ghost presence, uninterested in Horace's first profitable cotton crop in ten years.

"I hate myself for saying this, Deborah, but I don't think I can stay here any longer." Horace got up from the breakfast table and stood behind her chair, where he didn't have to look at her. "Jim's pathetic, but we were too happy without him. I'm working my hands to the bone building up Black Banks for another man, who wouldn't care if it all burned to the ground tomorrow. And yet, I don't think he would sell it—even if I had any money. It's all the poor fellows' got left. I'm sorry for my brother, but—Deborah, Lively has found a superintendent's job for me on Blythe Island. Do you think I should take it?"

She reached for his hand and pulled him to his chair. "Whatever is best for you is just exactly what I want to do, Mr. Gould, dear. Of course, I don't think you would be paid more than the salary Uncle Jim pays if you went to another plantation. But—you would be away from Black Banks. I know that will be easier for you."

He looked at her a long time, still wondering, after three years of married life, at her wisdom—her perception and her good common sense. "You're right on both counts. I wouldn't gain a cent. It's not a profit-sharing deal—it's just another salaried job. I'd get this big rock out of my stomach, though, if I didn't have to ride Black Banks knowing it doesn't belong to me and never will. But what about you?"

"I don't count."

"Oh, yes, you do. Sometimes I think you love Black Banks as much as I do."

Her eyes softened, then twinkled. "I do, but not as much as I love you."

Late that year, as soon as Jim's fields were picked, the cotton ginned, baled and on its way to Lively and Buffton in Savannah, Horace and Deborah and little Jennie left St. Simons and went to live in a tumble-down plantation house on Blythe Island, west of Brunswick. The first night in the drafty, damp bedroom, Horace was out of the sagging old bed five times. Once to kill a black snake coiled around the leg of the cracked marble washstand, once to chase a mouse—which he missed—and three times to reset the wooden firkins, the big dishpan, and two kettles from one cluster of leaks to another, for at three in the morning the rain had begun to pour down in torrents.

Deborah worked so hard during their first year as tenant supervisors of the worn-out farm that when she told him their second child was well on its way, Horace was more alarmed than he had been the first time.

"I'm killing you, forcing you to live in this Godforsaken place just because I'm too stubborn to work for my brother."

"There is no such thing as a *Godforsaken* place! God came right here to Blythe Island with us."

"Yes, I know, I know," he mumbled, ashamed that Deborah's simplicity about God sometimes irritated him.

"Besides, I'm young and strong, Mr. Gould, dear. You'll see when the baby comes—I'll be strong as a horse. A good horse at that!"

Jessie Caroline was born in 1848, and once more, Mary and Maum Larney, who had brought Grandfather along with them to Blythe Island for the big event, managed the birth easily, so that the new baby was crying with vigor by the time Horace got back with Dr. Troup.

"Some day he'll come for you and you won't bother to make the trip," Deborah smiled up at the doctor.

(223)

"The little one's as fine as a fiddle, Mrs. Gould, and so are you," Dr. Troup grunted. Then he chuckled. "I believe you make having babies easy for yourself, my dear, simply because you believe in babies."

"Oh, I do. I want dozens!"

The first night after the family had returned to St. Simons, Horace sat on the edge of the rickety bed beside Deborah and Jessie. "Honey, how did you happen to name her Jessie? I know the Caroline is for Aunt Caroline, but who do we know named Jessie?"

"It's a secret."

"Even from me?"

"Well, I think so."

"Don't you know?"

"He didn't exactly say I wasn't to tell *you*, I guess."

"Who's this mysterious 'he'?"

"Your papa."

"Papa wanted to name the baby Jessie? Why?"

"Well, when he was a young man at the North, he was terribly in love with a Scottish girl named Jessie, who broke his heart. That's why he took the surveying job in Florida, to get as far away from Jessie as possible."

"And the old fellow still remembers her enough to want his grandchild named for her?"

"Of course. Now, he has two granddaughters named for the two women he loved most—Jane and Jessie."

Horace kissed her lightly. "I swear, you know more about that man than I do. It's no wonder I'm a sentimental fool—but who would ever guess it of him? He's such a dour New Englander."

"He is not dour! He's tender and loving and kind and sentimental and romantic."

"I've always known he was kind. I should know. Now, go to sleep—you and Jessie." He kissed her again. "I love you, Deborah Gould."

"I love you, Mr. Gould, dear."

He looked at her, his face sad.

"Why do you look so sad?"

"Just wishing we could wake up to the sunlight on the

(224)

marsh margins at Black Banks. Can't you see it, Deborah? Sometimes I can close my eyes and see the Black Banks lane winding through those big trees—a good road, well-shelled, cared for, clean. Not like these muddy ditches we call roads over here. I can hear the marsh hens fussing at the sun for rousing them, see the old pileated woodpecker—the real cock of the woods—chipping off whole shingles from the pine out back by the peafield. I wonder if the same rambunctious mocker is staking out his breeding ground yet? Remember how he used to chase that poor flicker for no reason at all?"

"My dear," she whispered, pushing back a loose lock of hair from his forehead. "We have marsh hens and a river and sunrises and pileated woodpeckers and mocking birds and flickers here, too."

He hung his head.

"Don't be sad, dear husband. I can bear anything—anything at all if you're not sad."

"But we can't live here in this shell of a house forever!"

"We won't. I've talked to God and He's already working out His answer. You've cleared a little money this year—almost five hundred dollars. We'll go back to St. Simons some day."

"Where on St. Simons—how?" It still irritated him that she spoke to God as though He had time to bother about which house a family lived in. "Where could we possibly go?"

"I don't know, but we'll go. We're young yet. There's time."

"*You're* young—I'm thirty-five."

"And sleepy and getting cross. Good night."

About midsummer Horace raced into the old Blythe Island kitchen and whirled Deborah off her feet, shouting, "Good news! A letter from Mary with the best news in the world!"

She hugged his neck. "Well, read it to me!"

"Sit down, now—sit down, and listen. 'Dear Horace, I am too excited to bother with preliminaries. Mrs. Wylly

(225)

was just here with a marvelous proposition. The overseer she hired when John died has been cheating her and she let him go. Now she wants you to come back to St. Simons and take full charge of her plantation at The Village on a profit-sharing basis! You and Deborah and the children would have to live in the Wylly house with the old lady and her spinster daughters, but you would have the top floor all to yourselves. Papa told her I'd write to you at once, and now please hurry with your reply. This won't be like having you at Black Banks, quite, but it will certainly be second best. We are all waiting with bated breath. Hurry. Your affectionate sister, Mary.' Well, Deborah?"

Her eyes were shining. "You see? God kept His promise!"

"Can you bear living in the same house with the Wylly women?"

"You'll be there, won't you?"

He took her in his arms. "I don't deserve you. Certainly you don't deserve to be jerked around from pillar to post as I've done all our married life."

Deborah wriggled loose from his arms, ran across the kitchen to his planter's desk, took a quill from the glass of buckshot, opened the ink well, and pulled out the desk stool. "What are you waiting for, Mr. Gould, dear?"

36

Deborah was not entirely sure Mrs. Wylly or Margaret Matilda Wylly approved of her making new curtains for the third-floor living quarters at The Village, but gay, dotty Miss Heriot Wylly pulled herself up the three flights on her rheumatic old legs almost every day to see what new "fancy" Deborah had concocted.

"I declare, young lady, I never thought I'd see this

attic looking this way again." Miss Heriot gazed around the sloping rooms, some parts of which were so low that Horace bumped his head when he forgot to stoop. "We slept up here when we were children, you know. My little bed was right there in that corner by the window, where your Jessie sleeps. Oh, we had some happy, noisy times here in the attic, all right." She winked and nudged Deborah's arm. "I suppose you and that handsome husband of yours have some good times up here, too, eh?"

"Oh, yes, Mr. Gould can be very gay and playful, even when he's so tired, as he always seems to be these days."

Miss Heriot squinted at her. "Is Mama working him too hard, do you think?"

"He's just a very fine planter and can't bear to see land go to waste, Miss Heriot. Is your mother happy with us?"

"Happy as Mama can be. I swear to you, child, I haven't seen my mother smile but once since old Hazzard murdered my brother—in cold blood. In cold blood. Then went free as a bird and got himself a wife the very next year!"

"Uh, Miss Heriot, we were talking about whether or not your mother is satisfied with the job Mr. Gould is doing for her."

"Oh," she snapped her fingers. "Oh, yes, Mr. Gould. Isn't he a handsome, broad-shouldered, stately gentleman? Do you reckon he's as tall as Mr. John Couper was?"

Deborah smiled. "Not quite."

"Poor Mr. Couper. Had to leave St. Simons Island and go to die with his son on the mainland. But now, there was a man who knew how to keep his spirits up and in the face of all the tragedy he had to bear. A son and a daughter dead—poor Mrs. Couper gone. Never forget what he said at church the Sunday after they buried his daughter, Isabel—and you know, they buried her the same day the poor man had to sell sixty of his dear nigras! He loved his darkies, too, believe me. So, on this Sunday, his old heart was really heavy. He was standing there by his oak tree—that was before your husband's father became Frederica postmaster. I can see him yet, his fine-looking thatch of gray hair blowing in the breeze—did you know he was redheaded once?"

"No, I didn't. But what did Mr. Couper say that day, Miss Heriot?"

"Well, I can see him yet leaning against that big old tree. 'Miss Heriot,' he said, 'I'm just like poor Job. All my troubles have come down on me at once. But as the Lord has promised to provide for His lambs, I dare to hope He will do a little something for this old fleeced ram!' "

They both laughed, and Deborah said she hoped Miss Heriot's mother could learn to laugh again some day.

"Too late for that, my dear. Nobody laughs around this house any more but you and me. Do you notice that?"

"Mr. Gould laughs."

"Not much. Not any more. I'm not one bit worried about whether Mama is satisfied with your husband."

"You're not?"

"What good would it do? There's no one else who'd come. What I do worry about is whether or not your husband will see fit to stay with us till Mama passes. When she goes, I guess we'll sell. But right now, we're the beggars, not you folks."

Horace met Jim at the fork where The Village Road joined Couper Road. Neither man shouted a greeting.

"Where you headed, Jim?"

His brother's voice was taut, brittle. "I've got to talk to you, Horace—about me."

"All right. Can we sit our horses and talk here?"

"Might as well."

Horace waited for Jim to begin. If Jim had something to say, he wanted it to be what Jim wanted to say, with no urging from him.

"I want you to—come home."

"Home?"

"Back to Black Banks. It's—more your home than it is mine."

Horace's heart began to pound.

"Please, brother—please come back!"

"Papa says you had a good crop this year, Jim. Almost broke even. That's good for these times. You don't need me. Why pay me when you can make it all yourself?"

"Because I want people in the house!" Jim shouted. "I want your little girls to—to listen to. I wanta eat at the table with somebody I know! My God, I can't start dining with the niggers!"

Horace tried to remember this broken, embittered man as he used to be—adroit, attractively arrogant. He was still arrogant most of the time, but it was the empty, helpless arrogance of a defeated man who lashed out at everyone—especially the Negroes—to force attention to himself.

"I'll have to talk it over with Deborah, Jim," Horace said flatly.

"Naw, you don't! That little doll will do anything you tell her to do."

"I don't *tell* her to do anything."

"All right, all right, I know you're noble." He smiled crookedly. "I didn't mean that, brother. I just think Deborah will want to come—if you do. I can't imagine a wife like that, but somehow you managed to find one. Will you at least ask her? And—tell her I'm—so devilish lonesome rattling around in that big house, I—don't trust what I might—do, if you don't come back."

Without waiting for an answer, Jim spurred his horse and headed home.

"Would you go on supervising Mrs. Wylly's fields if we moved back to Black Banks?" Deborah asked when Horace told her. "She's depending on you."

He got up from his chair in front of the fireplace in the Wylly attic. "You know I would. She'd be bankrupt if I left."

"Then let's go right away!"

(229)

He looked down at her sitting with her feet tucked up in the chair. "You didn't hesitate, did you?"

"No."

"But Deborah, can we make the kind of home we want our children to have with—a man like Jim around?"

"We can try. And some day, beloved, your brother may decide to sell us Black Banks."

"Ha! For what?"

"For money. We wouldn't need too much for a good down payment. Don't forget we now have over eight hundred."

He smiled. "Where do you get that spunk, Mrs. Gould?"

"All the Irish have spunk."

"You know how Jim feels about selling Black Banks. Don't even hope for that."

"Well, I won't—not out loud anyway. But I've already told God I'm hoping and I can't take it back from Him. We'll move back, won't we?"

He sat down again. "Yes. I think I could manage it by September. I guess it's better after all, to have even a little bit of Black Banks than it would be to own all of any other place in the world."

"I'd like for our third child to be born at Black Banks," Deborah said. He looked so surprised that she laughed at him. "Did you think I was just getting fat, Mr. Gould, dear?"

Lizzie didn't wait for the move to Black Banks. Their third child was born in August, the month before they left The Village, and when Horace drove the buggy to Orange Grove to bring Aunt Abbott, he found her lying in the front yard beside her camellia bush.

She was dead.

37

Deborah made no effort to hide her grief. Neither did she permit it to interfere with their plans. Mary Abbott had trained her well. "When sorrow strikes, it's the natural thing to cry," her aunt had often said, and Deborah's weeping was like summer showers—sudden and frequent and brief. Always she smiled as she blew her nose and dried her eyes, and the days went on cheerfully. They were moving back to Black Banks, and she knew the last thing Aunt Abbott would want to do would be to interrupt that happiness. Sometimes she cried as she bathed the children, but her attention never strayed, and the little girls were not afraid of her tears. "They will know grief some day, too," she told Horace. "Children need to be taught that sorrow is part of life."

Deborah's return brought joy back to Black Banks, and Adam and Ca sang again as they worked. Down at the quarters the people talked among themselves of the possibility that with Master Horace back, they might ask for a barbecue and Jubilee at the end of the picking season. "It's lak' we's all been 'surrected from de dead, Miss Debbie," Ca declared. "Dat Mausa Jim, he hate singin', he hate laughin' an jokin'—he hate livin'! Ah wish you an' Mausa Horace would ax' me to do somepin' hard, 'cause dey ain' no other way to say thank you fo' comin' back."

"It ain' right, M-Mausa Horace," Adam said one morning as they were saddling Major for Horace's ride to the Wylly fields. "It ain' r-right, sir, fo' you to ride off to dat other lan'. Jis' lak it don' seem right fo' you not to be ridin' ole Dolly no mo'. M-Mausa Jim ain' doin' r-right b-by our place!"

"That's no concern of mine, Adam. Miss Debbie and the children and I only live at Black Banks."

"Y-Yes, sir."

"I've noticed something, Adam," Horace said. "Look at me. You've started to stammer when you talk. When did that begin?"

Adam grinned sheepishly. "Ah-ah-ah don' know, M-Mausa Horace."

"You didn't stammer before I left. Are you sure you don't know why you're doing it now?"

"Yes, sir."

"Nothing wrong you want to tell me about?"

A deep frown creased Adam's high forehead as he glanced at Horace and quickly away. "W-well, jis' a little, Mausa Horace."

"Something's 'just a little' wrong? Enough to give you a nervous habit like stammering?"

Adam picked up a magnolia leaf and began to fold it into squares.

"Adam! You've always been high-strung—you never could stand still for long, but you're worse than ever. What's wrong?"

He was tearing the folded leaf into ragged pieces.

"Look at me, Adam. Are you ready to get yourself a wife?"

The slender Negro moved a step toward Horace. "Oh, Mausa Horace, you a g-good m-man— you a *good man*!"

"Who is it, Adam? Who's the woman you want? Won't she have you?"

"Yes, sir, yes, sir, sh-she wanta' m-marry up wif me, b-b-but—"

"But what?"

"M-Mausa J-Jim, sir." He hung his head.

"That makes no sense at all. Jim would be glad for you to marry and have children. You'd increase your value to him. Why do you say my brother disapproves?"

"It—it be M-Mina, Mausa Horace. De K-Kings' Mina."

That was different. Adam was the most dependable Black Banks man, and of course, had been sent on errands many times to King's Retreat. Somehow he had managed to get to know Mina, one of Mrs. King's best girls.

"We's walked along together fo' time, Mausa Horace—fo' time!" Adam's face lit up remembering. "I ax' her d-did she lak' to t-talk to me, an' she say she sho' do lak' it." His expression darkened, and he twisted his thin hands together. "M-Mausa Jim, he say to f'git Mina an' git me a G-Goul' woman." His eyes filled with tears. "M-Mina be de onliest one ah wants, Mausa Horace."

It was not unheard of for Negroes from different plantations to marry, but it was inconvenient—risky, some owners believed. Jim would think so. Wouldn't like Adam wanting time off to go to Retreat. There was only so much Horace could say to Adam, and he choked back his resentment against his brother and all slave owners like him: good enough to their people, by their own standards, by their own feeling of superiority to the blacks. They fed them well, housed them adequately, clothed them warmly in order to keep them strong and able-bodied. Now and then a reward of a piece of bright ribbon for the women or some tobacco for the men. But when a Negro fell in love, it was funny—something to make small jokes about—but not to take seriously.

"Ah wish you own me, M-Mausa Horace," Adam whispered miserably. "Ah sho' w-wish you own m-me."

"Well, I don't." Horace snapped. "I don't want to own anybody!"

Before he might say something he'd regret, he swung into the saddle and rode off toward The Village for his day's work in Mrs. Wylly's fields.

During all the hot, labor-filled summer months of the year 1851, Horace felt himself growing more anxious over Adam, more restless over his own half-complete life, more uneasy over Jim's worsening disposition. The scorching heat that pressed down upon them all began to lessen as October gave way to November, but the heat of his own inner turmoil increased. Jim had begun to drink—not heavily—but enough to make him still more indifferent, less interested in the Black Banks crops. If there was to be a good crop next year, Horace knew he would somehow have to plant it, and the Wylly fields as well.

On a chilly afternoon in late February, he saw Captain Charles Stevens galloping down the Black Banks road, and ran out eagerly to greet his friend.

"Welcome, stranger," he called as the Captain, sporting a fringe of beard on his wide jaw, dismounted and came toward him, his big hand out. "You're looking mighty dignified and prosperous, Captain, in those new chin whiskers."

"Well, Gould, I figure it this way—when a man is about to add still another boat to his line, he needs to look the part. Miss Sarah hates the beard. Vows it tickles. But see? Not a sign of a mustache—just a little decoration on my stubborn chin."

Horace laughed. "What brings you here at this hour, Captain? Won't you come in?"

"No—no time for a visit." He was fishing in his inside jacket pocket. "I brought this letter for Miss Deborah—from England. I thought it might be important."

Horace examined the letter. "Bradford and Bradford, Ltd., Whitehaven, Cumberland County, England," he read. "Hm. Have no idea what it could be. Well, my wife's busy cutting out dresses for some of the people now, anyway. Change your mind, and come on in."

"I wish I could, friend, but I left a ruckus at home. Is it sinful to pray an old black woman will die soon? If my old Grace lives much longer, it can be the death of me."

"Is Grace still scaring your children?"

"Threatening to eat them now! Swears she used to eat little children back in Africa—liked them better than peanuts, she says. Insists white babies' meat would taste far sweeter. I think the hag is harmless—just old in the head. But she frightens my wife, and the children were screaming when I left." He swung onto his horse. "Just thought the letter might be too urgent to wait for Sunday, when your father collects the mail."

"You're a good neighbor," Horace said warmly.

"Things all right for you, Gould? Still hacking away at that Wylly land?"

"Still hacking away. Mrs. Wylly is very ill this week. The daughters will have to let the land go when she dies. I think they'll leave the Island. The two of them put together don't have as much get-up-and-go as the old lady."

"What happens to you when she's gone, Gould?"

"I don't know. Haven't the slightest idea."

"Oh, that's sad," Deborah said, as she scanned the legal looking document from England. "My uncle, Captain Robert Dunn, is dead."

"I'm sorry, my dear," Horace said.

"Well, I didn't know him at all, but he wanted to adopt me when my father died. Dear Aunt Abbott wouldn't hear of it, thank heaven—or I wouldn't be your wife. But he must have been a kind gentleman." She handed the letter to Horace. "Read it, Mr. Gould, dear, and explain it to me. It sounds dreadfully legal."

Horace scanned the letter, frowning.

"What is it, dear?" she asked. "Is it something bad?"

"Your uncle has left you a thousand pounds."

For a moment, she just stared at him. "A—thousand—pounds? Why, Mr. Gould, dear, we're rich!" He was still frowning. "What's the matter? Don't you like it that we're suddenly rich?"

"Oh, I like money all right—but not this way. It's my place to support you."

"But this is a love gift from a dear old man who meant well. We can—oh, my husband, we can make your brother an offer now—we have almost two thousand dollars! Do you realize God has given us almost two thousand dollars?"

"Supper on de table, Miss Debbie," Ca said from the doorway. "Soon as ah call Mausa Jim, ah takes up de johnnycake."

"Thank you, Ca. We'll be right there."

"I'm not hungry," Horace said.

(235)

"You will be—johnnycake. Your favorite. Oh, Mr. Gould, dear, let's talk to Mr. Jim right now!"

"No! No, Deborah. I'm not going to give him a chance to turn me down. Not a word at dinner about the money, do you understand?"

"Yes, sir. I understand. No, I don't either, but I promise not to say a word."

As soon as Jim sauntered into the dining room, Horace knew they were in trouble. His brother was dressed in his best cutaway coat—at least twelve years old, frayed, wrinkled, too loose across his shrunken shoulders. The gray waistcoat had a button missing. He had been drinking again, and he needed a shave, but his hair, stiff with Macassar oil, was slicked down on each side of a crooked part.

"Well, good evening, love birds." He bowed, then sat down ceremoniously, whisked open his napkin and looked from Horace to Deborah, a patronizing smile on his face.

"Good evening, Mr. Jim," Deborah said carefully. "I hope you're hungry. Mr. Gould says he isn't, but I think he will be. Ca has made johnnycake."

"Oh, then 'Mr. Gould' will regain his appetite, I have no doubt."

Horace tried to be pleasant. "How did things go today, brother?"

"Well, Mausa Goul'," he drawled, "de ole darkies, dey work fine in de fiel's today, suh."

Jim leaned back in his chair, a pathetic shadow of the old Jim who used to make everyone laugh when he imitated the Negroes. Everyone but Horace. Even as a small boy, he had felt uneasy when Jim put on his "darky act." Tonight, Horace wanted to hit him.

"Dey all chop an' chop wif deir hoes, an' dey all sing de ole songs lak' good, cheerful niggahs ought fo' to do."

Ca came in from the kitchen, carrying the johnnycake.

"Didn't you, Ca? Didn't all you faithful ole niggahs sing yo' cheerful songs all day an' beat yo' johnnycake an' chop yo' cotton?" Jim grabbed at Ca's long skirt, but missed.

Horace stood up.

"Sit back down, dear," Deborah whispered.

"No, Miss Deborah—let my brother stand. I want to look on him a moment. Doesn't he present a striking picture of the kindly, benevolent, aristocratic Southern planter? Look at him. My industrious, conscientious, *sponging* brother!"

Horace moved toward him.

"Brother!" Jim was almost shouting. "Brother—why don't you ask the old man if he'll buy Black Banks for you? You're never going to own your own land any other way.

Deborah got up quickly and took Horace's arm.

"You love the rotten land and I hate it. You make a profit on it and I go bankrupt. Now," Jim lowered his voice, "of course, I know you haven't made any money to buy it yourself. You're such a great-hearted, generous, Christian gentleman, you only want to work and slave for others. Very admirable, but not very practical. So, maybe the old man could be persuaded to dole out again and then you could be the Mausa an' de Missus ob deah ole Black Banks."

Jim's drunk, Horace told himself. My brother is bitter and lonely and defeated and—drunk. Keep still. Keep still.

"Or maybe you prefer to work for three old ladies who keep you built up with flattery! I don't know what I'd give for one little word of flattery. Maybe I'd give you Black Banks, brother mine, if you'd offer me just one word of flattery."

Horace's anger drained away faster than it had built up—so fast, he sat down weakly, Deborah beside him. "I'm not interested in having Papa buy anything for me, Jim. Will you let the subject drop?"

"Glad to. I was just having a little fun anyway. Papa couldn't buy this place. He didn't have any better year than I had. His *productive* son was off the old home place—working for three female fools."

Deborah sat with Horace before the fire in their bedroom until very late that night. Neither of them mentioned

Jim's outburst. She read to him for a while from her favorite poems by John Donne, hoping to quiet him, remembering Aunt Abbott's warning always to wait for a man until his balance returned or his anger cooled. Jim could push even a saint too far, she supposed, and her beloved was no saint. She had put him into God's hands, and he would be all right sooner or later. Even Jim could not push God too far.

"Do you want me to read a short poem about God?" she asked.

"No," he answered sharply. "I mean, not tonight, Deborah. I've got enough on my mind. I'll leave God to you for the present."

"Oh, but you can't do that."

"Why not?"

"Because He's everybody's God. Yours as much as mine."

Horace smiled wearily. "Maybe."

"Not maybe!"

"Well, all right—not maybe. But you do the praying, Miss Debbie, and I'll do the worrying."

"But we're one, Mr. Gould, dear, and praying and worrying don't go together. To *worry* when God said he was mindful when even one little brown sparrow falls to the ground is a sin."

"Then you have a sinful husband." He yawned. "And a tired one. I've got a big day tomorrow at The Village."

"The thousand pounds belongs to you, Mr. Gould, dear."

"I just want to go to bed now, Deborah, and not say any more about anything."

As soon as Mary learned about Deborah's inheritance, she rode to The Village and searched until she found Horace.

He helped her from Peter's aging back, kissed her lightly, and asked, "How in blazes did you know about the money?"

"Larney caught herself listening on the grapevine."

"Do you think they know what we dream at night, too? I'm glad you're here, though. I need you."

"Make Jim an offer for Black Banks right away!"

He jerked off a twig of scrub oak at the edge of the plowed field. "Forget it, sister."

"But Mrs. Wylly's not going to live long, Horace—she's past eighty and her kidneys are failing. That means she'll die any day. Then what will you do?"

"I don't know."

"Of course, if you'd let us, Papa and I would be paying you right now for all you still do for us at New St. Clair."

"I'm not interested in charity, even from you, and Papa."

She was silent for so long, she forced him to look at her. Her eyes were full of both love and challenge. "Horace, Horace, why are you against becoming a man?"

"I'm against not becoming my *own* man!"

"You think you are, but you're not. There's no reason on earth why you shouldn't make Jim an offer now that you have that money."

"I will not give him a chance to turn me down! Nothing would please him more."

"Brother, listen to me. Don't say one word until I'm finished. Deborah wants lots of children. There's another one on the way right now. She's the kind of woman who should have them. But are they going to grow up never remembering one home as being theirs? Which is more important—your silly pride or your children growing up with the security of knowing their roots are down in a special place that will always be home to them? Which, Horace? Which is important?"

He didn't answer, but he realized that somewhere a high gate, locked until this moment, began slowly to swing open. Somehow he must slam it shut. Was he going to live out the years of his life permitting his sister to push him toward every important decision?

"You have everything in the world to be thankful for, brother. Do you thank God every day for a wife like

Deborah? I'll bet you don't, or you'd be considering her now instead of yourself. You are even being given a chance to buy your own place and you won't make the effort because you're stubborn and proud—and afraid! Go on and get as angry as you like, but I love you too much not to try to pound some sense into your head. Doesn't it make sense what I'm saying?"

It made such good sense he felt lost—as though what he had depended on through every day since he returned to the Island had suddenly deserted him. Slowly, he walked to a big pine stump and sat down. If Mary would only leave now—right now—so that what appeared inevitable could happen to him alone. He buried his head in his hands and closed his eyes tight, as though to postpone the moment when he would have to look at himself as he had really been—proud of his own efforts, ungrateful, hurtling down the road, determined to call it the right one—pitying himself for being on the fringe of life when all the time he had forced himself to stay there because he had insisted upon protecting himself from humiliation. He had never felt more trapped, and it both helped and frightened him that he found himself blaming Deborah. Oh, not Deborah herself, but her quiet, natural little talks with God about him! He tried to convince himself that Deborah had run to Mary in an effort to force him to do things her way. The gate swung a little wider. That was not true and he knew it. Deborah would talk to no one but her God. Had Mary been praying for him, too? What made them think he needed their prayers? Wasn't he working as hard as a man could work? Hadn't he made important strides in improving their worn-out land? Weren't other farmers and planters riding to him for advice on crop rotation, seed selection, soil erosion? Hadn't he done better with the few acres of Wylly land this year than Jim had done with all of Black Banks? Wasn't the worn-out Blythe Island tract more productive because he had worked it?

He didn't look up when Mary rode away. "Why should I swallow my pride and ask Jim to sell?" He spoke aloud, but it was a mere complaint, he knew, not a rational question.

A wide-winged shadow darkened the thicket of cassina and water oak beside him, soared swiftly out over the greening cotton field and vanished somewhere in the woods. Horace stood up.

Was it weak for a man to pray? To ask for help when he couldn't help himself? Who would know if he tried? God would know, of course, and as he realized he didn't mind God's knowing about his weakness, his stubborn pride—a kindness settled around him, closing him protectingly into the bright silence. A light breeze moved the slender oaks in the little thicket and touched his face. A lone crow, separated from its flock, cried, off toward the river.

"God?" His voice was tentative, unfamiliar. "God?" His eyes were open, looking into the thicket. "I need help," he said simply, and waited.

In a moment, he caught a flash of color—red, green, blue—in the nearest sapling oak, as a nonpareil perched on a twig and sat motionless, a spot of brilliance—alive, but useless except for the beauty of its color and the music of its silvery song. If God cared enough to create that tiny bird only for its beauty, maybe He *was* interested in a man's living in a house he could enjoy, could love as he loved Black Banks. Nonpareils have a habit of sitting still for long periods of time, he knew, but this one stayed longer than any he had ever noticed before, and he kept his eyes on it, his heart opening steadily toward whatever whim of creation had brought the little bird into being.

When at last the flash of color was gone, he walked deliberately to his horse, pulled himself into the saddle and rode, not to the Wyllys, as he had planned, but home to Black Banks to find Jim.

A week later, in a quiet, unemotional, strictly business transaction, Jim sold him all of Black Banks, including the big house and the Negroes, for twenty-two hundred dollars.

"This down payment will be more than I'll need to get started in Texas," Jim said, signing the deed over to Horace, with a relieved flourish, reminiscent of the old Jim. "It's been so simple. I wonder why we waited so long, brother."

"It was my fault," Horace said. He wanted to run to Deborah, but Jim was important now. "What will you be doing in Texas, Jim, do you know yet?"

"I have no idea, but it's a new country. A man can start over there maybe. Who knows? I might try cotton again. Might even be fool enough to get married again, too."

"You—you're divorced from Alice?"

"Over three years ago. Didn't see any reason to shock the populace on St. Simons. But I'm telling you, just in case I'm idiot enough to try again. Wouldn't want you to think your lovable brother a bigamist." He held out his hand. "Good luck, Horace. I like you when I'm sober. Sorry I had that brief bout with John Barleycorn. It doesn't help."

Horace took his hand. "Good luck to you, too, Jim. I'm sorry you're not staying till the new baby comes."

"I'm afraid to. This one might be a boy. I couldn't take that."

"Are you sure you're doing the right thing to leave without saying good-by to anyone else?"

"They all know my trunk went yesterday; why prolong the agony? I know it seems a rotten thing to do, but I'm not up to a final goodby. Especially with Papa ailing. This one will be final."

"Then I guess you'd better ride on out. Deborah's due back from Rosemount any time. Mary might come with her."

"And leave Papa sick? Not our sister. You're right, though. I'm stalling."

"Want me to go out to your horse with you?"

"No."

They shook hands again, Jim picked up his carpetbag, settled his old beaver hat on his head, walked out the front door for the last time, down the wide steps and rode out of sight around the first turn in the winding Black Banks road. Horace watched from the tall window of his own house.

38

Jim's hunch had been right. The new baby was a boy, Horace Abbott Gould, and the celebration planned for the anniversary of his first month on earth was in happy preparation for days.

"Did you have a party when I was born, Mama?" six-year-old Jennie asked.

"No, we didn't, dear, but it wasn't because we weren't just as happy when you came. We didn't own our own home then and didn't have much money."

"Do we have lots of money now?"

"No. Your papa is still paying Uncle Jim for our house and land. But Papa's doing very well—better than most cotton planters—because he's such a good one. And he's just been appointed to the vestry of our church, too."

"Do you like it when I visit with you, Mama?"

"Yes, indeed. I like it as much as visiting with Papa."

"Is Papa old?"

Deborah laughed. "Not at all! He's older than I am, but forty isn't old."

"Is he as old as Grandpapa?"

"No—just half as old." She held up the pale blue voile dress with a pink ribbon sash at its high waistline. "Do you like your new dress for the party, Jennie?"

"Oh, yes! I like it because it's blue."

Her mother smiled at her. "Like your eyes and your papa's eyes."

"Who's coming to our party next week?"

"Oh, Adam rode all over the Island, inviting everyone to come and bring all their children. We're not only celebrating our new baby, we're celebrating our very own home at Black Banks, too."

Jennie hugged herself. "I don't know how I can stand to wait till next week, Mama—I'm so happy about our party, I think I might die!"

About midafternoon, Horace galloped up the Black Banks lane toward the stable in search of Adam.

"I've just come from Rosemount, Adam. You'll have to take another note around."

"Mausa James is passed—ah kin tell by yo' face, sir."

"No. Mrs. Wylly died this morning, but my father is still alive. Weak, but he's still living. There'll be no party, though—at least not for a long time, the way things look."

Adam's sensitive face wrinkled with sorrow. "Ah sho' be sorry t' hear dat, Mausa Horace. Maum Larney say we ain' gon' hab dat party a tall."

"Yes, I know she's been prophesying doom for days." Horace took a note from his pocket.

"Maum Larney be the seb'nth daughter to a seb'nth daughter."

"I know, I know. Here's the note. Take it around as fast as you can. There'll be a full moon tonight. Don't worry if you don't get back before dark. I trust you."

"Yes, sir. Ah knows dat."

Horace started for the house, then turned back. "Don't lose any time at the other places, but you might want to stay a few minutes at the Kings'."

The two men smiled at each other.

"Be careful of the new overseer, Adam. Mrs. King's at the North. You can tell Mina if you can get a chance to talk to her that you two can be married as soon as we get Mrs. King's permission when she comes back. I haven't forgotten my promise."

Larney was right. There was no party to celebrate the birth of their first son or the purchase of Black Banks. James Gould grew steadily weaker through the hot summer months, and on September 3, just as the sky began to clear after a brief afternoon thunderstorm, Mary and Horace stood by the big mahogany bed and watched their father give up his long struggle to stay with them. Mary shook his thin shoulder gently—once, twice—then tucked the coverlet up around the wrinkled old throat. She stood erect, her eyes dry, and said to Horace, making it a fact they could now accept: "Papa's gone."

Together, they walked to the window and looked out onto the fresh, washed world around Rosemount. Rain still dripped from the big oaks and from Mary's oleander hedge below. The sun was setting, polished gold clouds trailing it toward its resting place for the night. A ray caught a drop of water on the tip of a palmetto frond, and for an instant the light was fractured on the surface of that single drop into all the colors of a rainbow. Mary pointed to it and Horace nodded.

"Papa left everything to me," Mary said.

"No one deserves it but you."

"Everything but July—he left July to you, brother."

Horace winced. He didn't want to own his friend. But knowing Mary would never understand, he put it aside to think through later. Nothing must come between them now.

He put his arm around her shoulders and felt strength flow into him, and after a long time, when the sun was just a thin red arc over the cotton field to the west, Mary turned to him—still erect—and just before she burst into tears, she smiled.

PART FIVE

39

Winter almost missed coming to St. Simons Island in the year 1854 and, as usual when the weather smiled, the Islanders were confident of good crops. Like two brothers, Horace and Mary supervised the work at both New St. Clair and Black Banks. Larney's John, in spite of his advancing years, rode proudly as the head driver of both plantations, still commanding the respect from the field hands that Larney commanded inside Rosemount.

"How old do you think you are, Papa John?" Horace asked July's tall, gray-haired father one day as they rode together.

"Ah be gittin' on, Mausa Horace," John chuckled. "Look lak ah might be some older'n Larney, an' she 'bout as ole as de Black Banks riber."

John would never know Horace had asked his age because he felt so strongly that both John and Larney should be freed while they were still able to enjoy freedom. But they were not his to free. Mary loved Larney and John as much as he loved them, but she would see no point in changing things. The faithful couple would be looked after as long as they lived. To free them would seem like utter nonsense to his sister. July *was* his, and although his old friend had refused point blank when he offered freedom soon after James Gould died, the conflict in Horace had become so unbearable that he knew he had to try again.

The right time came the day that he and July went alone into the woods behind the Black Banks stable to bury Dolly. Adam had helped them hitch a team to drag the body of the beloved horse to the spot Horace had chosen to be her final resting place, then left the two friends alone. They dug the big hole in silence, and with ropes securing the once lively mare, July led the team while they eased her into the ground.

When the mound of dirt was in place, they laid down their shovels and turned their back to the grave. Finally July said, "You want ah should leave, Mausa Horace?"

"No, July. Let's sit down here with Dolly a while and talk."

"Yes, sir."

They sat on the carpet of oak leaves, Horace leaning his head against a big tree. "She was our best friend, wasn't she, July?"

"She sho' be a fine 'un, sir."

"Makes me wish I never had to ride another horse."

"Yes, sir. Make me wish ah neber had to take care of another 'un. Dolly lib a long time—thirty-two year!"

There were tears on both their faces. Neither man tried to hide them.

"July?"

"Yes, sir?"

"There's only one thing you can do to help me today."

"Mausa Horace, you knows ah'll do anything you say."

"I can't go on the way we are much longer. I manage with the others, but owning you is doing something bad to me inside."

July looked at him and then at the ground.

"I'm not doing it for you any more than for myself, July, but I've got to give you your freedom. Maybe it's more for me than for you. Don't refuse me again."

"Would—would ah hab to leave, Mausa Horace?"

Horace looked at him, surprised. "Is that why you turned me down before? No! I would hope and pray you'd stay with me. If I ever needed you, I need you now. I can't pay you much, but I would pay you something. If you're free, and still choose to stay, don't you see how much more it will mean to us both? You'll be staying only because this is where you want to be."

"Kin—kin we not tell nobody, Sir? Not my mama or papa? Not nobody? Kin it be a secret wif you an' me?"

Horace thought a minute. "Of course, if that's what you want. How about it?"

"Effen it's what you wants to do dat bad, yes, sir—dat's de way ah wants it."

They shook hands, still sitting on the ground.

"I promise on, my word of honor, no one on St. Simons will ever know but the two of us."

When Horace stood up, July jumped to his feet, too, and brushed the leaves off Horace's trousers and jacket. "Ah thanks ya', sir, fo' dat promise."

The two men looked behind them at the long mound of freshly dug sandy soil. "Makes walking away from old Doll a little easier for me," Horace said. "You always took such good care of her, July."

"Ah wish ah still could, sir."

"So do I." He put both his hands on his friend's stocky shoulders and looked him full in the face. "Thank you for all those years, July. And—maybe I thank you even more for all the years we have ahead."

40

Adam and Mina had chosen to be married according to the custom of their African ancestors. Smiling and holding hands, while the other Gould people stood in a circle singing and clapping, they had jumped together over a broom laid on the ground in the Black Banks front yard and so became man and wife. Every Friday since their wedding, Horace had driven with Adam to King's Retreat, then home alone. They had missed only one weekend, and that was this year, 1854, when Deborah gave birth to their fifth child, Mary Frances. Each Monday morning at dawn, Horace would drive back to Retreat to bring Adam home for his week's work at Black Banks. Why he had chosen to make the ten-mile trip, he knew Mary would never understand. Adam could be trusted with a horse, and he rode well. It was a waste of time for Horace. Still, he went. He joked with Mary and Adam about how he "served his own servant," but in his heart he knew he made the long trip every week to help himself.

"I think my heart is as heavy as yours on Monday morning when I come to bring you back, Adam."

Adam glanced at him out of the corner of his eye as he drove the buggy briskly away from Retreat, down through Anna Matilda King's avenue of oaks late in November. "Ah thanks ya', sir," he said hoarsely.

"Well, don't thank me! It's dead wrong for a man and his wife to be separated all week."

Adam didn't answer.

"I tried to buy Mina again last week when Mr. King came home from San Francisco. They can't get along without her."

"No, sir. Dey wouldn't do so good wifout 'er."

"But what about you?"

"You so good to me, Mausa Horace, ah git along. Might be ah couldn't see Mina a tall. But ah does, 'cause ob you."

They rode in silence for a few minutes, then Horace said, "I wish sometimes you'd tell me what you really think down inside when you're alone at night in your cabin missing Mina. Why is it your people can't tell us anything important, Adam? Is it because my skin is white and yours is black?"

Adam said nothing.

"I know that isn't it. I should keep my mouth shut."

"Yes, sir."

"Adam? Would it help if I gave you your freedom?"

The Negro stiffened momentarily, "Freedom," he breathed. "Freedom!"

Horace waited for Adam to speak again. Finally, he said, "Won' do no good fo' me to be free, sir. Mina ain'."

"But the Kings would be glad to have you work for them. You might have to work for nothing, but if I freed you—you could offer your services there. They're nice folk. They'd feed and clothe you."

For a long time there was no sound but the rattle and

squeak of the buggy and a blackbird's broken whistle repeating itself. Then Adam was crying, his slender calloused fingers gripping the reins so hard that the wide fingernails turned white.

"You've stopped stammering since you and Mina got married," Horace said, trying to pretend he didn't notice the muffled sobs. "I'll bet you'd lose your nervousness altogether if you never had to leave her like this. I'm offering you your freedom."

Horace could feel him trying to form words—words that could be spoken to the white man who owned him. "Do you want to think it over for a few days, Adam?"

Adam snuffed two or three times, coughed, sat up very straight, and said, "I done think, Mausa Horace. An' what ah thinks is what right does ah hab to—to freedom more'n Ca or July—or Maum Larney or Papa John or Matty—or any ob dem no-good fiel' niggahs? S'cuse me, sir, but you cain't free 'em all."

Horace remembered his promise to July. People would have to know about Adam. He would leave Black Banks to live at Retreat with Mina.

"Do you pray much, Adam?"

"Some days mos' all de time."

"I know you go up to Christ Church when we take the other people every Sunday afternoon, but do you talk to God during the week?"

Adam smiled slightly. "Dey ain' no other way t' lib wif things, sir."

Horace had never thought of praying about his own guilt—the guilt he had carried, unconfessed except to himself, through the years he had owned the Black Banks people. What would be the use to pray? Would God ever change the hated system that caused his guilt? Would God suddenly supply him with the money to free his people and begin to pay them? Only a few would stay, even for a small salary and food and shelter, he supposed, and then he would be bankrupt without their strong arms and their strong backs. Would God change the minds of his slave-owning neighbors so they would not ostracize him and his family? Even God couldn't rid a man of his guilt as long as the cause of that guilt was as much a part of his daily life as eating his meals and feeding his children and loving his wife. What good would it do to pray about a hideous, necessary, immovable guilt like his? He would have to go on living with the system. If Adam could, he could, too.

They rode the rest of the way to Black Banks in silence, but when they reached the stable, he thanked Adam. It helped that for once, his slave did not ask him why. They simply shook hands and on some ancient, near-primitive level, they shared a moment's equality.

41

What looked to be an all-night December rain was falling, and Horace sat reading before the Black Banks fire, while Deborah embroidered. She had grown even more beautiful with the passing of the years, and tonight she looked especially lovely in a yellow dress, with a matching ribbon in her thick, dark hair. She's being very quiet, he thought—a little too quiet and a little too prim. "You're thoughtful, Deborah. Are they private thoughts not for the ears of a husband who's tired of his Farmer's Almanac?"

Her gray eyes twinkled; she shifted her embroidery hoop, nonchalantly tossing to one side the long bolster slip on which she was working and sat up a little straighter, but said nothing.

"Miss Debbie, there's something afoot."

"Do you like the new slip I'm making? See? It has birds and what I call an Island tree. I'll have to move my hoop maybe a dozen times before I cover the whole design. I drew it myself and it goes all down the length of the bolster slip. Do you think it's beautiful, Mr. Gould, dear?"

"Indeed, yes," he smiled. "But won't all that needle-work scratch when one tries to sleep on it?"

"Oh, no one will sleep on it! It's for our guest room, for special occasions. Ca's Nancy will take it off each night before our guest goes to sleep and put on a plain linen slip."

"Guest, did you say?"

She put down her work. "Guest! My cousin Anna Evans, who lives in Canada and is just about my age—twenty-four or twenty-five—has written that she is very eager to see our Island, and I've written right back to her mother, my Aunt Elizabeth, inviting Cousin Anna to come down for a nice, long visit."

"Splendid," he said, propping his feet on the hassock, ready for a conversation. "When will she arrive?"

"Oh, Canada is a very long way off, so I don't think she'll be here for Christmas. Probably for New Year's—in time for my birthday, I hope. You'll like her, I'm sure. I expect to. She's a fine figure-skater, Aunt Elizabeth tells me, and is now through school and quite well-educated enough to teach."

"I don't think she'll find figure-skating too easy down here, but neither do I think the poor girl is going to be permitted just a—pleasant visit, so perhaps our lack of ice won't matter."

"Why, Mr. Gould, whatever do you mean?"

"A fine spirited young lady, eager for a visit to our Island, well-educated—ready to begin teaching? I hope you told her we'd pay her travel expenses, my dear."

Seeing her surprised embarrassment, he burst out laughing. "Let me enjoy myself, little Debbie. It isn't often I catch on to one of your schemes. Do you think that fancy new bolster cover will cause Cousin Anna to like us well enough to stay indefinitely—and tutor our children?"

She was laughing too. "Why, Mr. Gould, dear—you've just had a marvelous idea!"

Deborah wanted Anna's meeting with the children to be timed just right, and so they were not permitted to meet her boat. "After all," Deborah reminded Horace, as they rode toward Frederica early in January, "Cousin Anna is used to life in a city. We'll have to break her into our rural ways gently, carefully. And I'm glad she didn't get here for my birthday, do you know why?"

"No, why?"

"This way I can meet her in my beautiful new Pilgrim cloak you gave me." She snuggled closer to him on the buggy seat. "Am I pretty enough in it to please you?"

He slipped his arm around her straight shoulders. "You are even more beautiful than I expected you to be. You like the Scotch-plaid colors? I ordered it from a catalogue."

"All the way from Philadelphia! I love the colors—dark blue—black"; she traced the plaid with her gloved finger, "light and dark blue, a thin line of yellow—and that's magnolia-leaf green, I've decided. You know," she chattered on excitedly, "I want to make a nice impression on Cousin Anna. We've no choice but to make her love us all so much she just can't bear to leave!"

He chuckled.

"I'm serious. If she's in love with our Island, staying will be what makes her happy—and where else could we get such a splendid tutor for our children—for so little money?"

"Not much color for you tonight, Cousin Anna," Horace said, as he sat with their tall, pleasantly plain visitor on the west piazza watching the sun go down. "Our winter sunsets are usually like fire across the sky."

"I enjoy it this way, too," she said lazily. "It's the color of a dove's breast—barely pink, soft. It's a comfortable sky."

"Liking it better here with us?"

"I love being here with all of you—if only I could conquer my stupid panic over these creeping, crawling things! I know the children will stop tormenting me when I stop delighting them with my womanly shrieks. But why did the Creator have to place so much horror in the midst of so much beauty?"

(256)

"I guess we can't know about all that, Cousin. I wonder the same things myself sometimes."

"The bugs and spiders? Do they bother you, too? After all these years?"

He laughed. "No, I don't wonder about things like that. The South is to me the most naturally beautiful part of the United States—even with our snakes and bugs and hurricanes. There's a kind of peace here I never found anywhere else. But," he sighed heavily, "there's a wide streak of ugliness, too—horror, as you say."

She sat up, staring at him, characteristically intense. "If I'm speaking out of turn, forgive me, Cousin Horace, but do you mean slavery?"

He nodded.

"In Canada we don't think of men in your position minding it."

"I know," he said quietly. "But a few of us do mind—deeply. More than we admit—even to ourselves."

"In that case then, I'm truly sorry for you."

Deborah and the children came romping onto the piazza with big plans for a trip to the beach if the sun should be warm tomorrow, and quite courageously, Horace thought, in view of her history so far with the teasing children, Cousin Anna said she'd like that very much.

About midmorning the next day, they loaded the big bateau with quilts, a jug of lemonade and a jug of water, a hamper of picnic lunch and a change of clothes for two-year-old Horace Abbott, in case he fell down wading in the surf. Deborah chose Luke, a bright-eyed, strong-shouldered Negro boy, to make the expedition with them, and with Horace waving good-by from the Black Banks landing, they set out down the river toward the narrow strip of sand dunes and pine trees and cabbage palms called Long Island. The trip across was pleasant, even for Cousin Anna, except for one alligator sunning himself in the black sandy mud not forty feet from where they landed. To the children's disappointment, she recovered, and they laughed and sang songs all the way across the uninhabited little island to the wide sweep of ocean beach where they were to spend the day.

"It's nice here by the sea," Cousin Anna said, holding her arms up to the sky. "Not a sign of that spidery moss anywhere!"

"Oh, it doesn't grow this close to the ocean," eight-year-old Jennie volunteered knowingly. "No one knows why. But it doesn't. I miss it. The trees over here look undressed."

For two hours they picked up shells along the treasure-strewn beach, and because a trip to the ocean was such a rarity, the children forgot to tease in their excitement over what they were finding—angel wings, olives, jingles, whelks, moon shells, cockles, slipper shells and sand dollars. They crammed their pockets full and begged Deborah for towels from the picnic basket to carry home still more.

Just before lunchtime, Cousin Anna was standing alone, a little apart from the others, her tall body casting a long shadow across the pale gray sand.

"Look behind you, Cousin Anna!" Jessie shrieked.

"Jessie, leave Cousin Anna alone," her mother scolded.

"But, Mama, look!" The little girl was laughing so hard she almost couldn't talk. "Look—there's a big old—sand crab—cooling off in her shadow!"

This time Cousin Anna didn't scream. She was too horror-struck. The crab was crawling steadily toward her, leaving a scratchy trail in the sand, and as she inched away, it followed her.

Deborah called, "It won't hurt you. Just stand still. Or run—you can outrun it easily."

Cousin Anna couldn't run. She was too terrified to move. The youngsters were shouting with laughter, jumping up and down, clapping their hands. Suddenly, Anna threw up one arm and collapsed in the sand.

"Is she dead, Mama?" The children huddled together, their faces white and scared.

"No, but she's fainted from fright, and I want this to be a lesson to all of you! Do you hear me?"

Deborah splashed Anna's face with the fresh water Luke brought and slapped her cheeks and rubbed her wrists. "You see? She isn't pretending to be afraid of bugs and lizards and snakes and crabs. She *is* afraid—deathly afraid. And you'd all better ask God to forgive you and help you never to frighten her again."

Little Horace began to cry, Jessie and Lizzie stood twisting their fingers, and Jennie prayed: "Lord Jesus, we're awfully sorry we scared her—we love her, we want her to love us."

Cousin Anna moved her head, and Deborah whispered, "While you're praying, Jennie, ask Him to make Cousin Anna want to stay and teach you your lessons."

Anna's eyelids fluttered open. She looked at Deborah and smiled. "You can stop the prayers, Cousin. I'm going to stay."

42

When Cousin Anna had been a beloved, important member of their family for two years, another daughter, born on Christmas Day, was named Anna Deborah. "I don't see how she can miss being a special child with two names like those," her father declared, and from the first, Anna Deborah indeed was different. She was a healthy child, but quieter than the others, more thoughtful, almost too sensitive and tender. Not that she cried much, she didn't. But a dead wren found in the road, or a sick chicken or pig caused Anna more pain than most small children feel.

"She looks at me out of that thin little face with those wide, solemn gray eyes," Cousin Anna said to Horace, "and it's hard to know whether my own heart is aching for the dead bird or for little Anna."

Horace and Cousin Anna frequently had long talks together after supper, while Deborah and Ca got the children ready for bed. He found her capable of an admirable, almost masculine objectivity, and on one stifling August night, when they had taken their cold tea to the east piazza hoping for a breeze off the ocean, he said suddenly, "Don't be deceived by the peace and quiet and comfort of these years you've been with us. They've been wonderful years, the best I've ever known." He stirred his tea absently. "For the first time in its history, Black Banks is out of debt. But this Island is a part of the state of Georgia and Georgia is—in spite of some new railroads and factories—basically a Cotton State. And that means a state in trouble."

She looked at him thoughtfully for a moment; then Horace said, "It's hard to believe, but as sure as gun's iron, there's tragedy ahead for the Union."

He had never voiced it before. His way had been to remain silent, even when attending planters' sessions at Retreat, and especially at meetings of the St. Clair Club, when the air crackled with hatred and resentment of the North. Talk of secession had raged for over two years, but it was never spoken of on St. Simons as a tragedy. On the contrary, as the 1850's rolled toward the 1860's, secession came to be the magic word for solving all planters' problems. At the July meeting of the St. Clair Club, there had been an enthusiastic toast: "To the glorious, much-to-be-desired day when our beloved Georgia will be declared totally free and independent!"

Horace had not drunk to it; in the excitement, no one noticed. He had grown to hate the word "secession," and it was good to have Anna, a Canadian, to talk with. Her interest comforted him; her neutrality gave him room to think things through for himself without the danger of argument.

"There's no point in saying the South isn't in a bad way economically. We are. I've read everything I can get my hands on from the viewpoint of both sides; I'm

(260)

convinced the tariffs are still unfair, that the North—through its control of trade and manufacturing—gets forty cents of each cotton dollar, but there's got to be a better way to equalize the injustices."

"Do you have any ideas, Cousin Horace?"

"No. I'm neither a politician nor an economist. But this country's got some good ones on both sides. I couldn't be alone in feeling that we've got to find a way to remain a united nation. I mean—I'm sure I'm not alone even in the South on this."

"There may be others right here on St. Simons who agree with you."

"But like me, they keep their mouths shut, eh?"

"Keeping silent may be the best way for you, sir. After all, you're now our Justice of the Peace—maybe you should hold your peace." She smiled. "After all, what would be accomplished if you stirred up heated arguments among your neighbors? Only Mr. Thomas Butler King leaves the Island to mix about in the political world outside, and from what I've gathered, his opinions are so set in favor of the Cotton States' independence, nothing you could say would shake him."

"King is for peaceful secession. He's not a fire-eater, as so many Southern politicians are these days. We don't see eye to eye on owning slaves, but King tries for the middle of the road."

"Ah, there you have touched the sore spot, Cousin Horace. It is slavery, isn't it? No matter what they say, North and South, the infection *is* slavery."

He nodded. "Yes, it's slavery—especially in the new states. The right to own slaves has become synonymous with the right to own land. Why, back in the late twenties, when I was in school, it wasn't at all unusual for a Southerner to admit freely that the whole institution of slavery was immoral, wrong—that same day, somehow it should be abolished. I had one friend who argued this point, but great numbers of Southerners did not. Tempers very seldom flared over the question. To-day, if I admitted that I feel slavery is as rotten and evil as I believe it to be, it would infuriate most people. It would terrify many of the Negroes themselves. By now, the system has become the very breath of the Southern economy, the basis of Southern life. It's late, maybe too late, for anything rational to be done."

Anna thought a moment. "Even when I came down four years ago, we Canadians felt the hostility growing. But, Cousin Horace, American Northerners don't *know* Southerners. Naturally, living in Toronto, we read Northern United States newspapers—and Southerners are depicted as callous, relentlessly cruel monsters who beat their slaves, have immoral relations with black women and stay intoxicated on mint juleps. There may be some truth in this—I'm not an idealist where human nature is concerned—but I see no signs of it on St. Simons Island."

"Oh, Cousin Anna, *we don't know each other at all.* There is little or no communication between North and South. Each has a hundred excellencies entirely unknown to the other. If there were only some way for us to get acquainted, some kind of mutual affection would have to replace this hate that is pulling us apart! If we could only visit one another in our homes for long enough to find out that—good and bad—we *are* people— one country. I believe that's the only way anything can be settled, even slavery. Of course, it will take time to solve the slavery problem, and I know I sound like a typical planter when I say that, but it *would* take time. If I freed my people tomorrow, they'd be lost. We'll have to educate them, teach them trades, work out some kind of gradual lessening of both their total dependence upon the whites and the planter's dependence upon them. We'd both need help—lots of it—black and white. We'd both be lost. Do you know that if I freed my people, I'd never be able to borrow enough money to plant fifty acres of cotton next year? They're my most valuable possessions! My collateral. I hate it, but that's the fact. I don't know how many agree with me, but if I knew any other way to live—to support my family—before God, I'd do it. I'm sick to my soul of my own helpless guilt. I'd do anything to be rid of it." He dropped his head in his hands. "Anything but deprive Deborah and the children. The people would go hungry, too, and that is not a prejudiced Southerner talking. We exist on credit down here. They *are* my collateral. I couldn't borrow the money to pay them if I freed them and they wanted to stay." He looked up, smiled apologetically. "Poor Cousin Anna."

"Not at all," she said briskly. "I've come to love it here so much, I might be the only outsider who would understand what you're saying. I didn't understand before. I do now. I'm afraid I don't pity the fire-eaters, but I do pity you, Cousin Horace." She leaned back, watching the light fade from the sky. "I suppose you and the others who must feel as you do will just have to wait things out."

"I suppose so," he said wearily. "But unlike most of my neighbors, I don't think the Federal Government will permit the South to secede without a struggle. I have that strong feeling there will be trouble. A bloody, sickening struggle that could change everything forever."

"You agree with President Buchanan, then, that the Southern States do not have a constitutional right to secede?"

"I do. This country was founded on the principle of a *united* group of states. Once that principle is discarded, America is lost. In school at Yale many years ago, I came to know Yankees and I loved them. They might learn to love and respect us too, if only we could get to know each other—perhaps to work out the problem together. If we don't, we all have everything to lose, and absolutely nothing but tragedy to gain."

43

Christmas at Black Banks in 1859, the year Horace's second son, James Dunn, was born, was the merriest, noisiest, happiest time anyone could remember. The Negroes had their week's holiday from all but the most necessary work, and Horace, hiding his sense of foreboding that this might be the last merry Christmas for a long time, provided two pigs and all the trimmings for the biggest Jubilee on St. Simons. The older Gould children and their playmates from the quarters exhausted themselves with anticipation of what they would get for Christmas, what they would give to each other. They boasted loudly of how much barbecued pork each would be able to eat: "A halfa pig," little Anna thought. "Ah's gonna' eat two hafsa pig," Ca's six-year-old grandson shouted. And because the older Negroes had taught the Gould children how to do their rhythmical ring-shouts and ring-plays, the big back yard at Black Banks was alive with dancing, shuffling children of all ages and sizes, clapping black hands and white hands as they sang.

On the last night of Jubilee, Horace and Deborah and Mary and Caroline and Cousin Anna joined in when July organized a ringshout for everybody. The yard was strung with paper lanterns, and round and round the big bonfire of oak and fat pine, blazing in the mild December night, even old Larney and John shuffled along in the circle of laughing faces, as they sang together:

> If I live
> Sangaree.
> Don't get kill

Sangaree.
I'm goin' back
Sangaree.
Jacksonville
Sangaree.

As Ca and Deborah rounded up the children for bed, the Negroes from both Black Banks and New St. Clair stood to one side and sang Horace's favorite Sea Island slave song. He had always smiled through this song, enjoying it, admiring the strangely vigorous devotion of his people to their God, feeling their love for him, as they "giv' Mausa Horace a gif' ob his song." Tonight he couldn't smile when they began to sing. He could only lift his hand in a sign of gratitude for their gift. Almost always, he had joined in, trying to keep up with the ancient, complex rhythm. Tonight, he could neither sing nor smile, but he indentified with the lyrics as never before:

> My God is a rock in a weary lan'
> weary lan'
> in a weary lan'
> My God is a rock in a weary lan'
> Shelter in a time of storm.

> Ah know He is a rock in a weary lan'
> weary lan'
> in a weary lan'
> Ah know He is a rock in a weary lan'
> Shelter in a time of storm.

The storm broke even sooner than Horace had feared. Abraham Lincoln was elected President of the United States on November 6, 1860, and in the last days of James Buchanan's chaotic term of office—even before Lincoln could be inaugurated—South Carolina seceded from the Union.

"It's started, Cousin Anna," Horace said grimly.

(265)

"They're all so convinced Lincoln does not mean to leave slavery alone, that every single Cotton State will follow South Carolina out of the Union."

"Maybe not. There's still hope. Mr. Lincoln is a sane, sensible man."

"We can't take that chance, Cousin. I'm sending you back to Toronto while there's time."

"But what about the children's education?" she protested.

"We'll send the two older girls away to school. The others will have to make do on what Deborah and I can teach them until we see what's going to happen."

Early in January, Anna took Jennie and Jessie to Savannah on Captain Steven's little packet, *Sarah*, saw them safely settled in Madame La Coste's Boarding School and returned to her home in Canada. It was almost like three deaths in the family at Black Banks with the two girls and beloved Cousin Anna gone, but the real blow came a week later, when Fort Sumter was fired upon: Governor Brown ordered the Jackson Artillery of Macon to occupy the south end of St. Simons Island as a protection for the Brunswick Harbor.

"Mr. Gould, should we be terribly worried?" Deborah asked, when he read to her from *The Savannah Republican* that the Governor had also ordered State troops to occupy Fort Pulaski at the mouth of the Savannah River.

"Not yet, Deborah. I think not yet. Mississippi, Florida and Alabama are gone, but Georgia is still in the Union."

The January 18 issue of the Savannah paper reached Black Banks on January 21. Horace's hands shook as he read the big black headline:

GEORGIA CONVENTION VOTES 164 TO 131
FOR SECESSION

He let the paper drop and tried to realize that he was no longer a citizen of the United States. A hundred and thirty-one Georgians *had* voted against it. That was some consolation, but the State was gone. He fought to control his fury that he had been able to do nothing but stand by and watch it happen. He picked up the newspaper and read the rest of the story. After learning the vote, Georgia Senator Robert Toombs had left the Chamber of the United States Senate "with a harangue not soon to be forgotten." Toombs had defied the North to try to keep the South in the Union, shouting, "Come and do it! Treason? Bah!" Toombs, once reasonable and Union-loving, had then stalked furiously out of the Senate Chamber, walked straight to the United States Treasury and demanded what was due him in Senate pay, plus mileage back to Georgia.

Horace heard the front door slam, and before he could put the paper out of sight, Mary was in the sitting room, a letter in her hand, her face flushed and agitated.

He went to her. "Mary, what is it "

"You know perfectly well what it is, Horace. This is no time to try to protect your womenfolk—we're not that kind. But what's happened to the men of Georgia? How is it that apparently only one poor little dried-up Senator named Stephens kept sanity enough to act like a gentleman? To make sense?"

Horace moved a chair near the fire. "Sit down, sister."

"I don't want to sit down!"

"Well, what's that letter?"

"It just came from Georgia King. She acted as her father's secretary at the Georgia Convention and she says her poor father, still grieving over Miss Anna Matilda's death, tried desperately to steer a moderate course in the secession plans, but most of the men went wild. Stephens was fairly shouted down the instant he said the only rational thing anyone said all day—that the United States Government, with all its defects, comes nearer to what a good government should be than any other on earth—or something like that. Oh, Horace, Georgia King says most of the legislators were storming up and down shouting for revolution—wanting to break up the Federal Government—take fifty men and march into Savannah and seize the Customs House—march to Washington, burn down the Government buildings—seize the United States Treasury! Horace, we had intelligent, far-sighted congressmen once in this state—not lunatics! What's happened?"

"At least a hundred and thirty-one voted against it, Mary," Horace said helplessly.

Deborah stood in the doorway, her face pale, her gray eyes wide. "Is there any more trouble, Mr. Gould, dear?"

"Yes, Deborah. There's more trouble."

"Our Georgia politicians have gone stark, raving mad, Deborah!" Mary shouted. "We no longer live in the United States of America. We don't even have a country. I don't like the way the North treated us any more than those crazy men liked it, but Horace, this is no way to settle differences. This kind of insanity could lead to—Horace! Do you think it could lead to a—real war?"

"Yes." He tried to keep his voice calm. "Yes, sister, it could. Of course, there's always the possibility the Federal Government won't try to force us back in, but—"

"You don't sound one bit convincing. And even if they did try to get the Cotton States back in the Union by some legal means, these hotheaded Southern fire-eaters would do something to wreck it!"

Deborah, who had remained in the doorway, walked slowly into the room and stood between them. "I can see it's all very bad." She reached for Horace's hand and then Mary's. "But what can we three do but go on as we've always done? Being together, asking God to bring peace again."

"God has never stopped angry men, Deborah!" Mary said furiously. "Men so full of hate can't be stopped until they smash into something that stops them." She patted Deborah's hand and sat down. "I know it doesn't do any good for me to shout. I also know, in spite of their hotheadedness, that the South is going to come out on top, no matter what. After all, the paper said the U.S. Navy at Pensacola has already capitulated to our boys—and our Confederate Government isn't even set up yet. I don't like any of it, but if there's a fight, we'll win in time to avoid any real trouble for us here."

Horace stared at her. "You can't really mean that?"

"Of course I mean it. One Southerner is worth a dozen Yankees any old day! If they just give us time to cool off, things will be all right again—better than before, maybe—now that some of our grievances have been brought out in the open. Now that they know we don't intend to go on taking everything lying down."

He chuckled. "Mary, you're a Southerner, all right."

" 'Till I die!" She jumped up. "Well, I've had my say." Halfway to the door, she whirled around. "What did you mean by saying 'you're a Southerner, all right' in that snide tone of voice, Horace Bunch Gould?"

"You think with your emotions, sister. That's all I meant. Come on, I'll put you on your horse."

"We're going to be all right, Mary," Deborah called after her from the front porch. "No matter what happens, we are going to be all right here on St. Simons."

44

The Brunswick Herald's front pages were devoted almost entirely to news and stories of the heightened military activity along the Georgia coast. The Brunswick Riflemen, organized with enthusiasm and fanfare in October, 1860, were mustered into the Confederate Army in May of the next year under Colonel Paul Semmes, commander of Camp Semmes, south of the city.

Like women all over the area, Mary rounded up spare bolts of denim, shirting material, red flannel, ticking—even a contribution of over half their yield of goose feathers for use in the Confederate hospitals that were springing up across the eleven Confederate States.

It was now late in the year 1861, their fields were all

picked, and Horace and Mary were in his office at Black Banks, supposedly working on their accounts.

"Horace, you seem so uninterested in the war! How you concentrate on those old figures?"

"Because they have to be concentrated upon, sister."

"If you'd been with me in Brunswick last week when July and I carried our contribution over—if you'd heard those crowds singing—if you'd seen those brave, high-spirited boys packing to leave their families and sweethearts, you couldn't be so detached. They're marvelous, our soldiers—all of them convinced it will be over in no time at all. You should see them. They're like men preparing for a big hunting expedition! There's absolutely no sadness—oh, except for some of the older people. One of the ladies who sat next to me at the swing session said she prayed for hours on her knees every night. Of course, we must all pray, but our boys simply can't lose. Why, they're expecting almost no actual fighting. They're carrying trunks of clothing—dress suits, their best linen. Nearly every soldier in our area is carrying along his darky to look after him." She laughed. "Would you believe it, I saw half a dozen boys displaying their silver spoons and forks, vowing they would never eat one bite on Yankee soil except from Southern silver! Unlike our hotheaded Congressmen, they're going to show them in Washington how real gentlemen conduct themselves."

"In *Washington*?" Horace asked incredulously.

"Of course. They expect to take over Washington first thing."

"I see."

"Now, look here, brother—just because they turned you down for being forty-nine years old is no reason to be so lacking in fervor. You should be going around like the rest of us singing our new Confederate songs all day long—I'll bet you don't even know any."

"I've known most of them for years. The deckhands sang them when I was on the river boat. The Confederates just made up new words."

He had never mentioned the river boat in all the years

he had been home, and suddenly he was almost like a stranger to his sister.

He closed the black account book. "Well, Mary, this year of all years, it looks as though we're going to have a bumper crop of cotton."

"Don't you see? That's a marvelous sign. Everyone is saying King Cotton is going to win the struggle for us."

"I see the finest crop we've had in years going to waste."

"To *waste*?"

"How do we get the cotton to England? You know there's a Federal blockade all around us. Oh, a few men like Captain Stevens manage to run it now and then—but the Yankees are tightening it every day. You know all this."

"Horace Gould, where's your faith?"

"I don't know. I'd be lying if I said I did. Maybe if I knew what the Almighty thinks of us—North and South—I'd have an answer."

"Well, I can tell you!"

"You can?"

"The Almighty is on the side of the Confederacy! He couldn't be on the Yankees' side after the way they've treated us. Use your head, brother."

"The facts are all against you, Mary—God or no God. Even the Negroes sense it. They have a fine sense of history, those people. They know the trouble is really over slavery—they already smell freedom up ahead."

She laughed at him. "Your imagination is running away with you. Not by so much as a twinkle in one darky's eye can I see any difference in their behavior. Why, Horace, they can't read. How could they know all this?"

"I've taught Adam and July to read and I give them the newspapers."

"I'd say you were a fool, if Adam and July weren't so trustworthy. Oh, brother, brother—aren't you with us down here? Aren't you convinced we're in the right?" She forced him to look at her. "If you were young enough to fight, you would, wouldn't you?"

"You know the answer to that. I tried to get in as soon as they fired on Sumter."

"Then why is it I keep feeling far away from you? As though you aren't with me—with *us*?"

"Because I still love and believe in the Union."

"You can't now!"

"But I do. Listen, Mary, any self-respecting man would fight to his death to protect his family and his land and his state. I don't have to believe in the cause of a war to do that. General Robert E. Lee took command of the Confederate Armies with no more enthusiasm for the reason we're fighting than I have. But he'll fight to protect what's his. And so will I. When the time comes for older men to get into it—I'll be ready."

"Oh, but it isn't going to last that long."

"Maybe not."

"Anyway, that's all I needed to know." She sat on the arm of his chair, her hand on his shoulder. For a long time, they looked out the window. The woods beyond the yard were still, the oblique autumn sun filtering down in luminous shafts from the treetops to the carpet of brown pine straw on the ground. "I'm ashamed that I pressed you for an explanation, Horace. If anyone knows you'd fight to protect Black Banks, I know it." She sighed. "You have the most beautiful woods here of any place on St. Simons. The war seems very far away suddenly, doesn't it?"

"That's dangerous business, Captain—blockade running," Horace said to his friend at Frederica the next day. "I'm not asking any favors, just some advice. I've got to get my cotton to Liverpool. If we ever needed money, we need it now."

"Blockade running is dangerous *and* profitable, Gould. But if I can get your cotton through, I vow you will pay me no more than in the old days."

"You're a friend. What do you really think about the whole thing?"

Captain Charles stroked his chin whiskers and squinted out over the quiet waters. "I think we're headed for a long, bloody war."

"I wish I could do something. At least you can run a blockade now and then."

"You will be fighting in no time, Gould. They will lift the age limit—and they will evacuate all white civilians from this Island in less than two months."

Horace stared at him. "You really believe that?"

"I know it. I travel. I hear things. St. Simons is one of the most strategic spots on the Southern coast. Our growing fields and well-stocked barns can supply many soldiers with food. The Island is a perfect base of operation and refuge for blockade runners and raiding vessels. St. Simons commands the entrance to Brunswick Harbor, the largest on the Georgia coast south of Savannah. Oh, Gould, St. Simons is the key position for any chance the Confederacy has to hold this part of the coast! Mark my word, there will be no one left on the Island within two months but Negroes and soldiers. So, be ready. We have spent the last Christmas on our little strip of beauty for a long, long time."

Captain Stevens was right. In December, 1861, when Deborah's eighth child, Helen, was only a few months old, Confederate officers from the fortifications which had been built on Retreat plantation rode from house to house up and down St. Simons, ordering all white civilians to evacuate within one week.

"You'll be needed in more places than your own to help get them off, Mr. Gould," a young lieutenant told Horace. "Most of the able-bodied men are in the military. Captain Stevens will be on hand to help, and we've asked him to rent all the flatboats possible. Each family pays its own rental, of course. How soon can you be ready?"

"Three days should do it for us," Horace said. "Captain Stevens warned me. I've been expecting it."

The lieutenant laughed. "You're certainly the only one I've found with that much sense."

"Will it be for long, Lieutenant?"

"Not more than six months. Maybe not that. We'll lick 'em fast. Main thing is to evacuate quickly and smoothly." He turned his horse. "I hate to see you all go, sir. We've had some fine social evenings at King's Retreat in the last few months. A thing like this can take all the fun out of a war, can't it?"

Deborah was sitting on a big trunk telling an Irish "wee-folk" tale to the children when Horace said the time had come. Lizzie, eleven; Horace, nine; Mary Frances, seven; Anna, six; and Jimmy, two, went running excitedly to the yard and clambered into the old wagon, loaded with the few possessions they were taking along. Ca stood sorrowfully beside Deborah, holding Helen, the new baby.

"We're ready, Mr. Gould, dear. As ready as we'll ever be—to leave this blessed place."

Horace put his arm around her, but all he could say was, "I'm proud of you. I love you."

She clung to him, then turned to Ca, smiling as tears ran down her cheeks. "You won't have me around telling you what to do for a while, Ca. Just this one last thing—take the baby to the wagon for me, please?"

Ca was crying, too.

"Deborah," Horace said, "are you sure Ca shouldn't go along to help?"

"Mr. Gould, dear, Ca has children and grandchildren here. I could never live with myself if we forced her to leave them. It's bad enough to take Adam, but at least he and Mina don't have little ones yet. I'll get along fine with Adam's help."

She ran to where the other children waited in the wagon, shouting good-bys to the people, who stood around them, many of them crying. "All right, children, is everybody in?" Deborah forced a cheerful smile and made the quick, heartbreaking trip around the circle, shaking each hand, kissing the black children, who looked more frightened than sad, saying over and over—"We won't be long. Take care of yourselves and our home, now, and wait for us to come back. We won't be long."

Horace made the rounds too, and the last person with whom he shook hands was July. "You're free, July," he whispered to his old friend. "You don't have to stay here, you know."

"Yes, sir, Mausa Horace. Ah knows. But ah'll be right here, when you comes home. Dey ain' gittin' to our place, sir, effen ah kin stop 'em."

Horace gripped July's hand in both of his, hurried to the wagon, and pulled Deborah up into the seat beside him; Ca handed her the baby, and they began the slow, bumpy journey down the Black Banks lane, with everyone waving and calling good-bye and weeping.

When they reached the New St. Clair turnoff, Adam was waiting in the other wagon, loaded with hogs and chickens. Luke and Aunt Caroline sat in the Gould carriage alone. Mary and Maum Larney and John were nowhere in sight.

"Your sister refuses to come," Caroline said, wringing her hands. "I've tried everything, Horace—even to shaming her for making more trouble for you at a time like this, but she won't budge. Insists she can handle the Yankees, that she's changed her mind!"

Horace ran down the New St. Clair lane, motioning for Luke to follow with the carriage. He found Mary standing between Maum Larney and Papa John, in the black silk dress she had planned to wear to the mainland, giving orders as though it were any ordinary day. If Aunt Caroline had failed to convince her, he saw no point in trying.

"Why are they digging over there by the springhouse, Mary?" he asked almost casually.

"I'm staying here, but we're not taking any chances on those Yankees," she declared. "We've packed up the silver and Mother's good china and we're going to bury it so deep even their long noses can't find it."

"Good idea," Horace replied, then picked her up and carried her—kicking and pounding his shoulders—to the

(275)

carriage, climbed in beside her, helped Larney and John scramble in, and told Luke to drive back to where the others were waiting.

Half way across Buttermilk Sound, the flatboat which carried the Negroes, the hogs and chickens and the few pieces of furniture broke loose from Captain Stevens's pilot boat and, amid horrified screams and cackles and squeals, turned over, spilling Negroes and hogs and chickens and most of the furniture into the chilly gray water. Only the Negroes could be saved, pulled soaking wet, wide-eyed and terrified, over the side of the remaining flatboat. Mary helped rescue Maum Larney, but she still had spoken to no one.

"It's all right about our furniture," Deborah comforted Horace, when he had crawled around boxes and wet black bodies to sit beside her. "We're all still here, and that's what matters."

"The hogs and the chickens mattered, Deborah. They could mean the difference between hunger and plenty for you and the children if I have to leave you."

"We still have enough, Mr. Gould, dear, for no longer than we'll be gone."

"Co'se we's got plenty," Maum Larney scolded Horace, as she wrung salt water from her long skirts. "Larney's gon' plant a big garden anyway when we finds a place to lib." Her scolding seemed almost like old times, and Horace's heart lifted a little, until he heard Adam sobbing.

"It's Mina," Deborah whispered. "He doesn't know what's going to happen to Mina."

During the three miserable days they spent in makeshift quarters at the Dent's deserted New Hope plantation on the mainland, Mary would not even discuss with Horace where they might live. When he returned on the third night with the bad news that he could find nothing large enough for them all, he felt utterly alone without his sister's help. "I've found a furnished house in Blackshear for you and Aunt Caroline, with a room for Maum

(276)

Larney and Papa John," he told her. "Deborah and the children and I will live in Burneyville. I've rented a buggy for your trip to Blackshear. It will be crowded with the four of you, but you don't have any baggage except what Aunt Caroline brought. Can you share your clothing with Mary, Aunt Caroline?"

"Of course, Horace dear. We'll do fine," Caroline assured him.

Mary said nothing.

"I bought an old wagon, Deborah, for our things. We'll divide supplies with Mary and Aunt Caroline."

When it came time to separate, Deborah put her arms around Mary and kissed her. "I'll be praying for you every day, dear sister," she said. "For you and Aunt Caroline and Maum Larney and Papa John and for our homes back there."

It was a simple little speech, but everyone heard it, and Mary could hold out no longer. "I'm ashamed of myself," she said stiffly, her back erect, the skirt of her black silk dress whipping in the wind off the river. "I was not wrong—I was right to want to stay at Rosemount. Any Yankees who might make their dirty little tracks to St. Simons, *I could have handled—alone*. But I was wrong to sulk. All of you please forgive me. We should have stayed at home, but since we didn't, we're going to be all right. We're all going to be *all right*.

She hugged Deborah and the children, then ran to Horace and threw herself into his arms and cried. He held her until she jerked free, blew her nose, stood straight as a pine tree and announced: "Well, now, that will be enough of that until the Yankees surrender!"

Horace was able to stay with his family a little over a year—long enough to settle them into the drafty, cramped cottage in Burneyville near one of the few remaining railroads. He bought some pigs and a cow, rebuilt the ramshackle barn, repaired the house as best he could, cleared the available acre of ground and planted a garden. Two days after their ninth child, Angela La Coste, was born, he received his orders to report back on St. Simons no later than March 15. An overage regiment nicknamed "The Babies" had been formed under Major G. T. Smith, and by spring, 1863, Horace had lost all regular contact with Deborah and his family.

45

30 April, 1863
Near Dalton, Georgia

My Deborah,
When I will be able to post this only God knows, but in order to stay sane while we wait here in the hills of north Georgia, I must at least write for my own sake. I am well, fidgety, depressed with the waste of all this waiting. We expect to be moved to Dalton by summer and General Joseph E. Johnston is to take command. What comes them, I cannot say. I try not to think of even one hour from now. There have been several revival meetings since I have been here and many men claim they have found God. I have enjoyed attending, although the service is very different from ours. I'm afraid my only claim to religion these days is that I have to trust God to keep in touch with me. I know He is in touch with you, my beloved wife, and through your prayers, with me, too. Kiss our children for me and tell them to be obedient to you.

Your loving husband,
Horace B. Gould.

23 June, 1863
Burneyville, Georgia

My dear husband,
We are all fine and with the help of God and my

Doctor's Book, I intend to see that we stay that way. Children are dying all around us here, but our dear ones remain healthy and seem to get hungrier every day. It is not easy for us and I would be deceiving you if I said it was. But nothing is so hard for me as to be away from you where I cannot even look at your dear face. In case you have not received Mary's letter this week, I will tell you that faithful old Maum Larney is gone. She died in her sleep well into her eighties. Papa John has taken to his bed with grief. But it will encourage you to know that your sister, Janie, has come to live with Mary and Aunt Caroline in Blackshear while her husband serves the Confederacy. Janie brought extra dresses, and Mary is elated. Her old black silk was giving way. I promised Mary in my last letter that I would pass along this good news to you. It has been so long since I have had a letter from you, and although I hate coffee made from parched corn, and grow weary, along with the children, of monotonous food, nothing is really hard for me except not knowing that you are safe. I know you write when you can and so I can only pray that a letter gets through soon. The railroads are vanishing one after another. It is a strange time and we are both in strange places—but we are always together in God. With all my heart, I wish I had assurance that God is as real to you as He is to me. I need to know that you are aware of how close He stays to us both.

My dearest love,
Deborah A. Gould.

In the trenches at Dalton
24 December, 1863.

Beloved Deborah and children,

General Johnston has taken command long ago, and yet we are entrenched at Dalton, still waiting. There was snow last night, and my thoughts were back to my school days in New Haven. Tell Horace and Jimmy their father was the best shot of all with snowballs hurled wantonly at the face of the big Lyceum clock on the old Yale campus. Our children have never seen snow. Perhaps, when this is over, we can bring them up this way. To me, it does not compare with our Island, of course, but in the spring, especially, I found north Georgia fresh and beautiful. I have hopes once more that this may reach you and that yours may reach me. There is no real way to answer your questions, nor for you to answer mine in their proper order. I do not receive Mary's letters any more but of course I am relieved and happy that Janie is with her. Pray for me, my Deborah. I try to pray for all of you. I am writing on my knee as I lean against an embankment covered with crocus sacks to keep off the chill. It is hard to believe this is Christmas Eve, and harder to believe that Maum Larney is gone. I still need her. The Babe at Bethlehem chose a strange world to come into.

> Your devoted husband,
> Horace B. Gould.

> 7 May, 1864
> Burneyville

Beloved husband, Mr. Gould, dear,
Some months ago, I tried to assure you that God never loses touch with anyone. Excuse me, my dearest, but why is it that you feel you personally do not have a relationship with God when He is doing all possible to care for us? My prayers each night in this tumbledown shack always include, not only a plea for your safety and our quick return to Black Banks, but that you will come to realize that there is no way known to man to be far from the watchful eye of the Father. I miss our little church at Frederica, but I am learning that God comes to us wherever we are. Why not try Him and see? What can you lose, Mr. Gould, dear? Just say, "God? Are

You here with me?" He will let you know somehow that He is. The children are fine and so am I except that I cry as quietly as possible at night when they are asleep, from loneliness for you and from the strain of keeping my spirits up all day. By far the hardest part is not knowing whether you are dead or alive, sick or well. My prayers attend you always and God attends you in ways I never could, even were it possible for me to be there in those muddy trenches with you.

My deepest love always,
Deborah A. Gould.

3 August, 1864
In the trenches east of Atlanta

My Deborah,

Sherman is still trying to push around us with forces far larger than ours, but General Joe Johnston is proving to be a master of the strategy of evasion and delay, the only course left to us. Every day the armies are in contact, but so far I have not even been nicked. Fighting has mostly been digging trenches and rifle pits under the blazing sun. I have seen men die and I will never get accustomed to it, but I have grown rather immune to smelling death. And if ever I live on St. Simons again, I shall not mind the deer flies. No more time for writing now. A shell just passed over our line on its way to Atlanta. The people are living in cellars and bombproofs there. I am alive and well and I love you and the children.

Horace B. Gould.

In the trenches, Atlanta
12 August, 1864

Beloved Deborah,

There has not been time to receive your answer to my last letter, but this is my birthday and my thoughts are, as always, far away in Burneyville,

(281)

where you and my precious children wait out this dreadful madness. This senseless war, when American continue to kill Americans. I have killed too, and the memory of it will never leave me. The sky to the east is very dark and full of rolling clouds, but with a rainbow spanning the cloudy region. The contrast is meaningful to me—like our life before the madness and now. The rainbow also brings your love spanning the distance to me, my own darling wife. There is death and stinking sickness and misery all around me, but up ahead, if I live, is the hope that we will go home again. Paper is in short supply, so I will end this with all my love to you and the children. Pray for me, oh, pray for us all.

> Your devoted husband,
> Horace B. Gould.

> 3 September, 1864
> Burneyville

My darling, Mr. Gould, dear,

A good letter from Mary today, thanking me for keeping you informed about them in Blackshear. Paper is scarce here too. Her letters reach us in Burneyville more easily, but I know it is hard for her not being able to write to you. She and Janie and Aunt Caroline and Papa John seem fine. We are still getting along in our little house. We eat enough, although seldom a variation from collards or turnip greens, sweet potatoes, and a little meat. To save paper, as you can see, I am cross-writing this between the lines of your last letter and it breaks my heart to part with even a piece of paper your hands have touched. I never permit a day to pass without lessons and the children seem to learn well from me. Word has come that on orders from General Beauregard, Madame La Coste's school in Savannah must be closed and Jennie and Jessie are heartbroken to have to leave for life in Burneyville. I did not tell you until I knew a way would be provided for our darlings to come here. Dear Madame La Coste, so pleased that we named our Angé for her, is sending them with two young Cavalry officers from the garrison. God is taking care of us.

Your loving wife,
Deborah A. Gould.

7 September, 1864
Bivouac near Jonesboro

Beloved Deborah,

Such a small scrap of brown paper. I will be brief. General Joe Johnston was relieved of his command on 17 July, in favor of General Hood. Since then we have lost four important battles outright. The Union Army entered Atlanta 2 September. I have been given some leave and I will be en route to you when you get this. I am now a Captain.

Your loving husband,
Horace B. Gould.

For a long time, Deborah sat in the chair where she had read his letter, unable even to weep. He was coming home. She would see his face again. She would know the safety of his arms around her. She would hear his voice. It wasn't fair to let the children go on playing outside not knowing, but she had held back her weeping so long, maybe she deserved five more minutes alone. Tears began to stream down her face and she cried as hard and as freely as she had needed to cry for all the long months he had been gone. Then she leaned back in the dear Black Banks rocker—the one that had caught on the side of the flatboat and didn't get lost in Buttermilk Sound—and for the first time since March, 1863, when he went away, she rested.

The warm, yellow autumn sunlight picked out the piece of tin young Horace had nailed over the rathole in the floor. It glistened now and looked almost beautiful. She sat up suddenly. How would he get home? By train for some of the distance, perhaps, but all around Burneyville, the railroads were torn up, their rails hauled north for Confederate fortifications. Would he find a horse? Would he have to beg rides? Two of the Demere boys and Tip King had been forced to beg rides and walk. Maybe he would have to trudge for miles through the hot September days and nights and sleep in the woods! "Dear God protect him! Take care of your child, Horace Gould," she begged. "Bring him safely back to us."

"Mama?"

"Anna! What on earth are you doing hiding behind that cupboard, dear? I thought you were out playing in the creek with the other children."

Deborah saw Anna's lips tremble and her gray eyes fill with tears. "Mother isn't scolding, dear. You just startled me."

"I—I wouldn't have hid, but—you were acting so funny. I'm sorry, Mama, I didn't mean to do anything wrong."

"There, now, this is no time to cry. Oh, I take that back—it's a good time to cry." She held out her arms to the girl. "And if you encourage me just a little, I'll start all over again with you!"

"Is—is Papa all right?"

Deborah held her at arm's length, looking right into her eyes. "Yes! Papa's all right and he's coming home to us."

For a moment, Anna stared at her mother. Then her angular little face began to glow. "Can—can we go back to Black Banks when Papa comes?"

"No, I'm afraid not yet, dear. But all we need to do today is be glad and wait for Papa to get here. He might even be here by day after tomorrow!"

Anna didn't jump up and down, as Deborah knew the others would, but stood very straight, her hands clasped, breathing hard in her effort to contain her joy.

"It's all right if you yell and whoop, Anna. I feel like it."

"Oh, no," Anna whispered. "I'm too happy."

46

The children didn't recognize him when he plodded up the dirt road in his mud-caked boots, but Deborah saw him a long way off and ran to him. There were those few seconds in his arms, his rough jacket scratching her face as he pressed her head against his shoulder so hard, she had trouble breathing.

"Deborah! Deborah—beloved, beautiful Deborah," he said over and over, his voice old.

He was so thin and exhausted she almost resented the children swooping toward him like wild Indians. But he managed their hugs and kisses and laughed at them for saying his whiskers scratched, and after he had bathed and slipped on his old plantation work clothes that Deborah had kept clean and waiting for such a day as this, he devoted himself to the children until their bedtime. He told them enough about the war, but not too much, and somehow he managed to keep his spirits high until Anna, lingering after the others had said good night, hugged and kissed him again.

When they were all in bed at last, Deborah and Horace once more sat together before an open fire.

"Almost like being at Black Banks, isn't it, Mr. Gould, dear?"

"Almost." He sighed. "Oh, Deborah, don't stay over there. Come and sit on my lap. I have—to leave tomorrow morning. I'm lucky to be here at all. My transportation failed at the last minute. If it hadn't, I'd have had a whole week with you."

Tomorrow morning! Finally she asked, "How did you get here, my darling?"

"Two trips in broken-down wagons, packed in with

other soldiers trying to get home, too. Rode a mule for ten miles or so—walked the rest of the way."

She hurried to sit on his lap and took his head in her hands. "I should put you to bed, then, right away. I must not be selfish, but oh, let me hold you close for just a few seconds—long enough to last."

They clung to each other in silence until a log burned in two and rolled out of the fireplace, scattering live coals over the new rag rug Deborah had made. She jumped up and Horace brushed the coals onto the hearth.

"Now then, it's time for you to talk to me," he said. "What news do you get from the Island? Is everyone gone? I heard even our troops had been evacuated."

She frowned. "Yes, and I might as well tell you, my dear—before they left, they were ordered to blow up your father's lighthouse."

He leaned his head against the high backed chair and closed his eyes, but said nothing.

"They were afraid the Yankees would be able to use it as a target," she explained. "You know how wonderfully it showed up, even by daylight."

Without opening his eyes, he said, "Yes, I know. What else? Tell me everything bad first."

"Captain Charles Stevens is—missing!"

He looked at her. "Missing!"

"Believed to have been captured and imprisoned at the North. He was last seen trying to cross the marsh above Frederica. They even got his boats."

Horace took a deep breath. "What else?"

"Thomas Butler King is dead. He died at their refuge in Waresboro this year. His son Lord Page King is dead, too. Killed at Fredericksburg. And do you know, Neptune brought the body back somehow to Christ Church yard?"

"All the way from Virginia to St. Simons?"

"Yes, and in time for Mr. King to witness Lord's burial before his own death. Neptune has gone to war with Tip King now."

(286)

He said nothing for a long time, then asked, "Deborah, do you think you were wise to send Adam back to the Island?"

"Oh, yes, I do. The poor man was grieving himself sick not knowing about Mina. We hoped for a long time that she had refugeed with the Kings in Waresboro, but she didn't, and Adam became obsessed with the idea that Mina had refused to leave St. Simons because she thought he would still be there. Anyway, Adam was not ours to keep—he's free now."

"That's right." Horace smiled a little. "They're all free now. Adam and Mina—free, and able to live together under the same roof as man and wife." He leaned back and closed his eyes. "I'm glad, I'm glad, I'm glad—oh, Lord, how glad I am they're all free. I don't know what we'll do without them and I don't know where the money will come from to pay them to stay, but I'm glad they're free. A big struggle has ended for me. One I could never have ended myself." He reached for her hand. "Deborah, I'm so tired. Will you let me sleep about an hour or so and then wake me up?"

"No—you must rest all night, my darling."

"Then I won't go to sleep." He looked at her almost sternly. "Deborah, when a man has lived as I have for the past two years, he does not waste any of this he can possibly help. To make me sleep through the night would be like depriving me of a piece of bread if I were starving."

She bit her lip, fighting tears. "All right, Mr. Gould, dear. I'll let you sleep two hours and then I promise to wake you. But—could you bear to tell me quickly—are we losing the war?"

"Yes, as of now. Sherman is headed right across Georgia to the sea." His voice grew hard. "For the first time, I have a real incentive to fight. Maybe killing won't be so hard when I'm helping to keep them away from Black Banks. I'm on my way to Savannah tomorrow." His laugh had no mirth in it. "A very different Savannah from the one I used to know. Let me sleep right here in the Black

Banks chair, Deborah. I think I'd like that. But no more than two hours, promise?" He gripped her arm so hard it hurt.

Deborah tried to smile, but the tears were flowing again as she propped a pillow behind his head and covered him with a blanket.

47

With Lee engaged by Grant in Virginia and Atlanta lost, the Confederacy was sinking into its final agony when Horace rejoined his command fifteen miles from Burneyville. Sherman's men were rushing down and across his beloved Georgia, just ahead of him, burning and pillaging, whooping and shouting by the light of the flames from burning furniture, carpets, clothing, stores of rice and cotton. Sturdy plantation houses and barns flared, buckled and fell into smoldering ruins marked only by "Sherman monuments"—blackened chimneys standing all along the Yankee route to Savannah. What had they done to Black Banks? *What had they done to Black Banks?*

He was due to report at Savannah on October 1, 1864. There seemed ample time, even if he and his troops were forced to walk the seventy-three miles. In a week, by taking a short cut at Darien, they had bypassed Sherman's army, and back beside the salt marshes again, Horace felt new strength. For the first time since his enlistment, he was within a few miles of St. Simons Island, and with the Negroes free, he was free at last to begin to hate. The Yankees had accomplished what they set out to do. The Negroes were no longer slaves; most of them were roaming the countryside like unruly, lost children. The Cotton States were defeated. Why did the destruction have to go on? Confederate soldiers had received no pay in months. Food was running out. Their ammunition was almost gone and there was nothing left in the treasury. The soldiers' boots were tied around their feet with old rags, if they had boots at all, and with each weary, painful step through the dark mud of the salt marsh Horace felt his bitterness grow.

"It's harder for you down here, ain't it, Gould?" A freckled mountaineer from North Georgia tried to joke. "Now ya' know how we'uns felt with the fightin' up thar 'round our shanties. Co'se my shanty ain' no fine plantation house like yours, but a feller's house is his house, an' Yankees is Yankees, an' burnin' is burnin'."

After the first hot pain between his shoulders, Horace remembered nothing. He regained consciousness in a low-ceilinged, stuffy, strange room. The pain at the base of his neck was searing and his North Georgia buddy's words, " . . . burnin' is burnin'," followed each other back and forth through his clouded mind.

"I'm the Widder Dundle, an' you're in my house on the Altamaha River," an old woman's voice was saying wearily, as though she had explained to other men in pain and was girding herself to face the ordeal again. "You got shot goin' through the marsh."

He tried to figure it out. An advance patrol from Sherman's army must have been bivouacked in the woods beside the marsh.

"Jis' like they shot cha fer fun," she continued. "Your fellers tol' me them Yankees plunked chu an' let the rest go. Course our boys carried you here. They dug the bullet out. You bled like a stuck pig. I'm near outa' rags, too. Had me a time astaunchin' it."

Horace struggled to open his eyes. The hunched form bending over him swam from side to side, and the stench of his own wound sickened him.

"Shut yer eyes agin'," the old voice rasped. "Yer weak as a kitten. Be good effen ya'd jis' drop off to sleep a while. I'll wake ya' up in a couple of hours. See then effen I kin git some grub down yer throat someway."

Deborah tried with every ounce of her energy to stay cheerful before the children, but Anna was not fooled. The child did not ask why they hadn't heard from her father, but she ate almost nothing and her thin face grew paler, her gray eyes bigger, more haunted. Savannah was so close they had expected frequent letters, and then five agonizing weeks had crept by with no word at all.

"It's like Papa's ghost is in the house, Mama," Anna said.

"Hush! Don't even think such a thing," Deborah cried, and then comforted the little girl. "It's just that he was here so recently and for such a short time—it makes it seem as though you dreamed it. I—I know for sure Papa is all right."

"How do you know?"

"Because he's in God's hands."

"Doesn't God let other men get killed?"

"That's enough, Anna. Don't ask any more questions. We just go on believing and trusting God, and one day we'll hear." She kept her voice firm. "One day we'll hear."

It had rained for three days, and the children were restless and quarrelsome. To occupy them after their lessons, Deborah used up the last of her flour baking cookies. "Not very good ones," she laughed, "with no sugar, but I put the rest of our Black Banks cane syrup in the dough, and now we're going to cut up the canned plums into little pieces and make a funny face on each cookie."

They were a noisy bunch around the open hearth, shouting their ideas for pictures to decorate the big, flat cookies, when over the laughter and chatter Deborah heard footsteps on the front porch and ran to open the door.

"Be you Miz Goul'?" a drenched, skinny Negro boy asked.

"Yes, I'm Mrs. Gould. Come inside, child, out of the rain."

He stepped timidly into the room. "Ah got a message 'bout yo' husbun'."

The children grew as silent as death.

"Well, tell us quickly, please—what is it?"

"He be powerful sick at de preacher's house an' he say kin you come an' git 'im?"

"He's sick? Who is the preacher? How far is it?"

"Which queshun you want me to answer fus', ma'am?"

"*Where* is he?"

"At de preacher's house 'bout eighteen mile."

"Have you come eighteen miles to tell us?"

"No, ma'am. Ah come eight. Mah sixth cousin, he come ten."

Deborah took the boy by his thin shoulders. "Now, listen to me carefully. We'll give you something to eat and try to dry your clothes before you go, but get word back to Mr. Gould that we'll come for him just as soon as we can find a mule."

"Yes, ma'am. Ain' no use to drah mah clothes, dey'll jis' git wet agin. Anyway, ah got t' git raht back. Ah come wif de mail."

"Jessie, fix something for this lad to eat, and Horace—start hunting."

Thirteen-year-old Horace jumped to his feet. "Yes, Mama, but where will I hunt? I reckon I can make our old wagon roll, but where am I gonna get a mule?"

"Just begin asking. People are coming and going in Burneyville these days and—God knows we need a mule."

"All right," Horace said, pulling on his father's plantation jacket against the rain.

"And Horace, beg them! Tell them it can save your father's life."

At dawn the next day, young Horace helped his mother carry out the mattress from her own bed, and over it, in the rickety wagon, behind the ancient, borrowed mule, they spread a thick layer of crocus sacks.

"See to Mr. Jenkins's mule, Horace, while I finish making the bed," Deborah instructed, tucking her pillows under the mattress to keep them clean and dry. "We must be sure you have that old critter properly and safely hitched up. Thirty-six miles you have to travel in this rig."

"He's hitched up as good as I can do it with this worn-out harness, Mama," the boy said, climbing onto the driver's seat.

"That's bad grammar, son. Not hitched up as 'good' as—hitched up as *well* as." Because the rain was still falling, she threw her rag rug over the makeshift bed, stepped back and blew a kiss to Horace Abbott.

"All right," she said, smiling up at him. "Go as fast as you can. You'll do well to reach him today. Let Papa rest overnight and start back early tomorrow. And oh, my dear, God go with you."

Deborah managed to pass the long hours of that sleepless night by talking to God. "Lord, if that mule hasn't stumbled and fallen, if the wagon is still rolling, don't You think they could be back here before sundown? Take care of them, Lord; keep the mule moving and the wagon rolling. Watch over my husband and my son."

The rain stopped in the night, and when first light began at last to break through the clouds hurrying away toward the east, she admitted to herself that she could not face the children today; Jennie could look after them. She dressed quickly, threw her worn Pilgrim cloak around her shoulders, left a note, and was pulling on her bonnet as she unlatched the front gate. If she started walking toward them, she would know that much sooner.

Because the carpet of pine straw along the side of the rutted, muddy road was much easier to walk on, she held to the edge of the woods all morning, always in sight of the road. Her feet were blistered and bleeding before noon, but she rested only when she had to. At first, she tried to identify bird songs, but it was October and few birds sang. The day grew hotter, the woods quieter, and for hours she passed no one. A large rat-tlesnake, stretched in the sun, forced her to cut back from the road to pass it safely but did not slow her down. A deer crashed through a thicket a few yards away; the silence returned, and so did the strength to keep walking—more slowly, stumbling often, but still walking. "Don't let me step on a pine cone, dear Lord. I mustn't turn my ankle. Not now."

She chewed some sassafras leaves and when she came to a narrow fresh creek, knelt to scoop up water. Still on her knees on the sandy creek bank, water dripping from her chin, she heard the rumble of a cart or a wagon—far, faraway, but unmistakable. "Don't run!" she command-ed herself, as she scrambled to her feet. "Don't run, Deborah Gould—*walk*. If you run you might faint, and that would only worry him."

One careful step after another, and another, and an-other—unmindful of her bleeding feet, never taking her eyes off the road—she plodded ahead, until the old mule came in sight and she recognized her son alone on the wagon seat. Unable to help herself, she began to run and, in spite of young Horace's shouted warnings, kept running until she could grab the splintery side of the creaking old wagon and hang on for dear life, while the boy halted the feeble mule.

The thin, emaciated figure lying silently on the make-shift bed could not be her husband! She stepped back, staring first at her son and then at the sunken, closed eyes of the sick man.

"He's bad, Mama. I didn't know what to do for him. I just kept drivin'."

Slowly she approached the cart again and laid her hand on her husband's head. "Mr. Gould, dear? *Mr. Gould, dear*?"

"Is he dead, Mama? Mama! Is Papa dead?"

She saw the slightest movement of his eyelids as he struggled to open them, and jerked off her bonnet to shield him from the sun. "No, dear—he's not dead."

"Deborah?" The whisper was barely audible.

"Yes, my darling, it's Deborah."

His head rolled to one side and he lost consciousness again.

48

Later, she could never remember sleeping at all during that first month, but the day came when Deborah knew she had nursed him back to life. Soon he could walk with her in the woods around the Burneyville cottage. But he had changed.

"I didn't even have the satisfaction of being wounded in battle," he grumbled. "I just happened to be a nice moving target for some Yankee's pistol practice."

Deborah had to accustom herself to the fact that he didn't joke any more, not even with the children. She had conquered the gangrene in his wound; somehow she would conquer the bitterness she felt growing in him.

"It's more than bitterness," he said. "Can't you see, I'm trying to learn to hate? I died a little inside every time I've had to kill a Yankee, Deborah, but since they're going on with the slaughter after their cause is already won, *I've got to learn to hate* in order to go on too."

"Not while you're here with us, you don't. This is the time to rest and be quiet. Let God tell you what you have to do. You're too sick to know. This is the time to be thankful and glad, my beloved. You're still weak, but you're getting well. That's what matters."

He sank heavily onto a fallen log. "Yes, I'm getting well, and my orders are to rejoin my command in Savannah the minute I'm able." He covered his face with his hands. "I'm as able right now as I'll ever be."

"Mr. Gould, not once in all the years I've been your wife have I openly disagreed with you, but I'm doing it now. You are not strong enough in your body to go back yet!"

"My body's in much better shape than my spirit. Unlike the rest of the noble Confederate Army, I know when I'm beaten. They won't be getting much when their Captain returns, but I'm going back."

He reached his command in Savannah just in time to obey orders to evacuate the city before Sherman arrived; in time to run for his life, with the last straggling band of Confederate soldiers, across the pontoon bridge, minutes before it was blown up. And as he ran he began to be afraid as he had not been afraid before. Not of death, but of life.

27 December, 1864
In bivouac near Savannah

My Deborah,

I am well in body, but more depressed in spirit than at any time during the madness. We have just seen what passes for a newspaper and I copy a terse account of the Savannah celebration of the birth of your God, Jesus Christ:

To His Excellency President Lincoln:
I beg to present you, as a Christmas gift, the city of Savannah, with one hundred and fifty heavy guns and plenty of ammunition; and also twenty-five thousand bales of cotton.
Signed, W. T. Sherman,
Major General.

The end is near for us. I have heard the destruction on St. Simons is great. I know you are expecting a child, my Deborah, but even if I am discharged soon, in my present state of mind, I cannot come back to you until I have somehow returned to the Island to see for myself what they have done to our home. Do not beg me to come. I will have to refuse. How long we must sit in this stinking hole the Confederate Army calls a bivouac, I do not know. By spring, I may be free to swim, if necessary, back to St. Simons. I only know I cannot rest or pick up the pieces of my life until I have gone there first—alone. When you write to Mary, kindly advise her. I have not learned to hate. It is too late now to try. I am only empty and afraid and too old to delude myself that we will have anything ahead but despair. I wallow in it night and day. Only in that journey back to the Island do I have any faith at all at this point. I found myself there once; perhaps I will again. I am not fit to be with anyone who loves me now. I will come back to you when I have found out about Black Banks.

Your devoted husband,
Horace B. Gould.

49

On April 9, 1865, Lee surrendered to Grant at Appomatox, and General Joseph Johnston, reinstated after the battle of Atlanta, surrendered to Sherman on April 26 at Durham, North Carolina. Horace was mustered out near Savannah, so exhausted it took him two weeks to reach Brunswick. Eight-five endless miles on foot, sleeping at night in the woods beside the marshes, eating what he could find without a gun. Oyster beds were plentiful along the salt rivers, and an occasional sweet potato gave him a change when he was lucky enough to find one left behind in a deserted, untended garden.

He reached Brunswick in mid-May, on a morning so clear and soft it brought tears of homesickness as he wandered around the old Brunswick waterfront in search of a way to get across to St. Simons Island. He could see it, beyond the five salt creeks, stretching quiet and green and familiar, but still out of reach.

The Federal Government had set up offices in Brunswick, and the streets were thronged with strangers. He walked for over an hour without seeing one person he recognized—black or white. He was almost home, but he had never felt so far away.

Finally, he noticed a heavy-set man clapping his hands to summon a Negro. The Negro hurried, smiling, to the man's side, tipped his old hat, took a piece of money from the prosperous-looking gentleman and headed for a fair-sized bateau tied at the dock just below where Horace stood.

"Where are you going?" he called to the Negro.

"S'n Simons Islan', boss."

Horace's heart leaped. "Can you take an extra passenger?"

The Negro looked him over. He was unshaven, his ancient gray officer's jacket fastened with one remaining button, his mud-caked boots tied on with rags. "Yes, sir. Ah carry you—fo' money."

Horace had never heard a Negro ask for money in his life. "How much?"

"Fi'teen cent, Yewnited States money."

"I only have one Confederate dollar."

"Ah kin handle it."

Horace jumped down into the bateau, and they picked up the portly gentleman and began the winding, sunlit trip across the blue waters of the tidal rivers that separated St. Simons Island from the mainland.

"Shall we introduce ourselves?" the gentleman asked.

"Certainly," Horace answered. "I'm Captain H. B. Gould."

"My name's Eagen. A. M. Eagen." They shook hands. "Headquartered at Retreat plantation. United States Government-appointed friend to the Negroes."

"Yes, sir!" the oarsman chuckled, as though he and Eagen shared a secret.

"I see," Horace said carefully.

(297)

"Did you say 'Gould'? Ah! *The* Gould of Black Banks?"

"That's right." Horace bit off his words, not wanting to find out anything about Black Banks from an outsider.

"Coming home to see what's happened while you've been away, huh?"

"That's right," Horace said again.

"Well, you're the first old resident to come back, Gould, and you might just have a few surprises in store. But lemme tell you something. I'm your friend, too."

This was not the time to antagonize a Federal man. Horace gritted his teeth and kept still.

"Now, as I said, Gould, I'm set up at Retreat, and if there's anything at all I can do to help you, let me know."

To help *him* on St. Simons Island? That was *his* Island. *His home*. What right did this Yankee have to offer help? As they crossed the mouth of the McKay River, he caught the empty look of the rounded south end of St. Simons. His father's lighthouse *was* gone. Deborah had warned him, but the fact had no reality until now. Was Black Banks gone too? Would any of his people be there to welcome him? If they were there, was there anything left in him to command their respect now that he was no longer their owner? Suddenly, he felt he would give anything to see July, to try to tell his old friend how empty he felt. How sick he was over the total defeat, not of the Confederacy, but of the whole country. No one had won this war! Everyone had lost, and a grief heavier than his fear of seeing Black Banks engulfed him—grief, sorrow, pity for them all, black and white, North and South. Why did he especially want to tell July? He didn't know, except that July had always symbolized for him the quiet, deep, untapped strength and wisdom and importance of the black people. Horace needed him now—Maum Larney's strong, free son, July. He smiled inwardly. He had not freed July. His black friend had always been free. July, without a last name, had always known more freedom than he, Horace, had ever known, because July knew and accepted himself as

(298)

he was. If only the nightmare of this new uncertainty would suddenly end and he could wake up to discover it was time to meet July at the edge of the Black Banks woods again, to go hunting. Hunting for coon and wild boar and rabbits, not men.

"Now, I don't like to interrupt your reverie, Captain," the Yankee was saying, "but we do want you Rebels to know the Federal Government is going to do all in its power to make everything as painless as possible. And to prove it, how about a horse? You're not aiming to walk all the way from Retreat to Black Banks, are you?"

He was planning to walk. It had been so long since he had ridden, it hadn't occurred to him not to walk.

"I'll be glad to loan you a horse."

Horace stared across the flat, brown-green marshes, flowing like rivers between the creeks—marsh and creek, marsh and creek, forming the familiar pattern all the way to the sea. He wanted to hate this man, to tell him to go to the devil, but the tangy, earth smell of the salt marshes had stirred a memory of the man he used to be when he *was* Gould of Black Banks—when he possessed only the normal fears every man knows, before he became a stranger to himself, before he had learned to kill and to be afraid.

"Yes," he said. "I'd be grateful for a horse."

The bateau scraped against the sand on the bar at Retreat, and Horace waited for Eagen to climb out first. He and the Yankee walked up the wide beach toward the old Retreat house, its shuttered veranda and gabled roof as familiar as the King sand bar. There were Negroes about, but not King people. At least, he recognized no one and no one recognized him.

Eagen was babbling about where he would find the horse. "Around to the back of the old King cotton barn ... being saddled now ... we want you Rebels who used to live here to be treated right ... of course, you've heard of Sherman's Special Field Order Number Fifteen ... all of the Sea Islands have been given to the Negroes ... forty acres apiece ... the land surveyed off ... still, you're welcome to look around the old place ... and let me know if I can be of any more help."

As the Yankee talked, Horace felt that he, himself, had shifted to one side—to a position from which he could watch them both. He saw Eagen with a rope knotted around the head of an aging, ragged Confederate officer—pulling pleasantly with all his brute strength. How would he have known his land had been surveyed into forty-acre tracts and given away? How would he have known about Sherman's Special Field Order Number 15? "Thank you," he muttered, then turned and walked around the King house, across the weed-choked lawn toward the big cotton barn. A strange Negro—his hand out—was holding a sorry-looking horse. Horace fumbled for a coin, mounted and rode slowly down Anna Matilda King's avenue of oaks toward Frederica Road.

The beloved road seemed the same, except for the deep ruts and thin, worn patches of oyster shells. The trees still stood together on either side, their spring-green branches touching over his head. He let the old horse amble along. No need to hurry. No one was expecting him. He could spend the night in the familiar woods on St. Simons as comfortably as he had spent the last fourteen nights in strange woods. The sight of the De-mere house at Mulberry Grove was worse than his dread. Only its crumbling walls still stood, and stark, silent chimneys. He didn't stop. He could do nothing for his old neighbors, still somewhere on the mainland in a makeshift refuge, unaware of what had happened to their home.

Storm clouds were beginning to form, crossing and recrossing the sun—common on any Island afternoon. As he rode, he watched the woods: the light coming and going in them—a gigantic oil lamp turned up bright, then slowly dimmed, lighting the thickets on each side of the narrow road, then throwing them into ghostly shadow.

His sense of time was gone, but in what seemed only a

moment, he was shocked to realize that he was nearing Kelvin Grove. The two-storied pink tabby house would come into view around that stand of pines. He stopped, suddenly afraid it would not be there. If he feared so to see Kelvin Grove, how could he face what he might find at Black Banks? Eagen could have told him if Black Banks had been burned, but he had been afraid to ask. Afraid. Passing Ben Cater's Kelvin Grove meant he would reach Black Banks next. Coming abreast of the old Cater house, his blood ran cold. The yard swarmed with screaming, fighting children. What looked to be an entire Sunday congregation of black people filled the wide veranda, sprawling or lounging in the wicker chairs and up and down the front steps as though they owned it.

They do own it. "Oh, God!" he groaned, and urged the horse to a gallop. Once out of sight, he slowed again. Ben Cater's nice house! Only a few Negroes in a thousand would know how to take care of a house like Kelvin Grove without supervision. How could they be expected to know? They had been told what to do and how to do it for all their enslaved lives. Didn't it stand to reason that they would run wild now in a white man's place like undisciplined children? The freed Negroes needed houses, but where were the defeated Southern landowners supposed to live? The trouble wasn't over. It had just begun.

He caught the scent of jessamine and saw the thick old vine he had looked for each spring. He was almost there. *Black Banks.* The time had come. Reining the horse at the Black Banks lane, he sat for an instant, peering down the familiar, winding road, his heart pounding. Then he plunged into the dappled sun and shadow, through the woods toward his beloved house.

He saw the steep, sloping roof line first, looming tall and welcoming among the high pines and oaks. The reins fell from his hands, and the old horse rounded the last turn in the road at a walk. Tears began to flow down Horace's cheeks as the house came into full view, and he sobbed with relief, sitting the borrowed horse on the old road he no longer owned. He no longer owned the house, either, but it stood. *Black Banks still stood.* The dear house stood. What he had feared most had not come to pass. ...

Three shots shattered the quiet and a Minié ball slammed into the tree beside him, as a gang of angry Negroes raced out of the house and loosed three snarling dogs across the yard. During the moment in which he sat, too stunned to think, he was sure he heard someone shout his name, but another bullet split the limb above his head and he wheeled the horse, galloped back to Frederica Road and turned north in the direction of Rosemount.

Is front of what had been the New St. Clair house, he dismounted slowly. No one would shoot at him here. No one was living at Rosemount. For a long time he stood looking at the ruins, burned to the ground except for the crumbling first-floor tabby walls and sturdy blackened chimneys. He walked through the charred gate, still hanging by one hinge to the picket fence, across Mary's rose garden, over the rubble that had been the gracious front veranda, and stepped through the doorway into vacant, weed-grown areas with familiar dimensions and shapes— the rooms of his father's house. He climbed over a fallen slab of tabby into the roofless sitting room where he had told his father about the trouble at Yale, so many lifetimes ago. No tears came. He simply wondered that even the need to hate had gone from his heart. Down the wide hall, in the rubble of the collapsed stairway, he picked his way to Larney's kitchen. Her big fireplace stood as solid and defiant as Larney would have stood had she been there herself to fight off marauding Yankees. Her old iron spider lay turned upside down on the hearth, and one pot still hung on its hook.

He was glad his father was dead.

At the first sound of running footsteps down the Rosemount lane, he ducked behind a thick section of tabby wall and waited. He was unarmed. He could be cut down with no chance to defend himself. Through a hole in the crumbling tabby, he saw a man—a Negro—standing in the empty road, a pistol in his hand. As Horace crouched lower, the man raced out of sight around to the back of the house, and his footsteps crunched on the shell-littered ground as he ran inside the ruins, down the wide central hall and out to the front again. Horace thought of Deborah and the children. He shouldn't have come here alone. It could be months, even years, before anyone would find his body. He watched the Negro walk across the yard, then stop to scratch his head. His back to Horace, he stood there a full minute, as though deciding what to do next, then called, "Mausa Horace!"

Horace's mouth went dry.

July called again, not very hopefully. "Mausa Horace—be you here?"

The sunlight was gone suddenly, as though it had been blown out, and the sky churned above the empty Rosemount rooms in black, roiling clouds. Wind lashed across the ruins, stirring swirls of dust and leaves, blowing sand into Horace's eyes as he walked slowly out from behind the wall where he had been hiding. July turned, and the two men stood for a long moment, looking at each other. Too much had happened; too much had changed for a quick greeting. Then Horace ran the few steps to his friend and embraced him, unashamed of his tears. July was crying too. . . .

"July, you old hound dog," Horace said. "Do you have any idea how glad I am to see you?"

"Yes, sir," July grinned. "Ah knows how glad ah be to see you, Mausa Horace." His face grew solemn, pitying. "You—you sho' look lak you's had a hard time, sir. Be you all right?"

"I am now," Horace said, sitting down on a fragment of the old wall. "How did you know I was here?"

"Ah libs in mah ol' cabin at Black Banks, an' ah seen dem no-good niggahs take after ya', sir. Ah heerd 'em hollerin' an' shootin' an' ah try t' warn ya'. Den ah sees

(303)

ya' ride off up dis way. Ah figgered you come to yo' papa's place." As he talked, July kept watching in the direction of Frederica Road.

"What's the matter?" Horace asked. "No one's coming. Sit down. I've needed to talk to you. Tell me everything that's happened since I've been gone."

"Ah can't do dat, Mausa Horace. Dey ain' time. Ah tol' dem niggahs what lib at yo' house, ah'd come dis way t' he'p 'em fin' ya'. Ah jis' come to warn ya'."

"Are they still after me?"

"Yes, sir! Dey ain' got no sense. Deys from off somewheres." He held out his pistol. "You better hab de gun, sir. You needs it wussin ah does."

Horace took the pistol. "The tables have turned, haven't they?" Then he remembered Larney. "Your—mother is gone, July. Papa John is still all right the last I heard, but Maum Larney died in her sleep."

"Yes, sir, ah knows. Miss Mary, she wrote me a letter." He smiled a little. "Ah could read it, too, Mausa Horace."

"Good for you!"

"Yes, sir. Dat be de fus' letter ah eber got." He looked nervously in the direction of the road. "Mausa Horace, ah gotta go, but be you gon' buy yo' place back some day an' come home agin?"

"Is there any way I *can* buy it back, July?" Just hearing his old friend ask the question gave him the first small hope. He grabbed July's arm. "Have you heard of anyone else being able to do that? Have you?"

"No, sir, but ah's heerd dat wif enough money, a man might could do it."

It had begun to rain, big, heavy, sporadic drops, building up to what any Islander knew could become a downpour.

"Git de money an' come back to us, sir. Dey's some ob us ol' uns still here."

July was about to leave him, and he had found out almost nothing. "How long have they been in Black Banks, July?"

"Ober two year. It be all tore up inside, sir. Lak de little church house."

(304)

"The church? They tore up our church?"

July looked at the sandy ground, darkening now as the rain fell harder. "Niggah sojers. Crazy Yankee niggah sojers! But you come back, Mausa Horace—we kin fix it all up agin. Ah'll be lookin' eber day."

Horace grasped his hand.

"Don' ride back till after dark, sir—ah's beggin' ya'. Hide up at de church till it be dark."

July was gone, out of sight into the woods, his rapid footfalls covered quickly by the thunder and the wind and the pouring rain, as though he had never been there at all.

Riding toward the church through the storm, Horace almost doubted he had really seen his old friend. July was there and gone so fast, the loneliness had only been sharpened. He could find no explanation for the hope July had given him. A mere rumor, repeated by a loyal Negro, that with enough money he could buy Black Banks again, was not sufficient reason to give a sane man hope. But he hoped.

He saw the cross first on the steeple of the church. It had been knocked to one side, the steeple shattered by artillery fire. As he came nearer, he could hear the loose doors being driven by the wind against the outer walls. He rode straight up to the steps and sat for a long moment, feeling ill. The rain was slackening, but it had soaked through his battle jacket, and still dripped from the wide brim of his officer's hat. The church windows had been shot out. Why was it so shocking to see the ugly scars of war on a church? His nausea passed and in its place came anger. Anger that shook his soul as the wind shook the loose shutters and doors of the desecrated little building. He tried to reason with himself. War is war; one building is like the next when men go crazy. Black men, July had said they were. What difference did that make? He had seen the hideous handiwork of bands of Sherman's white soldiers—and of the men in his own company. There was no difference between the races in their capacity for violence. "A building is a building," he said aloud. At least they didn't burn it, and maybe they haven't even been inside. July could be wrong. Maybe they just shot it up as they rode past.

He tied the horse securely to an oak and climbed the rickety wooden steps. In all the years he had been a vestryman at Christ Church, he had never felt a part of it as he did now.

Inside the dark, musty sanctuary, he stumbled, and a family of mice raced past him out of a nest of old paper and blankets. His eyes adjusted to the shadows. The Union soldiers had bivouacked in the church. Some of the pews were turned up to make bunks; others had been chopped up for firewood. The floor was weathered and split and part of it burned out—all of it littered with paper and refuse and filth. Then he saw the altar. They had used it as a meat block on which to cut up the stolen cattle. A year or maybe two years had gone by since the soldiers left, but the debris, the dried entrails, the hacked-off hoofs and tails and heads were still strewn about the altar.

Feeling ill again, he rushed outside and down the steps. He couldn't ride away. July had told him to wait for dark. Suddenly, he fell to his knees, buried his head in his arms on the sagging church steps and cried, "Oh, Christ, help me! If You're still for us in this world in spite of the way we are—help *me* to know it now. Tell me what to do."

How he meant for God to help, he didn't know. He knew only that he would stay there on the wet ground until help came. Sherman's Special Order Number 15 was a fact. They had given away Black Banks. He was an intruder to be fired at from his own house by the men he had longed to see free. He tried to hate them—to hate the black men and the white Yankees. A man could bring God his hate and ask forgiveness. He had no hate to bring. He had nothing. No hate, no money, no property, no home, no way to feed his family. But he was there, before Deborah's God, needing help—and he would wait.

When he awakened, a chuck-will's-widow was calling through the darkness from one of the churchyard oaks. The storm was over. He had slept. Kneeling on the weathered step that had become his altar, he looked up at the blue-black sky—clear now, thick-spattered with stars. He felt rested for the first time since he left Deborah. Rested and ready.

Nothing had changed. He would still have to sneak back down Frederica Road under cover of the darkness and beg a ride to the mainland, but he was ready—not only to find a way to buy Black Banks a second time— he was ready to tackle his life again.

A man does have a choice, he thought. A man can choose despair or he can choose—faith. He had chosen.

Astride the Yankee's horse, he rode slowly out of the churchyard and down Frederica Road. He would like to tell July that he was himself again, that somehow he would be back, but that was impossible. He wasn't free to ride into Black Banks yet. Not yet. But he was free. As free as July.

As he rode past the Black Banks lane, he waved to the dear house, and in the clearing along Frederica Road where Mary Abbott's cotton fields used to be, he saw a thin new moon—rising.

Acknowledgments

All characters in *New Moon Rising* were real people, and—so far as could be determined, except for Linda Thatcher, Mrs. Shedd and the Livelys—real names were used. The Gould story was discovered in the main from an unpublished manuscript: "The Goulds of New St. Clair and Black Banks," written many years ago by the late Agnes Hartridge, one of Horace's granddaughters. His living grandchildren, to whom I am forever indebted for meaningful friendship as well as help, are: Mrs. H. B. Diggs, Mrs. Douglas Taylor, Mrs. L. W. Everett, Mrs. Jeff Powell, Mr. Potter F. Gould, Colonel James Dunn Gould and Horace's namesake—to whom I have dedicated the book—Commander Horace Bunch Gould, S.C., U.S.N. (Ret.).

An ex-Yankee such as I could never have managed without the freely offered assistance of many, many people. Along with the names already mentioned, I must add: Mrs. Allen Burns, a descendant of the Caters and Wyllys; Mrs. Albert Fendig, Sr., a descendant of the Abbotts; Mr. John Davis, a descendant of the ante-bellum Negroes who called themselves the "Wylly people," and Mr. Beeman Lee, descended from the "Hazzard people." For direct information about their parents, Mina and Adam Procter, I was greatly helped by their sons, Mr. Enoch Procter, Mr. James Procter and the late Mr. Willis Procter. Mr. Charles King, Mr. John E. Golden and Mr. Henry Morrison were invaluable to me in authenticating the customs and the peculiar coastal dialect spoken by their Negro ancestors, and my dear friend, Mrs. Mable Hillery, along with the other members of the Georgia Sea Island Singers, gave me firsthand access to the rhythms and lyrics of the Sea Island slave songs. For an informative tour of the Sea Palms Golf and Country Club, now located on the site of James Gould's old plantation, I thank the Club's General Manager, Mr. Sonny Bryan. For help in searching old documents in the vaults of the Brunswick Court House, I am grateful to Mr. Ralph Skelton, and for particular help on small but important details, Captain and Mrs. N. C. Young, Mr. F. P. Vanstory, Mr. Watson Glisson, Mrs. Lorah Plemmons and Horace's great-granddaughters, Miss Clara Marie Gould and Mrs. J. R. Bruce.

What I could not discover firsthand, I found through the always gracious cooperation of Mrs. Wallace Ledbetter and Mrs. Seward Knight of the St. Simons Library; Miss Theo Hotch, Miss Vivian Polk and Mrs. Harriette Hammond of the Brunswick Public Library; Mrs. Ruby W. Berrie of the Margaret Davis Cate Memorial Library at Fort Frederica National Park, St. Simons Island; Mrs. Barbara Bronson, Reader's Service, Public Library Unit, Atlanta; Miss Beatrice Fairchild Lang and Mr. Jimmie H. Gunter, Georgia Department of Archives and History, Atlanta; Miss Dorothy W. Bridgwater of the Archives Reference Libraries, Yale University, New Haven, Connecticut. I am indebted to the Fort Frederica Association and to the works of the late Margaret Davis Cate for much useful information.

For authoritative information and clarifying insight into life in nineteenth-century Savannah and the Golden Isles, I am permanently in the debt of my new friends, Mrs. Lilla M. Hawes, Director of the Georgia Historical Society, Savannah, and Mr. Richard Everett, historian at The Cloister, Sea Island, Georgia.

For a memorable trip in his pilot boat, I thank Captain Alfred A. Brockinton of St. Simons Harbor, and for patient and frequent explanations of river routes in the intricate coastal waters, I especially thank his bar pilot, Mr. Lawrence Gray.

Of course, I am grateful to my mother for her letters of encouragement as I worked, and as with the writing of *The Beloved Invader*, I again inadequately thank my beloved editor, Miss Tay Hohoff. I also thank my careful copy editor, Mrs. Peggy Cronlund. Joyce Blackburn, my best friend and most perceptive critic, toiled with me—night after night—over every line. And through still another book, Elsie Goodwillie has delivered a beautiful typescript.

Mentioned last, only so that it will be remembered, is my heart-deep gratitude to Burnette Vanstory, Coastal Georgia historian, Member of the Board of Directors of the Coastal Georgia Historical Society, and author of *Georgia's Land of the Golden Isles*, who did the main part of the comprehensive research—with love and care and a writer's sensitivity to my needs.

Horace managed, through a loan from Janie's husband, to recover and restore the Black Banks house and land. Later, all confiscated property was returned to its owners, but Mary lived with her father's relatives in Utica, New York, until 1870, two years before her death, when she repaired Larney's old cabin at New St. Clair and moved back to the Island. She is buried near Horace and Deborah—beside her father—in the cemetery at Christ Church Frederica, and on her momument is one chiseled rose.

I must not fail to report that fifty years later, in 1880, Horace received—along with the others who were forced to leave—an honorary M.A. degree from the faculty of Yale. In a privately published book, *Biographical Memoranda Respecting All Who Ever Were Members of the Class of 1832 of Yale College*, there is a page written by Horace himself, telling with customary Gould reserve of his life after Yale. He speaks briefly of his "seven unsettled years" and then, in one line, says it all: ". . . this Island has evermore been my home."

Thankfully, I hope this Island will evermore be my home, too.

Eugenia Price

St. Simons Island, Georgia
November, 1968

About the Author

EUGENIA PRICE is known the world over for her nonfiction as well as her bestselling historical novels based on the lives of people in the Southeastern United States. *The Beloved Invader,* her first novel, and the first book of her popular St. Simon's Trilogy was published in 1965. For this trilogy—*The Beloved Invader, New Moon Rising* and *Lighthouse*—she was awarded the National Endowment for the Arts Governor's Award and the Distinguished Science Award from Georgia College. In addition, she is known for her Florida trilogy and bestselling Savannah Quartet. A resident of St. Simon's Island, Georgia, Ms. Price is currently working on a new St. Simon's trilogy. Her most recent novel is *Bright Captivity*.

Heartwarming Books of Faith and Inspiration

☐ 28229 TALKING TO YOUR CHILD
ABOUT GOD, David Heller $3.95

☐ 27484 LIFE AFTER LIFE, $4.95
Raymond Moody

☐ 25669 THE HIDING PLACE, $4.50
Corrie ten Boom

☐ 27375 FASCINATING WOMANHOOD, $4.95
Helen Andelin

☐ 27085 MEETING GOD AT EVERY TURN, $3.95
Catherine Marshall

☐ 27943 BIBLE AS HISTORY, Werner Keller $5.95

☐ 27417 HOW TO WIN OVER DEPRESSION, $4.50
Tim LeHaye

☐ 26249 "WITH GOD ALL THINGS ARE $3.95
POSSIBLE", Life Study Fellowship

☐ 27088 MYTHS TO LIVE BY, $4.95
Joseph Campbell

Buy them at your local bookstore or use this page to order.

Bantam Books, Dept. HF4, 414 East Golf Road, Des Plaines, IL 60016

Please send me the items I have checked above. I am enclosing $_____
(please add $2.00 to cover postage and handling). Send check or money
order, no cash or C.O.D.s please.

Mr/Ms _____

Address _____

City/State_____ Zip_____

Please allow four to six weeks for delivery.   HF4–11/90
Prices and availability subject to change without notice.